The Murder of
Frau Schütz

J. Madison Davis

The Murder of Frau Schütz

J. Madison Davis

Walker and Company
New York

First published in the United States of America in 1988
by the Walker Publishing Company, Inc.

Published simultaneously in Canada by Thomas Allen & Son
Canada, Limited, Markham, Ontario.

Library of Congress Cataloging-in-Publication Data

Davis, J. Madison.
   The murder of Frau Schütz / J. Madison Davis.
      p.   cm.
   ISBN 0-8027-1055-7
   I. Title.
PS3554.A934636M87   1988   813'.54—dc19   88-14407

Printed in the United States of America

10 9 8 7 6 5 4 3 2 1

To my Father,
Whom I have never missed more.

· *Prologue* ·

Willi Kampfer wanted to throw off all his clothes and run away from this silly extra duty. The strap on his helmet chafed a spot just under his chin where his new electric razor had torn the whiskers rather than clipped them. His chin cup had filled with sweat, which burned like acid. Each piece of the body armor—the plexiglass mask, the heavy boots and gloves—weighed him down. Further, he wasn't sure that some of Waldheim's people didn't want violent confrontations: lots of news film, lots of "our Austrian" unjustly attacked, and lots of sympathy. Willi frankly didn't care who would turn out to be president, but he didn't want to be caught in between. Policemen were the first to get it, regardless of their politics, and any demonstration, no matter how seemingly benign, could turn bloody in seconds. There were too many people in the world willing to commit the kind of butchery Willi had once seen at the Vienna airport. It only took one.

He glanced down the line of his comrades toward a candy shop with a steel grid lowered over its front by a careful proprietor. The clock in the window said eleven-thirty. About now, he thought, his girlfriend Leni and he would have been anticipating lunch, hunger finally forcing itself between their flushed, damp bodies, demanding that they take advantage of the Milanese veal sautéing in the hotel kitchen. Instead of stretching his arms lazily and watching Leni pull her jeans over her brown and muscular buttocks, instead of rubbing his reddened eyes and inhaling the odor of her body on his fingers, he stood stiffly, arms at his side, wishing to God that Waldheim's people would get the rally going in the square behind him.

The demonstrators, whom the police were assigned to hold at the edge of the square, seemed restrained. An elderly man in a yarmulke was reading a set of instructions to the group. Some were quite young, about Willi's age, but bearded, with forelocks bobbing. A young woman, probably American, in a tight maroon top, gestured angrily at the elderly man, her breasts swinging from side to side. He raised his palms upward and spoke slowly. She shook her head. An older woman shoved in front of the younger and peeled back her sleeve, thrusting the tattooed numbers on her forearm in the woman's face. The American woman glanced from side to side, embarrassed, and the older pressed her advantage until the man stepped between them and spoke gently and carefully. All in all, Willi thought, they did not seem very dangerous.

The campaign band had begun playing popular old songs when the policeman next to Willi nudged him and pointed his chin toward a doorway. A man in a motorcycle jacket was gazing at his reflection in the glass. His hair was shaved close over his ears, but on top it had been shaped into a tall comb, like those decorating ancient Greek helmets. It was dyed green and red. "Do you think he's a Jew?" grinned the policeman.

"No," said Willi. "English. Their national folk costume. He thinks it's the queen's birthday."

The other policeman laughed, momentarily fogging his mask, then remembered it was important to look serious. The music had stimulated the demonstrators to prepare themselves. Placards appeared. The elderly man took out a bullhorn and began a chant to drown out the music: "Ne-ver! Ne-ver! Ne-ver!" Willi began to think of Leni again: the strong shoulders, the appendix scar, the delicate knees.

Suddenly, there was shouting behind them as well as in front. About twenty feet away, an old man waved a brown folder and gesticulated toward the speakers' platform. Three other older men, one carrying a Waldheim placard, shouted and pointed at the demonstrators. The man, however, insisted on trying to push his way toward the platform. He awkwardly bumped into a couple in front of him. The man with the placard grabbed at the old man's coat and jerked him.

"Christ," said Willi, "why don't they stay with their own crowd?"

They were beginning to shove at each other.

"You'd better break that up," said the policeman next to Willi.

"Fine. You get the next," he answered. Willi had just begun to wade into the crowd when the old man tumbled backward out of sight. Someone screamed.

"Gun! He has a gun!"

Willi charged forward. The crowd became as dense as cold syrup. He saw the man swinging his placard. He shoved and struggled as women cried out. Leni flashed across his mind and he wondered what he would do if the old man started shooting. He remembered bagging bodies at the Vienna airport.

When he finally broke through, however, the old man was harmlessly on the grass, holding his folder close to his chest with his right arm, ducking the jabs of the placard bearer. "Stop that!" Willi ordered.

"She felt a gun!" said the man.

Willi stood between the placard bearer and the man on the ground. "This is true?" he asked calmly.

"No," said the old man.

"I felt it," the woman insisted.

Photographers were now holding their cameras above people's heads. Flashbulbs went off. The old man closed his eyes and covered his face with the folder.

"She felt my arm," he said. "My arm." When the old man stiffly raised his left arm, Willi saw that the hand was prosthetic. He approached him cautiously and stood him up.

"Do you have identification?"

"I must let them know. They don't understand how important this is."

Willi thought he smelled brandy. "You are being drunk and disorderly. I must see your papers."

Four more policemen had broken through and were watching. The old man glanced at them and handed Willi a Brazilian passport.

"You are a long way from home."

"I lived in Vienna many years. What these people have forgotten—I have proof. I saw it."

"Don't come in here spreading lies about Kurt Waldheim!" said someone.

"Bastard!"

"Let us have him!"

"Quiet!" shouted Willi.

"Is it all right?" asked a policeman.

"You must go back to the protest," said Willi. "You need to stick with the other protesters."

"But I am not just a protester."

"Please. We don't want trouble."

"But—"

"Please." Willi extended his hand. The old man acquiesced. He began to limp in that direction.

"Make way!" shouted a policeman. "Make way!"

"But the demonstrators already know," said the old man.

"And they won't get angry at you," said Willi. "Do you need a doctor?"

The old man brushed the cut under his eye with the folder. "I've been through worse than this. If I hadn't lost my balance . . ."

"Why don't you let me get you a doctor?"

"What is the problem, officer?" The questioner had pushed his way from the protest. He was wearing a black coat and a prayer shawl.

"It's all over," said Willi, but the Jew stood in his way.

"Everyone must hear," said the old man. "Everyone must remember."

"That is exactly why we are here," said the Jew. "I am Rabbi Taubmann. Did I not see you at Bitburg? You were waving that folder."

"He shouldn't have gone to the cemetery."

"Agreed. Are you a survivor?"

The old man squinted. "A survivor. Yes." He sighed. "That isn't much."

"It's something," said the rabbi. "You are a witness."

The old man nodded.

The rabbi turned to Willi. "He is not under arrest, is he? You can understand how something like this is upsetting."

"He created a disturbance," said Willi. "I should take him in for questioning."

The rabbi touched Willi's shoulder. "What are you doing? Leave him alone. He's just an old Jew. You can understand what that means."

"He has been drinking."

"He hasn't suffered enough in one lifetime? Is that what you think? Look, Herr Field Marshal, we Jews don't take shit any more. He is the only one who was hurt." Taubmann brushed off the old man's jacket. The one-armed man looked around as if he weren't sure why he was in this crowd being dusted off by a rabbi.

Willi glanced at another policeman. "All right." He held out the passport. "I have your name. You get away from here. Now."

"But—"

"Come, friend," said the rabbi. "Come on."

Willi watched them leave. The old man limped noticeably as they slowly left both the rally and the protest. Damn, the policeman thought, I could have been with Leni.

In the street the two old men entered, a teenager was sweeping the sidewalk. Life was ordinary.

"Where do you live?" said the rabbi.

"In Germany. With my family. I came just for this."

"Your hotel?"

"I haven't gotten one."

"And no luggage?"

"My valise is at the train station."

"We will get it and you can share my room."

"I refuse to impose. I have credit cards." The old man looked behind him. "I came all the way for this."

"So did I. But we have made them notice, eh? And anyway it is probably bad for my heart to listen to more lies. I get too excited. Come on." The rabbi tugged at his sleeve. They walked on to the next street. They stood on the corner looking for a cab.

"I did see you at Bitburg, didn't I?" asked the rabbi.

The old man nodded. "I almost got arrested there also. I'm not good at this, it seems."

"The Nazis did that to you?" He touched the prosthetic arm.

• 5 •

"No. The British."

"Then you fought in Palestine?"

"No." The old man was lost in his own thoughts.

The rabbi said, "I was sent to my great-uncle in Canada in '37. But I lost my father and mother and three brothers. When we found out all that happened, I was determined to prove that the Nazis had failed. There would be at least one Jew in Germany, for one Jew would mean they had failed. I wasn't terribly religious, you know, but I studied hard. I became pretty Orthodox, considering my family. I wear the forelocks, the whole deal, because I want them to know I am Jewish when they see me. They must never forget."

"No."

The rabbi waved down a cab. As the old man climbed in, he bumped against the door frame. His folder tumbled. Photographs, mostly, but several papers scattered on the pavement. "Here. I'll get them," said the rabbi. He handed the old man the folder and picked up everything without really looking at it. The photographs were yellowed at the margins. As he handed them to the old man, the picture on top caught his eye. He studied it, then the man.

"Is this *you*?" he asked incredulously.

The man nodded.

"You?" He shook his head in disbelief. "So this is you. My God," said the rabbi. "My God."

· *One* ·

There was something else going on. Max-Baldur, Count von Prokofsk, couldn't put his finger on it, but it made no sense. He awkwardly raised himself from the bed and scratched his groin. His medals, the highest the Reich could give, vibrated in the silver tray on the dresser, playing an irregular tattoo. Distant bombing? A breeze? Or the quick jerk of raising oneself with only one and a half arms and an unbending leg? The medals grew quiet. Next to the tray lay the thick file covering the murder of Frau Schütz. The commandant of the work camp at Ostheim had engaged in a seemingly thorough investigation of the butchering of his wife, with detailed interrogations and half a dozen photographs. It provided murderers. It described in one cool line their punishment: "Hanged, before assembled prisoners, June 1, 1944." What more did Himmler want?

The Reichsführer was the head of all the constabularies in Germany. He could choose from the Gestapo, the SS, and the SD for a skilled investigator. Instead, Himmler had chosen Max, barely recovered from his wounds and a score of operations. It made no sense. But Max's polite protests had elicited only a tight smile from Himmler. "We are confident you are our man, colonel. We have faith in you." Why? Why not simply close the file? Why go outside his own organization and select someone from the army? Why choose a man whose stiff and throbbing knee made him wake in the night, sweating ice, and grinding his jaws to resist screaming? The battlefield had been so simple before the rapid promotions. The old longing for morphine rose in Max like a specter and made him shake. He would not sleep, he knew. He lurched to his feet and put on his robe. He would call Sergeant Klimmer from the telephone at the end of the corridor, then seek out Oskar Hüber. Max had to know if he was being sent into a mine field.

Forty-five minutes later, Sergeant Klimmer was picking his way through the streets, often running up blind alleys only to back out and try another route. Max awkwardly craned his neck to help "Kleini" guide the car past chunks of masonry and splinters of glass that still tumbled during the night from the damaged buildings. The tiniest breeze or the scurrying of a looter could bring down what was left of a pharmacy, a café, or an apartment house. Yesterday, a thousand Flying Fortresses and Liberators, accompanied by at least as many fighters, had swept over the city like an infinite, dark cloud. He remembered the sound of the bombing. *"What the Thunder Said,"* Max muttered. Lately fragments of *The Waste Land* had kept echoing in his head.

"Sir?"

Max took a deep breath and pressed the side of his face against the glass. "It looks clear," he said, but Kleini was already grinding the gears to forward. Like Max, the sergeant was a "hero," and if Kleini hadn't been short, barreled-chested, and curly-headed—"race-defiled" by remote Bohemian grandmothers—he too might have been interviewed, filmed, and photographed ad nauseam. Their bond had begun as no more than the friendship of men from the same region, the loyalty of a soldier to his young officer, but they were closer now than they could express. Each owed the other his life in several ways. Max wondered what his ancestors would have thought of this strange war, begun to prove the superiority of a race, but in which all men equally became victims under indiscriminate legions of airplanes and V-2 rockets. Since Kleini had pulled him bleeding and vomiting from the Saharan bomb crater, he had never felt his education, his breeding, his refined tastes meant anything. It had all melted in the pain. But the low-born Kleini had taken his wounding with a few swinish grunts and vague shrugs, and now he cheerfully went out after curfew and mastered a stubborn clutch with a wooden foot that could not feel the pedal.

They were in Oskar's neighborhood, according to the address Max had been given, but they weren't sure which street was which. The intersection with which Kleini intended to orient himself had been obliterated. In the dimmed headlights, three of the home guard were sharing a bottle. If they stopped the car and demanded to see a pass, Max intended to thrust the envelope of Himmler's orders at them as a bluff. But the gray-haired man and his boyish companions were in no mood for curfew duty. They stepped quickly into an alley. Max could barely see their languid eyes. They did not care if he was a spy, a saboteur, or Hitler himself. They were tired, thought Max. The whole universe is tired.

"This is it," said Kleini. "I'm sure it must be down there." A building had collapsed across the opening. Though the Reich gamely put old men, women, and children into the streets, they no longer had the strength or the will to clean up the endlessly renewed piles of rubble. "I imagine there's no other way in. Perhaps you'd better try tomorrow."

"No alley?"

"It's in a dead end."

"I'll walk."

"Your friend may not be home."

"I need to see him." He could hear Kleini breathing. "Really."

The sergeant shrugged. "I'll help you."

Max took the case folder off the seat with his good hand and awkwardly twisted himself to open the door. He stuffed the folder under his coat and clamped it against his chest with the stump of his left arm. By then Kleini had opened his door. Max took his cane, pushed against the floor, and slid out. "You go back to the barracks."

"That wouldn't be wise."

Max straightened himself. "I'll be fine."

"I'll wait for an hour, then. If you don't come out, I'll assume you are sharing old stories."

"Very well, but only an hour." Kleini nodded, but even in the dark, Max knew his mouth had the small twist that meant he would disobey and wait until Max came out.

Max moved toward the black maw of the cul-de-sac. A brick building had collapsed from the right and it seemed easier to negotiate the finer rubble to the left. It was tricky, however.

He couldn't see the pieces that rolled his ankle from side to side, and tapping with the outstretched cane helped only for the larger pieces.

"What are the roots that clutch, what branches grow/ Out of this stony rubbish?" He remembered the line from his English tutor, a Scotsman whose oystery eyes never stopped seeing the bombardments at Ypres and on the Somme. Max recited more lines as he continued to tediously pick his way, but he recalled only fragments: *"The Chair she sat in, like a burnished throne . . .";* *"The river's tent is broken . . .";* *"Datta: what have we given?"* The years before the war were similarly composed of odd shards that his detoxification had not pieced together. Periodically, his body still cruelly ached for the morphine that had made him believe he remembered everything, understood everything. *"HURRY UP PLEASE ITS TIME/ HURRY UP PLEASE ITS TIME."* Eliot would be amused, Max thought, at the idea of a man whose body had been shattered, blindly feeling his way among the rubble of a thousand-year Reich, able to recall only splinters of a poem: *"Stetson!/ You who were with me in the ships at Mylae!"*

The pavement now seemed clean. The file under the stub of his arm had shifted. He straightened it and it felt hot, like a rash. He moved forward slowly, climbed a stoop, and felt the number. Back on the sidewalk, he nearly tripped on a paving stone. He felt someone watching him through darkened windows but saw nothing to verify it. He rapped sharply at what should have been number 17, and when finally he heard the door open and a timid voice ask, "Yes?" he said only, "SS Lieutenant Colonel Oskar Hüber."

"Next door. Upstairs," said the voice quickly. "We don't know him." The door slammed. Max tapped his way to the next. No answer. He tried the knob. It opened. Closing it, he felt for a switch. Though the single bulb was dim, his eyes watered. He was in an aging foyer that smelled of the disinfectant the Afrika Korps used to kill lice. A jaundiced eye peeked at him through a cracked door. Max nodded. The door closed. He climbed the curved stair.

At the top was a wall and door peculiarly positioned to turn the second floor into an apartment. He heard a gramophone and American dance music. He hesitated, then knocked gently. The music stopped, and light blinded him again.

"My God!" said an overly cultivated voice. "Max-Baldur! Back from the dead!"

"Oskar?"

"Max! You made it!"

Max squinted to see if Oskar had changed from when they had last met, in a Viennese café just before Max left for Africa. There were flecks of gray in Oskar's close-cropped hair, but his eyes and mouth still had the bemused twist of a man whose greatest suffering had always been ennui, whose jaded attitude was granted him as much by inheritance as by experience. Oskar seemed much taller in the crisp black SS uniform.

"Are you going to spend the night in the corridor?" Oskar embraced him and pulled him inside. The file slipped from under Max's stub and tumbled onto the Persian rug. The papers fell to one side, but the photograph of the remains of Frau Schütz dropped on its edge, then slid under the claw-footed divan. Oskar quickly scooped up the file, and indifferently placed it on an end table. He then lifted the picture and held it level with his head. "My, someone *was* angry, weren't they?"

Despite all he had seen in combat, Max involuntarily grimaced at the memory of the photograph. "Put it away," he said.

Oskar perused his old friend as if startled by the sharpness in his voice. He indifferently popped it back into the file. "Another horror in a horrible world," he smiled. "I'm so glad you're here. Let me take your coat. Your hat."

"The Reichsführer's adjutant gave me your address," Max explained, "I thought perhaps you might know something. . . ."

"Me? It isn't what one knows that helps. It's what one instinctively knows. And you! As always. Rushing to business. A count should know better. A little diplomatic foreplay and then ask what you want to know. But that's what makes you a hero, eh? Charge!" He laughed and neatly placed Max's hat on the file. He gestured at a leather chair by a hot stove. "Sit."

"Thank you."

"Now is it aquavit? Schnapps? I have a very expensive cognac."

"Cognac would be"—Max paused—"*incredible.*" His eyes dropped as he recognized the ebullience in his voice to be from a more innocent time, when he and Oskar had attended boarding school in Vienna. He smiled. When he raised his head, Oskar was perusing him again.

"My," he said thoughtfully, "you are rearranged a bit. You *are* a hero!"

"I wrestled with a British shell. The shell won."

"And that's why Africa is theirs." Oskar shrugged as if to say "That's the way it goes." Then he added, "The wry humor of the hero. I don't understand it at all. I told you there were ways to enjoy yourself, especially during a war, but no, it's the conquest of the sands for you. March, march, march for the Fatherland."

"Please. I'm tired of being a symbol. I thought the Reichsführer wanted to meet me for more publicity. I dread it. But now I find myself in the midst of something."

"Enough of Herr Himmler, Max. There is more to life than a poultryman's dreams." He clapped his hands. "Breda! Lilli! It's all right. He is one of my oldest friends. We are breaking out the cognac."

A door behind a brocade curtain opened. A broad-hipped blonde swept it aside with a large hand. "You should have told us," she whined. "We were almost dressed. I ruined another pair of stockings!" She peeled off her jacket and skirt and plopped naked, except for her boots, on the divan. She stretched out, dropping her head on the armrest. The second woman, with heavy haunches and pendulous breasts, slapped the first's feet down and sat, asking, "So who is this friend of yours, Oskar?"

"Max-Baldur, Count von Prokofsk, recently Colonel von Prokofsk."

The first lifted her head and said casually, "I thought he looked familiar. Your picture was in the *Signal*."

"Several times," said Oskar. "And in newsreels. He is an important hero."

"But only a Wehrmacht one," said the heavy one distastefully. "Where are the cigarettes?" she demanded. "And the music?"

"At your command, ladies."

Max sighed. He was disappointed that Oskar was no different than he had been in school. They had been an unlikely pair then—the serious, thin scion of a minor Sudetenland manor and the worldly heir to a Viennese munitions fortune. Yet they had been inseparable. To Max's father, Oskar had been a bad influence with his knowledge of the city's back alleys and gaming houses, but Max knew he had used Oskar more than anyone recognized. The irritation on his father's face when Max mentioned "my friend Oskar" had been more rewarding from age sixteen to eighteen than any of the essay prizes or sports medals he had won. Oskar had faked his way through school and everything else. He was a connoisseur of connivery. A number of bad memories in which Max had borne the brunt of Oskar's wicked humor came back. Max had wanted to see him, of course, but he was troubled by the notion that Oskar had involved him with the murder of Frau Schütz merely as a joke, merely because Oskar worked in the Reichsführung SS and had the opportunity to foist off his friend on Himmler as a kind of detective. The times were too dangerous for pranks. Himmler had highly praised Oskar, as if he truly respected him, and Max had been fooled into thinking Oskar had changed. Yet, despite his high position, he was the adolescent he had always been. It was just another disappointment in a long, disappointing war. Max wanted to leave.

"So," said the thinner woman, blowing smoke at the ceiling and absentmindedly tugging her pubic hair, "how do you find the Reichsführer? He needs a chin, don't you think?"

The heavier one slapped her thigh.

"Ouch! Lilli! You left a mark!"

"You deserve worse!"

"Breda deserves a spanking," said Oskar. "She's so impudent!" He tossed back a glass of cognac. "Well? How do you find our chicken farmer?"

Lilli pointed seriously at Oskar. "You may be sorry one day!"

"Lilli is our prophet," said Oskar.

Max shifted to the front of his seat. "She is likely right. Listen, I am not really in a good mood. Perhaps if I came back—"

"Nonsense," said Oskar. "You haven't touched your cognac and I am just about to put on a Bix Beiderbecke. I got it straight from the Italian Front. Listen to this. You don't hear trumpet players like this in the Afrika Korps."

"Really, I did not come for this."

Oskar's gray eyes narrowed. "Ah," he said. "Serious matters." He suddenly dropped his bemused expression. "All right, girls! Into the bedroom!"

"But the Beiderbecke!" said Breda.

"Later. Old friends need to talk." He held out a decanter. "Take this. Drink. Amuse yourselves."

Breda looked bored, but when Lilli hefted herself up, she expelled a long stream of smoke and grabbed the bottle. "It's not as fun without you, dearie," she said as she closed the door.

There was a long silence. Oskar poured Max another cognac and squatted on an ottoman in front of him. He stared, waiting, until Max felt some of his old affection for Oskar return. It couldn't hurt to feel Oskar out. If the investigation were more than a joke, Max had to know.

"Can they hear us?" he asked.

Oskar shook his head. "Not unless they're leaning against the door. And they wouldn't. They are smart enough to know there are things they shouldn't know."

"Really, Oskar. Still chasing whores."

"They aren't whores. They're the finest volunteer secretaries in the SS." He said it as if he believed it. Oskar the chameleon. "They know how to please men. They know how to serve. Breda has been an invaluable spy. Lilli has less subtle ways of eliciting secrets. They don't even try to figure out the meaning of the secrets they steal."

"Oskar, you are going to come to a bad end."

He grinned. "Max, you have become your father."

Max laughed—a short but nonetheless real laugh. The first in a long time. He shook his head. "Hardly. How did we ever end up like this?"

"How do you mean?"

"You in the SS. Me with half of my body useless. You know, when I stand sideways, the right half of me looks like it always did. The left half is the bodily equivalent of the Reich: scarred, immobile, pieced together with scraps of string. From my left I could be Frankenstein's monster."

"They are badges of honor," said Oskar.

"That's what Himmler said. He showed me his duelling scar and was surprised when I said this"—he traced the healed white gash from ear to mouth—"was the result of shrapnel. As if I would mutilate my face like my father did."

"His isn't really a duelling scar, you know."

"Of course it was! He was a fool for nationalism. He made von Papen seem like a Frenchman."

"Not your father's. Himmler's. I have no doubt your father's scar was acquired in the proper way."

"A fool. And I, no less. I should have remained in Brazil instead of rushing back to prove my Germanhood."

"You would be an unknown collector of redskin mythology, Max. You're a hero."

"If you think, after this war is over, that my being blown up will keep my estates out of Czechoslovakia or whatever country they create to replace it, you're sillier than the Führer." He paused, thinking he had gone too far, but Oskar merely sipped his cognac.

"The Führer is a fool, your father was a fool, you are a fool, and I am a fool. Max-Baldur, you are dishearteningly disillusioned. The philosopher of cynicism."

Max wiped an irritating bead of sweat from just under the edge of his brow. "I've been through too much, Oskar, and I certainly feel like a fool. I've lost most of my arm, and most feeling, other than pain, in my leg. For most of the past two years I've either been happily dazed on morphine or shaking and vomiting as I try to be free of it." His voice quietened. He was ashamed of having spoken so freely. "And now I find myself ordered to find a murderer. I don't understand anything any more."

"I have always heard morphine has its claws."

"Icy claws."

"It isn't very easy to get these days." Oskar watched him closely for several seconds. "Cigarette?"

"I gave it up. Too much trouble with one hand."

"I see." Oskar lit, inhaled, and blew two long streams from his nose. "What disturbs you is that you have no experience as an investigator."

"Obviously. Why me? I have never investigated anything except the beliefs of the Carachacho Indians and my own scars. I asked Himmler why he insists on putting me on this and he casually dusts me off. Surely—" Max lifted his hand

• 15 •

helplessly. "If you did this to me, it isn't funny, Oskar. I beg you to come to your senses."

"Max, Max. You don't understand politics. You don't appreciate your position. It is an excellent opportunity. Why did he tell you that you were to become a detective, hmm?"

"I don't know. He said my reputation was unimpeachable. He said noblemen are born with integrity, and babbled about Prince Waldeck uncovering corruption. He said no one could suspect me of complicity in an SS cover-up."

"There, Maxy, did it ever occur to you to take him at his word?"

"Really—"

"Seriously. My friend, you are a celebrity. It is your reputation as a defender of the Reich Herr Himmler is using. He knows you have no experience. He knows you won't come up with anything more than that which was contained in the report from Commandant Schütz. But when you confirm that Communist prisoners killed Frau Schütz, no one will doubt you. It's legerdemain, my dear count. Publicity. You will strengthen the bridge between the army and the SS, which has always been strained. You will confirm the one is not so different from the other, that all Germans are in this struggle together. These things are more important than a murder."

"But why should anyone suspect anyone other than the prisoners? And, even so, there is no reason to accept my word."

"You are Wehrmacht. You are a hero. You are not even a member of the party."

"But why is there any doubt? Oskar, I too read about Frau Schütz's murder in the newspapers. I believe the SS as much as I believe anything in the papers. Who doubts the reports?"

Oskar searched with his eyes for an ashtray. When he saw Breda had shoved it under the edge of the divan, he opened the stove and flicked the butt into the flames.

"There are rumors," he said. "There is often corruption in these camps, and, being understaffed, always collusion between prisoners and guards. There are some here in Berlin who use internal scandals to improve their positions. It's the usual jockeying and our poultryman is protecting himself. What's the harm, Max? You take a little trip out to the camp at Ostheim. You look around, you listen to the witnesses, you get photographed looking at the murder site. Later you dictate a long, ponderous, and extremely tedious but properly German report, which no one will ever read. Personally, I recommend you do this quickly, before the Red Army makes Ostheim the capital of a Soviet Republic."

Fake it out, in other words, thought Max. Our eminent criminologists have independently verified the SS report. Germans, sleep peaceful tonight. "You'd be better than I for this kind of foolishness."

Oskar grinned and stood. "True. Which is why I'm a lieutenant colonel with an intact body. I did not pay for my rank with my limbs."

Max looked up sharply.

"More cognac?"

Max stared. Oskar indifferently refilled his glass.

"I don't believe it, Oskar. It is obvious I am no investigator. Anyone could see this. It will be plain I have been chosen exactly because I have no background. If there are rumors they will be confirmed by my selection. It is ludicrous. If I did bumble into something different from the report, I would be a worm in their apple. Whatever is going on, it isn't to discover who butchered Frau Commandant Schütz."

"Perhaps not, Max. But you've no need to worry. The investigation is a sideshow, and you have orders, don't you? You are a soldier. Obey. You'll sleep much easier if you don't imagine a universe filled with plots. There is no problem. Trust me."

"And these words come from you, the intrigue artist, who once left me with your father's mistress, when you knew he was coming home."

Oskar tipped his head as if flattered. " 'Enough of these sounds!' old friend. Do you prefer Breda or Lilli? Each has an extraordinary repertoire. . . ."

Max thought for a moment. He should leave. It was late. Kleini would be waiting with the car. But when he looked up at Oskar to say no, a nostalgia overtook him. He remembered Vienna in 1932 and the smell of anise cookies baking in the back room of an ethereal blonde's apartment. "Breda," he said, "would be *incredible*."

Oskar winked as he had so many times in the past, and, as he pulled back the curtain and left the room, the feeling of being young and carefree sagged. Max felt his age, his wounds, and the burning only morphine could cool. He was ashamed, not only for his longing for the past, which was as hazy as a book read in childhood, but for his having discovered nothing about his strange orders. He closed his eyes and the black-and-white photograph of the murdered woman was vivid on the back of his eyelids. When he opened them, Breda had entered the room. Pale and sleepy, she brushed cigarette ash from her left breast. "I am the lucky one," she said. "I get the hero."

· *Two* ·

The train crossed a shaky bridge over a narrow river that was probably a tributary of the Oder, then turned southeast and came to a stop. There was no clear explanation why. The troops guarding the cattle cars at the rear were scattered in the woods, and late in the afternoon, when Max asked Kleini to find out what he could, he came back with two versions. The engineer had heard that a British bomber crashed into the bridge near Pilica, but one of the sentries said that Poles had been encouraged to loosen the tracks and the line was likely being inspected by hand car. "There must be partisans," said Kleini. "Why else set up a picket line?"

"I don't like sitting like this. A train is too delicious a target," said Max.

Kleini smiled and Max knew he was remembering when they had slipped behind enemy lines to blow up an old colonial railway carrying supplies to British troops. Max had left it to Kleini to estimate the length of the fuse and he had timed it perfectly. The engine, steaming ahead at full speed, was directly over the explosive when it went off. The steam tank burst like a second bomb, hurling chunks of metal hundreds of feet in the air. Then the freight cars began to blow at random as each, filled with either gasoline or munitions, derailed or crashed into the cars in front, spewing orange and black plumes against the cloudless sky. When the explosions had settled, Max and Kleini had leapt onto the boulder they had sheltered behind and danced and embraced and wept with happiness. It had been so good to be a young warrior.

The compartment was stuffy and Kleini went outside and stretched out on a grassy hummock to doze away most of the day. Max, who had been studying the murder file for the entire journey, was nauseated by a pounding headache from the combination of the stench from the cattle cars at the rear and his tiredness from intensely concentrating on the meticulously catalogued details in each deposition and report. He assumed all the details were not important, but he was afraid that if he did not pay close enough attention to what he was reading, he might miss the one essential detail that might lead to the truth. Wasn't this how mysteries were solved? How could he know? In Brazil, in order to improve his Portuguese, he had read translations of S.S. Van Dyne and Earl Derr Biggers, but how real murders were solved was probably a great deal less tidy and much less rational than how Philo Vance or Charlie Chan would solve them. The haphazard way that Schütz and his officers had become convinced of the guilt of the three prisoners was probably more realistic and reliable than a tightly constructed plot.

Max closed the file in disgust, grabbed his cane, and limped along the track for fresh air, but now that the train stood still, the odor gathered around it like a cloud. The cattle cars contained Estonian and Latvian slave laborers being resettled after their factory in Germany had been leveled by Allied bombs, or so said the SS major in charge. "This smell is unbearable," Max said to him. "Worse than a sty."

"They *are* swine," said the major.

"Why don't you open the doors and force them to clean the cars?"

"They are used to filth," said the major. "They live and breed in it."

Max flipped a stone with his cane. "They are remarkably quiet. In the Sahara we always had difficulty getting the enlisted men to keep quiet. The sound carries for miles."

"Inside the cars it is very hot. They snort and root when we drop some food through the roof traps, but they're incredibly lazy. They sleep at the slightest opportunity. Like that." The major clicked his fingers and gestured at Kleini, snoring peacefully on the grass. A dragonfly hovered over his nose for a second, then zipped away. The major smacked his lips with distaste.

"Sgt. Klimmer deserves more than a nap," Max said coolly.

Max begged off dining with the officers and locked himself in his compartment with a bottle of mineral water and the case file. Despite its ponderousness, he had already read it three times: statements by each officer and two noncommissioned officers, a diagram of the residential area of the camp with a carefully drawn red Maltese cross where the body had been found, and photographs of the crime scene and grounds. One showed a scrap of paper with a tear in the center, soaked with blood, and with the words. "Röhm's Revenge" clearly and elegantly lettered in black Fraktur. Next to it lay an SS dagger, the symbol that a man had finally been accepted as a full member of the "knighthood." Except for the translucent smear on its blade, it was remarkably clean.

The second photograph, however, was nearly abstract, a Blue Rider nightmare with distorted and irregular elements. Without looking closely, Max mused, an ordinary person would dismiss it as a bad photograph, so poorly developed that one couldn't tell what it was supposed to represent. But Max had seen dozens of men blown apart. He had helped decide whether a fragment of a hand, a nose, a chunk of thigh, belonged in one grave or another. Each time he opened the file, the puzzle of this photograph transfixed him for at least a minute. He would rotate it until he thought it was right side up. Frau Commandant Schütz had come to a bad end. Whoever had wanted to kill her had wanted the satisfaction of more than killing her. It wasn't enough for her to be dead, because, obviously, most of the mutilation had occurred as the corpse lay dead on the ground.

She was at an angle across the photo, stretched from the upper left to the lower right. Her left arm reached into the pea plants, her fingers curled around, but not touching, a pea blossom. The fingernails were consummately well-manicured. Beginning at the wrist, however, was a gash winding cleanly to her shoulder, its gentle swerves in the photograph reminiscent of a country road seen from the air, with the flesh pulled back so that the white of the bones winked. The torso had been slashed through the blouse and stabbed until cloth mixed with bits of meat, breast, and skin. The abdomen had been gutted. The dark cavity glistened where the entrails had been. The thighs had been spread obscenely, and, like the arms, were flayed to the bone by meandering slashes, as if the murderer had intended to leave only a skeleton.

When Himmler had first offered him the photograph, Max had examined it quickly—the corpse was barely recognizable as human, after all, and this Frau Schütz was no one he had shared a cigarette or a meal with, no one he had reprimanded for failing to keep his rifle clean. The woman was of little more interest to him than Corporal Schwegger, who had patrolled the edge of the woods from twelve to eight searching for the escaped prisoners and saw nothing unusual, but had been forced nonetheless to write a five-page report on his evening's duty. Max, in fact, had no reaction at all to the body until he recognized that the odd twistings of flesh on top of the corpse's face were not, as he had thought, the entrails, but rather the curved, halved body of a fetus.

Once, when he was up the Amazon, somewhere near where it gets lost in the eddies and mists that begin the Orinoco, he had watched a Dutch anthropologist help a miner's wife, an Indian, through a breech birth. The child had finally emerged, greasy and white and still, and Max had sickened when he thought the baby was dead. But the Dutchman cleared the baby's mouth with his thick index finger and swatted its chest. It cried out so exultantly that Max plucked his notebook from his khaki shirt and wrote in youthful extravagance, "*Magnificat anima mea*: for the first time I have heard Bach." The mother, however, quickly noticed the child's extra finger on its left hand and she refused to touch not only the child, but the miner as well. She, and several of the Indians who worked with her husband, believed the baby should be abandoned to the jaguars. The husband seemed indifferent and the Dutchman wasn't sure he should interfere, but Max pleaded, begged, used every word he knew of the miner's Spanish and the Carachacho dialect. All his arguments about the sacredness of life and the innocence of children had no effect, either because of Max's inability to express these ideas in those languages or the nonexistence of such concepts in the culture. Finally, however, as the Indians grimly moved toward the child, Max shouted and turned their own mythology on them. They had six major gods. The deformed hand was a sign. If the child were destroyed, the river would rise in vengeance. The Indians seemed to interpret Max's desperateness as fear and were befuddled enough to make the mother suckle her son, at least temporarily. If the boy were lucky, when the miner eventually deserted his wife and son, as the prospectors inevitably did, the Indians might have gone on to protect this deformed child and his unlucky mother.

Max sat in his compartment sipping mineral water. Periodically, all the feelings that had washed over him in his desperate arguments to save the Carachacho infant flooded back. The intensity was too much to bear and not relieved by snapping the picture back into the folder. He was queasy, not so much from outrage or horror, but rather from feeling anything. He had been twenty when he argued for the infant. Nine years ago. A century. Part of him said Frau Schütz's fetus was lucky. It could never have its spirit and body broken by human stupidity passing for glory. And yet, it would also never feel the real glory Max had known when the Dutchman had finally forced the infant to cry. *Magnificat anima mea.* Sitting in the stifling train compartment with the smell of excrement and diseased flesh filling his gorge, again and again persuing the photograph and wondering if the train would ever move, he was nauseated by careening paradoxes a soldier hardens himself against and from which he had become even further detached over the past two years.

Finally, however, the train flexed, the catches between cars clanked, and the sentries clambered into the troop car. The stench of the cattle cars fell behind and Kleini tapped at the door. "If you like, sir, I will prepare your bunk."

When Max woke, the world was sheathed in fog. He dressed without calling the sergeant, congratulating himself on how adept he was getting with his good hand. It was already midday. He worked his way to the officers' dining car. There were only three of them on the train: himself, the SS major, and an SS lieutenant. The SS men talked mainly of a counter-offensive in Normandy. The major argued that the fall of Cherbourg was deliberate, an attempt to narrow the front so that the army could split the Allied forces with a panzer ax and drive them off the continent. The Americans in particular, he argued, were inexperienced and prone to fall for traps more subtle commanders might devise. The lieutenant insisted that no one was really concerned with the Western front. The real enemy was Communism. The Germans had let Cherbourg fall simply to avoid expending too much effort against the expeditionary forces. They would deal with the British and Americans as soon as the Russians were driven back to the Arctic.

Max mostly nodded. It felt pleasant to forget Frau Schütz and listen to pointless discussions. The fog swirled past, occasionally revealing a tree, a water tower, an empty train station with an unpronounceable name. The eggs and steak were delicious. The SS ate well. Their red wine was obviously French, if not particularly fine. Max stayed until just before dusk, when there was a brief moment of sunshine and the lush countryside rose like a green mist to the distant mountains. The three of them could have been strangers on holiday, swapping stories, discussing their hometowns, but when the sun was swallowed in grayness again, the major began to philosophize about the decadence of the old nobility and told how an effeminate Saxon prince had fawned on him at his arrest. "There was Jew in his blood, I'll warrant."

"They are everywhere," said the lieutenant.

"Not for long." The major tipped the wine bottle over his glass, shook it when nothing more came out, and reached for a cigar. "Colonel, surely you among the nobility have been aware of the rampant corruption around you. It must have outraged patriots like yourself."

Max immediately remembered a tirade his father had poured forth at a dinner long ago. "Not myself. Not personally. To be a Sudetenland German, to have lost most of our ancestral lands—we did not mix with the more notable nobles. And I spent many years in South America."

"So many possibilities for development there," said the major.

"And now you are investigating the episode at Ostheim," said the lieutenant.

"I'm not sure how much liberty I have to discuss that."

"Pah!" said the major. "Everyone knows. Something stinks out there. If I ever get to run a camp, there won't be any chance prisoners will get near my wife. If you want my opinion, the Reichsführer is just waiting for your report to get

• 24 •

rid of someone. If prisoners have free run like that, security has failed utterly."

"I can't say."

"Well, as you wish, colonel, but I sometimes think an open discussion would end all the silly rumors. There is much whispering that should be ended. I'm not saying where I heard it, but the Führer himself has great hopes for Ostheim, and is furious an ordinary crime has caused gossip in the SS."

"Gossip? Is this why I am sent?"

The SS major grinned. "Who knows? There is no reason to involve the army. It is, I must say, somewhat offensive. No insult to you intended."

"I understand." Max leaned forward. "I told Himmler that myself," he lied. "Perhaps you will let me in on some of these rumors."

"They are trivial," said the major. "Blatantly silly."

Max sat back.

"You don't seem the policeman type," said the lieutenant.

"No," said Max. He glanced out at the fog and the photograph of Frau Schütz seemed to be projected onto it. "And it is hardly an ordinary murder."

"How do you mean, colonel?"

Max wanted to pay them back for telling him nothing. "I really don't feel free to discuss it. I'm sorry."

There was a long silence.

"This travel!" said Max impatiently. "It exhausts me. I must lie down."

"The wine goes to one's head," said the lieutenant.

Max nodded amiably. "Very pleasantly, though. Good night."

"You should arrive at Ostheim near midnight, I'd guess," said the major.

"Sergeant Klimmer will wake me."

"Ah, but who will wake him?" he laughed.

The SS men then turned to each other as if Max had already left the compartment and began to talk earnestly about training programs. Max thought of Oskar and wondered how anyone so lighthearted could adapt himself to the religious intensity of the SS. Even when SS men relaxed, some part of them was weighing, calculating, assessing not just others but, most important, themselves. Usually their characters were filled

• 25 •

with the utter lack of doubt that came through in the major and in the report written by Commandant Schütz on his wife's murder. They did not qualify anything they said. If they allowed any ambiguity into their universe, all would be chaos. They were mystical at the core: substituting faith in their "knighthood" and its destiny for any quibbling over rightness or practicality. Captain Joachim von Rauschwald, Schütz's second in command, had written his report in this way, as if the truth of what had happened was much less important than that he had personally avenged Frau Schütz by hanging the murderers with nooses of barbed wire. He described the carrying out of this duty in more detail than he had accounted for his whereabouts the night of the murder. He even mechanically described the poor physical health of the killers: two were nearly insensible from typhus. He carefully mentioned that his double loops of wire had drawn little blood from the neck of murderer Komnoliakov, though gore streamed from the other two. If the wrong men had been hanged, this von Rauschwald would likely shrug. It was the victim's destiny to be a victim, and there could be no ambiguity in that. If orders changed, such men were blind to the contradictions. It was difficult to imagine Oskar Hüber as part of this cult. Oskar was a skeptic. He had always been. A man like that could neither see a "grand plan" nor accept the total submersion of the self in an ideal. How had the chameleon not revealed his true colors? Or could he conceal a profound faith behind a false superficiality? Could it be another trite case of the convert's being more religious than those who converted him? That would be the greatest joke of all.

The train ground to a halt well before midnight. An SS corporal rapped on Max's door and ushered in a driver wearing the red and white patch of a Byelorussian Waffen-SS volunteer. The train would be halted until at least the next day—the rain had undermined the tracks leading to Ostheim. The huge Byelorussian held out a note from Commandant Schütz:

Dear Colonel von Prokosk:
(He had misspelled Max's name.)
I apologize for the inconvenience. I am sending Sgt. Baranovitch. Though the trip is longer by automobile, it will be much shorter in time. It is annoying how these

bureaucratic matters often result in genuine human inconvenience. You will soon see how pointless this whole inconvenience to a hero like yourself is.

With the highest respect,
SS Commandant Major Bodo Schütz,
Commanding Officer, Ostheim

Kleini appeared in the doorway behind the messengers. He glanced at the SS corporal, then up at Baranovitch. "Sgt. Klimmer reporting, sir."

"We are leaving the train," said Max. "Pack my belongings."

The SS corporal stepped aside, but Baranovitch stood dumbly in place, his breathing audible as an aged bulldog's.

"And you, sergeant, you know this road well enough to drive it in the dark?"

"Very well. Sir. Very well." His accent was thick.

"Is it a good road?"

Baranovitch snaked his hand. "Back and forth, but I know it like my mother's face."

"Good. We will meet you outside. Go to the troop car, have some tea."

"I will wait by the car, thank you, sir." He saluted and left.

Max closed the compartment door and watched Kleini pull the bags from the upper rack. He thought for a moment, then pointed to his briefcase with his cane. "Kleini," he whispered.

"Sir?"

"The two pistols. Take one. Ride up front with Baranovitch. Watch him closely."

Kleini looked surprised, as if he hadn't yet realized that they were involved in anything more than a morale tour. "An officer's pistol?"

"Keep it concealed."

He nodded. Questions were forming, but he could not articulate them. "Sir . . . ?"

Max moved closer to him. "Kleini, you are the only man I can trust out here. If this Byelorussian tries anything peculiar, you kill him. If he doesn't, you try to get friendly and find out what he knows. I don't know what we are getting into, and I may need all the information I can get. You sergeants can find out how clean an officer's underwear is better than another officer. You understand?"

"This investigation is serious?"

"Maybe. The hair on my neck is prickling. If it isn't something the surgeons misconnected, we are in a minefield, Kleini. I have read the case file until my head feels like it will split, and that is all I can say. Until we know where the mines are . . ."

Kleini nodded. "We'll make it," he winked. "Didn't your doctor say you've got more lives than a cat?"

"I can't afford to lose any more. These are subtle mines this time." He raised the stub of his arm. "And we, my friend, are running out of parts."

Kleini stroked the tunic flat he had just folded into the suitcase, contemplated it for a second, then reached for the briefcase with the guns.

· *Three* ·

As the car swayed, its brakes screeching through the dark, Max was barely able to keep from sliding across the seat. Kleini gripped the dash with both hands. If Baranovitch were leading them into an ambush, he wasn't making the car very easy to hit. Max thought of Reinhard Heydrich. He had met him at a fencing exhibition two weeks before he had shipped for Africa. About the time Max had first been promoted, Heydrich was appointed Reich Protector of Bohemia and Moravia, only to be assassinated as his car rounded a curve in Czechoslovakia. He supposedly died chasing his assailants, but Max wondered if Heydrich's driver had simply smashed them into a tree—like Baranovitch threatened to do at any moment—and the "assassination" had been merely an excuse to crack down on the resistance.

Nausea was rising in Max's throat as he noticed the fine pink light to the east. The road seemed to be straightening and the outline of trees became visible. Baranovitch yawned and drove faster. For a second it looked as if he might drive through a stone wall that suddenly loomed ahead of them, but the brakes shrieked again, and when Max pushed himself upright after being thrown against the seat, he peered out through the windshield. Before him was a wood archway with the word "Ostheim" in black letters over the gate. The guards, wearing the Trident of Vladimir patches indicating Ukrainian volunteers, recognized Baranovitch and waved the car through. Baranovitch turned left and after a few hundred yards they came upon a second gate, this one guarded by two officious Germans.

"Welcome to Ostheim, Colonel von Prokofsk," said the corporal. "You will be taken to your quarters to freshen up, if you like. Commandant Schütz would like to see you as soon as possible."

"I do not wish to wake your commandant," said Max.

The corporal seemed almost offended. "Commandant Schütz rises at four."

"Ah," nodded Max. "Then let's not keep him waiting."

A row of low fieldstone huts lined a dirt parade ground narrower than a soccer field but nearly as long. A second line of wooden houses, a meter off the ground on stone piers, sat opposite them. A dozen prisoners on scaffolds were painting the wooden structures or replacing split boards. Most of the buildings were either offices or barracks. Corrugated walkways bridged a few muddy paths between the huts, though most of the ground seemed hard and dry. Baranovitch stopped at one end, gestured with his head, and grunted, "His majesty's inside."

Max turned and leaned out as the Byelorussian opened the door. "What do you mean?"he asked sharply.

"Sir?" said Baranovitch.

" 'His majesty.' What did you mean by it?"

"I meant only the highest respect." His lips pursed. His gray eyes were cool and hard.

Max knew he would only harden more if pressed. Glancing at Kleini, who was biliously pale from the ride, he smiled and whispered, "You should never let officers know what your pet names for them are." He winked. "Too often they try to live up to them."

Baranovitch's stone face did not change.

"You will take care of Sergeant Klimmer, eh? Klimmer always needs his breakfast."

"Yes, sir."

"I'll escort you, sir," said Kleini. "I don't think I can eat."

"I'll be fine, sergeant."

Max entered the building quietly and closed the door behind him. A political prisoner wearing a red triangle on his chest was sorting thick ledgers on top of a cabinet. When he spotted

Max, he bolted upright, dropped the book he was holding, and shuffled toward him.

"Good day, sir, good day. Can I be of assistance, sir?"

The prisoner smelled sour, like old beer. His eyes were jaundiced and bleary. Max looked past him.

"Commandant Schütz?"

"Certainly, sir, and whom shall I say is calling, sir?"

"Colonel von Prokofsk. I'm expected."

"Indeed you are, sir. Indeed expected. Follow me, if you please, sir."

Max thought it odd that a prisoner seemed to be the only person in the building. "A moment," he said. "Why were you stacking those ledgers?"

"It's my job, sir. I'm a clerk, sir."

"I assume these records are not confidential?"

"Oh no, sir. Though I assure you if they were I could be completely trusted. I am completely rehabilitated, sir. In fact, I am willing to do whatever I can to support the Reich and our master Adolf Hitler."

The obsequious clerk barely concealed a quaver in his voice. Max thought of street beggars he had seen in Manaus, masking their bitter hatred for foreigners with a cloying servility. This clerk, however, was so timid, at least in appearance, that Max found him even more disgusting than the beggars. He passed it off as part of his weariness. The clerk, after all, had asked nothing of him. "Very well," he sighed.

He was led past several empty desks to a heavy oak door. The clerk tapped his bony knuckles, then Max stepped past him and quietly saluted the commandant. "Heil Hitler."

Schütz snapped to attention like an eager recruit. "Heil Hitler!"

Numerous papers were scattered on his desk, and he appeared to have been working for some time. Yet, his uniform was crisp, his face alert, and the band of his remaining hair neatly trimmed. He stayed behind his desk and spoke in clipped tones. "Colonel von Prokofsk, I am pleased to make your acquaintance. Your heroism is well known to all Germans. Please, be seated. You are no doubt tired from your journey—an unnecessary one, you shall soon see."

"I am sorry to have to meet you under these circumstances," said Max. "May I express my condolences?"

Schütz shrugged. "These things happen," he said. "Please. Sit."

Max studied the commandant carefully. "I am certain it must be painful for you to have to go through an inquiry like this. Especially after you so carefully conducted an investigation of your own."

Schütz was expressionless. Max noticed a scratch just above the hairline over his ear. "It is not, I assure you, painful. What the Reichsführer deems important, I deem important, but, as I have expressed in several letters—I feel no need to keep this confidential—I am somewhat insulted. The whole matter dragging on in this way is an annoyance. I have important work to do here. This camp is barely two years old. The Führer himself is very interested in its success, I assure you. I cannot waste time on past matters."

"Commandant Schütz, this 'past matter' is the butchery of your wife."

Schütz blinked. "In the time of destiny, personal matters must be set aside. Nothing will bring her back." The commandant's gaze was unwavering. Max uncomfortably prodded the toe of his boot with his cane.

"Well," he said, "I have no particular intention of disrupting your work. I am merely here to carry out my duties. Personally, I fail to see the necessity."

Schütz stood abruptly. "Tea, perhaps? Coffee?"

"You SS officers are well-supplied. Real coffee?"

"I have been saving some for a special occasion. My wife was very fond of it."

"If it's not imposing."

"I wanted it myself. It is no imposition." He pressed the buzzer on his desk, then reached into a drawer. The prisoner-clerk came in.

"Yes, my commandant?"

"Go to the mess. Tell them to brew a half liter of this." He held out a small cloth sack. "Make certain not a speck of it is lost."

"Yes, my commandant." The clerk scurried away. Schütz sat, laced his fingers over his midsection, and stared.

Max uncomfortably peered about the room. "The building seems sturdy. I would think a camp like this would only be temporary."

"That is shortsighted thinking. These camps will be part of the new world order for some time."

"I meant that the Russians have advanced quite well recently."

"We are in no danger of the front."

"They are not that far now, I understand."

"A temporary setback. The Slavs are subhuman. This is scientifically proved."

Max straightened his back. He was sore from the jolting ride. "For subhumans, the Reds have been quite successful lately. Even Gobineau or Julius Streicher would have to admit that."

Schütz's eyes flashed. It *was* possible to anger him, violently. He spoke through his teeth. "It is this kind of defeatist attitude which led to Versailles. You, you aristocrats, you army types, you have no vision. You cannot see the ultimate victory. A temporary setback to you means we have lost." He slapped his desk, then pushed out his hand as if shoving something away. "We will sweep them back, back across the Caucasus and into the plains of Asia. Someday Ostheim will be the westernmost of a chain of camps developing this wasteland called the Soviet Republic. Camps will stretch across the continent like an archipelago across an ocean. And who will rule this great chain? Me. Yes, me. Under my Führer. Me. Because I am loyal to my Führer. Me, because I have the vision to see this and because I have worked for years to make it true."

"Indeed," said Max quietly. "As a German, one can only hope that your vision of a Soviet defeat will come true."

"It shall. Mark my words. Any day those stinking Bolsheviks will collapse."

"I hope so. We all hope so."

" 'Room to live.' That's what this war is about. And I will provide the means to make those vast spaces livable. Roads, schools, grain elevators, mines, factories. As the indigenous population is displaced, the Aryans will reclaim their homeland." He seemed to be looking through Max and smiling at what he saw. "Yes," he said quietly. "It shall be. It shall be."

Max prodded the toe of his boot with his cane and shifted in his chair again. Eventually, he said cautiously, "Commandant

Schütz, you seem a well-informed man with obvious connections. Do you know why I have been sent here?"

Schütz's eyes grew steely again. "To investigate this murder."

"No. That isn't what I mean. Why have *I* been sent? Let me be blunt. Before the war, I studied anthropology. I have no experience in crime. There is some motive behind my assignment that is not clear. Would it not be to my benefit to know this?"

"Quite possibly. But I can tell you nothing. I suspect you are merely here to add another stamp of authenticity to my conclusions. Caesar's wife must be above suspicion."

"Excuse me?"

"Those closest to the Führer must be purer than Parsifal."

"Ah."

"In a world of political intrigue, rumors must be stopped. You will prevent a minor annoyance, that's all."

"I can count on your complete cooperation, then?"

"Naturally."

"And you will go through all details of that evening and the subsequent investigations?"

"No, Count von Prokofsk."

"Excuse me?"

He spread his hands over his desk. "I am very busy, here. We have some five thousand interns. I am responsible. In a month's time we may have three times as many, or so I hope."

"Commandant, I come with orders from the Reichsführer." Max tapped his pocket.

Schütz smiled. "Don't misunderstand. I will put Captain von Rauschwald at your disposal, if necessary. However, I expect that you will have to rely almost entirely upon yourself."

"But I would think it is essential that I get full cooperation from everyone involved."

"You will have no problems if you are reasonable. I promise you."

There was a weak rap on the door. The clerk had returned with an antique silver pot of coffee. He scurried about, placing the tray on a map table against the wall. The odor immediately filled the room. "How delightful," said Max.

"As I said," beamed Schütz.

The clerk, nodding, gave them their cups and backed out of the room.

Max inhaled the steam rising from his cup, then balanced cup and saucer on his thigh.

"The fool should have gotten you a table," said Schütz.

"No," said Max. "I must learn to live with myself."

"So must we all, eh?"

Max tasted the coffee. It was very weak and obviously adulterated. "Very good," he said. "I haven't had as good since Brazil."

"It is superior, isn't it?"

"May I ask a question, commandant? Oh, not on the murder."

"Naturally. I want you to feel free with me, though I find no need for your being here."

"This clerk of yours. He is essentially unguarded. He moves about in your offices. He is alone with you."

"And you ask why?"

Max tilted his head to one side.

"Because they are animals. They must never see that we fear them."

"But your wife was murdered."

"And like mad dogs, the murderers were put out of their misery." He placed his cup carefully back in his saucer. "They cannot know how much we despise them until they know we shall never fear them. Never." He thrust a squat finger forward. The set of his jaw was like Mussolini's.

"Ah," said Max.

"Never," said Schütz.

· *Four* ·

"**H**e asked me if I would begin today, but I said no. This irritated him." Max paused and looked through the fencing at one of the nine perimeter watchtowers. The midafternoon sun had raised thousands of gnats and flies from their hiding places.

"From what they say in the barracks, I'd say irritation is Major Schütz's specialty," said Kleini. "He doesn't like us, I take it?"

Max glanced over his shoulder. "He was polite, but barely. He'll get worse. I don't think it's personal. Typical SS. He's desperately sure of himself because he was so unsure of himself before he had a uniform. He was probably a baker or something of the sort before National Socialism."

"Close," Kleini smiled. "A sausagemaker."

"Really?"

"Unless Sergeant Duitser was pulling my leg."

Max paused and gently tapped his cane against Kleini's shin. "You see? That's what I mean. Enlisted men know the officers better than they know themselves. I need your eyes and ears. Did you, by any chance, get a grip on why I was assigned to this?"

"No. I think Duitser may open up, though."

"Keep at it."

Kleini suppressed a yawn. "A warm day."

"Humid."

"I tried to nap but couldn't." He brushed at the insects hovering in front of his face.

"Nor I. My leg was throbbing." They reached the corner and looked down the long side of the fence. The garden was at the far end. They glanced in its direction for a moment, then peered across the dog run and barbed wire toward the back of the prisoners' huts.

Kleini spat. "I hate these places. They smell. It is hard to believe we have come to this."

"Well, we will do our job and get back to Germany."

Kleini shook his head. "No, colonel, you dismiss it too easily. You have been out of touch. Don't think those tales you heard were part of the morphine. They are real. They are worse. These are bad places under the control of worse men."

The word "morphine" struck Max like a fist. "There are excesses in every war, Kleini. You have seen enough to know that."

"But you have not really seen these camps. You don't really know what is going on. I have friends. While you were laid up, I heard things. If they're only half true . . ."

"Come, come. You act like the Nazis were the first to mistreat the innocent, like Germany invented injustice. History is full of juggernauts rolling over the innocent. Prison guards always get out of hand."

"Perhaps so," said Kleini, "but someday we may look back on this, and then we will know how much we avoided seeing for ourselves."

"It is very difficult to know the truth about oneself."

"You are just mouthing truisms, colonel." He straightened up and turned from the fence. "I'm sorry. I forgot myself."

"No," said Max. "No. You must speak freely. I need your honesty. I need your brain."

"Brain!" Kleini snorted. "If I had a brain, *I'd* be the officer."

He prodded Kleini's belly with the handle of his cane. "And if you had a very small one, perhaps you'd even be a count, eh?"

They strolled on, ignoring the vicious dogs that paced just beyond the wire, and the distant voice of someone shouting orders in the compound. To the left, in succession, they passed the barracks of the large Byelorussian and Ukrainian contingents, then that of the Germans. At the end was the mess, then the commandant's office. Just beyond, as if dropped out of a movie set, was a set of six small cottages, each with a stone fence and flower boxes in the thatch roof dormers. The cottages lined three sides of a lawn, lush and green, with white chairs and tables. Children were tossing a red ball to a Pomeranian, then chasing the dog and wrestling it away from him. Two women smoked placidly while a woman in prison dress brought a tray.

Max and Kleini paused, studied the strange vision, then looked at each other.

"*Summer surprised us, coming over the Starnbergersee . . . ,*" Max murmured, "*we stopped in the colonnade . . . and drank coffee, and talked for an hour.*"

"What?"

"A poem," said Max. "About memory gone unreal."

"Your Scottish tutor, again," said Kleini. "You said you hated him, but you seem to remember everything he taught you."

"Perhaps because I hated him. When one is young, one wants Keats, Byron, Heine. Instead of Shakespeare to teach me English, he pounded me with Eliot. Now modern art does not suit the new Germany, crumbling though it is. In twenty years literature may forget Mr. Eliot. One is better off learning dead poets."

They reached the edge of the large garden. There were dozens of rows of potatoes, cabbages, and other vegetables. Three prisoners, guarded by a very young Ukrainian private, were carefully stepping between the rows and putting rocks in burlap sacks. They began to work faster when they saw Max and Kleini approaching. In the pea patch, under the corner guard tower, there was little sign of the murder, except for a small circle of trampled plants. Max contemplated the area for a moment. The photograph flashed across his mind. Kleini plucked a drying pod from a pea plant and munched its contents.

"Terrible soil."

"Yes," said Max. He poked around in the dirt.

"They won't get good potatoes."

"No." He turned over several rocks. "This is the point at which I should find a button that will reveal the killer."

Kleini lifted his head toward the guard tower. "Is that how it works?"

"Supposedly."

"And the guard that night, he heard nothing?"

"Supposedly."

"That is hard to believe."

Max gave up poking. He cleaned the tip of his cane with his hand. "Very hard. Even on a moonless night, he should have noticed something, and if it were too dark to see, why would Frau Schütz be stumbling in the pea plants?"

"A secret meeting?"

"Perhaps."

"Or the body was dumped here."

"Ah."

"The guard, maybe he was asleep. Or drunk."

"If they follow standard practice, they are supposed to signal each other at regular intervals."

"But who knows out here? Perhaps they worked out something to let themselves sleep."

"That," said Max, "you can find out. You move in your circles; I will move in mine."

"You are beginning to enjoy this, I think."

Max squinted.

"I can see something in your eyes."

Max shook his head. "We are just here to confirm the report. We mustn't make too much of it."

"Colonel, you are a poor liar. You like a good game. You had the same expression when you leaned over a map of an enemy position. You haven't been interested in anything for months, but now there's a glimmer in your eyes. I know you like an old shoe."

"Nonsense, I—"

Something rumbled, then thumped, then subsided to a tinkling like broken glass. A prisoner stood staring at the rip in the bottom of his sack as if it were inexplicable. The stones he had been carefully gathering were piled at his feet. The guard charged forward, swearing in Ukrainian. The prisoner mumbled quick, apologetic phrases out of his toothless mouth and poked a brown finger at the guilty tear. The guard pointed at a crushed potato plant, then, exploding with anger, smashed his rifle butt into the prisoner's jaw. The man collapsed like a rag. The guard shouted and kicked him. The heavy boots thudded against the fallen man's side. The other prisoners dropped their heads. The guard pulled the bolt on his rifle and aimed it downward.

Time seemed to freeze as Max shouted. A blur charging across the garden rows smacked into the guard's side, sending him sprawling. The rifle discharged. Kleini awkwardly rolled off the guard and tossed the rifle behind him. The guard looked up and raised himself on his hands, hissing something that Max could not hear. Kleini kicked upward, rotating his body on his shoulder. He caught the guard in the face with the toe of his wooden foot. The boy fell back, his legs twisted under him, his helmet comically cocked, his eyes rolling in shocked confusion.

When Max reached Kleini, the sergeant was sitting upright, puffing. He glanced upward and gestured toward his boot. "I've broken it now." He exhaled. "Damn it." The wooden foot was twisted completely to the side.

"Are you all right?"

"It's not easy to run"—he coughed—"with that thing."

"You did well."

Guards were running from the tower. The two standing prisoners stared at Max in astonishment. The private, recovering his senses, raised a weak hand to the blood dribbling off his forehead. Max limped over to the prisoner who had dropped the stones. His jaw was smashed. Max felt for a pulse in the bony wrist and couldn't find one, though he could hear the rattle of wet breathing.

Max stood to face two Byelorussian guards. "Take this man to the infirmary," he said.

"What is this?"

Max recognized the low voice of Sergeant Baranovitch. "This guard was going to shoot a prisoner."

"And?"

"And I ordered him to stop."

Baranovitch leaned over the private, who stuck out his lip in bewilderment.

"He crushed the plants," he said, swallowing hard.

Baranovitch nodded and prodded the supine prisoner with his toe. "He won't live. You should have let him finish."

"I have given orders that he be taken to the infirmary, sergeant."

Baranovitch pursed his mouth as if his great slow brain were considering what sort of fool he was dealing with. "Yes, sir, my colonel." He waved in the two guards, then directed the two prisoners to sit.

Kleini, who had hopped up on one leg, flopped the boot containing the wooden foot back and forth. "I knew it," he muttered. "The damn straps."

"We'll get it fixed," said Max, and telling Kleini to put a hand on his shoulder, he helped him hop toward the stone fences around the cottages. It was much farther than it seemed, or else the humidity and the eyes watching from all directions made it seem so.

When Kleini finally settled onto a bench just inside one of the walls, he muttered, "The lame leading the lame."

"We'll get a car."

"My God," said a throaty female voice, "his ankle is broken!" The woman was very fat, with a buttery complexion. She had thick fingers, which she pressed against her doughy chest.

Kleini, still breathing hard, raised the "broken" leg and waved it so that the foot flopped. "Wooden," he said. "Can't break an ankle you don't have."

"It came loose," said Max. "We are sorry to intrude on your teatime. I am Colonel von Prokofsk, and this is Sergeant Klimmer." He touched his cane to his hat bill.

"Oh, I am so pleased, Count von Prokofsk. We were so looking forward to meeting you at dinner. I am Frau Ursule Frank. Dr. Klaus Frank is my husband. You have met?"

"Not yet."

Another woman, after shooing the children back, stepped around Frau Frank. She was slender, somewhat tall for a woman, with bronze hair and full lips. When she smiled, Max noticed a gap between her front teeth. She extended her hand and then, suddenly, dropped it back when she saw the pinned sleeve of Max's tunic. He quickly, however, blocked its retreat with his hand, and raised it (along with his cane) to just below his lowered lips. "I—I am Frau von Rauschwald. Bette von Rauschwald."

"Max-Baldur von Prokofsk," he said, "but, please, both of you must call me Max."

"Oh I think nobility is so elegant," said Frau Frank. "The new order can never replace such sophistication; it must simply incorporate it, don't you think?"

"I'm afraid the only nobility left—like me—is not of much consequence."

"My husband," said Frau von Rauschwald, "would never agree with that."

"Nor I," said Frau Frank. "Surely your man here needs some help. Shall I ring for my husband? He will come immediately. Can you join us? We were having springerle and chamomile. We would be honored."

"I would not impose."

"Never," said Bette.

"Done, then!" chirped Ursule, who in horrified fascination blinked at the blunt end of Kleini's leg.

He had removed his boot and was fingering the straps of his foot. "Don't bother your husband," he said. "This buckle tore through. I will poke a hole with my penknife and it will do, for a while."

"Well," she said, "you will join us then?"

"I don't much belong at officers' teas," he said. "I must get back to the barracks."

"You are certain you'll be all right?" asked Max.

"Don't be silly, colonel."

Frau Frank took Max's arm and they walked around the cottage to the enclosed lawn. "You are very familiar with your sergeant, Count von Prokofsk. I am surprised a man of your rank and stature doesn't have a lieutenant as an aide."

"Sergeant Klimmer could be a lieutenant any time he wishes. I would see to that."

"He refuses?"

"He says he is a simple man, more suited to obey orders than invent them, and to be sergeant is enough misery."

Frau von Rauschwald leaned forward to speak past Frau Frank. "You are close."

"He saved my life more times than I'd like to admit. It's a coincidence we travelled so far from where we were both born, only to meet in Libya. If there had been no war, we would only have met if he got a job mucking my father's stables. Yet, now, he's an excellent typist, he's courageous, he has good sense, and he has all the skills, except a full education, of a gentleman's private secretary or valet."

"You are generous with inferiors," said Frau von Rauschwald.

"I consider him my friend."

She moved ahead to pull out a chair.

"You ladies are too solicitous."

"And what opportunity have we had for company?" said Frau Frank. "I will fetch a fresh pot of tea."

"Have Magda do it," said Frau von Rauschwald.

"No, no," said the fat woman over her shoulder and headed for the cottage opposite. "I won't waste this chance to serve a count."

Max bemusedly stretched his fingers on the marble-topped table. "She makes too much of me."

"We see no one in this place," Frau von Rauschwald sighed.

He watched her brush a bright strand of hair from her strong cheekbones. She caught him staring at her, so he quickly looked at the children who had gathered several yards away to stare at him. "Yours?"

"Greta, on the end. And Hedwig."

"They are five, six?"

"Greta is six. Hedwig is seven."

"You've been married for a while, then."

"Forever," she said matter-of-factly. "Go away, children. Go play with Hermann." She smiled sweetly. "You won't put that in your report, will you?"

"What?"

"That Ursule's son, Little Klaus, named their dog after Field Marshal Goering."

Max pursued his lips. "I would have expected a rounder dog."

She tilted her head to one side and he thought she was pretty. He didn't want to think about that, so he perused the cottages. "It is so pleasant here. One wouldn't know we were in the middle of a war."

"You wouldn't say that if you were in my seat. And today we're lucky. The wind is blowing toward the prisoners' compound."

"Ah." The memory of the cattle cars came back. "Perhaps you'd rather sit here, facing your home."

"No," she said. "I prefer to face the truth."

"That is somewhat surprising."

She was startled. "Why?"

"Because you are obviously embarrassed at my, ah, condition. You mustn't feel awkward at my being such a mess."

"It was only momentary," she said, looking him straight in the eyes. "I was surprised. I expected another bald Prussian. You surprised me. That's all. I am comfortable with wounds. One must be."

"And here we are!" Frau Frank slid a tray onto the table. "I have brought the honey too. Nothing too fine for our visitor."

"You are too kind," said Max. Frau Frank chattered about how difficult it had been to get anise seed for the springerle, surprisingly difficult, and butter. The last shipment of butter turned rancid within a day of arriving because, she supposed, of train delays.

Max heard two shots fired in rapid succession, then a third, about a thousand meters away. Neither of the women, however, paid any attention to them. Frau Frank had moved on to her recipe for Scottish shortbreads. Frau von Rauschwald closed her eyes and breathed deeply, her nostrils almost grasping at the warm air.

"Very good chamomile," said Max, putting down his cup.

"An old woman sold it at the gate one day. She had picked the flowers locally. God knows where she came from. There is nothing for miles. The villages are all relocated. I am so pleased you are pleased, Count von Prokofsk."

"Call me Max. I insist."

"You are so refreshing!" said Frau Frank. "Neither Klaus nor I are much for ceremony."

Bette von Rauschwald opened her eyes. "Lila loved chamomile."

"And apple cake," said Frau Frank.

"Lila Schütz, you mean?"

They nodded.

Max lifted a springerle, then placed it back on the table. "You know, ladies, if it isn't too painful, I would be indebted to you if, at a time not inconvenient to you, you would tell me about Frau Schütz. What she was like personally. What she thought about. Her habits."

Frau Frank glanced at Frau von Rauschwald, who was indifferently fishing for an insect that had landed in her cup. "It was a terrible thing," she said. "I don't know what Bette and I could add to your investigation."

"Probably nothing," Max reassured her. "I just think people who die need to be remembered, and who they are is more a matter of whether they liked chamomile than where they were born, or how they died."

Bette looked skeptical, but she spoke, almost to herself. "When it happened, I thought, 'This was inevitable.' It was still a shock, but inevitable."

Max waited for more, but she did not go on. Frau Frank picked up the thread. "Lila was a free spirit. She embraced life. Threw herself forward and enjoyed food, drink—"

"Men," Bette added.

Frau Frank leaned forward and whispered. "She wasn't very particular about the hygiene of her men, if you know what I mean. She required several treatments from my husband."

"Ah." He was quiet for a moment. "Did the commandant know?"

Bette shrugged. "Everyone else did."

Frau Frank patted the table. "He would have to be blind as a bat, and deaf as a rock."

"Which he is," said Bette.

"He seems, ah, preoccupied," said Max.

"He's an obsessive clown," she added sharply, then abruptly walked off toward her children.

Max and Ursule watched her go. One of the little girls was crying. Bette stroked her head gently, then leaned over and kissed the scraped knee. "She's a pretty thing, isn't she?" said Frau Frank. "And so unhappy here." She put her hand on Max's forearm. "Schütz makes it hard for everyone, Bette's husband not the least. Lila was 'friendly' with Captain von Rauschwald."

"Ah."

"Really it was disappointing. He was lucky not to catch anything. She was definitely beneath him. He has aristocratic ancestors, like yourself."

"Perhaps better than mine."

She rocked back in her chair. "You are too modest, Max." She said "Max" as if she were tasting the word. "Enough of poor Lila. More tea?"

· *Five* ·

Max finally escaped Frau Frank's endless pot of chamomile and eulogies for scarce foods. He sought out Kleini and found him snoring in an upper bunk in the noncommissioned officers' barracks. Max closed the door quietly. He crossed the dusty parade ground back to his own room. The throbbing in his leg and a thudding in the center of his forehead seemed to make sleep impossible, but he closed his eyes, and after what felt like a few minutes, opened them to the angular shadows of late afternoon. Glancing at the time, he realized he had slept for over two hours. For a moment, he felt relaxed, comfortable. He left his bed, limped across the wooden floor to the washbowl, and pressed a damp cloth against his eyes.

Not wishing to spoil his mood, he did not look at himself in the mirror. Too often lately, the sunken eyes of the morphine addict stared back, and all the physical pain and the humiliations of suffering swelled in his memory. In Africa, he had discovered how easy it was to die. He had watched it a thousand times: the subsidence of pain, then the eternal black stare. Despite all the inborn resistance and fear, it was easy to appreciate, even desire, that release. Morphine was the next best thing to dying: no emotion, no discomfort, no pain. The pleasure of corpselike apathy. The stare that penetrates the world. Supplied by his doctors, it became his private way of dying when life crawled over his skin like a million beetles. It was so much easier to die than to live that he did not fully understand why he had chosen to fight the addiction and resurrect himself. Life had not changed. In fact, what attractions it once had were lost after the drug wore off. Addiction was like a romantic love, with life afterward always much harder than life before. Now, always, a spectral woman with cool arms and an enclosing breast beckoned to him from a door to oblivion. It was too easy to want her again. It was impossible to believe time would dull her attraction. He sat on his bed, sweating profusely, his damp undershirt pasted to his chest and back. His dark mood did not pass. He heard a clattering in the next room, and someone humming. He scratched the stump of his left arm, then pulled off his cold shirt.

Though the officers and their wives usually dined in their cottages, or on special occasions in the single officers' hall, tables had been set up on the "village" lawn, as the evening was balmy and the broken clouds not overtly threatening. As Max approached, he could smell hot vinegar and onions. A prisoner was pouring water into goblets. Two men in SS officers' tunics leaned against a wall sipping from pewter cups. Max was early, but before he could discreetly slip back to his room, they spotted him. The tall blond with a patch over one eye approached him. The shorter one, with a bulldog face, poured himself another drink.

The blond saluted. "Heil Hitler. And welcome. We meet at last, Count von Prokofsk. I am Captain Joachim von Rauschwald." His hands were thin, but very strong. His single eye was bright and analytical.

"Pleased to meet you, captain." It was necessary to look up to speak to him. "I met your wife earlier," Max volunteered, then added, without knowing why, "quite by accident."

"Really? Was this after the incident in the garden?"

"Yes."

"You should not bother with our foreign volunteers. They know how to handle our . . . customers." He was amused with himself. "Come, have a drink. It is only a plum brandy, but, alas, it serves tonight as our predinner cocktail. Our fortifier."

"Thank you."

"And this," he gestured at the shorter man, "is Lieutenant Pevner. After dinner, he will move on to the night watch."

Pevner cocked his eyebrow as if to say "That's how it goes."

"A pleasure," said Max. Von Rauschwald arrogantly plucked the water goblet from the head of the table and flung the liquid in an arc behind him. Some spattered on the chest of a prisoner, who merely adjusted the fork von Rauschwald had displaced.

"I am early," said Max.

"The wives are feeding the children. They don't quite trust the nannies."

"Ah."

"And our noble commandant never touches drink. If he did, we might not have to settle for this. All business, our Schütz. Business and mineral water." He raised his cup and sipped. Max did likewise. It went down his throat like a flash fire. His eyes watered.

Pevner sniffed. "Not elegant. But effective."

Von Rauschwald sneered at the lieutenant. "He means not elegant as we, of noble blood, deserve."

Pevner turned away, but not before Max observed him rolling his eyes.

"In times like these, elegant is less important than effective."

"Hear, hear," said Pevner. "Now that Vitebsk has fallen, it is only a matter of time before the Reds get Minsk. We'd all better be drunk if they overrun us."

"Speaking of drunk," said von Rauschwald, "our eminent physician is in fine form again."

The bandy-legged, rotund doctor nearly fell on his front step as Ursule Frank tugged his arm. He pulled loose and reeled toward the table. "Now his 'effective' makes our 'effective' pitiful. We'll be out of grain alcohol before the week's out," said Pevner. Dr. Frank, ignoring everyone, plopped into a chair at the far end of the table and waited for the food. He mopped his brow with the edge of the table cloth, then let his heavy arms dangle at his side.

"Does he do this often?" asked Max.

"Regular as death," said Pevner. "You see, my dear count, only misfits are assigned to Ostheim. Those not useful any place else. Our doctor has fallen to sleep during operations. He confuses laudanum with flowers of sulfur. Captain von Rauschwald"—an icy glance from the captain made him twist his mouth with amusement—"was, like you, wounded and unfit for combat."

"And your commandant?"

Von Rauschwald interrupted with a violent sneer. "Herr Schütz is a *wurst-maker,* with big, but nonetheless idiotic, plans. Who would want to be the czar of Russia when one could own a few hectares in Bavaria? Germany's had enough of dreamers and, so, they are exiled like the rest of us. Only Schütz believes Ostheim is of any importance. He complains about his corps of rejects—us—constantly. He sees it as a plot to ruin him. He despises having Ukrainians and Byelorussians and Lithuanians in his command."

"They are pigs, after all," said Pevner. "No sense of discipline."

"We might as well enlist Jews."

"It only proves we are losing the war," said Max cautiously.

Von Rauschwald shook his head sadly. "There will be others, and the sausagemakers won't be running things then."

"And Frau Schütz," asked Max, tossing back the last of his brandy, "was she like her husband?"

"God no," said Pevner, "it was a sorry thing to see a woman like her tied to him." There was a mistiness in his voice that did not seem to come only from the brandy.

In the silence that followed, Max studied von Rauschwald peering at the lieutenant with his disdainful eye. Eventually, he became aware of Max examining him. "Frau Schütz was a meat-grinder's wife," he said coolly. "They deserved each other."

Pevner walked away, as if to avoid saying more.

Heads turned. Schütz had rounded the corner of his headquarters. The clusters of people scattered about the lawn gravitated toward their places, Max noted, grimly stiffening their backs. Conversation was muted and Frau Frank prodded her husband, who looked up through half-closed eyes, wiped his forehead with the tablecloth again, then settled back in his seat as before. Schütz grasped his chair at the head of the table. "Please," he said. "Sit. Colonel von Prokofsk, you will sit on my right." Von Rauschwald sat on Schütz's left, opposite Max. Bette sat next to her husband. The wife of a Lieutenant Kurzner sat between Max and her husband. The others were scattered down the table to Frau Frank at the end. They all seemed to be waiting for the commandant to speak. Even the three prisoners who stood a few meters from the table were leaning forward, anticipating the signal to serve.

"You have had a good day, I trust?" said Max.

"Endless paperwork. Endless," said Schütz. "An early interruption throws my whole schedule into chaos."

"I would happily have waited," said Max. "I thought you would prefer to see me as soon as possible."

Schütz, as if he did not care what Max's explanation was, merely barked for the soup. "And where is my water?" he added. "Where? Idiots!"

Frau Kurzner, a round-faced woman with spectacles, lifted her spoon even before the soup had arrived and said, "Commandant Schütz has really gone to some trouble for this meal. Isn't that right?"

"The weather is nice," he grunted. "And we were due for one. There has been too much confusion since my wife, ah, left us. We deserve a few pleasantries. Morale and all that."

"The commandant is a very good host," she nodded.

Schütz pointed toward the prisoners' compound. "That is why I entertain so many guests." People laughed halfheartedly, as if on cue, except for Bette von Rauschwald, who stared into the soup before her.

"When I was at Buchenwald," he went on, "we had extraordinary facilities and incredible cooks. Some day our meals here shall rival the best restaurants in Paris, which, by the way, I hear are vastly overrated. You have eaten there, of course, haven't you, colonel?"

"Only once, between trains, at a tiny bistro. It was nothing special: a very good soft cheese."

"I am surprised," said Schütz to the entire table, "you hereditary types, I thought, had nothing else to do but eat and gamble."

"I do not gamble," said Max curtly. "I prefer to have a more precise idea of the outcome of what I do."

"I find myself rather fond of cards," volunteered von Rauschwald.

Schütz grunted. "This would hardly make one a nobleman. Any more than adding a 'von' to one's name." Dr. Frank correctly assumed that this was another of Schütz's jokes and emitted a burp of a laugh. The others, however, were caught between trying to let Schütz see they were laughing and not offending von Rauschwald. Their faces were tortured and several were preoccupied with stirring the green flecks in the cream of asparagus soup.

"Our colonel," added Schütz, "is a *genuine* blue blood, not exactly a Hapsburg, but authentic." Von Rauschwald closed his eye and shivered with fury. He too, thought Max, was capable of great violence.

"Unfortunately," said Max gaily, "we were granted the worst lands in the Holy Roman Empire. One must conclude that the founder of my house was not the most valuable member of the emperor's armies."

Frau Frank, who had already finished her soup, pressed a napkin against her lips and chortled, "He is so modest, don't you think? And with such obvious heroism in his blood!"

"A regular Siegfried," said Schütz.

"You must tell us about your exploits in the war," said Lieutenant Kurzner. "I have wanted, since the beginning, to take part in combat. I would give my arm to be able to wear those palms." He pointed at the band on Max's sleeve. The word "Afrika" was embroidered between two palm trees.

"Believe me, it isn't a fair trade. A cuff-title doesn't look half as nice on an empty sleeve."

"I didn't mean 'give my arm,' I meant—"

Frau Kurzner cut off her husband. "It is a beautiful cuff-title and you wear it well, colonel."

"Thank you, madam."

"Our Kurzner is full of notions," said Pevner.

"Idiotic notions," said Schütz.

"Heroic notions," said von Rauschwald sharply. He was so irritated he had not tasted his soup. Bette, however, was eating as if she were alone in an empty café, idly counting the roses on the wallpaper.

"Do you know," asked Max, "what combat soldiers are dubbed in common parlance? 'Front-line swine.'"

"Outrageous," said Kurzner.

"Not really. The battlefield humbles one," said Max. "One comes to know how little separates us from the beasts. There are terrible prices to be paid, and not just the obvious physical ones."

"But it is glorious that men like you willingly do so," said Kurzner. "Some of us never get the chance to contribute."

Frau Kurzner patted her husband's arm. She obviously worshipped him. "I've told him a thousand times his work is also important."

Schütz lifted his soup plate without looking at the prisoner who swooped to take it. We are here given the opportunity to begin the renewal of the barbaric east," he said. "It is unfortunate we have been temporarily driven from Africa, which would have offered similar opportunities. Imagine a string of these camps stretching all the way to the Great Wall. What a dream! What a space for the Aryan peoples to reestablish their culture!"

The diners had plainly heard this many times before, and though most of them smiled and nodded, only Frau Kurzner seemed sincere. The doctor appeared particularly revolted, either by the speech or the alcohol curdling the soup in his stomach.

"We have humble beginnings here," said Schütz. "I recognize this. I presented the concept of Ostheim to my superiors for years. They tried to ignore me, all but Ernstberger, that is. He was excited by the prospect. I wrote to Himmler, to Kaltenbrunner. When Höss was given Auschwitz, I telephoned him. So few men have the wish to foray into the future! I finally implored the Führer himself. He alone had the wisdom to know what I was talking about. He penned a note, and Ostheim was born. Have I shown you the note? It hangs in my office." Schütz's eyes gleamed. Max shook his head. Schütz twisted toward him as if confiding. "Yet there are those who would like to see me fail. That is why my staff consists of such notables. That is why I am not given a rank commensurate with my position. That is why you are here, dear colonel. There are those who wish to besmirch the entire concept." He struck the table once with his fist. The china rang. "They will not succeed. Everything will be put to rights once the Führer sees what a success we are creating in spite of the hindrances."

"Ah," said Max. He noticed Dr. Frank reach desperately for the crystal decanter of wine.

Blood sausages, cabbage in red wine, and boiled potatoes were placed on the table. The diners ate intently. Several of them remarked how lucky they were that Max had come. Meals like this were not available every day. Pevner toasted Max in gratitude, but Max noticed that he, like most of the others, split his sausage lengthwise and inspected it carefully. Frau Kurzner clumsily excavated a piece of bone with the tip of her knife. As the wine continued to circulate, the general tension abated somewhat, but whenever Schütz spoke, Max could almost hear the teeth grinding. Von Rauschwald was the worst. His passionate silence was broken only when someone asked him a direct question. Bette von Rauschwald continued to act as if she were at dinner alone.

"The Count von Prokofsk had quite a little adventure today," remarked Pevner. He had a wicked turn of mouth.

"Oh?" said Schütz.

"You did not hear, my commandant?"

"Hear what?"

"In the garden, the count and his sergeant saved a prisoner."

Schütz peered at Max amusedly, a piece of sausage skin dangling from the corner of his stuffed mouth. "Saved? For what?"

Someone laughed. "It was nothing," said Max. "A private broke a man's jaw. Sergeant Klimmer—at my insistence—stopped him from shooting the wounded man."

Von Rauschwald glanced back and forth between Max and the commandant.

Schütz swallowed. "You interfered?"

"Yes."

"How absurd!" said Schütz.

"Soldiers must learn to control themselves."

Dr. Frank erupted in laughter. "I wondered why this creature was brought to me." He nearly toppled his chair and blinked when he caught his balance.

"I did not think," said Schütz bluntly, "you were here to interfere."

"The private was a Ukrainian. I would not let my own men do such a thing."

"Here, only my rules matter," said Schütz. "What you do with your soldiers is of no consequence. You have no command here but your sergeant. Remember that."

Von Rauschwald took sudden interest in the discussion.

• 54 •

"This is not the Afrika Korps," he said. "The prisoners out-number us twenty to one, and we remain in charge only so long as we know that they are not men. They are no better than ants, colonel. The slightest insubordination must be crushed out of them. We are not dealing with warriors. We give our guards free rein to handle the cattle as they see fit."

"Perhaps the Afrika Korps needed free rein also," said Schütz, wiping his jaw.

Max took a deep breath and pressed his good knee against the underside of the table to anchor himself. "Meaning?"

"Meaning you and your men were driven out of Africa, weren't you?"

The entire table waited for Max's reaction. He knew he should strike Schütz in the face. All those tinkers and chimney sweeps and printers who forever gave up their Sundays in pastry shops, their nights in warm beds. All those men who wet themselves rather than run. All those cooked alive inside tanks. All those buried by the wind, in the same sterile sand that entombed Carthage. He knew he should feel anger. He should have erupted. But he didn't. Not because Schütz might have been trying to provoke it, but because even those men to whom he had been so close seemed as remote as Scipio Africanus or Belisarius. *The wind,* he remembered the old Scotsman hissing, *Crosses the brown land, unheard.* When you think about what you should feel, you are not feeling it. Schütz's taunt struck fog and dissolved in it.

"We had our victories," he said.

"You certainly did," said Kurzner. "Great victories!" The lieutenant stopped short of disagreeing with the commandant.

"You are here to verify my report on Lila's death," said Schütz. "You will do that, and not trouble yourself with other matters."

Max placed his fork on his half-empty plate and signalled the prisoner to take it away.

"You are wasting food," said Schütz. "My dear count, we cannot afford to waste food."

Bette abruptly stood and flung her napkin onto the table. "Tell him how to eat, now! Go ahead!" She kicked her chair backward and walked away.

Schütz was momentarily stunned, as if no one had dared

speak back at him for years. As he watched her walk away, he smirked. "The Frau *von* Bitch is upset—again." He waved away the prisoner who had been hovering Max's plate near Frau Kurzner's ear. "It is time for the torte. Bring on the torte."

Max hoisted himself to his feet and spoke to von Rauschwald. "Your wife should not walk about alone."

"There is no danger," said the captain. "I cannot deal with her moods."

"I will go after her," Max said. "My doctors have said I should pause in midmeal. I can only eat so much at a time. Forgive me. I am not intentionally rude."

Schütz prodded his torte with a fork. Whatever satisfaction he derived from driving Max from the table he kept to himself. The politeness he had adhered to in his office had disappeared in his need to prove before everyone he was the only authority in Ostheim. Max was the only person at dinner who did not seem to be either afraid of Schütz or emotionally raped by him. To Schütz, Max was a risk. One insubordination leads to another. He was someone over whom the commandant had no absolute control, who might reveal Schütz's power as an illusion induced by Ostheim's isolation.

The sun was setting. Max lost sight of Bette behind the cottages, and scanned the fence and towers before he saw she had strolled into the garden. He watched her pause on one leg to shake a stone from her shoe. She moved on to a row near where Frau Schütz had been killed, stopped, and stared at the darkening mountains beyond the fences. She did not look back as he approached, though she must have heard him lurching his stiff leg over the rocky ground.

He cleared his throat. She barely moved her head. The sun disappeared between two unimpressive peaks. A breeze fingered the loose hairs at the back of her neck.

"You are not afraid to come out here," he said, announcing himself.

She shrugged. The boots of a guard climbing the nearby watchtower clunked.

"And there is where the prisoners cut through the fence."

The guard reached the top. A second started down.

"Don't you believe Lila Schütz was murdered by prisoners?"

"Why shouldn't I?" She tossed her head.

"Then why would you be so casual about coming here?"

"Why should Lila's ghost bother me any more than the others?"

"I would think you would not wish to join her as a spirit."

"Perhaps I already feel like one. Life, real life, is a memory. Ostheim could be hell, couldn't it? But one gets used to anything."

"You don't seem used to it."

"Perhaps you want me to be afraid. Would that make me throw myself into your arms?"

The guard was clanking something against his spotlight. "That would be difficult," said Max, "since I've lost one."

Her head dipped. He knew he had affected her. "Sorry," was all she said.

"Don't be."

"Why are you out here? You're missing more of Major Schütz's table talk."

"I think, if I may be so bold, that I would be a little more concerned if prisoners had begun cutting through fences and murdering. I don't think I could be so indifferent to taking a stroll through my friend's blood." He closed his eyes momentarily. The words had gotten out before he absorbed their full meaning. He had been splattered by his own friends' blood. He had tasted it. He had been blinded by it as if it were acid.

"What do you want with me?" she said tonelessly. "It's not enough I have to put up with all the rest? Now you've been sent by Himmler himself to drive me mad?"

He spoke quickly, not so much to surprise her, but because a sudden thought startled him. "You all think Schütz murdered his wife."

She turned and searched his eyes. "I—I don't know."

"But you think so."

"I don't know. Where did you get this notion?"

"It may be a notion, but you believe it."

She pressed her temples with her fingers and squeezed her eyes shut. "Yes. All right," she whispered. "It's true. Is that what you want to hear?"

"You all believe it."

"I don't know. I think Joachim believes it. Dr. Frank is too far gone to believe anything. We don't talk about things here. We talk about anything else. Anything. We pretend we're doing something honorable. We pretend we're von Rauschwald when we're really just Rausch. Schütz is a swine, less than a swine. He is capable of anything. We all know he is capable of anything. When we return for dessert, Schütz will be waiting. He likes to get everyone's stomach full and then tell how he used to handle things at Buchenwald. His favorite story— well, no, why spoil your fun? It goes with torte like a good Turkish coffee. He's probably waiting for you now. Go ahead. It's dark, and he's usually in bed by now. He's waiting just to tell you his favorite stories."

Max reached out and automatically took her by the shoulder. He would have held her until she calmed, but she spun away. The sensation of her soft blouse sliding out of his grasp was so acute that he contemplated his fingertips. She stopped several rows away, her back to him again. Her white blouse was tinged blue in the dimness and someone was calling out a list, probably of names, somewhere in the prisoners' compound. He thought to leave and even began to pivot on his bad leg. He stopped.

"There's no need to go back," he said. "I have never been much for tortes."

She said nothing. Her head was bowed. Was she weeping? The guard tested his spotlight, flashing it twice over the dog pens, then shut it off.

Max had an urge to touch the back of her blouse. He lifted his hand to do so, but dropped it to his belt, hooking his thumb over it. "So," he said, "I am sent because the SS may have a murderer in its ranks. Am I to assume someone here in the camp has been sending hints, or more, to Berlin?"

She did not move.

"Are you that person?"

She spoke, but it was inaudible.

"Excuse me?"

"No!" she said sharply. She moved her head from side to side as if desperate, then charged at him. "Can you be such a fool? Maybe Schütz killed Lila. Maybe not. What's another murder more or less? There's a war on. The SS is full of murderers. We've been dragged out here and caged and Schütz is the lion tamer who makes us dance for the amusement of Berlin. The day before Lila was killed we posed in front of our cottages: the perfect German women feeding strudel to the children. Afterward, Lila took the cameraman into the back of his truck. I'm tired of pretending. Tired to the center of everything in me. That's why Frank crawls into his bottle. That's why Lila hefted her skirt for any man who could get stiff. That's how we escape. Schütz may or may not be Lila's murderer, but he's a murderer of souls. That's why we hate him. We—"

Her words were cut off by a sob. She flung herself against Max and buried her face in his collar. He was rocked backward by the force of it, but managed somewhat awkwardly to keep his balance, partly because she had clutched the cloth in both hands under his armpits and pulled him toward her. His hand hung suspended above her head, as he tried to understand what he should do. He was thinking about feeling again, and because of it, not feeling. He closed his eyes and gently touched the back of her head, sliding his hand down to her nape. "I'm sorry," he said, then not sure why he had said it, opened his eyes and added, "I mean I didn't understand the situation." That sounded even stupider, so he squeezed her closer against his chest. He could feel her warm breath through his clothes.

"Listen," he whispered. "The war won't last much longer. Soon everyone will know it's all but over. Hitler will be sent on a permanent holiday and we'll all go back to bread and cheese. It's only a matter of time. I'm going back to Brazil at the first opportunity. I'll take a punt deep into the jungle and I'll find the Carachachos. They'll squat on the ground, nibble on a roast monkey, and tell me how Cuzumbalo or Kirimamo has stolen another pig from the Zuino Indians upriver. And that will be the only kind of war they know. And that will be the only kind of battle I'll hear about the whole time I'm there. They won't even know the world's been at war. They'll only know about Kirimamo's pig. There must be some place you and your husband can go after the war, some place whose image you can cling to until you are free of Ostheim."

She lifted her head. He slid his hand out to her shoulder and felt the sharp bones underneath. She sniffed. "Do they really eat monkey?"

"Absolutely."

"But monkeys are so filthy."

"I suppose so. So are hogs. All animals are filthy before we prepare them."

She looked up at him. It was just light enough to see the tears in her eyes and the impression his shoulder braiding had made on her cheek. "You are not what you appear to be."

"No?"

"No."

"And what do I appear to be?"

"I don't know."

"Please. I'm interested. Be frank."

"Cold. Formal. Distant. Like a portrait. Like a ceremony."

"Ah." He lifted his hand from her shoulder and backed away.

She reached out with her right hand and caught his empty sleeve. "And now you put on that mask again. The hero."

He felt warm, then cold. He was sweating and his breath seemed to be growing short. He wanted to be away from her, but she held his sleeve tightly.

"But you aren't that way. You hide behind it. I can tell from the way your sergeant looks at you. He knows you. I can tell because you're like me. You're afraid to lose control. It attracts you, but you fear it."

"You think so?"

"I know."

He studied her for several seconds. "You too are scarred," he said lightly and reached up to touch her face. But he had no hand to touch it with and he stared at the stub of his left arm pressing against the inside of his pinned-down sleeve as if he had never seen it before. She too looked at it, but instead of being washed in the sudden horror he felt, she leaned over, took it in her hand, and pressed it against her cheek.

He pulled away. "We must go. We have been away too long."

"If you say so," she said. She crossed her arms and they walked back silently.

· Six ·

As they reached the stone wall of the "village," Max could feel his leg tightening. He mentally prepared for the last of the dinner. He did not want to appear any different than before he had left, yet how could he reconcile the stark photograph of Frau Schütz with enduring insults from her likely murderer? Furthermore, he sensed that Schütz was not the sole cause of his unease, and that disturbed him even more. Max told himself that nothing significant had happened in the garden, but he was afraid his suspicion of the commandant might make him just awkward enough for the others to think that, indeed, something important had transpired between him and Frau von Rauschwald. He self-consciously smoothed the front of his tunic as if searching for any outward sign that might imply he had changed, and was reminded of the first time he had sex.

The act itself was a blur. He was fifteen; she was the beefy daughter of a falconer. They were in the stable hayloft, or perhaps the barn. She had teased him, as he remembered it, then casually flopped back on the hay, hefting her skirts, revealing what he had only seen carved sanitarily in marble. Whatever had then happened had not taken long. Her thighs were so large, he would later be unsure he had actually penetrated her. His strongest recollection, however, was of the feeling that tormented him afterward. It wasn't quite guilt, though it definitely wasn't delight. He was more awed. At what? That the sky hadn't cracked? That the swallows in the rafters were indifferent to what had transpired below them? Despite the inevitable way the falconer's daughter had gone about it, it was impossible that Max was no different. He had changed. He had metamorphosed or been born into a second life. He knew that. Though he had carefully picked the fragments of hay from his sparse pubic hair, though he had turned his clothes inside out to make certain there were no seeds to reveal his pants had been down, he was certain everyone would see an obvious change. The flush of his cheeks or the dryness in his throat would make it obvious both to his father and hers.

When the men returned, the bushy-headed falconer dangled two bloody rabbits in Max's face and said, "So, young von Prokofsk, what think you of this?" Max stammered something positive and waited for their response. They *must* have been able to see it, smell it, augur it from the reedy quaver in his voice. Yet, all afternoon, the men had talked pleasantly of the merits of one bird against another, barely noticing the boy with them, utterly insensitive to the fear that had seized him each time one of them turned to him.

That feeling was in him again. Only this time, he kept reminding himself that nothing had passed between Bette and him. He also knew that even if the reverse were true, there was no way to see it in his eyes, his halting walk, or the color of his cheeks. All these rationalities did nothing to ease him, however, and he blamed it on the morphine. It had suppressed his feelings for so long, his body was now releasing even those adolescent emotions that were no longer relevant. Bette, on the other hand, despite the rawness she had shown in the garden, seemed to be turning inward, sealing herself in a chrysalis, glazing herself in, as inscrutable as the texture of an insect wing in amber. There would be no touching her.

"The torte was despicable," said a voice. Max, startled, instinctively reached across to where he would normally be wearing his pistol. He dropped his cane and nearly lost his balance.

Captain von Rauschwald stepped from the shadows of the wall and picked it up. "There was a texture," he said, "that was more akin to sawdust than ground walnuts."

"So you've taken to lurking in the dark," said Bette casually. Max straightened himself and felt foolish. You carry more old habits with you than you know.

"I have interrupted your conversation," said von Rauschwald. His face was concealed by the blackness under the bill of his hat. He studied the end of his lit cigarette, then flicked it away. It struck the ground in a shower of sparks. "It must have been quite a talk. Our beloved commandant gave up on you almost as soon as he gulped his dessert, thirty minutes or more ago."

"Frau von Rauschwald," said Max, "has been helpful in letting me know more about this camp, Frau Schütz, various little things."

"Undoubtedly."

"For instance," said Max, continuing quickly in order to find another subject, "I find it quite incredible that women and children have been brought to this remote country. Despite the pleasantness of their company, and the island of home life it creates, I would think it is a strain, and potentially dangerous."

"My dear count," said von Rauschwald, "one cannot underestimate the morale value of having a loyal woman at one's side. Or so our commandant says."

Bette said nothing. She crossed her arms, lowered her head, and marched for her cottage.

"A loyal woman," muttered von Rauschwald. "Nothing is a better asset."

"Indeed," said Max. "You seem a well-matched couple, if you don't mind my saying so."

The captain paused. Max wished he could see that intense single eye, in order to get some clue as to what von Rauschwald was trying to discover by scrutinizing him. "We are like, shall we say, music. Even our discordances create a beautiful effect."

Von Rauschwald stepped into the light. Max noticed the pewter cup in his left hand and the strong smell of plum brandy. "Please," he said, gesturing toward the gate, "join me for a drink before the family compound lights go out. I believe Frau Frank insisted that some of the torte be saved for you, but I recommend it only for termites."

Max did not wish to get closer to von Rauschwald. If it were to appear that they had become friends, Schütz, who obviously

disdained his second officer, might become even less coopera-
tive. Further, Max suspected the captain only wanted to be
able to claim a real nobleman as his friend—whether it was
true or not—in order to lend credence to his own elevation
from Rausch to von Rauschwald. It seemed imprudent, however, not to stay on his good side. If, indeed, there were
suspicions that Schütz had murdered his wife, von Rauschwald likely encouraged the spread of them. There was no
doubt what his sharp looks at his commanding officer had
meant. Also, if Max somehow found any evidence of Schütz's
guilt, he would need all the Rauschs or von Rauschwalds he
could get. Schütz would be a dangerous adversary.

"Very well," said Max. "But only a nightcap. I must begin
tomorrow."

"Certainly," smiled the captain. "I suppose I am imposing a
bit, but insomnia frequently troubles me."

"Provoked by your injuries?"

"No." His face hardened in the same way it had when Schütz
had baited him.

"You are lucky. When the weather changes, my knee . . ."

"I sometimes think I feel a piece of shrapnel in my head,"
he said, "but it is impossible, or so say the quacks. In any case
I have resolved not to be one of those aging veterans who
shows his scars to his children and complains about constipa-
tion. I have a life to build, even if it is to be on rubble. There
will be a Fourth Reich, and I intend to be among those who
build it."

"You think positively. That must be difficult to sustain."

"I need to. One must accept the truth and move on. One
must know the obstacles well and move forward nonetheless.
Merely because certain fools have botched the war does not
mean that National Socialism is doomed."

"It has defied all predictions in the past," said Max, grateful
to be talking as if he were at a cocktail party where nothing
germane is ever said. "You have lovely children, by the way."

"Yes," von Rauschwald said, as if it were inevitable. "I was
very careful in selecting their mother."

"Ah."

They had rounded the end of the wall, and the dining tables
were now visible. Prisoners, watched by the grumpy Sgt.
Baranovitch, were scrubbing them down, turning them side-

ways, and carrying them toward the officers' dining hall, a hundred meters beyond. At the edge of this activity, perched on top of a round lump in the grass, the dog Hermann lifted his head. It took Max several seconds to recognize the lump as Dr. Frank, prostrate, arms and legs splayed out like a parody of Vitruvian man.

"My God!" said von Rauschwald, charging at the sergeant. Baranovitch saluted, but otherwise watched implacably as the furious captain closed the distance between them.

"Why is that man lying there?" shouted von Rauschwald.

"He is drunk, sir."

"He is drunk? So? Are we to suppose he is to lie out there all night?"

"If he does not wake, sir."

Von Rauschwald threw his pewter cup in Baranovitch's face. It plinked against the edge of his helmet, just above his eyes, then tumbled into the darkness. Baranovitch merely wiped his face with his enormous hand. "Have you considered how this swine makes us look? Here, in front of the prisoners? He represents the German people, the Aryan race. Have you considered this, you shit-headed idiot? Have you considered you might be responsible should he catch pneumonia and die?"

Baranovitch glared dumbly.

"Well?"

Baranovitch's voice rolled out of his throat like thunder. "Have you considered, captain, sir, that Commandant Schütz may have ordered us to leave him there?"

Von Rauschwald glanced back at Dr. Frank, then thrust his face up at the sergeant's. "You will not play games," he said through gritted teeth. "You will have him removed to his cottage at once!" Von Rauschwald turned and nearly collided with the last table. Losing all control, he kicked at it until the startled prisoners dropped it. He then struck one of them on the shoulder with his fist. The man tumbled to the ground, curled into a fetal position, and wrapped his head with his arms. Von Rauschwald kicked him twice, then, apparently not satisfied with the prisoner, swung a fist at the upright table leg, cracking it below the claw foot.

Max, momentarily stunned, had not moved since the tirade began. Now he eased forward. The fallen prisoner, apparently unhurt, scurried to his comrade's side, who looked around anxiously. The guard in the closest tower, upon hearing the disturbance, had fumbled with his spotlight. Von Rauschwald had fallen to his knees, breathing hard and holding his hand, in a circle of bluish-white light. The brightness put Baranovitch into silhouette, but so far as Max could tell, the sergeant had watched it all without reaction. They stared at the panting von Rauschwald. He slowly turned his head to look at Max.

"It is—It is inconceivable that the world is populated as it is." He gasped for breath. "It is inconceivable that the best are cheated of their natural rights by Jews and sausagemakers." He took several more breaths, then faced directly into the light. "Turn that off, you idiot!"

Von Rauschwald stood up, still holding his hand. Baranovitch slung his rifle over his shoulder, silently crossed to Dr. Frank, and unceremoniously grabbed him by the ankles. With a grunt, he dragged him across the grass to the door of his cottage. Max noticed the curtains move, as Baranovitch opened the front door, hefted the doctor by his lapels, and dumped him inside like a sack of potatoes.

"Come," said von Rauschwald. "I promised you a drink."

"It is late," said Max.

"One drink."

Max nodded. Calmer now, von Rauschwald wiped the inside of his cap with a handkerchief, which he then nonchalantly snapped at his knees. He moved along the wall, searching for his pewter cup, found it, and, silently extending his arm, directed Max toward his cottage.

The low ceiling of the parlor was spanned by round beams. The heaviness of the furniture, along with the broad fireplace that covered nearly the entire wall, dominated the room. There was space only for one chair, a huge buffet, a settee, and a table. A portrait of the Führer watched from the wall opposite the smoldering fire. On the mantel, several photographs and two certificates were on display. Otherwise, except for the stag's heads carved on the corners of the buffet, there were no decorations. It was ten times more claustrophobic than the rooms provided the single officers, thought Max, but then, presumably, there were also bedrooms and a kitchen through the door at the end.

"Please. Sit," said von Rauschwald, pointing at the chair. Max, however, took the settee, assuming that the chair was the captain's usual place. Von Rauschwald unlocked two doors low on the buffet. From one he removed a round, flat bottle. From the other, two goblets. "I have something I hide from the others, but I feel like you are the kind of man who can keep a secret."

"In most instances," said Max.

"You are cautious." The captain placed his hat on the buffet. "It's a good quality to have." He poured two large drinks. "Armagnac. It is not a particularly remarkable one, but is sufficiently pleasing to remind one of cognac. To be reminded of the better things in life becomes enough after a while. I pleaded, I begged for cognac from a lieutenant I knew in France. Finally, this arrived. I did not pay him what he asked. I shall likely never get another bottle again. I may regret not paying cognac prices for Armagnac."

"You honor me with your treasure," said Max. "You needn't have given me so much."

"No, you honor me."

Von Rauschwald seemed pleased with himself. He hesitated as if deciding what to do next.

Max sipped. The drink was very fragrant, rising in the nose like a warm mist. "Delicious."

"And will likely medicate us against the effects of our dinner."

"I had no problem with the meal. It was plain, but—"

"Those damned sausages. Schütz has some notion they are the quintessential German food. We will be better Germans if we eat sausages. God knows what may be in them. Schütz watches over the grinding himself, when he's not planning more additions to the camp. He can't free himself of his old profession."

Max brushed the back of his head against the picture frame above the settee. He glanced up. Hitler seemed to be staring at him. He almost said excuse me. "And you, captain, what did you do before the war?"

Von Rauschwald swirled his drink. "Me? Why, I dabbled. Rather like you, I suppose."

"I suppose so."

The captain abruptly stood. He took one of the photographs

from the mantel and thrust it at Max. "Look," he said coyly. "You will recognize the gentleman on the left."

"The Reichsführer."

"Yes. He personally congratulated each of us at the initiation."

"The initiation?"

"Yes, the awarding of the dagger. I was lucky enough to be among those who received this honor at Quedlingburg, at the tomb of King Henry the Lion."

"Ah."

"Himmler was nearly in tears, as was I."

"You look quite happy."

"It was one of the finest moments of my life." Von Rauschwald's expression suddenly darkened. "Six months later, a French mine ended my career. This, after the French army had collapsed."

"Our careers have changed. They have not ended."

Von Rauschwald snatched his picture back and placed it carefully on the buffet. "As long as I am here, it is ended. I would do anything to get back into combat."

"You sound like Lieutenant Kurzner."

"Kurzner is only interested in the decorations. In the glory. I, well, I enjoy the war. Incredible to say, but why not admit it? Combat is a man's greatest sensation. You're alive, alive, alive! Not like stewing here. No matter what one does here, it is never enough."

Max paused for a moment and contemplated von Rauschwald's outburst. The captain was like a piano string, tightened until it was ready to snap. The Armagnac, perhaps, made Max willing to ask what he had momentarily held back from. "Would you spread rumors about Schütz's complicity in his wife's death?"

Von Rauschwald stared at him. The single eye stabbed through Max like an awl. "Did Bette tell you that?"

"Your wife told me nothing."

"There is nothing to tell. Three prisoners killed Frau Schütz. What possible question could there be?"

"Ah."

"So that's it. You're not here to investigate Frau Schütz's death. You're here to find out who is gossiping about it."

"No."

"I'd suggest you talk to Frau Frank, or that little swine Pevner. I am of the SS. I have my oath. Despite my distaste for the mistakes that allow an idiot like Schütz or a mental degenerate like Pevner into our sacred order, I am loyal." He stood. " 'I swear to you, Adolf Hitler, as Führer and Chancellor of the German nation, loyalty and bravery. I vow to you and *to the superiors whom you shall appoint obedience unto death,* so help me God!' This is the oath I live by, Count von Prokofsk. I cannot speak for others in the SS."

Max nodded. Von Rauschwald poured himself another Armagnac and drank it quickly. "I am sorry," said Max, "to have suggested it."

Von Rauschwald remained with his back to him.

"You understand I must probe," Max said, trying to assuage him. "I am serving the Reichsführer."

Von Rauschwald did not move.

"I went too far, perhaps."

Von Rauschwald shook his head. "These stuffy rooms. This stifling camp. We should do what we are here for and stop muddling around."

"What do you mean?"

"Schütz. We are here to eliminate the enemies of civilization. Instead, he muddles about with his schemes, as if he could turn apes into constuction crews."

"It is late," said Max, masking his distaste.

"No. I have something you will enjoy. Wait." He fumbled with his keys and opened the central door of the buffet. He removed a gramophone from the compartment. *"Tristan and Isolde!"* He reached through the small door at the end of the room and brought in several recordings. "Wagner! The genius of the German spirit." He cranked up the gramophone and fidgeted with the needle. He reminded Max of Oskar Hüber and the night in Berlin. Max also remembered Breda, whom he did not wish to remember.

"You enjoy music," said Max.

"It is the highest expression of the true self. All men of breeding appreciate music."

"I am very fond of Mozart." He thought of Chopin, but did not think the mention of a Polish Frenchman would help his relationship with von Rauschwald. "And Bach also."

"Mozart? It is frivolous, though."

"Frivolous?"

"It is superficial. Tricky sometimes, but without substance. No, the age of such frippery is over. Such music contributes to the sapping of the German spirit. Typical Austrian silliness."

"You can hardly call the Jupiter Symphony silly. Besides, especially in times like these, a lightening of the spirit may be a good thing." Max felt vaguely uncomfortable, as if what he had just said had no truth in it. "Surely you don't think so little of Bach."

"Bach is a pygmy beside Wagner."

"Well, if you insist."

"I do. One gives oneself over to Wagner. Wagner reaches into the profundity of German being and awakens all the reservoirs of Aryan memory."

"I am not saying it is inferior to Mozart or Bach. I am merely saying I prefer to listen to them."

"That is because you do not yet understand how to let yourself flow with Wagner. You should become Wagner when you listen to him. You cannot know it, as you can Bach, until you feel it. Consider this"—he lifted a record—"the love-death theme. Who can deny that the act of love is an act of dying? Oh, not in the cheap sense that a climax is a 'little death' as the French say, but in the sense that one's identity dissolves. The rapist yields to the force within him, and is, therefore, raped. The killer yields to the power within him and his identity for those seemingly infinite seconds fades into oblivion. Love is a kind of death in which you give yourself away. Death is the ultimate giving away. We Germans understand this. This is why we are superior. We do not assert the individual over the race. We give ourselves—with pleasure— over to our destiny. It does not matter if Hitler fails and ends up in Holland like the Kaiser did. The quest is what matters. The seeking after power and purity. The proof of our superiority is that we gave ourselves over to him, totally, despite the possibility of failure."

Max grew uncomfortable. He had begun to see some connection with giving himself over to morphine. He cut off von Rauschwald. "This is all too mystical for me. I have never been much for religion."

Von Rauschwald smiled. "Of course. Otherwise, you would have graced the SS with your courage. I suspect you are merely veneered by your education, as I was. Underneath you have a heart of good German oak. Listen. Listen carefully, but do not analyze. Drift with its tides."

"Afterward I must go. It is near midnight."

Von Rauschwald placed the needle reverently and rapidly took his chair to make certain he was already in place when the first quiet chords began. Max pretended to be staring at the hearth, but actually observed the captain. Von Rauschwald was transformed. Gradually he relaxed. As the music swelled, his face became more peaceful. The condescension that always played about his lips, the icy hardness in his eye, seemed to diffuse as the eyelid descended. At first, it was like a man praying. He even seemed to grow paler, though it may have been a slight change in the color of the lightbulb, as the voltage in the line was drawn to something further along, like one of the spotlights. He then reminded Max of a man bleeding to death, and the peace that had overcome him disturbed Max more than the fury he had shown in the courtyard. When the music ended, von Rauschwald did not move for nearly a minute. The scratching of the needle seemed like it would go on forever. When he finally opened his eye, it was so sudden Max's heart skipped a beat.

"You felt it," said the captain.

"I—I see what you mean."

Von Rauschwald stood. "No, then you didn't. It is not to be understood. It is not intellectual."

"I mean I felt it in a way I had not before."

"Perhaps another?"

Max pushed against the settee arm. "No, I could not appreciate it. I am exhausted. I must sleep or the investigation will never be finished."

"Some other time. I think we are much alike. There is an affinity in our bloods."

Max adjusted his cap. "Thank you for having me here. It is very pleasant."

"It is a sausagemaker's idea of a home," he said, sneering.

"No, really, it is similar to my father's hunting lodge," he lied. "It brings pleasant associations."

Von Rauschwald looked around as if the room had qualities he had not known. "Another time," he said. "I have several more records."

"Thank you," said Max. "I would be honored."

Despite the lateness of the hour, Max was surprised at the sounds from the prisoners' compound. Dogs were barking; men were yelling orders. Perhaps a surprise search for concealed weapons was on. Or two prisoners had been fighting. He remembered how Kleini had joked once that the only time enlisted men set about punching each other was when their sergeants needed sleep. Max thought about everything that had happened since he had arrived. Schütz was a swine, there was no doubt of that, but was that a reason to suspect him of killing his wife? Did someone, von Rauschwald in particular, have the notion of smearing Schütz until he was transferred? The SS was, he had always heard, full of connivers who'd stab you with the hand with which they'd just patted you on the back. It wasn't impossible that Bette was sent by her husband to plant questions about Schütz in Max's mind. Max had merely, conveniently, got the idea before she had had the chance to present it. On the other hand, what influence could Max have with the SS? If he did, indeed, return with a report that accused Schütz, the SS was likely to close ranks like Jesuits under attack by Lutherans. He had left Oskar Hüber's apartment too quickly, without finding out anything. If only Breda and Lilli hadn't been there, he might have been able to grab Oskar by the lapels and force him to reveal what he knew. No determination. Where had it gone? He had left humiliated. He did not understand why he didn't hate Oskar. There had been enough cruel schoolboy tricks in Vienna to last a century. Maybe von Rauschwald was right in some way: the German nature was to give oneself over to something, to someone, no matter how destructive.

Max's leg hurt. He stopped midway between the family quarters and the commandant's offices and listened to the noises in the prisoners' compound. There was a reciting of names, then the sounds of counting. A guard coughed in one of the towers. A door clacked shut. He was thinking it was like sneaking out of his dormitory room and sitting on the roof tiles outside the attic window and listening to the noises of Vienna on a spring night. There was even the sound of laughter coming from somewhere behind the cluster of offices and barracks. He missed the smell of the pastry shop in the next street and the puttering of automobiles. As if it were forbidden to enjoy even the memories of life before the war, however, insects began to harry him. He continued to his room, knowing even before he tried that he would not sleep. It wasn't just that Ostheim had grown even more Byzantine since he had arrived, or the feeling that some essential clue to the whole mystery might have presented itself already. If he could come to understand this camp, would he understand the German ethos better? Would he know himself better? Or was Ostheim, with the self and the national soul, like von Rauschwald's music, not to be intellectually grasped? There was a chilling fear in him that Ostheim seduced. Schütz's strange enclave begged people to let go, to give in, to yield. Sleep, Ostheim, morphine, death—even the feel of Bette von Rauschwald's neck, which still pulsed on his fingertips—they were all interrelated. Max could not be certain what would happen if he let himself slip.

· *Seven* ·

Max twisted on the light to his room. On the dresser next to the washbowl was a plate, covered with a lead crystal dome. A note, scrawled on pulpy yellow paper, lay beside it:

Colonel von Prokofsk,
   Frau Doctor Frank pointed out to me that it would be an injustice should you not enjoy any of the torte. Perhaps your walk will increase your appetite. Sleep well.
                    Commandant Bodo Schütz

Max lifted the glass dome. A strong smell of chocolate rose from two large portions. He studied the cakes for a second, as if waiting for a cruel joke by Schütz to materialize. He carefully replaced the dome, unbuttoned his tunic, and sat on the bed. He scraped mud and grass from the heel of the boot on his stiff leg with the toe of the other. The wad resembled a sea urchin lying on the floor. He wondered if it were partly held together by Lila Schütz's blood, then kicked it away. Getting his boots off was the most difficult part of getting undressed and Kleini usually helped. Max was too tired to get into all of that right away, so he swung his legs onto the bed.
   He watched a tiny moth batter itself against the bulb. He thought he heard someone snoring, though it might have been the wind. Max was tired to the bone, but he wasn't sleepy. Even when he closed his eyes, he was too intensely attuned to

every noise, every smell, even to the texture of the coarse blanket under him. He should have listened to more Wagner and drunk von Rauschwald's Armagnac until he passed out on the settee. He smiled and mouthed the end of the pub scene of *The Waste Land:*

> HURRY UP PLEASE ITS TIME
> HURRY UP PLEASE ITS TIME
> Goonight Bill. Goonight Lou. Goonight May. Goonight.
> Ta ta. Goonight. Goonight.
> Good night, ladies, good night, sweet ladies, good night,
> good night.

Had he got that right? He laughed and said "Goonight!" in order to hear himself. What sort of accent was that? A Sudeten German repeating the lessons of a Scottish tutor in a poem with Cockneys written by an expatriate American. *Good night, sweet ladies, good night.*

Breda, then Ursule Frank, then Bette flashed across his mind. He knew he would not sleep. There were too many shadows nudging at him. He awkwardly raised himself, cut off the light, and sat in the dark. He didn't feel any more comfortable, but he had to stop letting himself get distracted. It was hard to think systematically after all that had happened since his return to Europe. The rushed commission, the invasion of Africa, his father's angling to get him on Rommel's immediate staff, the battles, the wounds, the anesthesia, the operations, the morphine, the morphine, the morphine . . . Then the newsreels, the magazines, the prewritten morale speeches to troops lined up like liniment bottles in a pharmacy. A warm handshake from Streicher, an embrace from Goebbels, a wet kiss on each cheek from Goering. Then Himmler. Then Ostheim. Max had been like the child of a movie star, led about and displayed. He wasn't certain he knew how to think logically any more. And he did not trust his feelings, when they infrequently appeared. "I am a child again," he thought. "I don't understand the adult world."

Yet he could not accept that. He had been trained as a scientist. If he had lost every skill he had developed in analyzing the culture and customs of the Carachacho, there was nonetheless some nostalgia in him that was constantly pricking him to get back to himself, to think and feel as before.

Very well, he said to himself. A method. Professor Dreyer always said that science is born only when a precise method of inquiry is formulated, and only after that can insight take over. So first, reinterview everyone whose statement is in the file. What do I watch for? Any inconsistency, of course. Any omissions. Any distortions, either emphasizing or minimizing anything in the statements. Take nothing for granted. Test them, prod them, watch for when they are uncomfortable, stretch their patience. I provoke their tempers. I find the sores, and I salt them until the web of interrelationships is exposed. Accumulation of data is the key. This is just another village up the Amazon. It is a village of people less happy, less homogeneous than the Carachacho, but it is nonetheless a village.

That would take care of the murder, and, in the end, it might be true that the prisoners did it, or Schütz, or more likely, that Max would be unable to prove either way. The second problem, however, could not be frontally attacked, and might ultimately be trivial. One cannot go through the army without seeing dozens of irrationalities. Yet this particular one continued to seem like more than a bureaucratic mistake. Why had *he* been chosen to investigate? Why not one of the SS Legal Department, who normally did internal SS investigations? Max sought for some time for a method that might force von Rauschwald or Schütz to tell him more, and rejected each one as too straightforward to unravel what, if it were intentional, must be Byzantine in its creation. There was little choice. He would try to get in touch with Oskar Hüber again. Oskar had known something, and, as in the old days, was amused by the reactions of those from whom he withheld information. Max had to find some way to get it out of him, though he was so far away. Was there even a telephone in this place?

Those were the plans. Simple. Clear. When in war, select the objective and move against it without hesitation, without doubt, knowing full well you may fail, but knowing that uncertainty is the greatest cause of failure. Max should have felt more at peace, but did not. He fantasized arresting Commandant Schütz, or slapping him in front of his guards until he apologized for insulting the Afrika Korps. He also recalled, several times, how Bette von Rauschwald had pressed the stub of his arm against her face. He ran through his mind each word of his conversation with her, then mentally watched her having tea with him and Frau Frank.

He felt feverish, and had another sweating spell. He uneasily spent the entire night awake, endlessly studying each gesture, twist of the mouth, each intonation that Bette von Rauschwald had used. She disturbed him more than Schütz but he didn't know why. Bette was some sort of third puzzle and he couldn't see how it related to the others, or even why she was a puzzle. When the noise of the dawn roll call fully woke him, he opened his eyes and said, "I have lost the night."

He rolled over and dropped his legs to the floor. Sleep or not, he would begin. This business had to end, and it would not end any more quickly if he put it off until he could sleep. He stiffly crossed to the washbowl, leaned over, and blinked. There was nothing under the crystal dome. The torte was gone. He lifted the glass. A sticky spot of filling proved it had been there. He scanned the table, the floor. He patted the bed for crumbs. He hadn't eaten it. He was certain he hadn't eaten it. Had he? He checked the window. Still locked from the inside. He opened the door. To his left was one door, then a solid, stone wall. To his right, a succession of doors down to the tiny foyer with a desk, a smiling orderly, and Kleini, flapping his hands as if he were telling a joke.

The orderly cut short his laugh when he saw Max. He tapped Kleini on the arm, and the burly sergeant came up the corridor. "You're up early, sir. Rest well?"

"A moment," said Max. He limped down the corridor to the orderly, who, as he got closer, looked more like a boy than a man. "Corporal," he said.

"Yes, sir." The corporal saluted.

"Who came into my room last night?"

"Excuse me, sir?"

"Someone came into my room last night."

"When, sir?"

"I don't know when."

"I have been here since midnight, sir. No one went in."

"This is impossible. Someone was in my room. They stole my torte. You must have been sleeping."

"No, sir," said the corporal. "I never sleep on guard duty. Never."

Kleini came up behind Max. "A torte?" he asked in his ear.

When Max looked back at him, he suddenly recognized how ridiculous he might seem.

"Corporal, did you steal the colonel's cake?"

The boy's eyes widened. "Oh no, I would never do such a thing. No, sir. Never. And I never sleep here. Never. No, sir. Never."

"A rat," said Max. "Mice, perhaps." The boy was much too frightened by the accusation, and probably too jumpy to have done it. "I'm certain it was a rat. You must report a rat in the quarters, so that sanitary measures can be taken."

"Yes, sir. Immediately, sir. I'm very sorry."

"Don't be," he said absentmindedly. "Rats, like taxes, are inevitable."

"Thank you, sir. I will have the creature found immediately, sir."

Max nodded and brushed past Kleini, who was eyeing the boy suspiciously. Back in his room, he touched the smooth knob atop the glass bell. Kleini came in.

"I will need to bathe," said Max. "Help me off with these boots. While I am bathing you will locate the four enlisted men I am to interview today. What time is it?"

"About six."

"We begin at eight. Two-hour intervals." He opened the drawer and looked for any sign that his intruder had also gone into the file. He could not be certain. It lay there as before. He flipped to the eyewitness reports. "Sergeant Külm first. Then Sovolevsky, Koshak, and"—he did not even attempt the long name—"this one." He held out the statements. "At lunch, I will let you know whom I will question tomorrow."

"If they are on duty?"

"Get their superiors to release them. Say it is at Schütz's behest. And check on a stenographer. No. Forget that. They may speak freer without one."

"To an officer?"

Max shrugged. "Well. Maybe not. But we must try. What have you learned?"

"Nothing big," said Kleini. "I'm only just getting to know them."

"Whatever it is, tell me. It takes many threads to complete a tapestry. Can you get me some tea?"

"German tea."

Max made a face. "It will do."

"And something to eat? There are some pretty fair fried cakes."

"I'm not up to food."

"It would be a good idea. For your strength."

"You should have been my mother, Kleini. Just the tea."

"I'll see to the bath."

"Good."

He paused in the door. "A rat?"

"A very big one," said Max. "With two legs."

Kleini touched the door as if feeling for a bolt. There was none. He thought for a moment, then left.

Max drifted in the sensuous warmth of the portable canvas bathtub. The soap was harsh and the steam rising from the water had a metallic smell, but it was pleasant, very pleasant. Frau Schütz had never been murdered; Herr Schütz was a cranky, but lovable, schoolmaster; Ostheim was Manaus; and a harmless boy in lederhosen had stolen the torte for his sister. Those silly canvas bathtubs! He had been dismayed when Kleini said it was the only alternative to the slippery floor of a shower, but now he was in it, he hoped never to see a porcelain bathtub again. In Libya, he had once been so disgusted with the sand in his hair, under his fingernails, in between his buttocks, he had set up the canvas tub in the open in the middle of Rommel's tanks, and sat in the water smoking a cigar until he had sunburned half of his body.

Max regretted telling Kleini he could take care of himself while the sergeant arranged the interviews, because he had trouble getting out. He slopped most of the water over the sides, slipped, and ended up on his hand and good knee. He eased himself out of the puddle to the long mirror by the row of sinks. He was gaunt, but ruddy—the water had been very hot—and the scars on his body meandered like cracks that exposed the white clay under a painted vase. Except for the clean bullet scar, a white dot under the ribs, he was unmarked

on the right. On his left, however—ironically the more vulner-
able side of the heart—he was marked from head to toe: the
long line from ear almost to chin, the blunt end of his upper
arm, the horizontal line running one quarter of the way
around where his lower rib used to be, the vertical cut over
the hip, the indentation in his thigh where a chunk of flesh
had been blown away, and the patchwork scars circling the
knee. "You have used up eight of your lives, Max the Cat," one
surgeon had said. "And you still have your brain, your eyes,
and your balls. What more does a cat need?" Max lifted his
penis and looked at it in the mirror. Strange foreign object,
he thought. And what good are you, anyway?

He turned away. He felt invigorated, as if he had slept for
days, and he wasn't going to let staring in the mirror put him
into one of his moods. He was a cat, he was nimble, he was
going to traipse through the investigation and surprise them
all. They didn't know they'd bought a cat in a sack. He'd
managed, with some grunting, to get himself almost dressed
when Kleini returned to help him with his boots. He felt
dapper, so he carried his cane. He was even pleased with the
small office—normally used as a storeroom for old documents—that Schütz had set aside.

The interrogations, however, quickly dulled his spirit. He
was forced to begin with Koshak, a soft-spoken Ukrainian
private whose German was so rudimentary that Max had to
repeat his questions several times and often couldn't fully
understand the answers. The written affidavit Koshak signed
made him sound quite literate, as if Schütz, unhappy with
the unnatural sentence structures and strange grammar, had
edited it. That in itself was suspicious, but despite endlessly
twisting Koshak's words in order to get him to contradict
himself, Max ended up with only a private whose German
degenerated in the course of the badgering and whose exasperation at forcing his tongue to conform to the foreign
language resulted in copious sprays of spit. No, Koshak had
not slept. No, he had heard no sound. No, he had not looked
directly into the garden. Ordered to watch the perimeter of
the woods across the clearing and the outer fence, he had
watched the woods and strolled along the fence. Yes, he had
smoked. He knew that was against the rules, but everyone,
even the officers, did it. If you had a cigarette, you'd better

smoke it or someone would steal it. Besides, it made you more alert.

Sgt. Külm had no problems with German. He spoke of his dogs tenderly, even when he described how they were trained to rip out a man's throat. One of them, "Clausewitz," had been nursing a sore paw. That was why Külm was out later than usual. He was in the pens, trying to muzzle Clausewitz, when the dogs at the far north end of the run sounded agitated. He went outside, couldn't see them, and walked along the outside of the run. He was halfway to where the run ended—by the tower—when the dogs, thinking a prisoner had gotten too close to the wire, came charging back. That was when they began barking. When he spoke to them, they calmed, and he walked back. He later decided that the dogs had gotten agitated when the prisoners had been cutting through the wire. The dog run was only along the east fence, between the prisoners' barracks and the headquarters, family quarters, etc., and the prisoners had been far enough along the north side that the dogs noticed them, but didn't feel threatened.

"And you think," asked Max, "that the reason the prisoners cut where they did was the dogs?"

"Naturally."

"But if they had stayed close under the towers, rather than midway between, would they not have been much harder to spot?"

"But they would have been near my babies."

"There's another tower at the other end."

"It's another hundred and fifty meters. Each step is another chance of being noticed."

"Ah." Max made a note. "And what is the chance your dogs could be distracted?"

"Distracted?"

"Yes. Nowhere in the report is this asked. A piece of meat? A cat? A bitch in heat?"

"Impossible!"

"You think so?"

"Utterly impossible!"

"Not even for a nice chunk of meat?"

"Not a chance. And who, do you think, has a nice chunk of meat these days?"

"Ah."

After Külm, Max rocked back in his chair and stared at the wall. What was the point? Well, true, he had only struggled through two interviews, but he wasn't learning anything he didn't already know from his reading. Külm had been even more precise and certain of what had happened on June 2 than he had been when he had given his statement. Like a parent instructing a child—or a Carachacho trying to make an anthropologist understand his values—there would be a tendency, unintentional but nonetheless important, to smooth out all the ambiguities. Were the dogs actually agitated or did Külm simply walk in that direction because of restlessness? When he heard of the murder, suddenly the vague urge became remembered as a specific reaction. Something like the butchery of Frau Schütz couldn't take place without the dogs knowing it, or so Külm would want to believe. If there were anything hidden about this murder, it would likely lie in what people wanted to believe, in the gray areas of fact made black or white by the attempt to perfect imperfect memory.

When Kleini arrived with lunch, Max was on the verge of changing his approach. He was watching a spider drop from the roof beam on an invisible line. When the door opened, the spider was blown against the wall. Kleini set down the tray. A semicircle of rye bread, a chunk of hard cheese, and a tin flask sat upon it.

"So," said the sergeant, "how goes it?"

Max shrugged. He lifted the flask and smelled beer. He poured half a glass. It was thin, light, and reminded him of Brazilian beer. It was probably watered down. "No surprises," he said.

"Did Schütz do it?" asked Kleini, sawing at the bread.

"What do you mean?"

"What do I mean?"

"No, I know what you mean. Why are you asking?"

"This morning, after I found Sovolevsky, I helped a detail glaze some windows. I overheard something. I offered a cigarette. Puff, puff, I hear that one of the corporals is taking bets on Schütz being arrested. My smoking buddy wants inside information. He'll even split his winnings with me."

"Where are the odds?"

"Two to one."

"Not bad. We 'hereditary types' love odds like that."

Kleini offered the bread. His cocked eyebrow asked "What?"

"Nothing. It is obvious, though, that quite a few people believe he did it."

Kleini spoke with his mouth full. "Nearly everyone. The bet is on whether he's arrested."

Max chewed his bread. It was tough as a cotton shirt. The cheese, however, was surprisingly mild. "Do they believe he did it himself or had someone do it for him?"

Kleini shrugged. "Either way. They don't seem to know anything we don't know, but I can try to loosen a few more tongues. It would help if I could get some cigarettes. Better yet, some schnapps."

"That would be difficult, but I'll see."

The spider was dropping from his rafter again.

"Why do they suspect him?"

Kleini struck his chest as if clearing a lump from his throat. "Nothing special. Frau Schütz was a whore. If you had the sausage, she had the sack. More than one man looked nervous when I asked who had given her a poke. Finally, Duitser said it was better not to know."

"Meaning it was safer Schütz not know."

"Absolutely."

"Schütz is not a lovable fellow."

"So I gather."

"On the other hand, that doesn't mean he's a murderer. I was thinking of Peter Kürten."

"In Africa?"

"No. Düsseldorf. 1930 or so. They called him the Düsseldorf Ripper. According to what I read, he was charming, a real ladies' man. Yet, he indiscriminately killed women for sexual pleasure."

"I remember! God! My brother and I used to fight over the latest newspapers."

"I think even his wife had no suspicion until he told her. Like Kürten, this killer of Lila Schütz seems pathological to me. We mustn't rule out someone merely because he is lovable, or not lovable."

Kleini swallowed his beer and sat back. He grinned slightly, then fingered a scratch in the table. "And the captain's wife? How lovable is she?"

"Bette von Rauschwald?"

Kleini looked smug.

"There is nothing between us."

Kleini nodded.

"No. I talked with her. I wanted to find out about Frau Schütz."

"There is nothing wrong with scratching an itch," Kleini said. "It's a sign you're getting better."

"I tell you, sergeant, there is nothing between us."

"So now it's 'sergeant.' More bread?"

Max sighed. "Very well. I just don't want more rumors flying. I'm not doing anything with Frau von Rauschwald. What are the rumors?"

"You were seen in the garden, embracing. You walked together. You left her house late last night."

"I was with the captain."

"I'm just saying what they said."

"Doesn't it strike you as peculiar that a woman can be carved up in the garden and no one sees or hears a thing, yet I allow myself to console an unhappy woman and everyone sees it?"

"Not everyone. Most of the men seem to like it. Von Rauschwald is a prig, so they say, and they'd like to see him wear horns. One fellow told me how much they were tickled by Schütz, all straight and proper, barking orders when they knew Lila was in his cottage, resting up from a night of waving her legs over some Byelorussian's back. They'd like von Rauschwald to be treated the same."

"Bette is a faithful wife?"

"Listen, colonel, what do bored men talk about? Women. They have a whorehouse here, did you know that? Ostheim has all the comforts of home. But even that gets boring. There's a lot of fucking going on here, not all of it according to regulations."

"It's to be expected in a place like this. Everyone's like an overwound clock." Max held up a thumb and forefinger. "Bette von Rauschwald is this far from a breakdown, I suspect, and needs to get away." He swirled his beer. "What do you know, specifically, about who is poaching in whose forest?"

"Nothing much. A joke the other night that Kurzner likes a boy now and then. Nothing but a joke maybe. Not like the stories I heard about Frau Schütz. But with all this loose talk, you might want to know that the interest in you and Frau von Rauschwald seems mostly because there hasn't been anything to say about her in the past."

"That's interesting," said Max, "but of no personal importance. In fact, it may be unfortunate, concealing, as it does, another set of possible relationships and motives. All facts, however, are relevant to the case." Kleini tried to catch his eyes, but Max diverted them and studied the spider. He laughed.

Kleini glanced up at the spider. "What is it?"

"I was thinking of my English tutor."

"Not more modern poetry. Don't you know any poems about birds and flowers? Remember birds and flowers?"

"Oh no. He once told me the story of Robert the Bruce."

"Who?"

"A king of Scotland."

"He wrote confusing poems, I suppose."

"No, but he was persistent. Lunch has changed my mind. Let's have Sovolevsky and that other one. Even if we don't get Schütz arrested, we'll go through the motions."

Kleini shrugged, and finished off the cheese. Max briefly tried to envision Bette in bed with another woman. Frau Kurzner? Frau Frank? Like wrestling a wad of butter. No. He couldn't imagine it. Underneath all her raw nerves, she was deeply in love with her husband, he thought. And why not? He was tall, handsome; the eye patch gave him dash. It was foolish to imagine otherwise.

The spider continued making its web, clumsily and slowly, but without ever stopping.

Nearly two weeks passed. Max's notes piled up. The shells of two flies and a fat brown bug hung in the spider's web. By July 2, the Russians were converging on Minsk and the railway connecting the city to Baranovitchi was cut off. Von Rundstedt was relieved of his command in France, which seemed to lift the spirits of some of the SS men, but the Allies continued to advance in France and Italy, and on the Byelorussian fronts.

The day Baranovitchi fell, a week later, Max saw the big sergeant who was its namesake beneath a guard tower holding two young soldiers. Their faces glistened with tears. By the fifteenth, the litany of fallen cities began to sound like a chant: Vilna, Caen, Pinsk, St. Jean-de-Daye, Brest Litovsk, Rossignano, Leghorn, Idrica, Lida. The official news played up minor victories as major ones, but the rumors emerging from the communications room held no optimism. If that weren't enough, the Soviet offensive in the Ukraine was moving steadily west. They were already north of Ostheim. If they ever struck decisively south, the camp was doomed.

The single officers' mess became a room of food-pokers who grimly refused to talk about the war. The nervous glances, with everyone trying to avoid everyone else's eyes, made dinners seem like appointment time in the waiting room of a specialist in terminal illness. Max was certain his father, debilitated as he must have been from the cancer, had faced the last months of his life better than these young men were handling the imminent surrender, but he did not know, as the Count von Prokofsk had died shortly after Max's first battle. Max had been thinking of the old man when he heard the whistling of the British shell that had put him in bed for two years. Old men, young men, commandants' wives. Some die, some are spared, a truth that never made any sense. Everyone was ultimately drawn into the vortex. Everything met its end.

The investigation, like the Third Reich, was floundering. Despite his long workdays, studying notes even at meals, he found little that clearly revealed anything. He had gone through almost everyone who had seen or dealt with Lila Schütz the afternoon, evening, and night of her death. His image of himself grilling the witnesses until a crucial, heretofore unappreciated fact revealed the fabric of the lies, became a fantasy. He was plodding, plodding, plodding. He didn't have the experience to know when it was useless to continue questioning. He couldn't tell if anyone was lying or not. What tormented Max most was the irrational belief that a real investigator would have known. In breaks between questioning, he would walk to the communications hut and attempt to contact Oskar Hüber by telephone. He was hardly ever in, and if he had been, he had just gone out. Max left messages and hoped that Oskar's supernatural luck wouldn't finally run out during an Allied bombing.

Max had also held off interviewing Schütz himself. Since Schütz was considered the prime suspect by so many, Max told himself he was saving him for last, when all the data had been assembled and he could catch him in half-truths or lies. Yet he often admitted to himself he wasn't sure he had the stomach to match wits with the commandant. Surely, a real policeman would relish the opportunity to unmask a culprit. Like a tiger smelling prey, he would be tensing his muscles to spring. Max just didn't feel like he was hunting. As despicable as Schütz was, there was no reason to make him into a murderer. The facts were quite straightforward. Schütz had been seen, several times, in his office during the period in which the killer or killers had been slaughtering his wife. It was therefore unlikely he could have participated in the crime personally. Surely a jealous husband would want to be in on his revenge, wouldn't he? The murder could hardly be called impersonal.

Time after time, Max came back to the facts of the second of June. Lila Schütz had eaten lunch at the usual time. About one-thirty, she carried a tray of wild strawberry tarts to the Franks', where all of the officers' children were playing inside with the dog Hermann because of an unseasonable drizzle. She left, however, almost immediately, and was seen by a Pvt. Kierczik headed in the direction of her husband's office and the cluster of noncommissioned officers' barracks. Where she went for the next hour was unknown, though, at just after two, according to a Lithuanian supply sergeant, someone had hurriedly started one of the three officers' cars normally parked behind the cookhouse and driven off. The guards at the gate to the headquarters and family compound reported, however, that between two and four only von Rauschwald had been driven through the gate, so if Lila Schütz had taken the car, she hadn't really gone anywhere.

No one noticed when the car was returned, but Lila was next seen at just after four. The rain had let up slightly and several soldiers taking a break behind the prisoners' huts to the east of the dog run saw her on the opposite side, taunting one of the bigger dogs. She was holding a long, dry branch, inserting it between the wires and driving the dog to a near frenzy by poking it. When the dog bit off most of the stick, she tossed the rest in. She laughed broadly, then walked away.

The soldiers noticed mud on the rear of her skirt. One of them (after dragging this much out of a Pvt. Sebastian, Max could not get him to say who) made a remark about her spending three-quarters of her life on her ass. About five, she was back at Frau Frank's, complaining about the weather. She told a joke she had heard earlier—something tasteless about a general with piles—complained about making dinner, and went home at precisely 6:20 in order to make certain their new maid had Schütz's dinner ready at seven o'clock.

Shortly after eight, she angrily charged across the courtyard toward headquarters. Rounding the stone wall, she bumped into Frau Kurzner returning from the infirmary. Lila dropped a small bottle. They felt in the wet grass for a few seconds, then Lila found it. From what she said in passing, Frau Kurzner thought she was angry about Schütz's being late for dinner again. The small bottle seemed to be pills, though it could have been something else. Lieutenant Kurzner was down with the grippe and Frau Kurzner thought maybe it had spread to Commandant Schütz. Kurzner also thought she heard Lila talking to someone, probably male, but it could just have been Lila angrily muttering to herself, as she commonly did. This was the last time she was seen alive. According to Schütz's statement, she never showed up at his office. He came home to a dry dinner, just beginning to burn in the low oven, at 9:27 (or so he said). By the noise, one soldier thought the commandant had beaten his maid with a shaving strop. There was no sign Lila had ever returned home.

Sergeant Külm, checking his dog Clausewitz at nine-thirty, had noticed a woman going between the single officers' quarters and the first of the noncommissioned officers' barracks. He couldn't say it was Frau Schütz. It might have been Bette von Rauschwald. The woman was too tall to be Frau Kurzner, and too thin to be Frau Frank, but he only got a glimpse of her. Later, when he checked Clausewitz at eleven, he had heard the agitation of his dogs. About fifteen minutes after that, just as Külm got back to his bed, the escape alarm sounded.

A surprise inspection of Prisoner Barracks F had revealed three empty bunks. A general roll call was begun under the direction of Captain von Rauschwald, who had taken over for a flu-ridden Kurzner. Pevner arrived shortly after, and by one-forty they had confirmed three men were missing. During the lengthy roll calls of numbers, one of the prisoners inexplicably bolted from the lines, was shot, and fell into the concertina wire. Von Rauschwald ordered the body to remain on the wire for a week, as an example. Eventually the captain produced the numbers of the three escaped prisoners, who were found the next day, after Schütz threatened "severe punishment" for each tenth man. Two escapees were in the infirmary suffering from typhus. A senior block inmate and two barracks orderlies under him dragged the third, screaming incoherently, from the ranks, into which he had supposedly slipped after the previous roll call. They were the chief suspects in the murder of Frau Schütz as her body had been spotted by Sovolevsky at 2:25.

Corporal Sovolevsky had relieved a Private Tag in the outermost western guard tower. Although it was possible that prisoners might attempt to escape in that area, it had never happened in the two-year history of the camp. Those attempting to escape would not only have to get past the tower at the northern corner of the family compound (with the dog run ending beneath it), but the guards continuously walking along the parallel fences of the northern side of the family compound and the outer perimeter. In between was a clean, open space that had once been dug out in a search for good building stones, then refilled. Sovolevsky had sat with his back to the camp, overlooking the fences, watching the forest, the distant hills, and occasionally scanning the fence line with his spotlight. Max noticed his fingers were yellowish, so he probably smoked, though the corporal would not admit it. At 1:12 Sovolevsky had heard rustling in the distant brush and telephoned the nearby towers. Eventually, he spotted a low, dark animal foraging. It was bearlike, he thought, though he didn't see how it could be one. Wolves had been seen in the area once, so he telephoned the gate to warn Corporal Schwegger and the others patrolling along the woods. More likely than wolves were the frequently reported madmen who lived in the woods like beasts, eating whatever they could get their gnarled hands on. Possibly it was just a peasant wrapped in a dark blanket hunting berries; Sovolevsky couldn't say. Other than that, nothing eventful had occurred until about 2:20.

Koshak had yelled out to him in Ukrainian, then German:

"Lights! Lights!" Sovolevsky fired up his spotlight and scanned the outer perimeter and the woods. Seeing nothing, he swung it around in the direction of the shouts. Koshak was already standing in a circle of light from the other tower. He was pointing his rifle toward the garden. He had seen cuts in the fence behind the spirals of wire, and the stiff fencing was bent outward, toward him. Sgt. Baranovitch came down from the tower over the end of the dog run, leaving Pvt. Ulnya with the light. Sgt. Külm ran into sight. They did not approach the fence, as the electricity had likely been turned on when the alarm for the escaped prisoners had sounded at 11:15. They could see nothing.

Sovolevsky began a systematic search of the area, sweeping the light in wide ovals, beginning first at the end closest to him. Thirty meters from his tower was the brothel, identified in the report as "the closest structure." He saw two whores, angered by the racket, closing the tiny windows at his end. There were no soldiers inside, as far as anyone knew, because of the alarm and Sovolevsky saw no one around the house. He began to sweep the garden. It was the crazy angle of three of the pea stakes that first caught his eye. Schütz, he remarked, kept a true German garden, too tidy to produce tasty food. He did not see the body at first, but kept hovering the light around those skewed poles. Something flashed: Jewelry? The hilt of the knife? The flayed bones glared in the light.

Who got to the body first was not clear. There was much confusion when it was recognized as a woman. Baranovitch eventually got to the scene, however, and dispatched two men to discover if any of the prostitutes were missing. He ordered the others to move back. Although they had trampled much of the surrounding area, they had not forgotten to avoid most of the plants. "Our commandant would be angry to lose his peas over a dead whore," Baranovitch later stated, but a search of the area revealed no distinctive footprints, and nothing dropped. When they finally recognized, at just past three, that the victim was wearing good clothes and was clearly not one of the brothel girls, Baranovitch arranged a circle of lamps and sent for an officer. Before Lt. Pevner showed up, Baranovitch edged up to the body and studied the knife planted in its left breast. He recognized it as the ritual dagger given to officers who had taken the final oath of allegiance to the SS. Baranovitch had remarkably little curiosity about it or about the note, elegantly printed in Fraktur letters about five centimeters high: "Röhm's Revenge."

Max had forgotten Röhm, but the interview with Pevner jogged his memory. Ernst Röhm had been the head of the SA until the summer of 1934, when he had, according to Pevner, gone into collusion with the French ambassador to assassinate Adolf Hitler. The executions that followed ended the heyday of the SA and made the SS the Führer's Praetorian guard. The army, along with most of Germany, had been delighted that the uncontrollable and sordid SA had lost its power. This was all common knowledge, and Max remembered reading about it in a Brazilian newspaper. Though occasional doubts were expressed that there had been any significant putsch planned by Röhm or anyone else, most people seemed to think that the swift and bloody sharpness of the SS response was proof enough that something serious had been in the wings. Hitler, after all, had personally arrested his old friend Röhm. What Pevner said that Max did not know, however, was that evidently the SS had failed to find every traitor in the SA. Periodically since 1934, SS men had been found murdered, with the words "Röhm's Revenge" nearby. The deaths were not linked in any way, nor, it appeared, was it possible that the same individual had carried on a personal course of revenge: the killings had taken place in many locations and were quite different. They were a clear indication of the many enemies of the state who still lurked in the shadows.

Was Frau Schütz's murder another instance of SA revenge? A woman had never been such a victim so far as Pevner could remember. If she had been, it was hardly likely that anyone among the staff had done it. None of the Byelorussians, Ukrainians, or Lithuanians would have been in the SA. The SS troops, most of whom were young, were unlikely to have been in the SA. There could have been some family affiliation with the SA, but then why join the SS? Coercion? Perhaps someone whose sympathies lay with the SA had been sent over to the SS from the army simply because concentration camp guards were needed. It was worth checking the personnel records, Max thought, but he didn't expect anything to come of it. The prisoners executed for her murder had not been Germans, and were, therefore, unlikely SA members, though they could have been acting for another prisoner—or staff member. Perhaps the three escapees were merely convenient culprits. On the other hand, maybe the note and dagger were intended to throw everyone off the scent. That's what Schütz had concluded.

Damn! There were too many possibilities. Max slammed his hand on his desk and rubbed his eyes. His head hurt. The seemingly extraordinary usually has a mundane explanation. The Carachacho told their children that Pummaksoy, the flesh-eating god, hid in the river near midday, waiting for a nice tender child. They all knew of children who had gone to the river on a hot day and never returned. But children drown, they are kidnapped by other tribes, and some of the most poisonous water snakes, particularly the one called "the Flower-Spitter," are much more active in a noonday sun. The true explanation was far less memorable than the mythology, however. A lurking SA avenger was dramatic, but about as real as Pummaksoy.

There were only a few witnesses left he wanted to interview: Schütz, of course, and Klaus Frank. He had scheduled the doctor three times, but Frank "forgot" his afternoon appointments and claimed emergencies in the mornings. Max also wanted to interview Frau Frank and Bette von Rauschwald. The doctor's wife had frequently asked Kleini about "the Count" and likely wanted another excuse to serve tea and cookies. When Max had seen her near the communications room one day, she had invited him to lunch. He shouldn't have refused, he now thought. People are often more relaxed in a social setting than in an interview, especially if they have few opportunities to socialize. Frau von Rauschwald, on the other hand, had just about dropped out of sight. When he saw her one afternoon with the other wives and their maids receiving new food stores, she had only nodded politely, flushed when he bowed in her direction, and avoided his eyes. She was still obviously embarrassed by how she had acted on his first evening in Ostheim.

Though the women had no involvement in the specific events of that night, and, therefore, were not included in Schütz's report, they each might know something about Lila's habits, her boyfriends, and where she might have been between the time she was last seen alive, at about nine-thirty, and the discovery of her body. Ursule and Bette might know more than they thought they knew. And they both seemed pretty open, unlike Frau Kurzner, though she was also worth a try. At the very least, Bette could tell Max if she had been the woman Külm had seen going between the two buildings.

Max had just stood up to increase the circulation in his leg when there was a sharp rap on the door. Kleini came in. "Lieutenant Colonel Hüber wants you," he said. "On the telephone."

· *Eight* ·

In the communications room, an SS private first class and a dour, bespectacled woman sat before three large radios, a switchboard, and a double-padlocked metal cabinet containing the coding machine. When Max burst in on them, they spun around, then pointed at the receiver lying on what looked like an old school desk. Max snatched it up.

"Hello," he said. "Hello."

"Hello," said a woman. "This is Colonel Hüber's office, Reichsführung SS. Who is speaking please?"

"This is Colonel Max-Baldur von Prokofsk." He spoke sharply and probably too loud, but there was a faint buzzing on the line. "I have been trying to reach Colonel Hüber for over a week. Please put him on."

The woman's voice became less formal. "Max-Baldur," she said.

"Excuse me."

"How are you, Max?" She had lowered her voice. "This is Breda, Breda Epp."

He visualized her indifferently brushing cigarette ash from her upturned breast. His mind went momentarily blank and his throat tightened. "Ah," he finally forced out. "Breda. Yes. How are you?" He paused. "How is your friend Lilli?"

"Very good," she said. "You are doing well?"

"Quite." He glanced back at the two behind him. The private was putting on his earphones and copying a message. The woman was unashamedly listening. Max's ears felt warm.

"I must speak to Colonel Hüber. Please put him on. This is not for personal calls."

"I see," she said flatly. "Don't be so hard. Don't you think I deserve another chance? I only wanted to give you a standing invitation for when you come back."

"Ah. Thank you." He was even more ashamed. She did not deserve this icy treatment. "I—I will make a point of it. You are very kind." As intended, his words sounded hollow, but she apparently accepted them.

"That's more like it. You know you don't want to leave it at one try. I know I don't. Here is Lieutenant Colonel Hüber. Good-bye." There was a click.

"Hello?" said Max. He turned to the woman. "I've been cut off. Hello?"

"SS Lieutenant Colonel Oskar Hüber."

"Thank God," sighed Max.

"Max! It really is you. How goes it? Ostheim is sufficiently entertaining, I trust."

"Extremely tedious. There is much I need to know, Oskar. You didn't tell me a thing."

"Oh?" Oskar sounded satisfied. He was playing his old games again, but what were they?

"Hold on." Max turned to the communications people. "Please leave me alone. This conversation is confidential."

They looked at each other. The private removed his earphones. "We are forbidden to leave the room. If you would like us to transfer the call to the officers' quarters—"

Max hesitated. Time was slipping away. "Oskar?"

"Yes."

"I cannot speak completely freely, understand? But you must speak freely to me."

He made a noise of agreement, which, with Oskar, had always meant "if it suits me."

"Please," Max pleaded. "This isn't a question of where you've hidden the professor's lecture notes."

"Very well."

"Why am I investigating this, Oskar? I want a straight answer."

"Because I recommended you."

"You? For God's sake, why?"

"Because you seem to be the right man, Max."

"Oskar, choosing me makes no sense. It has not from the beginning. You can't put your friends in situations like this because they are your friends."

Oskar laughed. "You have been away so long you no longer know me, old friend. We gather all sorts of intelligence here. That's what I do. In searching for an appropriate man, your name leapt out of the files. You're exactly where you should be."

"But why?"

"Because you're a hero. You're moral. You will do what is best for Germany."

"And what is that?"

"Whatever you do. Look, your word will put the case of Frau Schütz to rest."

"I have considered that, Oskar, and I do not believe it. Since when has the SS been worried about getting the approval of anyone? I have seen the look on SS men's faces when your legal department noses around. Not only would they get better results than I, they would be much more convincing to the Reichsführer."

"That is not what Himmler has said to me."

"I do not care what Himmler said to me or to you. I did not believe it then. I don't believe it now." He had forgotten his listeners. He lowered his head and voice. "Please, Oskar. Help me out. I am fed up with the whole situation."

The faint buzzing on the line rose to a sharp crackle, then faded. Oskar's voice became clear again.

"—the right man in the right place. This will become a great opportunity for you."

"Nonsense. What great opportunities are left in Germany?"

Max could almost see Oskar's bemused smile. "You shouldn't say things like that over the telephone."

"Fine. I would be happy to discuss it face to face in Berlin. I tried to."

Oskar was calm. "You *are* upset, aren't you? The camps are a bit distasteful, aren't they?"

Max didn't answer.

"Very well, Maxy, I will tell you something. I shouldn't do it over the telephone." He paused. "No, I can't. Breach of security. I will send a coded message immediately. Schütz has been keeping a secret. You will know why it is worthwhile to keep investigating. You will know why it is worthwhile to keep investigating. You will know that what you've been wanting for a long time has been tossed in your lap."

"No games, Oskar. We're too old for games."

Oskar laughed. "We mustn't tie up the lines any longer."

"One last question." Max sternly glared at the woman, who now pretended to be not listening. He decided to risk it. "Is there a suspicion in Berlin that the husband was somehow involved in the murder?"

"What? You mean Schütz? You can't be serious."

"Of course I am."

"Is there something in the water out there? Where did you get this idea?"

"It seems a common impression here."

Oskar silently thought. "Is it possible? We had heard all was not well with that couple, that there had been some scenes in public places in Weimar. When we first heard of the murder, I remember someone joked that Schütz's school for wives had produced its first failure. I didn't think there was any real possibility of this, however."

"Yes. Anything's possible."

"I thought you didn't want to play games."

"I'm not playing games. I don't know anything for certain."

"But you think—?"

"I don't know."

"That could be quite an octopus."

"Meaning?"

"I don't know, Max. I'll think about it."

"But am I to follow the threads wherever they lead? Is that what's intended?"

"Whatever amuses you."

"Oskar, you are not helping."

"Take your time. You will know why."

"Oskar—"

"Breda is my secretary today. Did you say hello?"

"Yes." What had she told Oskar? Did they laugh about it. Was Oskar teasing?

"She has asked me when you'll be back. You must have made an impression, Maxy. Good-bye."

An impression. Oh, yes, he had made an impression. There was no doubt about that.

He cradled the receiver and remembered that Oskar had

said something similar when Max had stupidly confessed his love for a prostitute he had met on a streetcar in the Ringstrasse. After taking her to dinner several times, Max had asked Oskar what he thought of reforming such a woman and Oskar had said something like, "It depends what an impression you made and I would venture you have made an extraordinary impression." Over the next few weeks, Oskar had watched with quiet amusement while Max made a fool of himself. When Max had finally seen how ludicrous he had been, he had nearly converted to Catholicism simply to be able to take the vow of celibacy. Perhaps, he now thought, he was foolish not to have gone through with it.

"Good day," he barked at the woman. Outside, he paused on the parade ground and looked around him. The bleakness of Ostheim, even in the bright sunlight, was more obvious than ever. The painting and patching that was constantly going on only made it more obvious. Squat stone buildings. Fences. Towers. A great cloud of black smoke meandered upward from inside the prisoners' compound. Across the hard ground, Sgt. Baranovitch wiped the inside of his helmet. He strolled toward him.

"Heil Hitler!" Baranovitch saluted.

"Heil Hitler. At ease."

"More questions, colonel, sir?" His voice rumbled like distant thunder.

"No, sergeant. Nothing important. Go on with what you are doing."

"The sweat soaks the straps," he said. "The leather swells."

"Leather isn't what it used to be, I suppose."

"Yes, sir."

"What are they burning over there?" Max pointed with his cane.

"Prisoners, sir," said Baranovitch.

"Excuse me?"

"Prisoners. There is typhus. It's the most sanitary way."

"Ah."

"We won't get the bridges finished," he mused.

"The prisoners are not good workers, I suppose."

"No, sir. We get something out of them, but they don't last long."

"Not if you shoot them for stepping on a potato plant."

• 98 •

"One shot makes fifty work harder."

"I suppose it would." Max shrugged. "When things go bad in a war, they go worse for prisoners."

Baranovitch nodded.

"So, sergeant, what did you do before the war?"

"I am a blacksmith, sir."

"Ah. You look like one. And you volunteered when?"

"Bolsheviks burned my house. My uncle, my brother burned with it." Baranovitch's eyes narrowed. "To get my hands on Stalin's throat, I would do anything. Anything."

"I'm sorry about your family."

Baranovitch said nothing.

"Sergeant, can we ignore the formalities for a moment and speak off the record?"

Baranovitch replaced his helmet and cocked an eyebrow in assent.

Max saw there was no one in hearing range. "I would be interested in your impression of the commandant."

"I like him."

"Not many seem to."

Baranovitch shrugged again. "He knows how to handle Communists: use them for what they're worth, then throw them away."

"Ah. And what do you think of this talk about Schütz and his wife?"

"He was too lenient."

"Meaning?"

"A Byelorussian knows how to keep a woman in line. You Germans—excuse me, with all respect—do not."

"Don't apologize. I wish you to be totally frank."

"The slut got what she deserved."

"Ah. And do you think Schütz did it?"

Baranovitch stared at Max as if he were trying to understand the full implication of the question.

"I mean," said Max, "that some people have said they wouldn't be surprised if he were behind it."

"No."

"No? You wouldn't be surprised?"

"No. He didn't do it."

"Why? Are you certain?"

"If you don't kill her the first time she fucks around, why do it a dozen times later? A good beating was all she needed."

"But maybe it all built up inside him."

"I have seen him angry. He does not store it."

"And if the prisoners did not kill Lila Schütz, who do you think might have?"

"I don't think," said the sergeant bluntly. "They did it."

"Ah," said Max. Baranovitch's face, never friendly, had hardened even more. It was clear that he had nothing more to say. "Thank you for the talk, sergeant." Before turning away, he added, "I feel I can trust you. I would like to think you could feel the same." He didn't mean it, but Baranovitch would be a pit bull against an enemy. Max hoped his words would at least make the massive sergeant hesitate before siding with Schütz against him, if it should come to that.

"A friend," said Baranovitch suddenly.

"Excuse me?"

"A friend. It's the kind of thing a good friend should do: end the humiliation. Lance the boil." He made a twisting, stabbing motion with his fist.

Max studied him until he looked away.

"And you, sir, said you had no questions." He grunted.

Bowing his head slightly, Max smiled. He headed toward Schütz's office. He would arrange the appointment to interview him personally. Despite all the gossip, there was nothing definite against him. There was no sign that Schütz had in any way reported anything other than the facts of the day of his wife's murder. He had, it is true, not mentioned anything about Lila's personal life, but that was not only understandable, it would be ordinary courtesy to the dead. Weren't such things commonly done by police to protect the family? Or was that only in books? Max felt better. He was somewhat less suspicious now that Oskar had seemed surprised that anyone seriously thought Schütz might be involved. He also felt that maybe his nervous misgivings were all unjustified. Oskar had promised to tell him why he had been chosen for Ostheim. It couldn't be all that dark a secret.

Max climbed the stairs to Schütz's office one by one. When he went inside, the prisoner he had seen on his first day was poring over a long ledger. The man nearly jumped when he noticed Max. A loose sheet of paper dropped to the floor.

"What are you doing?" said Max sharply.

"Nothing, sir," the man said, in a heavy accent.

"You don't act like it is nothing."

"I was checking the records, sir. It is part of my duties."

Max moved to the paper. "What is this?" He poked at it with his cane.

"The commandant's orders," said the prisoner.

"Let me see it," said Max.

The prisoner hesitated.

"Pick it up."

The man held it out. Max rested his cane against the desk and read the paper: "The following prisoners are deemed to have been infected with typhus and are therefore, of necessity, to be removed from contact with the other prisoners." Three neatly typed columns of numbers filled the bottom, followed by Schütz's signature.

"This many people have typhus?" asked Max.

"Yes, sir."

"And why do you have this list?"

"I am entering the names of the dead." His bony finger pointed at the ledger.

"But they aren't dead."

"They will be, soon, sir."

"It's true that medicine isn't as available as it was earlier in the war," said Max, "but you underestimate some men's ability to survive. Suppose some of them should survive the attack?"

"I can change the book."

"It doesn't seem very sensible," said Max.

The prisoner stared.

"Is the commandant in?"

"No, sir. New prisoners have arrived from Rumania. He always inspects new prisoners."

"Ah. You will take a message then. Colonel von Prokofsk would like to meet with him tomorrow, at his convenience, for approximately an hour. Is that clear?"

"Yes, sir."

"Will you write it down?"

"I will remember, sir."

"You're certain?"

"I have lost the ability to forget."

A chill slithered up Max's body. The prisoner's eyes were empty as the sockets of a skull. There was nothing behind them but a soulless, mechanical doll who went about his tasks without thinking. They were eyes that condemned everything to trivialization, as if they saw beyond and through present time. They were the sunken eyes of a prophet whose words cannot be believed: *I Tiresias, though blind, throbbing between two lives . . .*

"Who were you?" said Max, without knowing why.

The prisoner immediately understood. The past tense was for time before the war; the present was war, the now that did not end and the future was either nonexistent or not worth the bother. "I was Gissinger, the best poultryman in Teresva. People laughed at me."

Max waited for him to say more, but when he didn't it gradually made sense as the entire explanation. Max left, without another word.

Clouds had moved in low. Even the slightest peaks of the distant hills became obscured. The moisture pressed down the smoke from the burning of the typhus victims. The air became hazy and acrid. A dust like sweet charcoal coated the nose, tongue, and throat. In the middle of the parade ground, Max was nauseated. He slid his cane under his sleeve, holding it in his armpit with the stub of his arm. He held up a handkerchief to breathe through, but the taste was still in his mouth, the burnt-candy paste still in his nose and lungs. He couldn't settle on what to do. He certainly had no desire to eat. He felt dirty, but disliked bathing in the evenings. He considered visiting in the family quarters, but knew he could never relax there observing them, knowing they knew he was observing them, politely sipping chamomile all the while. They would be eating, anyhow. He strolled as far as the compound gates, occasionally passing through patches of clear air. He looked out at the main gate with its towers on either side. Just beyond it, fading in and out of the smoke and fog, he saw the main camp infirmary, a white wooden hut on stone piers. It was no bigger than the single officers' quarters. He wandered back along the fence. The dogs, trained to recognize uniforms, neither barked nor snarled but alertly watched him. Everyone else was watching him too, he felt, but, less honest than the dogs, they observed him out of the corners of their eyes, waited until he was out of sight, then rushed to speculate whether Max was the sort who could successfully bring down Schütz.

The orderly in the officers' quarters saluted. He looked too gray and awkward to be a soldier. His hands shook even when he stood at attention. He was wearing an Iron Cross that had a W in the center instead of a swastika. Max gestured at it with his cane. "The Great War."

"Yes, sir." The old man beamed. "Under von Hindenburg. There was a general!"

"My father fought in the Alps. Do you always wear your medal?"

He looked sheepish. "I know it's a little irregular, but I am proud of it. I am proud of my country."

"Ah." Max smiled. He remembered a young anthropologist rushing to the steamship office as soon as the French declared war. "Don't worry about me," he added. "You may wear it on your pajamas if you wish."

He saluted again. "Thank you, sir. A good night to you, sir."

"Good night."

In his room, Kleini had left a tray. A local buckwheat bread, cheese, sliced white sausage, and a corked bottle of dark wine. Max replaced the cover, unbuttoned his tunic, and settled on the bed. It was getting dark. He sniffed. Either the smoke had penetrated the room or it still coated his nostrils. He quickly lifted his shirt and inspected under the band of his trousers. No sign of typhus-bearing lice. He thought for a moment about the writing of his report and decided it would be better not to go back over all the details covered in Schütz's report, but only concentrate on assessing it. He sniffed. That would be quicker, and would get him out of here in a few days. Why did Oskar seem to think he should drag it out? Oskar obviously had no idea that Ostheim was not exactly the central European equivalent of Rio. Max sniffed again and decided to try the wine to clear the taste. There was no corkscrew on the tray, however. He took a thick pencil from the drawer and shoved the cork inside. His first sip from the bottle made him wonder how the smoke had penetrated the glass, but the second was somewhat better. He considered making notes on what to ask Schütz and the doctor, but instead dozed off.

Sometime after midnight, the old orderly rapped on his door. Behind him was the SS woman in spectacles, who so much resembled Himmler at first glance that Max thought she was the Reichsführer's twin. He blinked. The woman was still there. Max had fallen asleep so easily, he didn't really believe he was now awake. "Message for your sight only, Colonel Count von Prokofsk. From Berlin." She clacked her heels and thrust forward a sealed yellow envelope.

"Thank you," said Max. The woman did not move. "You may go now."

"If there is a reply?" The disdain in this woman's voice was probably the usual SS contempt for the regular army. The higher the army rank, the more certain they seemed of the holder's decadence.

"If there is a reply, I will call for you."

"Very well, colonel. May I remind you that this category of communication is to be destroyed after reading?"

"I know what the word 'secret' means," he said sharply. "Are you waiting for a tip?"

The eyes behind the thick spectacles widened at the insult. "Heil Hitler!" she said sharply.

"Heil Hitler," mumbled Max. She spun on her heels. The old orderly seemed amused.

Max closed his door. "Well, Oskar, why am I here?" He pinned the envelope against the table top with his stump and wiggled his finger under the seal. When he spread it out, there were only two words, typed in capital letters:

THE FÜRER.

· *Nine* ·

Max once more went without sleep. He passed through phases in which he was furious with Oskar and his penchant for conundrums. He swore he would write a report in which he would say only, "I know nothing definite to refute Commandant Major Bodo Schütz's report. Respectfully submitted, Colonel, etc." No more than fifty words. Himmler hadn't specified the length of the report, had he? Then Max would let his intrigue for the puzzles swirling around him take over. In the camps of the Carachacho, after all, he had spent many hours trying to make inexplicable behavior fit a coherent cultural pattern, and his military experiences, combat, and even two foggy years in and out of the operating room, hadn't completely changed him. He would get caught up in the idea of turning the tables, figuring out what was going on, and shifting it to his advantage, though what advantage there might be he could not grasp.

"THE FÜHRER"?

Max tried various theories. Schütz seemed to think he was close to Adolf Hitler, at least in the sense that Hitler had supported the founding of Ostheim. Suppose it was true. Suppose he knew something important. Oskar had said Schütz was keeping a secret. Suppose Lila found out and it became necessary to make certain she never revealed it. Lila is murdered by conveniently absent prisoners. But what could Schütz know? How could he be close to the Führer? Schütz seemed the kind of irritant that any superior would do his best to get rid of. Max suspected Schütz had actually been given Ostheim to get him as far away from Buchenwald as possible. Max had seen it happen before—an inferior officer who is such a pain he gets promoted or transferred or both, merely to get him out of the way. Schütz's dream of colonizing the East certainly fell into that category, especially since the East was steadily closing in on the West. If Lila knew something that had brought about her death, then how could it be exposed? Lila was dead. Schütz had no reason to talk. Maybe, on the other hand, it was not something Lila had found out, but something about Lila herself. Could she have bedded down with someone important, maybe even Hitler himself? Hitler was obviously very attractive to women. Max vaguely remembered that an English woman—what was her name?—had killed herself over him. Had Hitler said something in bed? Suppose the Führer had unusual bedroom interests that Lila might have made known. Suppose she had tried blackmail and Schütz had taken care of the problem. My God! All of these possibilities were so ridiculously farfetched, Max laughed out loud at himself for thinking them. Oskar had seemed not to have an inkling that Schütz was everyone's favorite bet to have killed Lila. Whatever the rumors were, they weren't connected to this message.

Damn you, Oskar Hüber, damn you. What have you gotten me into?

He stared at the paper for another hour or so, then slowly tore it into tiny fragments. It was strange how one could be sent off to a highly rated gymnasium in Vienna and then become attached to a calculating, pleasure-seeking, self-serving, and manipulative character like Oskar Hüber. Oskar Hüber, amused at Max's first loves. Oskar Hüber, who never took anything or anyone seriously. Oskar Hüber, who must have laughed out of the side of his mouth when they presented him his SS dagger and he recited the oath to Adolf Hitler. Somehow, however, Oskar and he had always ended up laughing about Oskar's latest prank, even if Max had been the victim. Also, whenever things had gotten out of hand, Oskar always figured a way to save Max. Once, Oskar had even taken a brutal caning by Professor Kleinfeld that really belonged to Max. The professor had drawn blood. Oskar had laughed about how furious Kleinfeld had gotten when he accepted the beating without crying out. "His veins were big as aqueducts," Oskar had said, "and the sweat flew off them like they were leaking." This was also the same Oskar who had set Max up with Old Man Hüber's mistress when Oskar knew his wildly, but justifiably, jealous father would be coming home early. Who could fathom the human mind? Kant, Bach, Eliot, Goethe, Kinchachua the Carachacho shaman, Adolf Hitler, Oskar Hüber, Bodo Schütz: these were all the same species?

Max had half finished the leftover wine when someone rapped. A bleary-eyed orderly, at least thirty years younger than the old one, stood in the corridor. "Sir, Commandant Schütz has sent instructions that if you wish to see him today, you must do so in his office in thirty minutes."

"In thirty minutes? What time is it?"

"Four-thirty, sir."

Max looked at him incredulously, then scratched the stump of his arm. The orderly tried not to appear to be staring, but he was. "Very well, fine. Is Sergeant Klimmer here?"

"No. Shall I send for him, colonel?"

"There isn't time. Thank you."

Max peered at himself in the mirror. He looked bad. He began to sweat. The chills came over him. Schütz certainly knew how to choose the time and take the high ground. Max's fantasies of grilling the despicable little commandant had become as idiotic as Schütz's vision of himself as czar of the eastern camps. Max splashed water on his face. He hoped the morphine shakes didn't show up again when the sweats abated.

When he arrived at Schütz's office, the prisoner clerk Gissinger was dozing. His head hovered a few inches above an open ledger and his pen had bled a pfennig-sized spot at the end of the name he had been entering. When Max closed the door behind him, Gissinger woke without being startled. His pen moved on as if he had been awake all along. He was faking, however, as the ink in his pen point had dried. "Excuse me, sir," he said. "I was so wrapped up in my work, I did not hear you come in."

"Undoubtedly," said Max. "I am here to see the commandant."

"He expects you, sir. I will announce you."

"No need." Max passed Gissinger and headed for Schütz's door.

The clerk panicked. He scurried out from behind Max and nearly bumped into him as the oak door swung back. He stood on his toes and tried to call out over Max's shoulder, "The Colonel von Prokofsk has arrived, Commandant Major Schütz."

Schütz looked up from his papers. He glanced at Max, then stood. "I thought I told you to announce him when he came."

"I tried to, sir," said the clerk, "but—"

" 'But'? What is this word 'but'? When I give you an order, you are to obey it to the letter! Don't you like work here? Perhaps you would prefer the gravel pits. A weasel like you belongs there, doesn't he?"

Gissinger simply blinked.

"Answer me!" Schütz slapped his desk. His pen holder jumped.

"Yes, sir, I am a pig. I belong there. I am grateful you have me here instead, but I will willingly go to the pits if you say so, Commandant Major."

Max was once again repulsed by the clerk's fawning. It again reminded him of the toadying of the beggars in Manaus, who bowed and scraped for strangers, then cursed them in Portuguese and spat on the ground as soon as the foreigners were out of earshot. At least, however, they retained some rough sense of manhood in their hypocrisy. Gissinger, however, gave him the feeling that he was as hollow as he seemed: skin and bones, but no human being. Max was disgusted by him and drifted away from the clerk as if he had just found out he was carrying a disease. "I told him not to announce me."

Schütz sneered. "And that is supposed to excuse it? I gave him specific orders."

"Yes, sir, you did, sir."

"Shut up," barked Schütz. "You speak when you're spoken to!"

Max, staring at Schütz, walked up to his desk. "The clerk was hard at work. I did not wish to take him from his work. I went past him before he had the chance to react. Now did you want me here at five, or not?"

"And I," said Schütz, "am not hard at work? Is interrupting him more important than interrupting me?"

Max dropped into a chair, pulled the case file from under his half arm, and snapped it on the desk. "I have cooperated with you. It is five. Now, do you cooperate with me, or do I write my report without you?"

Schütz growled deep in his chest, then exploded. *"But it is not five! It is four fifty-seven!"* He pointed at the wall clock. His eyes bulging, Schütz's breath could be heard in quick hisses.

Hieronymo's mad againe, Max thought. He slowly pulled his watch from its pocket, and snapped it open. His voice was calm and haughty. "I believe you're right, commandant. No, *were* right. It has just become four fifty-eight. My rudeness is unforgivable. I admit it freely. Shall I go out and come back in two minutes?"

Schütz clenched his fists and leaned on his desk. He looked like a poor medieval statue of a sitting lion. He glared until Max thought his eyes might pop out of their sockets. Max picked at an imaginary piece of lint on the hem of his tunic.

The commandant suddenly thrust a finger at the clerk. "Get out! You have no business in here."

"Yes, sir. Very good, sir." The door closed.

Schütz mopped his bald head with a handkerchief, then crossed to a narrow sideboard and poured himself a glass of water. He drank it and returned to his chair. Max listened to the clock ticking.

Schütz rocked back in his chair. "I have called you here now because it is the only convenient time. Another shipment of prisoners may be brought from the front today or tomorrow. I don't have time for your Wehrmacht games. You have interviewed everyone connected with the crime?"

"Nearly. I have yet to interview you, for one."

"And you have, of course, verified my report."

"Insofar as I have examined, I find the facts have been scrupulously assembled. There is no new evidence of any major significance."

"And thus you have verified my report."

"I said that so far I have verified the facts, Commandant Schütz. I am ordered, may I remind you, by Reichsführer

Himmler himself to come to an independent conclusion as to the interpretation of the facts."

"But you have found nothing, colonel, to contradict me, and therefore, you must end this, this annoyance."

"I have not completed my investigation. There are still several aspects I wish to look into."

Schütz, who had been simmering, boiled over again. "Who is behind this? Have you been told to drag this out? Ah, yes, they are always trying to bring me into disrepute. I will not allow you to succeed. There is too much at stake, my little count. I demand you wrap up this investigation within the next five days. Five days, that's all I will allow. Is that clear?"

Max stared at him. He wanted to crack him across the face with his cane.

"Is that clear?"

Max came to his feet without thinking, as if he had never been wounded. He stuck his cane into Schütz's belly as if it were a sword. He spoke quietly between his clenched teeth. "You are not here, Herr Schütz, to ask me questions. You are not here, Herr Schütz, to make demands of me. If you wish me gone, I will be happy to go," he prodded with the cane, "if and when I receive a written order from either the Reichsführer or his superiors. You have no control over me, Herr Commandant Major. None whatsoever. I will answer neither your questions nor your commands. I am here to question you, and you will answer me, or I will make certain that you'll dine on your own shit. Am I understood?" He prodded once more, hard enough to make Schütz's chair tip backward.

Schütz was flushed and breathing hard. His veins were throbbing in his throat and forehead. He was either growling again, deep in his chest, or grinding his teeth. If he came out of the chair, Max thought, the only chance was to try to catch him across the face with the cane, otherwise Max didn't stand a chance. Instead, he gently pushed the cane aside. "I have always obeyed my superiors," he muttered. "Even when they are making an error."

"Are you saying your superiors make mistakes, commandant?"

"I am saying they can be ill-advised."

"Really? The SS? You shock me."

"But that is not my business." Schütz diverted his eyes. "I obey to the death."

"Very good," said Max, sitting. "We understand each other." He rested the cane against the arm of his chair.

Schütz sniffed. He was like all bullies, thought Max. They collapsed when confronted.

"Now," said Max. "I find no need to ask you about the night in question. You were seen in your office several times before nine-thirty, when you went home to an overdone dinner. Later, during the attempted escape, you were in the prisoners' compound. I can accept all this for the moment."

"I had no opportunity to kill her."

"Please. Don't interrupt. It remains to be seen if you had no opportunity. I will be the judge of that."

Schütz sneered.

"Oh, I will, major. Be certain of it." Max spread the file on the corner of the desk and opened a fountain pen. "What did you know about your wife's sex life?"

Schütz seemed puzzled. "Is this the Wehrmacht idea of a joke?"

"Answer the question."

"We were very happy."

"I see. And this is why she frequently lifted her skirts for other men?"

"What has this cheap slander to do with her death?"

"Maybe nothing. This is not for you to judge. Were you aware she was quite a pleasure-seeker?"

Schütz stared.

"I will not recite the list of men who have been suggested as your assistants in satiating Frau Schütz."

"You tell me who and they will pay." There was ennui in the commandant's voice, as if he were reciting the regulations for filling out barracks rosters.

"It isn't that easy. According to common rumor, you might well need a camp to punish them all."

"It is all a lie."

"You know it isn't."

Schütz spun his chair sideways and stared at the portrait of Adolf Hitler over the sideboard. "All right." He inhaled. "She was a woman of great appetites. It started at Buchenwald.

The first few times I confronted her. I hit her. Once, twice. I broke her collarbone."

"Why didn't you divorce her?"

"I came to a recognition. I looked at her, wearing that sling, and suddenly knew that she was perfect for me. She had no respect for the conventional bourgeois mentality that brought Germany to the edge of ruin. What is the duty and morality of a wife? We all know what that is. The Party makes it clear. But there are also people who are above morality. If there are to be supermen, why not superwomen?"

"Why do I find your realization quite unbelievable?"

"It is the truth," Schütz protested. "You, you probably are full of antique notions of duty and respect. You are the kind of person that the new Germany has had to drag along in its wake."

"I am not at issue. I simply find it hard to believe that you would allow your wife to fuck anyone she took a notion to."

Schütz sneered again. " 'Fuck' you say, as if a natural need were detestable. Every word you say is so bourgeois. Jewish weakness, as Nietzsche puts it."

"So you were pleased Frau Schütz was cuckolding you?"

"Now it's 'cuckold'! Ha! No. I was pleased she was above the ordinary run of woman. I deserved a woman like that. Germany deserved her."

Max sat back in his chair. "Your logic, commandant, is a wonder."

"Are you saying I'm stupid?"

"No. Not at all. I am just unable to appreciate some of the New Germany's concepts."

"And they send you to question me!"

Max mused for several seconds. "And when exactly did Lila throw off conventional morality?"

"At Buchenwald. There was much, shall we say, playing around among the staff: wives with other husbands, even wives with wives. After six months there, Lila began to circulate among the men."

"And you would argue that this made all the wives there patriotic Germans?"

"Of course not. Most of them were mere thrill-seekers. They liked to think they were *in love*. Romance, you know. Something out of a French Jew's novel. The very reason they did it was conventional. Lila had no need of love. She took what she wanted for herself, just as we have taken Europe for ourselves and will soon take the world."

"And you were aware of the frequency of your wife's activities here at Ostheim?"

"She often described them to me, in private moments. But I did not take much interest otherwise. I am a very busy man."

"And you? Do you have as liberal an attitude toward sex as your wife?"

"Are you not wandering from the purpose of your investigation?"

"That, I remind you, is for me to decide. She was pregnant."

"I know. I was pleased. Another warrior for the German nation."

"But the child may not have been yours."

"She assured me it was."

"And you believed her?"

"Women have ways of preventing errors like that."

"Why would a superwoman care?"

"So that only the finest breedings can occur. Pleasure is one thing. Mating is another."

"Forgive me if I am astonished by your professed naïveté!"

"Lila assured me." He said it as an article of faith. Doubt was impossible.

Max paused a moment, then added, "You must appreciate that Lila's behavior might seem a powerful incentive to murder."

"In an ordinary man," sniffed Schütz.

"And is quite contrary to the pristine image of SS wives given in the press."

"That is merely to handle the residual emotions left in the populace. Not everyone in Germany is a National Socialist. Not everyone is yet willing to give up the old ways. For the time being, we feed them what they want."

"Not everyone may be a National Socialist, but they've certainly gone along."

"Destiny cannot be resisted."

"Ah." Max pretended to be writing something. Without looking up, he said, "Still, it seems that the Reich has made a considerable effort to remove prostitutes. It now seems they were Nietzschean superwomen." When he glanced up, the fire in Schütz's eyes could have withered grass.

"One other thing on this subject," said Max. "Do you have any specific knowledge of who may have enjoyed your wife's, ah, destruction of bourgeois values?"

"Pevner was always mooning over her. She laughed once and told me it was because he thought he was in love. She had done things he had never experienced. Am I supposed to tell you what?"

"Not now. Who else?"

"She usually didn't name names. Senior Colonel Kreuzer, who inspected the camp last year."

"Who else here?"

"Who knows?"

"Von Rauschwald?"

"Yes."

"Is that why you dislike him?"

"He is a shit. It has nothing to do with where he sticks his pisser."

"Why then do you dislike him?"

"He is another petty queer who joined the SS merely to be important. He takes on airs. He sticks 'von' on his name like it means something. He's a fart who thinks he's a peacock."

"What do you mean by queer?"

"He thinks he's elegant. He prisses."

"He doesn't seem that way to me."

"Well, he wouldn't, would he?" Schütz grinned. "Lila enjoyed humiliating him. And he kept coming back for more. He'll be out of the SS as soon as I can arrange it."

"And this has nothing to do with jealousy?"

"He's a fart. How can one be jealous of a fart?"

"Ah." Max thought for a moment. "I assure you, Commandant Schütz, that I will not insert irrelevant gossip into my report. Frau Schütz's sexual activities, if they are not relevant, will not appear."

"Do as you wish," said Schütz. "You are, supposedly, in charge. For the time being."

"For the time being," said Max.

"There are further questions?"

"Oh yes," said Max. "The dagger. The one that was found in her chest."

"I know which one you mean," he said nastily.

"I find it somewhat peculiar that the dagger is not more specifically discussed in the report."

"It is clearly stated that the dagger was mine."

"And that it was stolen. Was it?"

"Yes."

"Out of your home?"

"Yes. Several months ago. Our housemaid at the time did it. She admitted it under interrogation."

"But you did not recover the dagger?"

"She told us, at first, that she had sold it to a prisoner, but as he was already dead, I believe it was just a ploy. Further questioning had her saying she had thrown it over the fence to spite me, but that was also, I think, a ploy. She was protecting another prisoner. I made an example of her before the assembled prisoners, but no one came forward."

"Is it possible she did not steal it?"

"No. I'm certain she did. She was in our house twelve hours a day. Who else?"

"Your wife. One of the other officers' children. Perhaps someone else's servant. And where would the prisoners have hidden it until leaving it in Lila's body?"

"You are foolish. No matter how many times one searches the compound, they still have things hidden." Schütz went back to the sideboard for more water. Max noticed that he poured without the slightest tremor in his hand.

"I think you will agree, however, in looking at this entire situation from the outside, there are several appreciable oddities about this business of the dagger."

Schütz sat and sipped his water.

"For one thing," Max continued, "the dagger is ceremonial. It wouldn't cut goose grease." He reached into the folder, took out the photograph of the mutilated body, and shoved it at the commandant. "It could not have been the instrument or instruments used to make these long, even cuts." Schütz glanced at the photograph. If he were disturbed, it didn't show.

"I suggest in my report that razors or scalpels stolen from the infirmary may have been used. The dagger was merely a way of insulting me."

"Ah," said Max. "Yet none of these were found."

"When we replant the garden next year, I would not be surprised to find them buried there. This is all in my report."

"And you did not interrogate the suspects as to these weapons? Did they have the opportunity to get razors or scalpels? Why did they hold the dagger so long—at, I presume, great risk—before using it?"

"Two of the murderers were nearly unconscious from their typhus, the third was uncontrollably weeping and denying everything. There was no point in dragging out the inevitable over a few details, just to satisfy some army colonel's curiosity."

"Believe me, major, I have no curiosity about you or anyone else. Need I remind you whom I represent?"

Schütz sipped his water.

"I raise only questions that others may raise. You may resent this, Commandant Schütz, but you have no choice in the matter. Are you aware that a great many people suspect you of having butchered your wife?"

Schütz flung his drink against the sideboard. Pieces of glass scattered like gravel. Several drops of water landed on the face of Adolf Hitler, then slowly trickled from hair to eye to nose to chin. "I knew it," the commandant fumed. "It is a plot to undermine Ostheim. And you are one of the conspirators."

"I conspire at nothing."

"You are ruining me."

"I am investigating. That is all. I don't care whether Ostheim goes to hell, or you go to hell, or you become the next Führer. I'd rather be in Bavaria or Vienna or Brazil."

"You are playing into their hands!"

"Whoever's hands you're fretting about will be better served by letting the rumors drag on. If your report is to have any credibility, my report must be thorough." Max paused to let the thought sink in. If Schütz bought it, and if he were guilty, he might be tempted to try to explain too much in order to use Max's report in his favor. "Let me explain what I see as possible points that could be directed against you, assuming you killed, or arranged to kill, your wife."

"I didn't. I won't have you say I did. I have too much of importance to do here."

"First, it was your dagger. You say it was stolen. Yet, isn't this an object of great significance to SS men? Would you not be more careful with it? It is a sacred symbol to you and yet you do not keep it with you at all times?"

"It was one hundred meters away. In my home."

"Christians wear their crucifixes around their necks at all times."

"Very well, I admit I had two. I had a duplicate made in the eventuality the original was lost. I have known others to do the same. It is just a precaution."

"But isn't there great sentiment connected with the original?"

"Of course," snarled Schütz. "It is more than sentiment. It is the symbol of my oath to serve my Führer. It is the emblem of my knighthood. To lose it would be disgraceful. To appear in public without it, however, would be worse." Schütz paused. "It is only a symbol, after all. What really matters is in my heart and soul. Having a duplicate is like having a duplicate uniform. That's all."

"I suppose you can expect things to disappear occasionally when prisoners work so freely in your headquarters." Max gestured at the closed door and the clerk behind it. "And among your families."

"They must know we do not fear them. They are merely slaves and must be treated as such. Nothing they can do must be allowed to have the slightest effect upon us."

"Even the butchering of Lila?"

"Not even that."

"If one wished, one could make quite a bit out of that. It is as if you know the prisoners did not do it."

Schütz fumed again, but his eyes seemed to tighten, as if he were finally taking Max's words seriously.

"Also, that was your dagger. And you would have known about Röhm's Revenge, whereas the prisoners may not have."

"That was just a ruse to point the blame away from them."

"Also, in my opinion, Herr Commandant, your conspicuous indifference to what should be a great personal tragedy does not speak well for you." Max tapped the picture of Lila's corpse to emphasize the point.

Schütz almost laughed. His voice was as condescending as if he were speaking to an idiotic child. "Doesn't it? Would an outpouring of bourgeois emotion be more to your liking? Lila deserves better. She was a hero of the Reich. I will not spit on her memory by cheap public displays." He flicked the photograph back at Max, who calmly picked it up and slid it into the folder.

"Nonetheless, it is hardly credible."

Schütz stiffened. "Enough of this. When can I expect your report to be completed?"

"When I have finished it."

"What could possibly remain to be done? You have all the evidence. Despite your intention to undermine the eastern camps project, you have only cheap speculations in attempting to smear me. I see no reason you cannot write your report in the next two days."

"No."

"Why not?"

"I intend to interview several others. There may be something overlooked. Frau Frank, for example, may know something about Lila's personal life that may prove important."

"All she knows is how to stuff things down her throat."

"And then, I am concerned that there are no interviews with prisoners."

"Prisoners?"

"Yes. Why did they kill your wife? These three likely had friends. What do the friends know?"

"She discovered them trying to escape."

"I doubt that."

Schütz slammed the arms of his chair and stood. He said nothing, so Max continued. "If escaping, why did they cut their way into the family and command compound? Why not go through the outer fence? Then, why choose a spot so close to the center, where they are more visible to both towers, when they could cut through much less noticeably close up under the tower?"

"They are subhumans!" said Schütz in exasperation. "They don't think normally!"

"Even a rat can be clever. More important, in this photograph, you will note how the wire is cut."

"So?"

"The prisoners, according to your conclusion, climbed over, or more likely, through, the spiral of barbed wire. In the space between the wire and the fence, they cut the fence and bent it outward to give themselves an opening."

"So?"

"I find it hard to accept that they snaked their way through the concertina wire, when they had the means to cut it. Also, with only a few feet of space to stand in, between the coils and the fence, why would they pull the fence wire outward? It would be simpler, especially with the wire behind you, to push it in. Also, how could they know that the fence would not be electrified?"

"You are making arguments out of smoke, colonel. I do not appreciate it. They toss something against the fence, no sparks. The fence, in any case, is only electrified when the alarm goes off. There is not enough oil to run the generator at full capacity at all times. Perhaps they did not cut the concertina wire because the patrolling guards might notice it."

"These same patrols would not notice the fence?"

Schütz shrugged. "There are some things one can never know, colonel. Such as why they did what they did. Such as why they chose my Lila to kill. Raising these issues only complicates matters unnecessarily. Which you know. Which you must be deliberately doing for those against me. Probably with von Rauschwald's assistance."

"Commandant, I am simply saying it is more likely the fence was cut from the inside and pushed outward. If they were your prisoners, then they were already inside."

Schütz thought. "Possibly."

"Or they were not prisoners at all."

"No. Not possible."

"There are many dubious men in your command."

"No. The Slavic mind is too easy to predict. These Ukrainians and so forth would never kill in an elaborate way."

"If the Slavic mind is so easy to predict, perhaps you should be explaining to the General Staff why our armies are having such difficulty with the Reds."

"Traitors and bad luck. Don't be naïve. The tide will soon shift. It's much overdue."

"And what of the possibility one or more of your Germans killed Lila? You have a command of the wounded, the unsuitable, possibly the deranged. Also, what if someone loved your wife?"

"So he minced her? You *are* a fool. You are grasping at

spirits. You have found nothing, so you are trying to make something. I demand this investigation of yours be concluded by July twenty-first, at the latest."

Max closed his folder, took his cane, and rose. He stared Schütz in the eye. "You may demand what you wish. I will go on as I feel the need, or until my orders are countermanded. I intend to begin tomorrow in the prisoners' compound. I expect a proper escort. Now, I expect I am in need of some breakfast, so we will adjourn until some other time."

"There will be no other time. You are merely stalling."

Max reacted without thinking. He swept his cane across Schütz's desk, pushing onto the floor a file of papers and the flat porcelain paperweight decorated with the lightning-shaped *SS*. "There will be a time any time I ask for it, Commandant Schütz, or I will make certain to accuse you of the murder. Are we clear, commandant?"

Schütz stared.

"Well!?"

"I will get you for this, my little count," he muttered. "I will get you, make no mistake."

"Then we understand each other," said Max. Simply to twist the knife, he winked before he spun on his heels.

· *Ten* ·

As Max left Schütz's offices, he heard the commandant shout for his clerk, then, at the top of his lungs, demand that a call be placed to Berlin. Max neither hesitated nor looked back, but closed the outer door and marched into a surprisingly warm and yellow sun. He glanced at the communications office to his right, where the dour woman would be scrambling to get through to whomever Schütz wanted. At the far end of the parade ground, a squad was assembling, evidently to relieve the guards in the prisoners' compound. Behind them, six men were unloading a supply truck. He thought for a moment that they had all noticed him when he came out, so he tipped his head slightly and stepped down from the porch.

His leg was sore, but even that felt good. In the Afrika Korps, he had been promoted upward so fast that he had never felt as important or as commanding as each new rank implied. "Colonel" had come when he lay flat on his back and vague figures dressed in white had cleaned him and propped him up for other vague figures who, decked in ribbons and braid, had shaken his hand and pinned more medals to his hospital shirt. The lights for the cameras had been cold and infinitely white as the Arctic. Today, however, he felt lightheaded. He had handled Schütz. Even when he had lost control, his anger had been useful in putting Schütz in his place. Maybe it was lack of sleep or of breakfast, but he had met the challenge. He hadn't had to think about feeling or reacting. He had simply done so. "Colonel Max-Baldur von Prokofsk," he said to himself with satisfaction, then limped toward his quarters. He noticed the wind was blowing toward the east and the smoke from the burning in the prisoners' compound was very thin, almost nonexistent.

He asked the young orderly if he had seen Sgt. Klimmer. The boy said no and Max was surprised. Kleini always came in the mornings to help Max dress, or just to check on him. Max once called him his "mother hen" because Kleini took care of Max with more solicitude than his orders required. Kleini's not being there didn't bother Max too much, however. He considered ordering up another bath in the canvas tub, or even a shower. He even considered going to the officers' mess for breakfast and ignoring their surliness, but it was likely past serving time. He decided to munch on the cheese and bread left in his room, then to go after Dr. Frank. He was pumped up and ready. This was not going to be another day for the doctor to dodge him.

Tossing his cane on the bed and flipping his hat on the dresser, he lifted the cover off his food. There was nothing there. The cheese, the bread were gone. Only a few crumbs proved they had been there at all. He looked around the base of the wall for rat holes and saw nothing. He called in the orderly and asked who had been in his room. The orderly said, "Why, no one, sir." He smiled and asked if the boy had helped himself to his food. The boy said no, and he asked again, this time making it clear he wasn't angry if he had. The orderly earnestly said he hadn't. He hadn't gone into any of the rooms. His attention had never been diverted. He had not left his post. He did not know if the building had been checked for rats, but he would report the possibility right away. After the orderly left, Max tried to imagine why anyone would sneak into his room—once while he was asleep—merely to steal food. It must be rats, or a number of mice. He looked for droppings and found none. A quick rat? One who could lift and replace the domed cover?

He thought of the folder with the photographs, statements, and notes on Frau Schütz's murder. He had better take it back to the little office. Yet, if someone were getting into his bedroom, then surely that office would be no problem. On an impulse, he reached in his dressing kit and took out his talcum. Placing the folder inside the dresser drawer, he discreetly as possible sprinkled powder on the folder, the top edge of the drawer, and the handle. He then went to the orderly.

"Private, I want you to keep a good eye on my room."

"Yes, sir."

"I am leaving some important papers in the drawer and I don't want them disturbed."

"You may count on me, sir." The boy seemed very proud.

"Say, private, I seem to have missed breakfast. If mess has ended, where can I get something?"

"I'm certain they will not refuse you, sir."

"Ah," said Max. "Oh, and have you seen my sergeant yet?"

"No, sir. Would you like me to inquire after him?"

"Thank you. No. I'm sure he's keeping busy. At ease. Remember: never take your eye off the door."

Max turned to leave, then came back. "Private?"

"Yes, sir."

"How old are you?"

"Eighteen, sir."

"You don't look eighteen."

"I come from a small family, sir." The rapid blinking betrayed the lie.

"Ah," said Max.

After a bitter brew the gaunt cook called "coffee," and two cold and leaden potato cakes, Max went on to the noncommissioned officers' barracks. The sergeants slept four bunks to a room. In two rooms, men were snoring loudly. In the third, Sgt. Külm sat in his underwear on the edge of his bunk spit-polishing his boots.

"Good day," said Max.

"Heil Hitler," saluted Külm.

"Carry on." Max strolled in and patted one of the tightly made bunks. "They seem comfortable."

"What?" said Külm, who looked up, then added, "Oh. Yes, sir."

"How are the dogs?"

"Tired. It was a long night. The dogs are always needed for new prisoners, but they are not properly fed. Perhaps you could speak to the commandant."

"You haven't told him yourself?"

"Yes, sir, but, you know, different voice and all that. My dogs do the work of twenty men. More, but they don't get rewarded for it."

"Supplies are short everywhere."

Külm shrugged. It didn't matter. The dogs were too valuable to discount with a remark like that.

"I am looking for Sergeant Klimmer, my aide."

"Haven't seen him, sir." He spat on his boot and rubbed vigorously. "Not today."

"Yesterday?"

"Last night, sir, just after dinner. He was going with Sergeant Duitser into the compound."

"For what?"

"To sightsee," growled Külm. "It's lovely this time of year."

"Ah. And have you seen Duitser?"

"No, sir."

"Thank you, sergeant. If you were out late you ought to get some sleep."

"Don't like sleeping in the day." Külm spat on his boot.

Max left, stood on the parade ground several minutes, and observed the few clouds that had appeared. His leg began to tingle. He squinted up at the sun and decided to walk to the infirmary. The guards at the gate to the compound eyed him suspiciously as he avoided the deeper ruts made by vehicle tires, but did not challenge his right to pass. As his blood flowed more vigorously, the sleep in his leg gradually faded, but he began to sweat. He paused for a moment to concentrate on how he was feeling and recognized the perspiration as being from the effort and not a residual whining of his body for morphine. He was breathing hard, his heart was pounding, his mouth was pasty, but he felt energetic, almost dizzy with a strange mixture of tiredness, pride, and power. Even if the commandant managed to get him removed from the investigation, Max had reduced him to sputtering about revenge. Schütz could never get those moments back; Max could never lose them. He knew what the soccer player feels when the ball skips into the net, what the whole nation had felt when France capitulated.

The infirmary was further than it looked. After he had crossed the grassy patch at the end of the prisoners' huts, he paused again to watch three truckloads of prisoners come in from whatever labor they had been doing outside. Sitting on the roof of each truck cab facing to the rear, a single private with a machine pistol slung over his shoulder held the stave in front of him and further braced himself against the precarious swaying of the truck by pushing his boots against the cage. The cattle trucks had been topped over with a wooden lattice and the men inside had been so packed in they could not sit. The visible ones were pressed against the outer crossbars; indeed, almost seemed to be sleeping upright against the wood. They were uniformly gaunt, with the sameness of a row of skeletons in the physical anthropology laboratory of a university. They were a colorless, characterless mass, except for the brown, red, and black triangles sewn over whatever hearts they still had.

One of the trucks swerved closer to the infirmary, the soldier hopped down, and a prisoner bloody from the thigh down was pulled out. He clawed and grasped at those inside, who peeled his grip from their arms, their legs, the wooden staves. The soldier, along with two prisoner orderlies from the infirmary, dragged him out onto a stretcher and he was carried inside. The truck ground its gears, lurched, then pulled away.

The infirmary was larger than it looked from inside the headquarters compound. The walls were made of planks with marks and notches on them that indicated they had been part of some previous building. As Max reached for the door, he noted that the frame itself had evidently been part of a sign, as three Cyrillic letters were just visible under the white paint. Inside, directly opposite the door, a gray and haggard woman with abnormally wide eyes watched him cross the creaky floor. She had been squeezing out a bloody sponge with which she had cleaned the floor after the injured prisoner had been carried through, but she dropped it into the bucket beside her with a plunk and stood, her bony arms crossed on her chest.

"Yes, sir," she said dully. "Can I help you, sir?"

"I would like to see Dr. Frank."

"I will fetch him, sir."

"If he is busy, I am willing to wait."

She gestured at a door to her left. "Please go in. You will be more comfortable in there, sir."

"Thank you." Near the door to her right, Max noticed another smear of blood. "You missed one," he said casually.

The woman scurried to it. "Oh yes, sir, I am so careless, sir, yes, sir." Max watched her for a second, rubbing as if she were trying to scrub rust off iron, then went in. He had expected chairs, a sofa—an ordinary waiting room, in other words, but found a combination office and examining room. The desk at one end was covered with papers and a stack of books. The tomes were placed at odd angles, as if they had been absent-mindedly stacked on each other in the heat of writing a diagnosis: *Introductory Pharmacology with Particular Emphasis on Plants Indigenous to Silesia, Studies in Teratology, La Technique chirurgical dans l'age moderne,* and, uppermost, *An Analysis of the Racial Characteristics Defiling the Aryan Population of Central Europe.* Max opened this last volume to a plate showing three skulls with respective measurements of volume, circumference, and diameter. He remembered the calipers one of his professors had always carried under his arm. This same professor had offered to send Max to Heidelberg to work in the collection of skulls for racial studies. Max, however, had been lured by tales of primitive cultures and religions. When he closed the book, dust exploded off it. All of the books were dusty. He touched the papers on the desk and rubbed the powder between his fingertips. Only the small area in front of Frank's chair was not dusty. The blotter was festooned with small stains and circles made by wet glasses.

At the other end of the room was an examination table and a row of cabinets with locked doors. Max dropped into a chair along the wall. He had barely sat when Frank came in. His bleary eyes uncertainly focused on Max and his lower lip flapped like a walrus's as he licked his mustache. "It's you," he grunted. There was blood on the sleeve of his crumpled white coat and a yellow stain on the pocket.

"Yes, Dr. Frank," said Max. "It is time we talked. You're a very difficult man to pin down."

"Busy," he said. "Don't get up. Do you have cigarettes?"

"No."

Frank grunted again and dropped in his chair. He opened a desk drawer and took out a brown bottle. "Wine?"

Max shook his head. "I've just had breakfast."

"Wine's a better breakfast." Frank's hand quivered as he

• 126 •

poured the golden liquid into a beaker. He held it up. "There. Looks like a piss sample, eh?" He swilled it down. "Tastes like one. Local."

"Ah."

Frank belched. "So what's your problem? Headaches? Can't sleep?"

"Both, and I need a new arm and leg, but that's not why I'm here."

"I have nothing to say on Lila Schütz."

"Oh? Why not?"

"She's dead, the bitch. Can't do anything for the dead. They don't need anything."

"What do you mean?"

"They're free. No more lies."

"And what were Lila's lies?"

"Who knows?"

"You might. She was your patient."

"Everyone in the world is my patient."

"Meaning?"

"Meaning Ostheim is the world, or might just as well be."

"And you're the only doctor."

"Of course. I'm sent here for my sins. What did you do to get in?"

Max prodded the toe of his boot with his cane. "You are mixing your metaphors, doctor. Ostheim can't be both the world and hell, can it? Hell is a place outside the world."

He grunted. "All places are the same." He tapped his head. "The universe is in here."

"Then it's a drunken universe for you."

Frank reached over, lifted his bottle, and adamantly poured himself another. "Better than yours," he finally said.

"Perhaps," said Max, "but it would seem I am not neglecting my duty."

Frank laughed. "Do you know, Herr Hero, that that is exactly what my wife says? You've been talking to my wife. Maybe you can give her a poke for me. If you can catch her between meals."

"I wouldn't classify you among the starving, Dr. Frank."

The doctor rotated his desk chair. "True. Do you know Lila used to call me 'Ursule's capon'? She used to warn me to sleep with one eye open." He drew his finger across his throat.

" 'Slit! You'll be in the oven!' she'd say. Then she used to come over here and demand a pelvic examination. 'My cunt is sore,' she'd whine. No wonder! But she'd fool me. It wasn't sore. It must have been leather. She'd just want to get me all worked up. As soon as she was on the table, she'd say, 'Kiss it and make it better. Oh please. Kiss it and make it better.' Hmmph! She was dead meat long before the prisoners got her."

"And did you?"

"Did I what?"

"Take her up on her offers."

"Once, when I was stupid."

"Why did you stop?"

"She laughed at me. She told Ursule I had balls the size of beans."

"And was Ursule angry?"

"Who knows?"

"Were you?"

Frank shrugged. "They *are* the size of beans. Aren't yours?" He laughed and coughed simultaneously. "The bitch couldn't help herself. She's glad to be out of her misery."

"Do you mean she was unstable? Perhaps insane?"

"I don't know."

"You don't know? You're a doctor, supposedly. In normal circumstances would you advise her to get treatment?"

Frank cleared his throat. "In normal circumstances, I would have suspected either a nervous breakdown, addiction, or a brain lesion. But normal circumstances hardly apply."

"Meaning?"

"Meaning there's a war on. Look around you. Perhaps the bitch did the only thing possible. I know I do."

"It seems alcohol has made you a philosopher."

"Oh, you, like you have the right to judge."

"What do you mean?"

"I'm no fool. I may be a drunk, but occasionally my eyes clear. Did you know your surgeons made you the subject of an article?"

Max was stunned.

"Yes. They described in minute detail their work in your chest and hip. You're lucky to be alive."

"Of course. But that hardly equates me to you."

"Only in the sense," said Frank, "that you did not get through all of that without help. I know what pain is. Judging from the pallor of your skin, I'd say you've only been off morphine for—what?—three months."

Max said nothing.

Frank sat back in his chair and laced his fingers over his belly. "You were lucky to get it. There's not much of it around any more."

"What I went through wasn't easy," said Max.

"Hardly worth the trouble. What we have is in that cabinet." Frank pointed. "Help yourself. The key is behind the door."

Max was shaken. It was true he had been addicted to the drug, but was it that visible, even to an alcoholic? "It was not willingly. It was necessary, but I have put it behind me."

"All the same . . ."

Max straightened himself in the chair. "All right. You are very observant. So what can you tell me about Lila Schütz?"

Frank grunted. "Back to that, eh?"

"How often did she have lovers? Who were they? Who was the father of her child? Who would have killed her?"

"I don't know anything like that. Men don't leave their signatures on the *mons veneris.*"

"But you're observant. You must know something."

"She had syphilis, possibly gonorrhea. Hard to tell."

"Whom did she get it from?"

"How would I know?"

"You're the only doctor. You would have treated him."

"Two or three men get the drips every month. Pevner got it. Kurzner. Frau Kurzner." Frank squinted. "Wait. Isn't this all confidential?"

"Himmler himself sent me, doctor."

Frank shrugged. "Enlisted men? I'd have to look in my files for that."

Max dragged his index finger through the dust on Frank's desk. "Your records are well kept?"

"I suppose not. And it's hard to remember. She was going through the treatments. Mercurol irrigation." He pressed his forehead. "Pevner. The Kurzners. One of the sergeants, a German. Let's see . . ."

"Von Rauschwald?"

"He's no sergeant."

"No. Was he under treatment?"

"No. He has never set foot in here. I've never even received his medical records. He's sound as an ox."

"But I was led to believe he was one of Lila's lovers."

Frank shrugged.

"And the commandant?"

"I've treated him only for the grippe, and a sprained ankle."

"But surely she would have infected him."

"If they engaged in intercourse."

"Wouldn't they?"

"Colonel, sometimes I think you're an idiot. Husbands, wives, they're only married. It doesn't mean they screw. Anyway, not even Lila could want to rush into bed with our lovely commandant."

"But it would only take once."

"If he was unlucky or didn't use protection."

"He thinks he was the father of the child."

"That happens, especially with the protection available now."

Max had a sudden thought. It was so startling that he clacked his heel against the floor. "Isn't it true that syphilis goes to the brain?"

"Eventually."

"And doesn't it produce madness?"

"Yes."

"And could such a madness produce homicidal tendencies?"

"Certainly."

"Ah."

Frank was now the startled one. His puffy eyes widened. "Schütz?"

"Why not?"

"I don't know."

"Look at his grandiose plans for Ostheim. His inability to face up to our defeats. How could anyone be so emotionless about the butchering of his wife?"

Frank settled back in his chair and poured another drink. "You act as if his madness were extraordinary. Look around you. What is the measure of madness? In this place, only sanity is mad. Every day the prisoners go out and build roads and bridges we will be blowing up as soon as the Russians get near." He peered into his drink. "I," he added morosely, "who was trained to patch people up, can only put them out of misery. I should have been a vet."

"Putting all your philosophy aside, doctor, could not Schütz be exhibiting the symptoms of syphilitic madness?"

"It usually doesn't work this quick. Lila only got it sometime in late winter or early spring."

"She could have gotten it from him. He could have had it for years."

"I don't know."

"But what form does the madness take?"

"Delusions. Paranoia. But it isn't that precise. Medicine is guesswork. Diseases don't always act the same. Defining madness is like defining God. Try to put your finger on mercury."

"But it's possible."

Frank shrugged. "Still, it's a shame—"

The roar came without warning. The building was engulfed in a great wind of noise that seemed to lift it off its piers and drop it again. Max rolled to the floor instinctively as the roof planks exploded in a succession of holes. Glass shattered in one of the cabinets. Splinters filled the room like a thousand matches. Max barely had time to lift his head when a blast, infinitely louder than the roar that preceded it, lifted the infirmary and listed it toward Max's left. Cabinets, chairs, the examining table slowly began to migrate down the pock-marked floor. Frank, still sitting at his desk, his eyes fully open for the first time since Max had seen him, was soon pinned in his chair against the wall. The medical books, his blotter, his lamp, and papers broke over him like a wave. The wine in his glass splattered in his face and when he desperately clutched at the tumbling bottle, his fat hand only knocked it against the wall. "Shit!" he yelled and Max could see his lips moving as whatever followed was swallowed in a second roar. Again the ceiling and floor were polka-dotted by bullets and the splinters tumbled in a blizzard. Again the earth seemed to split as an explosion tossed the building and dropped it.

There was a moment of near silence in which the only sounds were the ringing in Max's ears and the fading of the planes as they banked away and up. Then he heard screaming, running, orders shouted in halting German. The roof beams were creaking. A truck started. A liquid dribbled from inside

a damaged cabinet, pattering on the floor and snaking downward until it dropped through one of the bigger bullet holes.
Max sat up. The escape alarm whined, then wailed. Would
there be another pass? He looked for better shelter and was
startled by the warmth flooding his side. He had been hit in
the stump of his arm. He numbly stuck his finger in the hole
in his tunic. The flash of pain was reassuring. He ripped the
cloth. The bullet had passed between his arm and side, ripping
the skin of both. The blood was out of proportion to the wound,
he thought, like an unstaunchable shaving cut.

He looked up at the light streaming through the ceiling
holes. The running and shouting noises had quietened and
the planes could be heard moving closer. He waved his half
arm. "Come on, you pigfuckers," he muttered, "there's still
some left." He rolled down the sloping floor until he was under
the examination table. How many bombs did the Russian
fighters carry? He didn't know. He did know that one direct
hit on the infirmary would leave pieces the size of mah-jongg
tiles. The image of the Belgian entomologist teaching that
game by the light of a lantern in his tent had just popped into
his mind when the guns opened up: rifles, machine guns, then
the hammering of the fighter guns. They were coming in from
a different angle this time, strafing from the northeast corner
and crossing diagonally away from the infirmary. He kept his
head low, however, and though no more bombs were dropped,
the vibrations caused more shifting of the furniture. A cabinet
door opened and several bottles crashed down. He smelled
ether and thought, "Good. I'll be burned alive. That will at
least be different."

The roar of the planes faded and the gunfire slowed, then
ended. Shouting. Running. Someone laughing. Someone bel-
lowing in a Slavic language. A single shot. The escape alarm
rising to full pitch. Someone screaming in pain. Max sat up
under the examining table, his back against the desk. "Dr.
Frank?" he said. "Dr. Frank?" He crawled up the floor, dragging his useless leg behind him. He cut his hand on a bottle
neck and whatever had been in the bottle burned worse than
his wound. He was surprised by the amount of light coming
in. He looked up and saw that two roof beams had dislodged.
If they had come all the way down, he would have been
crushed. When he awkwardly raised himself on his right

knee, with his bad leg stuck out at an angle similar to the fallen beams and braced against the desk, he smelled the sharp odor of a body completely relaxed. The end of a beam had crushed Frank's head. He looked like a wet clay figure that had been dropped. One eye was at the same level as his mouth, while the other was where it belonged. Both seemed to be staring at the wine that soaked his white coat.

Max had no reaction. He thought nothing. He felt nothing. He struggled up the floor to the door. A cabinet blocked his way, so he pulled himself on top of it. His weight made it slide downward some more, but it lodged against the chair (which was caught against the bookshelf) and he rolled off the other side. He paused to catch his breath and noticed the bloodstain he had left on the cabinet. He would need an antiseptic. He opened the door and fumbled inside. He came out with a handful of hypodermics without needles. He leaned over to see better. A bottle of iodine had broken and stained most of the other bottles. He noticed, however, the common shape of morphine vials. He picked one up. He stared at it for a second, then glanced at the distorted face of Dr. Frank. He quickly thrust three of the vials into his tunic pockets, along with one of the hypodermics, then crawled past the door and over the body of Frank's wide-eyed assistant.

· *Eleven* ·

When he tumbled out of the shattered front door, Max saw that prisoners' barracks "C" had been ripped in half. "D" was burning. A crater where the first bomb had landed and dislodged the infirmary was twenty meters away. A close call. The other crater had swallowed all of barracks "C" that had not been scattered over the compound. Two soldiers picked up a fallen comrade by the arms and were helping him limp toward the infirmary. When they saw it angled over like a trapezoid, they looked at each other and waved down a truck, which was bringing a dozen more soldiers to help assemble the prisoners in ranks in front of the barracks. One prisoner lay, apparently dead, in the middle of the grassy area, but men ran past him as if he did not matter. Max limped away from the infirmary toward the gate towers. He remembered his cane was still inside with Dr. Frank. Eventually, however, he reached his goal: the steps at the bottom, a place to sit.

He took a handkerchief from his pocket and clamped it between the wounds with his stump. The blood had stopped flowing, but he felt some stinging, particularly under his armpit. He watched a technical sergeant order prisoners to help pull some patients from the ward in the infirmary, then Baranovitch order them back into line for a roll call. The sergeant was the only one who seemed to know what he was doing. Other soldiers were running back and forth as they got new ideas of what they should be doing. Some nervously watched the sky. It was obvious that not only were Schütz's troops unprepared for an attack of any kind, but they had not even a theory of what they were to do when one occurred. Baranovitch grabbed one who was running past and was infuriated by whatever he said. He shoved him so hard the boy fell down.

The pilots had obviously not been part of anything significant. For one thing, they had strafed and bombed the area in which they were most likely to kill their own comrades. Secondly, two lightly armed fighters couldn't do any significant damage, unless they pinpointed Schütz's headquarters, and there was little point in that. The commandant of Ostheim was hardly a major military figure; he is hardly, thought Max, a minor military figure. He is hardly a military figure at all. The pilots were probably hunting for something to harass and had stumbled on Ostheim. They would soon be back with their comrades, swilling vodka and exaggerating what they had done that day. Perhaps they were reconnaissance for the next Russian offensive. Perhaps they were intended to look like reconnaissance for an offensive in order to divert troops south from the straight line to Berlin. Max idly wondered what the planes had been like. He had never seen a Russian fighter. But then, he had never been strafed indoors before. It wasn't so different, actually. The pilot couldn't select you as a target. It was always probability whether you were hit or not. Sheer happenstance.

"Colonel, are you all right?" A very pale, probably albino corporal loomed over him. The crookedness of his nose revealed some not-very-successful plastic surgery.

"It's little," Max said. "Nothing. Take care of the others." He had stumbled on a couple of the words and had mumbled the rest.

"How much blood have you lost, colonel?" said the corporal.

"Not much. Really. I know when I'm in trouble."

The corporal scrutinized him.

"Really. I'm tired, that's all. I did not sleep last night. That's all."

"I'll take you to the doctor, sir," said the corporal.

"No," said Max. "Stick to your post. The doctor's dead."

The corporal took three steps, then peered down. "Excuse me, sir, but did you know Egon Haldenstam?"

"Pardon me?"

"In Africa. Egon Haldenstam. He repaired engines. He is my brother. My family has not heard from him since the fighting in the Kasserine Pass."

"I'm sorry, corporal. I don't know him. There were so many."

The corporal's head dropped somewhat. "My father says he is dead. Too." He began climbing again. "Thank you, sir. Tell me if you need anything."

Max said "I'm sorry," but the corporal was already gone. *He who was living is now dead/ We who were living are now dying/ With a little patience.* So many went out, so few came back, and the few that came back were less than when they went out. Max settled back against the stairs. They were comfortable. He could almost sleep. The wind steadily blowing from the west made a scrim of the smoke from the barracks fire. The chaos still going on in front of him became a shadow play as figures darted back and forth with buckets. They became Carachachos, naked except for their headdresses with their great plumes from jungle birds: *Huf-ta-ta-ta! Huf-ta-ta-ta!* Their golden bodies glistened and dripped like roasting pork as they danced close to the fire and then away. *Huf-ta-ta-ta! Huf-ta-ta-ta!* The initiates were brought forward out of the dark, their faces streaked with white clay and the blood of a howler monkey. They came forward, emotionless as ghosts, carrying the knife that would make them men when the small, bloody piece of foreskin was cut away. *Huf-ta-ta-ta! Huf-ta-ta-ta! Cailleooto mingehoyo!* This is a boy! *Caillauooto kumasoyto!* This is a man! And then the great shout of all the men, the cry of the howler monkey, sucked into the infinite void of the jungle.

"Deutschland, Deutschland, über alles, über alles in die Welt . . ." Max opened his eyes. Men were still running, some with buckets, others with rifles. The soldiers gestured at the fire, gesticulated wildly, kicked at the bucket carriers who were too slow. Meanwhile, straight ahead, standing motionless in the river of smoke, files of prisoners had been organized by an officer. He was short, possibly Pevner. Sgt. Külm prowled the front rank with three of his dogs on a leash. In the third row, however, was the singer, reeling and spinning and bumping into prisoners and nearly knocking them down

and getting louder as he moved out of the smoke: *"Deutsch-land, Deutschland, über alles, über alles in die Welt . . ."*

A guard grasped at the man, but was pushed away. The man stumbled forward and threatened the guard with his bottle. It was only then Max recognized the Wehrmacht uniform and Kleini's squat form. Kleini emerged from the rows of prisoners and lurched across the open area. His voice was clearer and stronger, though it often choked out in the last syllable of a phrase. He tipped back his bottle, squinted up the neck as if it were a telescope, then continued singing. Max, who was moving toward him as quickly as he could, was only halfway there when Kleini lost his balance on the edge of the bomb crater and fell in.

Max stumbled, then slid down the slope of the hot crater. He clambered up the other side and jerked Kleini by the neck. "What are you doing?" he said. "Wake up."

Kleini's red eyes flickered. "Colonel," he said. "I have had a dream. I dreamt I had no foot and we were in Europe."

Max sat beside him. "Oh God, Kleini, you're drunk. Why are you so drunk? It's things like this that keep you from getting promoted."

"But I dreamt I had no foot and you had no arm and—"

"And you *have* lost your foot, Kleini."

Kleini laughed. "Where? Where have I lost it? Oh, help me find it, colonel. It itches and drives me crazy!" He blinked. "You are bleeding again. Not again." He struggled, trying to get up. "I can't help you. They got me."

"Are you all right?"

"Of course I'm all right. I'm drunk." He threw up on himself. Max shook his head and mopped at the slimy vomit with the bloody handkerchief. He flung the cloth into the puddle of brown water that was filling the bottom of the crater.

"Why did you do this? I've been looking for you. Is this where you've been the last few days? If Schütz wants to, he can have you demoted."

"He can kick me into the pit." He looked at his boot, the one that contained his wooden foot. "I can't kick anyone. I'm lucky. I'm innocent, colonel. I can't kick anyone." His face quivered, squinched up painfully, then burst into tears.

"Oh, Kleini," said Max. He slid over next to him and put his arm around his shoulder. "Calm down, Kleini, calm down."

But just as the crying would subside into weeping, the convulsive heavings would begin again. "Shhh," said Max, "shhhh." He pressed his cheek against Kleini's wet and curly hair, as if the sergeant were a little boy. "You are all right. The war will end soon. We'll go home and raise apples, eh? Great red, juicy apples. You'll find a strong woman and have seventeen children, eh? And I'll be their godfather. They can say their godfather was a count. How about that?"

Kleini abruptly rolled away and pounded the earth until his hands bled. "Children? I will never have children! Never! Children are for dying! Children are for dying!"

"Kleini! Kleini!" Max grabbed him by the hair. "Stop it! What is the matter with you? It was only a few bombs."

Kleini pressed his face into the dirt. When he raised it, yellow flecks of clay and soil clung to his lips and nose. "The fucking Bolsheviks. They woke me up. Then they left too soon. I wanted them to kill me, but they left too soon. I don't want to be a German, colonel. Can you make me a Jew, colonel? I want to be a Jew, then it will all end for me."

Max let go of him and looked away. "For God's sake, Kleini, how am I going to get you out of here and back to your room?"

"Aren't you precious," said Kleini grimly. "The Count Max-Baldur von Prokofsk, now colonel. Promoted and promoted and promoted almost from the day he set foot in the desert. He has shaken hands with Hitler himself. He has received direct orders from Herr Himmler. He has had tea in bed, while all the newsreel cameras recorded all the officials who came to pay him homage. Why not? You look the other way. You don't care about anything but your medals."

"You're drunk, Kleini. Remember who saved your life."

"And didn't I save yours? Eh?" He rolled onto his back. "It's all right, Herr Count, we are eliminating the scum of the world. There will be only Germans left, and you are the best of the Germans, Herr Count. You can pretend you don't know what's going on."

"Let's get you back and cleaned up. . . ."

"No. I never want to be clean." He began to sob again. Max slid over and embraced him again. Suddenly, he grew very calm. He spoke in a monotone.

"You told me to get close to the men. I did. And Sergeant Duitser said I should go with him because a new group of prisoners was arriving. There is—There was a village in the hills that the Hungarians claimed something about. They were saboteurs or something. Maybe they hid Communists. I don't know. They marched them here, about fifty. Most of them were women or very old. Not many were fit for Herr Schütz's building projects. After all, this is a labor camp. Work is good for you. It builds character. It sets you free. So Duitser says, 'Watch this' and all the people are lined up three deep on the edge of the pit."

"The pit?"

"Where they burn them. There is a hole, colonel. It was dug out by hand. It burns all the time, even if it is just a smoulder, and then they get it going again with brush cleared from the perimeter."

Max gingerly pressed his stump. The bleeding had stopped.

"And Schütz comes along the line and an old man sticks out his hands, begging, I guess to be let go and Schütz pulls his pistol and shoots him and his brains splatter on everyone around. Von Rauschwald is there and he laughs and you can see all the Ukrainians are smiling though they are pretending to be at attention. Schütz then says they are all disease-ridden and he orders them to strip and they all do and throw their clothes on the fire. Von Rauschwald points to an old woman trying to hide her breasts with her hands and jokes about how low they hang and everyone laughs, even the prisoners who are there to help maintain the fire."

Kleini sniffed loudly, then spat a gob of phlegm.

"You can tell me this later."

"No," he said. "I am drunk. I must tell you now. I won't be able to again. So then, Schütz goes along the row with a piece of yellow chalk and he makes an X on all the foreheads of old men and very young boys. He does the same with most of the women, though the one they were laughing at, he puts the X on her nipple. Then Schütz leaves, telling von Rauschwald to get the workers registered. Von Rauschwald orders the X's to remain by the pit, and I think, 'God, they're going to shoot them,' but I also think this is war and maybe they are shielding saboteurs, I mean, these people don't have to look dangerous to be dangerous. I mean, colonel, you remember the boy who killed Fritz Sauer in Benghazi, he was sweet-looking, an angel's son. . . ."

"I know."

"Then von Rauschwald stands to the side and eggs on the Ukrainians until they drag one of the able-bodied women out of line and they throw her on the ground and fuck her. She fights the first one and he really hurts her but when the second jumps on, she lies there like she's dead, staring up at the sky, until one of the men jumps out of line screaming and the guards beat him to death with their rifle butts. It's all happening so fast I don't do anything. I stand there and say, 'Duitser! My God!' and Duitser holds my arm and says, 'You get used to it. Wait.' "

"And von Rauschwald watched all of this?"

"He gets all red-faced with laughing. He points to one of the Lithuanians, a young boy, and he makes fun of him because his prick is showing through his pants and they drag him over and he is thrown on top of her and he is finished in just a few seconds. Then there is the fourth and the fifth and then one of them rolls her over and fucks her ass and there is blood all over her ass and thighs and she lies there like she's never going to get up but she does, she gets back in line, and they march them away."

"And there's no explanation?"

Kleini jerked away and stared at Max. A drool of spit hung from the corner of his mouth. "What explanation do you want? Duitser's? We saved a prisoner the first day we were here. What explanation did Schütz give you then? That the Ukrainians have to be given their way? That everybody needs to blow off steam? That—That—" He covered his face with his hands. "They were in a frenzy then. And they made the women put down their babies on the ground and they fixed bayonets and stabbed those with X's, sometimes slicing off parts of their bodies first, so that some of them jumped into the fire before they had been touched, before one of the soldiers rammed his bayonet into their ass or cunt, or cut off your tits or balls and threw them in your face. There was so much noise I couldn't hear. I turned away, and when the screaming stopped, there was only the sound of those babies crying, and the thuds as they kicked them into the fire, betting on who could kick them furthest."

"My God."

"They saved the last for me. They tugged at my arm."

Kleini almost panted, he was breathing so hard. His eyes were fixed on the puddle at the bottom of the crater. "But I am lucky, colonel. For a moment, just a moment in the middle of all that shouting and pulling, I wanted to. I really did. Why not? Everyone was doing it. Can you understand how much you want to do what everyone else does? But I can't kick anything. I have a wooden foot. My foot saved me. My uselessness saved me." He broke down in sobs, and Max embraced him again.

"Oh, Kleini, Kleini." Max peered up at the sky. It looked like it might rain. Surely it would rain. What was in his head? He knew that political opponents had been arrested, especially Jews. He had read about that in the papers. Well, after all, many of them were enemies of the National Socialists and a few momentary excesses were normal in difficult times. There were all the dreams; Germany could dream again. All the young and handsome men reestablishing the German nation: culture, jobs, pride, industry. Schütz had nothing to do with that. Schütz had turned his project for the colonization of the East into an excuse for perversion. This was not German. It could not be German.

And yet, Max knew that he had been denying something he had known, but had been careful not to admit. When you wondered where the Jews and trade unionists and Communists and gypsies had gone, you gave them some vague space in the East. But as the armies had been driven back from Stalingrad, none of them were brought back. Well, that would make sense, you wouldn't want them back, would you? They'd be spies and saboteurs. And if there were some cruelties, well, he had seen worse in war, hadn't he? There was the lieutenant who had pulled a Britisher from the tangle of his jeep by means of a pickax in the chest. Wasn't this the same? Wasn't it similar? And wouldn't war bring out the thuggery in any population? And? And? And?

And there was still the feeling he had kept his eyes shut. That he hadn't wanted to know. And now that he knew for certain—could not deny that he knew—he was baffled at what he could do about it. Schütz and Ostheim had to be an aberration. They had to be. Even the SS wouldn't play football with babies. Surely the SS notion of knightly purity did not include inciting Ukrainians to gang rape.

"We shall see about this," said Max weakly, but Kleini had passed out against his chest. He laid him gently down, rolled over and began to clamber up the slope. At the top, he saw that the barracks was smouldering, with only the end wall left standing. A roll call was going on. He spotted three men, one wearing a cook's apron, crossing the grassy area. He signaled to them.

"My sergeant," he called out. "He bumped his head. He's unconscious."

Max had shown no anxiety in his voice and the three resignedly ambled toward him. A thin private, missing two fingers, slid down to the snoring sergeant, looked at the vomit on his chin, and waved the others down to help him. They dragged him out, then one went to the infirmary for a stretcher. Kleini continued to snore, all the way to his quarters. They unceremoniously dumped him on his bunk and left. Max wet a cloth and wiped the sergeant's chin. He loosened his clothes, but did not attempt to undress him. It was hard enough to handle his own uniform. "The Englander," mumbled Kleini. "The Englander."

"What?" The only answer came as a snore.

Wearily, Max wandered back to his quarters. In the corridor, he paused outside his door and listened. He heard nothing in his room, but he quickly snapped the door back, hoping to spot a rat. Nothing. He looked around. There was no sign the food thief had returned. The talcum on the drawer was undisturbed. Max flopped back on the bed and stared at the roof beams. As he landed, one of the morphine vials pressed against his hip. He sat up, pulled out the three bottles, and stared at them in his hand. There you are: sweet oblivion, he thought. He considered hiding them under his mattress, then in the drawer, and finally decided to put them into his shaving kit. He was so tired, he felt nothing. He was incapable of the effort of memory. He again collapsed on his bed and was only vaguely aware of the man barking orders to a squad outside.

He dreamed he was in his father's study. The old man's white mustache stuck out so far it almost touched the shelves on each side. "Max-Baldur," his father asked, "where have you been?"

"I have been to Brazil, father."

The old man turned his head. The mustache just missed knocking a lamp off a table. "Max-Baldur, you're far too young to travel on your own." Max crossed to the pier mirror. He was ten and wearing shorts.

"Father, I have two arms."

The old man had settled into a leather chair and was reading. He grumbled something unintelligible.

"Father, my leg is normal."

The old man grumbled.

Max held up his new arm. He took a heavy book from the shelf to test it.

"Max-Baldur, that book is very rare. Don't handle it with your new arm."

Max placed the book on his father's desk and opened it. Goethe's *Faust* had been printed one large, red Fraktur letter to a page. He noticed the bookshelf towered upward, as if the ceiling were seven hundred meters high, and each book was a part of this *Faust*. He wanted to ask his father if *Faust* was the only book they had, but the old man was grumbling as he read, his mustache swinging horizontally or vertically, depending on the course of the argument he was having with himself, and inexplicably missing the lamps and knickknacks as it moved.

Max heard a car. He went to the French doors and spread the curtains. A limousine drove up the steps and onto the patio. Hitler was driving, dressed as a chauffeur. A woman was in the back, smoking a cigarette in a long, jeweled holder, and trailing an enormous red silk scarf. "Father, look, it's Lila Schütz."

"No," said the old man. "It's Isadora."

"Excuse me," said Lila, "is *Faust* the only book?"

"Yes, Frau Schütz," said Max.

"Isadora!" shouted his father.

"A pity," said Lila. "I wish there were others."

"I'm sorry," said Max.

"Drive on!" said Lila.

The car roared across the patio, down the stairs, and across the lawn. The scarf, whose end finally passed the French doors, fluttered up and blocked Max's view, but when it came down, Max saw that it had become entangled in the rear wheels of the car. The dead Lila was flopping against the gravel roadway as the car sped away. The chauffeur did not seem to notice.

The old man looked up from his reading: "You see, Max-Baldur, Isadora!" and Max was suddenly a hundred years old. It was winter and he was trying to rub his hands together, but he could not find either hand. "Isadora stole them," he called out. "Isadora!"

He felt something cold and damp against his side, and he knew he wasn't asleep. The light in the room was dim and a silhouette blocked his view. "What?"

"Sit still," said a woman.

"Bette?"

"Sit still," she said. "You should have cleaned this immediately."

"It's fine."

"There *is* infection in the world. Even heroes get infections. This might sting." There was a split second of cold that turned to fire.

"Ouch."

"Just a minute. There."

He gritted his teeth and hissed through them.

"I'm finished," she said.

"These things always hurt worse later."

She sat without speaking. He still could only see her outline.

"What time is it?"

"Nine-thirty or so."

"At night?" He tried to sit up. She pushed him back. Her hand remained on his chest.

"There is no reason to get up."

"I—I feel rude."

"That's silly. You're wounded."

"Not very much."

"It's still a wound."

"Why is it so dark in here? I can barely see."

"I threw my scarf over the lampshade. I didn't want to startle you. You see? It worked. I got off your jacket and shirt before you woke."

"I was exhausted."

She nodded. He awkwardly looked from side to side to avoid staring into the shadow of her face. Her hand, though light upon his sternum, moved. He twitched as if a tiny electric shock had come off her fingertips.

"Did Schütz send you to look after me?"

"No one knows I'm here." She turned her head. Max could see the silhouette of her profile. "I've wanted to come to you."

"To come to me?"

"Yes."

"Why?"

"I don't know." She faced him again. "But they told me you were hurt and I was afraid it might be worse than anyone let on. So I came." She stood and rinsed a cloth in the washbowl.

"But you've wanted to come to me?"

She nodded.

"Is it something about Lila?"

She seemed startled. "No. Why would you think that? Surely women have come to your room before."

Max blinked. His heart skipped several beats. "That isn't really true," he said. "You may think so, but it isn't really true."

She made a noise he couldn't decipher.

"Excuse me?"

She had covered her mouth with her hand. She was crying.

"What is it?" He raised himself off the bed and crossed to her. "What is it, Bette?"

She flung her arms around his neck and stifled her crying against his shoulder. He could feel the warm tears trickling down his chest. He yielded to the impulse to place his hand on the back of her neck, just as he had in the garden. It was downy and warm. He pressed his face against her ear and breathed in her fragrance. "Please," he said, "tell me what it is. I don't want you to cry. I don't want you unhappy."

"I was afraid you'd been hurt, really hurt." She sniffed. "Someone shouted that one of the men injured was you. They didn't say how much."

"It's nothing. It's like a bloody nose. They wanted the rest of my arm, eh? You—You worry too much about me."

She suddenly turned her face and tried to meet his lips. He pulled back. "You don't want me?" she asked.

"It isn't that," he said. "I just don't think it would be the thing to do."

"You don't like me."

"No. I like you very much. From the very first time I saw you I liked you very much." He was surprised not only to have said this, but also to mean it.

"But you must have had many women. Won't you make me one of them?"

Breda's face painfully flashed across his mind. "I have had women, as you say, but not as many as you might think. Is it common for SS wives to throw themselves at guests?"

She spun away from him. "You're a pig. Like all the rest. Lila used to say that. She was right. I'm the fool. She said there was no reason to sit around this place baking bread."

"Baking bread?"

"Being the perfect housewife."

"She may have died from her foolishness."

Bette reached for her sweater, which was hanging on the chair. "Well, if you're feeling better, perhaps I should leave."

"Don't," he said. The word escaped before he had time to think. He lifted her hand off the sweater and kissed it. "I—I have thought about you very much. I am glad you are here and grateful for what you are offering, but it wouldn't, it couldn't, be a good thing."

"What is left that is good?" she said. "One night can make no difference."

"Do you know what goes on in the prisoner's compound?"

"I don't want to know."

"But you have some idea?"

She said nothing.

"If what my sergeant told me can be verified, I may have to call attention to it. It may cause many problems for your husband."

"That means nothing to me."

"You have children. In the heat of this moment you may love me, but afterward?"

"I am not here to be in love. I was in love with Joachim once. And then he went away. What they returned to me was not the same."

"War changes us."

"Yes. It changes the world."

"They have killed women and children. They have brutalized them."

Bette pulled away. "Why do you insist on playing the fool? I don't want to hear about it. Schütz is always babbling about how he wants to make Ostheim an important camp, one like Buchenwald and Auschwitz. Don't tell me you're shocked by what goes on. They march many people in, but few go out, and then only to be worked to death on a building project. I came here because you were hurt and I stayed because I too want to lose myself for a time. Just once. That's all. I wanted to make love and kill the world, for a while, any amount of time. But I've only made myself cheap and stupid." She reached again for her sweater. He grasped her arm so tightly that she struggled for a moment.

When she stopped, he said, "I have been shot and blown up and cut and carved and sewn back together until I hardly know if I have an original part. I could be Frankenstein's monster for all I know. I never knew between operations if my doctors were lying. I never knew whether I would ever touch a woman again. And worst of all, I didn't care. I didn't even care whether I would live or not." He squeezed her arm even tighter. "Now you're here and you're offering yourself and I want you more at this moment than any woman I've ever known, but I'm not sure. No. I'm afraid." He dropped her arm, spun away from her, and sat on the bed. "I'm afraid."

She watched him for some time, then stepped in front of him and knelt. "You were wounded?" she said, nearly choking.

"Of course." He raised his stump. "What do you think this is?"

"No. I mean your manhood."

"That? No. It wasn't touched."

"Thank God," she said, closing her eyes with relief. "I thought I had—"

"But that doesn't seem to matter. The last time I tried, well, I couldn't. There should be nothing wrong, but I couldn't. There. I've told you. Only you and the other woman know."

"Did she humiliate you?"

"No, but the more she tried, the more impossible it became. I just can't go through that again. So please, go."

She took his hand, examined all the fingers, and kissed the tip of each one.

"Please," he begged.

"No. You don't understand me. It isn't so much the sex I want. It is the tenderness, the lying side by side. I just want to snuggle and feel warm. I just want to feel close to someone comfortable. I feel comfortable with you."

"I haven't been with a woman for over two years, Bette. Except the one and that—"

"And that is the past. Lie down."

He shook his head weakly.

"Lie down." She gently shoved him back.

When he did, she pecked him on the forehead, the lips, the throat, his chest. He closed his eyes and allowed himself to drift, as if he had just injected himself with morphine and could feel it spreading throughout his system. She carefully removed his boots and socks. He opened one eye to see her unbuttoning her blouse, then closed it. Part of him was reciting all the logical reasons not to do this. He could alienate von Rauschwald, whom he might need in dealing with Schütz. He could cause a new scandal, jeopardizing the investigation. He could cause Bette, who didn't deserve it, to be thought of in the same way as Lila. Another part of him was ignoring the rational reasons to stay away from her and simply screaming. He did not want another episode like the one with Breda. He did not want another woman to know he couldn't be a man. He did not want to give himself over to any feelings. If he yielded, for even a moment, he might succumb again to the living death of morphine, the fine, better-than-sexual pleasure of the opiate spreading over the body like a hundred warm tongues.

And yet, he had stolen the vials, even as the infirmary might have collapsed upon him.

And yet, he was lying here, quietly watching her unbutton her blouse, waiting breathlessly for the wife of Captain von Rauschwald to climb up next to him.

It was simply impossible to do otherwise.

· *Twelve* ·

It was slow. It was quiet. He drifted in and out of a sweet drowse as she stroked his chest, kissed his scars, explored each twist in his ear with her finger. Sometime later, maybe an hour later, her hand finally moved to the buttons on his trousers and quickly, effortlessly undid them. Feeling goose bumps on his arm, she covered them both with the blanket, put her thigh over his, and pressed the moistness between her legs against his hip. The sensation was startling. Fears scrambled through him again, but were superseded by a dryness in the mouth, shallow breathing, and the pleasant vortex of acquiescence. She pulled back her thigh and reached down to his knee, dragging her fingernails along the inside of his thigh all the way to his groin. There she took her hand away, paused, then traced the midline of his scrotum with her fingertip. When she finally wrapped her long fingers around his erect penis, she moaned at the feeling of it. He briefly had the sensation he was going to urinate, that his penis was twice the size of his body. Warmth spread through him and he arched his back. The semen splattered on his belly like molten solder.

She pressed her groin against him again, slipping her thigh between his, then rocked against him, kissing his eyes, nose, mouth.

"I'm sorry," he whispered.

"For what?" she grinned.

"For not waiting."

"We are not finished yet."

"Ah."

He pulled her against him. Her small damp breasts squinched as they flattened against his side and he sputtered, laughing. She pressed her face against his chest and giggled. He smelled her hair and quietened.

"I love you," he said.

She lifted her head. Her eyes were quizzical, as if she did not understand him. She smiled in a kindly way, however, and nuzzled him under the ear.

He looked away. "It was a foolish thing to say."

"It was a nice thing to say. A woman likes to hear it."

"Even if it isn't true?"

"It was true when you said it."

"How do you know?"

She touched his lips. "It wasn't your facade speaking. It was you, inside."

"Psychology."

"Something like that. I believe you loved me when you said it. Even if it was only for that moment. You can tell me it wasn't true—and maybe it isn't, now—but I want to believe it. Nothing you can say will change my mind. I need to believe it." She did not say it sadly, or desperately, but with determination. It was settled, and nothing could shake her belief.

"You're right," Max sighed. "I meant it. Perhaps I need to love someone. I felt a certain desperation. I wanted to do something for you. I wanted you to know how grateful—that isn't the word. Am I sounding like my facade, as you call it?"

She tickled his left nipple with her fingers. "Usually you sound this way. But I see through you."

He was suddenly uncomfortable with his nakedness, as if they were being watched.

"You shivered," she said, clinging closer to him. "Do we need another blanket?"

He kissed her forehead. "No."

"You're not cold?"

"No. I'm quite comfortable."

She kissed his collarbone.

"I should do something for you."

"For me?"

"I mean, it happened before—it seems to have happened before—I did anything for you."

"Your feeling this way is enough."

"But—"

"But what? It isn't a man's place to worry about such things. I feel marvelous. I feel delicious. I feel happy for the first time in years. That someone like you would think about pleasing me is enough. I just want to lie here forever. To touch you. That is enough." She cupped his tender penis. He jerked as if touched by ice, then relaxed. "When you are ready again, later, I will please you again, but I only want to lie here and cuddle. If you wish only to sleep, I will be happy too. That is enough for me. That is all a woman needs, most of the time. I told you all this before we started."

"Men and women never tell each other the truth, do they?"

"In bed."

"Especially not in bed."

"I'm pleased, Max. Why don't you want to believe that?"

"I feel like I haven't, God, I don't know, done my duty."

She rolled away from him. "You damned soldiers."

He reached for her. He was startled by the quick sting of his new wound. He hissed through his teeth.

"What is it?" she said.

"Nothing," he said. "I just want you to understand. Maybe duty isn't the word. You don't know how much you've given me. I want to give some of it back. Much of my life ended when I was wounded. In this one evening, you have given a very important part of it back. I love you for that. As long as I live I'll love you for that."

She sat up and looked down at him. She took his face in her hands and kissed him wetly on the mouth. "I do see through you, and I see your heart. It's nice of you to be so grateful for so little. Most men would not." She flung back the covers. "We must dress your wound."

"It's fine."

"No. You need a bandage. Call the orderly."

"He will see you." A thought came to him. "Did he let you in?"

"Don't be silly," she said. "How brazen do you think I am? You call for the bandage; I will hide under the bed."

"I don't really need it."

She shoved him toward the door. "I know what you need. Haven't I proven that?"

He smiled, clasped her behind the neck, and kissed her. Then, like two children working on a prank, they gathered up her clothes, and tossed them under the bed. He stuck his head into the corridor. The old man was dozing. He took the towel from beside the washbowl and walked to him. Startled by the naked colonel, he claimed to be "only resting my eyes" and rummaged up a roll of gauze and a bottle of three-percent carbolic acid. The odor of the latter filled the bedroom as Bette gently wiped it on and around the flesh wounds.

"You are good at this," said Max.

"I did volunteer work when—when Joachim was in France. You were lucky."

"That you worked in a hospital?"

"No. Five centimeters over and it would have gone through your lung. Ten and it would have struck your heart."

"A kilometer over and I wouldn't have been hit at all."

She began wrapping the bandage just above the end of his stump. "This day wouldn't have ended like it did if you had died."

"No," he mused. "But at least I would be rid of Ostheim."

"And me."

He caressed her ear. "Frau Frank. How is she?"

"She made quite a scene. Schütz had the bad taste to describe the body."

Max recalled the doctor's twisted face. He grimaced.

"I hurt you."

"No. He's a master of bad taste, Herr Schütz."

She split the end of the bandage with her teeth. The movement was so violent she might have been tearing Schütz apart. "He's a pig. Forget him."

"He's why I'm here. At least, I think he's why I'm here."

"It's the only thing I'll ever be indebted to him for."

Max studied her tying the bandage.

"There," she said. "If we had tape I would do this one." She touched the raw spot on the side of his chest. "But it isn't much more than a scrape."

"Do you still think Schütz is behind Lila's murder?"

"I have never said he was."

"But you suspect him."

"He's a pig. I believe him capable of anything."

"You have watched him for these last two years—"

"Eighteen months. Joachim did not bring me out immediately, but Schütz insisted."

"Insisted?"

"This is a colony, remember? Married men need their wives, he claims. The SS used to think marriage was unnecessary. Like Jesuits, the men were to be untainted, but now we women are useful. We prove that the SS has family values. Unmarried officers might develop undesirable interests in each other, so they are encouraged to sire future gauleiters."

"They don't want them like the SA."

She didn't understand.

"The SA was rumored to be full of homosexuals."

"So they said. I pay no attention to politics."

A vague idea was forming in his head. "Have you heard of anyone in this camp who may have such interests?"

"If I tell you, will it be part of your report?"

"Not unless it's important."

She knelt and rested her head upon his thigh. "With you, I think sometimes, there is no forgetting your 'mission.' You did not make love with me just to get information, did you?"

He leaned over and cupped her shoulder. "No. And I was hardly the seducer. How can you say that?"

"I'm sorry. I forgot. You are too honorable."

"Are you being sarcastic?"

"No. I mean it. You are what you are."

"Don't believe all those fine words from the newsreels."

"I've never seen your newsreels. I thought you'd be another bald, ugly Prussian. With a monocle."

"I remember." He lifted his stump. "Of course, I'm not exactly Vitruvian man. I'm missing more than my hair."

She kissed his knee. "You're not missing what's important." He was flattered when he thought she was referring to his sex, but, after a few seconds, she added, "Under it all, you are still sensitive. You still have a sense of goodness. In some men, that can be obliterated, but not in you."

"Don't try to make me a saint. I don't know what goodness is. I've done my share of killing."

"But you never enjoyed it. You accepted it, but you didn't

take pleasure in it. Oh, you try to pretend to be burned out, but there's still a flicker in you or you wouldn't be suffering."

"Just because you've seen me nude, you think you know all about me."

"Yes. Am I wrong?"

"I don't know anything any more. I was so young once. Now I feel like I've lived through the whole thousand years of the Third Reich. There's not much storm and stress left in me."

"No. I think you are the last believer. When all is said and done, you will still be a patriot. You still believe in the German people. You can be betrayed a thousand times and still believe."

"That would make me somewhat of a fool."

She kissed his knee again.

"Ah," he said. "Why don't I mind your thinking I'm a fool?" She gave no answer. She had vivisected him. He was too naked. He changed the subject. "Well, a woman of such insight must know much about the people in this camp. Are there any homosexuals? I have heard the men joke about Kurzner."

"Ursule once joked too. I think it was just teasing. What difference could it make?"

"Probably none. Perhaps Lila could have been a homosexual's rival. The murderer or murderers made certain that 'Röhm's Revenge' was stuck to Lila's chest. Perhaps someone who had a lover in the SA was wreaking some kind of vengeance."

"After all these years? Kurzner would have been a schoolboy when Röhm was shot."

"I know. It doesn't make sense, maybe. That note bothers me. There isn't any reason for it. And yet, it was obviously carefully made, artistic even."

"Dr. Frank once said he was in the SA."

Max lifted her head off his thigh. "Are you sure?"

"I think so."

"Do you think he could have killed Lila?"

Bette almost laughed. "He could barely walk on most days."

He thought about how Frank had said Lila had teased him. Frank would certainly, as a doctor, have been capable of cutting up Frau Schütz, and he would have had access to the scalpels. Max had seen the most gentle men implausibly become vicious killers on the battlefield, yet nothing seemed more implausible than that the distorted face in the infirmary had belonged to the mutilator of Frau Schütz. "I suspect you're right."

"Schütz is the real madman in Ostheim," Bette said. "Do you want me to go? You seem preoccupied."

"No. Please. I'm rambling because my mind's in a spin. I could hardly anticipate this evening."

"Thank you," she said.

"Climb up here." He patted the bed. "You're too tall to be all curled up. It must be getting chilly down there."

"A little."

She snuggled under his arm and licked, just once, the skin above his nipple. He felt somewhat guilty as he had brought her up beside him to find out one more thing.

"When—when you say Schütz is a madman, do you think it is an unusual madness?"

She squinted inquisitively. "There is such a thing as ordinary madness?"

"I don't know what I'm saying, or how to ask. Only Dr. Frank could have known for certain, and he didn't." Max knew that what he was going to say might destroy this comfort that had gradually accrued between them, but he had to pursue it, the investigation aside, for Bette's sake, as well as his own.

"What is it?"

"Lila may have had syphilis."

Bette was remarkably calm. "Poor Lila. Small wonder."

"Anyone who came into close contact with her may have contracted it."

"Schütz?"

"Yes. And others."

"Good God!" whispered Bette. "She was always hugging the children! Could she—?"

"It isn't likely, but—" The silence hung.

"But?"

"Your husband."

"Joachim?"

"He was intimate with her it seems."

Bette laughed again. "Don't be ridiculous."

"I'm not. Dr. Frank was certain of it. He begged your husband to come in for treatment, but he wouldn't."

"Because he didn't have it."

Max leaned forward sympathetically. "There's nothing to be ashamed of, Bette. If he passed it to you, you merely need to seek immediate treatment before it progresses."

"Is this why you hesitated when I came here? He didn't have it," she said sharply. "And he couldn't have had an affair with Lila."

Max was nearly angry. "Oh, I see, you might sleep with me, but your husband's without sin."

She slapped him and turned. "I know what I know. Perhaps I'd better go."

Max grabbed at her. She pushed his hand away. "No," he said, "I didn't mean that. It's just that—"

She would not face him. "Some great investigator you are! There are no eggs in the basket, count."

Max blinked. "What?"

"It wasn't only Joachim's eye that was lost in France. He pisses like a woman, Max."

"My God." He gaped at her back, trying to find the right words, but before he had the chance to speak, she had covered her face with both hands. Her body was shaking with sobs. He suddenly knew how much she had once loved her husband. He remembered how tenderly she had handled her children and he knew it was partly because they represented an earlier, more idyllic period in her marriage. He also remembered how barely polite they had been to each other and understood how the bitterness of his loss had destroyed whatever love had previously existed.

"Bette," he said softly. He awkwardly dragged himself closer and pressed his face into her hair, her neck. She spun around and desperately embraced him.

"He didn't want me here. He had no choice, though. He may have pretended to have a thing with Lila. He even pretended to ogle our maid when we had visitors, but it was impossible. Hopelessly impossible."

Max shushed her. "I'm so sorry," he said. "I've been a real fool. I'm sorry. Don't cry." He was swept by waves of tenderness, anger, humiliation, desperation, sorrow, pity, and love. He felt the wetness of her face and nose against his throat. He grasped the hair at the back of her head and lifted her away from him. He watched her red eyes flick back and forth, searching his as if to divine his feeling.

"You mustn't tell anyone," she pleaded. "I will do anything."

"Know that I do love you," he said slowly, and she pulled him on top of her, wrapping her legs around him and pressing her hips upward. The war ended then. There were no guns, no flags, no ideologies, no murders, no mutilations, no starvation. Only that bed, only a man and a woman and all distinctions dissolving as they drifted into sleep.

· *Thirteen* ·

Max woke about four-thirty. The room was totally dark. He heard a flapping, like a flag on the stern of a moving ship, and knew that the window was open. He reached for Bette and whispered her name. The only answer was the sound of the curtain dropping back against the window frame. He climbed out of bed and stumbled toward the window. She had, he presumed, escaped through it, but couldn't get it shut from the ground outside. He could see the silhouette of the fence wires against the night sky. Someone was moving along the dog runs with a flashlight, probably Külm. The shadows seemed to murmur the secrets they concealed. In the jungle, no matter how uninhabited it might seem to the untrained eye, you always knew it was filled with life, chattering or clicking or blinking. "There," Kinchachua once said, his eyes wide in the light of his family's fire, "is the jaguar. Hear? That is what he says when he is lonely." The invisible cat cried again, and Max had heard it this time, though the jaguar sounded far away. "He flees," said Kinchachua. "He sees the spirits of the dead." Ostheim, thought Max, might appear to be open, but it is really a jungle.

"I need the eyes of the jaguar," he mumbled.

He squeezed the bridge of his nose between his thumb and index finger. His nose was stuffy and there was pressure behind his eyes. For some time he wallowed in a profound sense of futility and tried to understand it. His failure with Breda he had accepted with a determined resignation. With all her expert manipulations of finger and tongue, he had somehow never gotten involved in it. The whole episode had taken place on the other side of a mirror, as it were. He had observed it emotionlessly and his body was someone else's. He had accepted his impotence with moments of anger or horror that he might never make love again, but they were no equal to the depression that was filling him now. He scratched at his genitals and felt the crusty grains that had dried on them. He put his fingertips to his nose and inhaled the earthlike smell of semen, sweat, and woman. He felt silly that he had told her he loved her. He barely knew her. For all he knew, she could have murdered Frau Schütz. Why not? The whole camp was filled with madness and death. Nonetheless, the thought only filled him with a greater longing to have her back.

> *Datta: what have we given?*
> *My friend, blood shaking my heart*
> *The awful daring of a moment's surrender*
> *Which an age of prudence can never retract*
> *By this, and this only, we have existed*

Am I reborn? he asked himself. If so, then I am suffering some kind of postpartum depression.

He shook his head. "You are too moody, Max-Baldur," he told himself out loud. "Like a true German." Would his emotions ever stabilize? A new foreboding was overcoming him. She had sneaked out of his room, in the dark, and set out for her home. What if her husband had waited for her? What if someone else had waited for her? In the dark. With a knife. No. It was impossible. It couldn't happen again. She wasn't like Lila Schütz. No.

He dressed himself. He strapped on his pistol, and set out toward the family cottages following the route he thought would be most likely for her, clinging close to the buildings, ducking into the shadows. Near the entrance to the officers' dining room he encountered a guard and borrowed his flashlight. He scanned the ground between Schütz's offices and the fence enclosing the lawn in front of the cottages. Quickly, then, he swept his light over the grass and circled the entire cluster of homes, in case she had tried to sneak in from the rear. Again, nothing. He thought to go back to bed but made for the garden at a speed that was not normal for him. He stumbled against the slightest irregularities in the ground, but somehow managed to keep upright. When he reached the edge of the garden, he was breathing heavily. His hand was shaking when he flicked on the light and peered up successive rows. Plants, dirt, rocks. Plants, dirt, rocks. Nothing. Max, he thought, you're acting like an idiot. You *must* be in love.

He was lowering the flashlight when something glinted. It took him a few seconds to situate the beam so that he could see the reflection again, but once he did, he moved up the row very carefully, so as not to lose it. When he was only a few meters away, however, the point of light disappeared. He backed up until it appeared again, then came unsteadily forward with a lowered head and torso. When the reflection disappeared this time, he was close enough to note its place adjacent to a potato plant. He prodded the soil with his toe. Nothing. He checked the location of the plant and poked again. The scalpel popped out, as if it had given up hiding.

Max dropped to one knee and picked it up. Other than some grit adhering in the parallel grooves in the handle, it was remarkably clean. He suddenly thought he shouldn't have touched it. It could have been checked for fingerprints. It still might. He placed it on the ground and reached into his pocket for his handkerchief. He had left it in his room. He gave up and put the scalpel in his jacket pocket. It had, after all, been outdoors for weeks. There was no likely evidence left on it to prove it had been used to mutilate Frau Schütz, though it was highly unlikely to have been dropped there at any other time. He stood and tried to locate it in relation to the place where the body had been found. He wasn't sure how far it was, but it was a long way, too far to throw, roughly halfway between the body and the brothel in the northwest corner. It made sense that whoever had killed Frau Schütz had escaped in that direction, an idea that didn't conform with the report's explanation that the prisoners had gone back through the hole they had cut.

The sky was lightening. Far across the compound, he noticed a light go on and decided it must be Schütz's office. A group of prisoners under the bulldog gaze of Sgt. Baranovitch were already raising scaffolding alongside one of the outer

towers while two of their comrades stirred paint. Max decided
to continue on to the brothel. On the night of the murder, he
remembered, Corporal Sovolevsky had taken special care to
sweep his light around it. Someone, however, after dropping
the scalpel, could have hidden behind it or under it, for like
the infirmary, it was wooden and built upon stone piers. The
person, or persons, could have remained under it for some
time, then slipped away in the confusion. He circled the
structure slowly, occasionally bending over to try to see under
it. As the sunlight weakened underneath, the grass gave way
to a narrow line of low, spreading weeds. Beyond them, the
dry, rocky dirt seemed undisturbed. It occurred to him that
under the shelter of the house might still remain the tracks
of whoever had crawled under it. On the west side, supporting
himself against the wall, he dropped to his knee and squinted.
Going on all fours was impossible with his stiff knee, however,
and even with the flashlight he saw no sign of human disturbance other than a brown fragment of glass.

He felt someone watching him, and saw that the tower
guard was leaning over. He looked like Corporal Schwegger.
Max put the flashlight back in his belt and raised himself. He
tapped his fingers against his hat to say hello, then leaned
over to dust off his knee. Schwegger indifferently saluted.
When the corporal turned to look out toward the brush line,
Max set out across the wide space between the brothel and
the outer fences. He strolled along them for a hundred meters
in each direction. There was no sign of any breaks in either
row of the fence wire, nor in the concertina wire beyond.
Furthermore, all the wire was weathered a uniform gray,
speckled with pinpricks of rust. None of it therefore had been
patched or replaced, probably since it was erected.

Had the prisoners cut their way into the family compound
with the intention of escaping through this previously untried
fence? If so, they had unfortunately encountered Lila in the
garden, butchered her, then hidden under the brothel when
the alarms sounded. With the guards on the alert, it was
impossible to attempt these fences, so they—somehow—went
back into the prisoners' compound where they were caught.
The scenario seemed preposterous. Prisoners might be able to
steal a scalpel and wire cutters, yes. But why risk cutting
through two fences? Why linger to mutilate the woman who

has bumbled into your escape? Why risk returning to the prisoners' barracks? Why not stay under the brothel? And then, to believe two of the men were infected by typhus and too weak to walk only eight hours afterward, well, that was just another implausibility. He would just as soon blame it all on the prisoners and go back to Berlin, but he knew he would be lying. And then suppose someone else were murdered? It could be Bette next time, for who could know the motives for the killing? Max had to find out more.

He noticed movement in one of the brothel windows. Someone had closed the curtains. He crossed back and climbed onto the porch. He considered whether to knock, then simply walked in. He scanned the small sitting room. A lumpy sofa. An art deco lamp. An armchair with a yellowed antimacassar. A burgundy carpet with a path worn across its Oriental pattern. Wilted flowers in a milk glass vase. A funereal odor.

"Good morning," said a raspy female voice. It belonged to a haunchy woman in nothing but a loose shirt. Her thighs were doughlike and pale. Her shins were hairy. "An early officer," she shouted over her shoulder. "Hop to it." She clapped her hands. She looked Max over. "I don't believe we've met. You must be the hero. We don't see many regular army uniforms."

"I have a special assignment."

"So I hear. Won't you have a seat? Schnapps? I have a little bit of dobostorte. It's only a day old."

"Really? I would think you couldn't get the ingredients."

"One of the privates brought it. He was on leave. He's in love with Ilse." She winked. "Very young."

Max remembered Vienna. "We've all been young."

"Believe me, these girls will make you feel like you're sixteen. I've trained them all myself."

"You give them training?"

"Well, I give them advice. They all know it's better to be in this area of the camp."

"Ah."

"Let me fetch the dobostorte while you're waiting."

"No, please. I'm grateful, but I am here to make inquiries."

Her heavy-lidded eyes flickered. "Ah, then, afterward we will entertain you, yes?"

"Do not be concerned. I will pay you for your time."

"Pay? We are not paid here. We enjoy serving the Third

Reich. Of course, we accept little gifts—not required, of course, but if Dagmar here pleases you, for example"— she gestured at an emaciated girl in a faded robe who had just straggled in—"you might want to give her a tin of beef, some hard candy, cigarettes. Money is of little use to us here." Two other women peered over Dagmar's shoulder. Both were gaunt, but not as much as the first. They were worn-out and sallow, but none of them were as skeletal as the regular prisoners. Despite the exhaustion in their smiles, one was biting her lip in what she must have imagined was an erotic manner. "Don't just stand there, girls, come in. Come in."

The lip-biter moved in rapidly and reached out to run her fingers down Max's chest. The other two moved up close to him as if in imitation of her, but were only reaching out when he backed away. He shuddered, but put on an awkward smile to cover it. "Please. No. I am not here for that. I have no interest in that."

"Ever?" asked the haunchy woman. She glanced at his crotch.

"Not this morning," he said sharply.

"Perhaps Hanna. Where is Hanna? That bedbug!"

The woman started for the door, but Max shouted. "No! None of you. No one. Please sit down. I have only questions."

The shout froze them. The big woman looked a little confused, but she moved her hand to indicate all of them should sit. "Good," said Max. "This is totally part of an official inquiry, though much may not appear in my final report. Do you understand?" They nodded. "So I want absolute frankness. No one will be harmed by telling me the truth. I have orders from the Reichsführer himself. Do you understand?" They nodded.

"We are here to serve you," said the haunchy woman. "Aren't we, ladies?" They all agreed.

"I want to know about the night Frau Schütz was murdered."

The three whores looked at each other, then to their madam. "But—but none of us was here, general," said Dagmar in a heavy accent.

"You weren't here?"

"What she means," said the madam, "is that they weren't here. There were all different girls then."

"Where are these girls?"

The madam hesitated for a moment. "They were"—she shrugged—"transferred."

"To the regular compound?"

"Yes."

"But you were here."

"I have always been here."

"Always?"

"Since the second week of the camp. The commandant major saw my file. He knew I had experience in this line of work. He wanted a place of recreation for his troops. He said they had a very pleasant one at"—she squinted, trying to remember— "at wherever he was before. So I was to pick out a few girls, and so forth."

"What is your name?" asked Max.

"Here, I am called Tanya. This is easier for Germans to say. My name has never mattered since I don't know who my parents were." She tapped the number tattooed on her forearm. "This is the only name that matters." She laughed, revealing a gap where her right canine should be.

"Well, if none of you ladies were here that night," said Max. "It is only Tanya to whom I need speak." They turned to the madam for guidance. She waved them out. Before leaving, each nodded and politely said, "Please come back, sir." Max thanked them.

When they had gone, he thought for a second, then sat opposite her. "They are well-trained," he said.

"Maybe," she said. "Dagmar is too new. Needs a little meat on her. She'll get better. No one wants to be on the roadwork. Or passed from one barracks orderly to another. The prisoners are worse than the guards." She stopped short. "Of course."

"Of course."

She leaned forward. "If I may be so bold, I would be very pleased to handle you myself. I know many things about Germans, but most of all I know their preferences. You are the masters of war. I am the mistress of pleasure."

"Stop it," said Max curtly. "Your words do not excite me or even interest me. You have whored it up so long, I suppose, that you can't speak like a normal woman. I am willing to make allowances for that as long as you tell me the truth."

She was startled, bewildered. "And what truth is it you wish me to tell?"

Max rapped his cane on the floor. "The truth. What happened on the night Frau Schütz died?"

"Nothing," said Tanya. "Nothing unusual. It was an enlisted men's night."

"Excuse me?"

"Enlisted men's night. They have two nights a week. Noncommissioned officers have two, and officers get three. Which days are determined month by month."

"Every month?"

"Yes."

"Why?"

Tanya shrugged.

"Who was here that night?"

"Who knows?"

"What do you mean?"

"Twenty to twenty-five come through on an enlisted men's night. All of them might as well be the same. Who can remember one particular night?"

"But it was the night Frau Schütz was cut to pieces only a few hundred meters away!"

"It may have been the night Baranovitch insisted on trying out every one of us. It may have been the night Ulf Wiedemann passed out drunk on the steps. Who knows? Life here has a certain sameness."

"And how many girls do you have?"

"There are five rooms, excluding this."

"And each girl will take on four to five men a night."

"Not always. Officers' days are slower. They are more sophisticated. We get to practice some special things."

"Like what?"

She grinned. "Like the knotted scarf. Like—"

"Never mind. No. I guess I have to know. Was there anyone who was notably interested in extreme practices? Who might have abused your girls?"

"Of course. An officer has the same cock a corporal has. And every cock finds its own way to crow, as my first husband used to say."

"I understand," bluffed Max, "that the commandant comes here frequently."

"He founded our establishment. Why wouldn't he?"

"Was he here the night of the killing?"

"I don't know. He comes often. I can't remember."

"Why aren't you candid with me?"

"A good whore keeps her legs open and her mouth shut. To kiss is unhealthy; to kiss and tell can be fatal."

"Has anyone actually hurt one of your girls?"

"Nothing permanent."

"I want to know who."

She thought for some time, rolling her tongue around inside her mouth.

"Who?" he demanded.

"General, I can't say."

"You must say."

"I can't say." She crossed her heavy legs. Her pasty thigh had a fading yellow bruise about the size of an egg. "I know where you come from. But I know you are just army. They are SS. Oh, most of them are just Waffen SS, or foreign volunteers, but I know the difference. You will write your report and go home. I will be left here. Besides, it's unethical. A priest or a lawyer wouldn't tell you his client's business, neither would I."

"Because of what you may know, you might end up like Lila Schütz."

"We all die."

"Not like that."

"Listen, general, if I knew something dangerous, do you think I'd still be here?"

It made sense. Max was angered by the sense of it. "Stop calling me 'general.' You know I'm not a general."

She winked.

"You say all of the girls who were here that night have been transferred?"

"Yes."

"Is that normal?"

"They wear out. Or they don't make the men happy any more. And, of course, if there's any disease . . ."

"Did those girls get a disease?"

"One caught mumps, of all things. Died of it."

"Venereal disease?"

"I taught them how to check."

"There is no way to check, except with a laboratory."

"You work up a little drop. If it's clear—"

"It means nothing."

"Well, if you say so. But who is the expert? It's always worked for me. Some of them get careless, though. As soon as we know, they're gone."

"I want the names of all the girls who were here that night."

"I'm not sure I remember. You won't need them."

"I want to interview them."

"By séance?" She laughed. "They're all dead."

"How do you know?"

She grinned. "They never send me a postcard."

He started to ask if she knew who might have given her girls a disease, but knew she would evade the question. In any case, with the parade going through each night, who could guess? Instead, he demanded the four girls' names. It took her a long time to come up with them, but she did. She could not remember the real names of two of them, but he was certain that somewhere in Schütz's files was a record of transfers and assignments. It did seem odd, she said, now that she thought about it, that all of them were transferred within two weeks of the murder. Usually they were switched one at a time over a long period of time. When it had happened, she had to train all of the new ones at the same time, and it was annoying.

"One final thing," said Max. "On the night of the killing, was it possible that someone hid under this house?"

"How should I know?"

He gave her a sharp look.

"Not meaning to be impudent, sir. There's plenty of room for a man under there. We had a technical sergeant here about a year ago. He used to sneak underneath. He'd worked a couple of holes in the floor. All he had to do was ask and he could have had a royal performance, but he preferred to peek like some little boy at his mother's keyhole. One night I pretended to be talking to the commandant, and I did a dance all around the peephole, so the sergeant would be looking up. Then I stood right over it, opened up like I was about to do something special, and pissed like a fountain." She cackled. "I think I heard him hit his head when he jumped. I saw him walking guard with a plaster, just here." She pointed over her eye. "But he said nothing, because he thought Schütz was here."

"Who was that sergeant?"

"You have no sense of humor, general. Does it matter?"

"I'll be the judge of that."

She shrugged. "Technical Sergeant Dieter Becker. He cut himself sharpening an axe and died of a septic infection. Or so I heard."

Max nodded. He stood. "If you would only trust me, I can guarantee your safety."

"No one can guarantee that. You're old enough to know that, aren't you?"

"I am sorry to have disturbed you so early in the day."

"All times are the same to me." Max had opened the door when she added, "Why don't you come back? It's a pleasure to have a real count for a change."

There was something about the way she inflected the word "count" that stopped Max. He turned. "Real count? Do you mean there are counts who aren't real?"

She said no, but too hastily.

"Do you mean a 'von' who isn't a 'von'?"

"Why would you think that?" She had lost her indifference.

"And is von Rauschwald frequently here?"

"I am not naming anyone specific. I would never name anyone specific." She licked her upper lip. "Please. You mustn't say I did."

"I won't," said Max, running his fingers down the door frame. "Here are a few marks." He held out the money. "Divide it among your girls and yourself."

"Oh, we have no use for money." She never took her eyes off the bills. "It is not allowed for prisoners to have money."

"I'm sure you'll find some use for it," he said quietly, thrusting it into her hand. "Good day, Tanya." He tipped his hat, closed the door, and headed for Schütz's office.

· *Fourteen* ·

Max intended to explore the prisoners' records. Schütz's original report on the murder said very little about the three executed men and nothing about the brothel. Max suspected that the brothel itself would not be unusual in SS practice—some provision was usually made for soldiers in isolated posts—yet Schütz's references to it in his report were always sanitized with vague wording: "the closest structure," for example, or "a utility building." Perhaps this was only to avoid rubbing SS noses in the fact that they ran whorehouses. Perhaps, on the other hand, there was something Schütz preferred not to admit, even to himself. That he was one of the men who received "special treatment" at the hands of Tanya and her girls, for instance; or that it was at the whorehouse he discovered he was carrying syphilis; or that there was some other secret the transferred girls had known. What would they have known, however, that Tanya didn't? This kind of thing wouldn't be in the ledgers carefully tended by Schütz's clerk, of course, but there might be something to indicate a relationship between the three escaping prisoners and one of the women.

Max paused between the brothel and the family area, looked toward the garden, and played with several ideas. Maybe the prisoners had broken through into here in order to help one or more of the women escape. Maybe one of the whores was the wife or sister of one of the three and killing Lila was a way of avenging her honor. And Lila was conveniently there to be murdered? Not likely, but if it were true, then Schütz would have a reason, however slight, to want not to have the whole story revealed. And the prisoners would finally have a personal motive for mutilating Frau Schütz. It momentarily suited Max's sense of irony to think seriously about the possibility that Schütz had executed the right men, and the whole investigation was meaningless.

Max was distracted by a movement at the rear of one of the family cottages. Ursule Frank, her hair disheveled, wearing a wide dressing gown, draped wet clothing over a rope stretched from a young linden to a hook on the wall. He remembered he had not expressed his condolences and set off in her direction. She had hung up a pair of long underwear, a white shirt, and a single pair of socks when she turned to go back inside. She saw Max as she did, however, and paused, holding the door half open with one hand, while gathering her dressing gown around her throat with the other.

As he got closer he could see her nostrils were reddened and her eyes puffy. "Good morning, Frau Frank."

"Good morning, Count von Prokofsk. We haven't chatted for some time."

"No," he said. "I'm sorry for that. I've been very busy."

She nodded vacantly.

"It's very early to be doing laundry."

"The doctor's burial clothes," she said. She attempted a half smile. "They need to be dry by noon. I wanted to take him back to his family in Swabia, but they say there are no trains for shipping the dead."

"Ah. The railways to the north have all been cut. You should have had your maid wash them."

"It was one last thing I could do." She seemed on the verge of weeping, but inhaled and stared at the distant hills.

He said nothing for several seconds. Someone was blowing a whistle in the prisoners' compound. A dog barked sharply. "I did not mean to disturb you, Frau Frank. It is just that I wanted to express my condolences. I sympathize with your loss."

"Thank you," she said. "That is very kind of you."

"It is the least I could do." There was another awkward silence. He had seen much dying in Africa with its hand-maiden grief, but he recognized he had never experienced any around women. His mother had died giving him birth. He had no aunts or sisters. He felt as uncomfortable as if he had caused the doctor's death. It was, somehow, men's games that had brought about Frank's death. Wearing a uniform somehow made Max an accomplice of the Russian pilots. "When my father died, I kept refusing to believe it was true. It is so difficult to accept the injustice of a strong, vigorous man's passing."

"My Klaus," she said, "was not very strong, I know, but that was because, at heart"—she placed her hand on her breast—"he was good. In order to be strong, you must have ice in your soul. He is at peace now."

"I barely knew him," said Max, "but I feel I understood what was troubling him."

"That is kind of you to say. You noblemen always know the right words. Please, you have eaten? Won't you come inside? I have nothing but two apple cakes, but I would like to share one with you."

"I would be intruding."

"No." She smiled weakly, but her eyes were pleading. "Little Klaus has gone out. I don't know where. I don't know whether he slept at all last night. The cottage is so empty this morning, so quiet. When Klaus snored, he drowned out all the sounds of this place."

"Little Klaus misses him?"

"He's at the funny age. He said he hated his father. Who knows what boys think nowadays? I don't think he grieves. That is what the Nazis have done to my boy. Please. Join me."

"Very well," said Max, "but you mustn't let me overstay my welcome."

"You could not," she said.

The kitchen was roughly equal in size to the von Rauschwald parlor, but seemed larger because the cabinets were white and the narrow dining table didn't seem to fill the space like the heavy furniture of the von Rauschwalds. Ursule hefted the enamel laundry pot off the stove and set it on the floor. She checked the fire, then put on a kettle. "We will have coffee," she said. "Lila used to get it for me. I have been saving it, but that is stupid. Saving it did nothing for Klaus. You'd think a doctor's wife would know that no one is guaranteed more life than anyone else."

Max started to say he didn't want to use up her coffee, but he had a sense that she was honoring him.

"Klaus," she said, "he did not suffer, is that true?"

For a second he felt the terror the doctor must have known when he found himself pinned against the wall by his own desk, bullets and wood exploding all around him. "He made not a sound. He didn't know what hit him, but even before that, he was as courageous as I have seen a man, even in combat."

"You are lying," said Ursule. "He was not a brave man. That was why he drank."

Max thought of the morphine he had stolen. "There is no one who is brave enough to face certain things."

She placed the apple cakes in the center of the table, and awkwardly settled onto a chair. "He was good at heart. That was why he could not face this place. And Schütz, he was always pestering him at first. He wanted Klaus to do experiments. Klaus had never wanted to do medical research. He didn't know anything about it."

"Experiments? What kind of experiments?"

She raised her fat hands. "Who can say? Turning Jews into Danes. Schütz only said that if this were going to be an important camp, then medical research was important. He never said what kind. That was up to Klaus."

"But Klaus never did any?"

She shook her head. "And Schütz threatened to have him sent to the front. But there were no doctors to replace him. Imagine Klaus at the front! He was no soldier. He was no scientist either. Schütz seemed to think any doctor could experiment."

"Vivisections? Postmortems? Nothing like that?"

"Who needs postmortems? He knew what they died of. He once told me he saw diseases here you couldn't see anywhere in the world, and it wasn't just the hereditary ailments some of the isolated peasants cooked up with their incest. There were nutritional diseases, he said, and infections from malnutrition, that he'd never seen, even in medical books."

"When there are shortages, it is always prisoners who suffer first."

"After a year or so, he finally gave up. He just put them out of their misery when he could." She stood and checked the kettle. "One bubble after another."

"I am in no hurry."

"I don't mean the water. When he could not help them, he released them. An air bubble." She made a motion like pressing a hypodermic. "No more suffering." She threw her head back. "Sometimes I thought he would do it to himself. Sometimes when he didn't get home until late, I thought he had, and every footstep I heard was a soldier coming to tell me."

"We all want to be out of our misery on occasion." A lieutenant had once told Max how he had shot one of his men in the head rather than permit him to suffer after having his guts ripped open by a mine. It seemed an act of kindness. But a doctor casually pumping air into patients' veins seemed, if not criminal, tasteless, immoral, a violation of something sacred. Max could think of no real distinction between the acts, however. After all, a physician would more likely have a better sense of a patient's chances than a lieutenant. Both men taking this role upon themselves reminded him of Kinchachua, the shaman, who would attempt to absorb the bad spirits (the illness) of others into his own body. The lieutenant and Dr. Frank had both taken something evil into themselves in order to relieve others, but unlike the shaman, whose strength would allow him to dance out the illness that the sick were unable to resist, Dr. Frank had been consumed by the demons he had absorbed.

The water boiled and Ursule poured it into a pot with the coffee grounds.

"Before Dr. Frank, ah, passed on, he told me he was once a member of the SA."

"Yes. Not for long. It was hard enough being called away in the middle of the night for births, but then to spend nights carousing with the brownshirts, well, he made his excuses, and after a while his uniform didn't fit."

"I suppose he was shocked when the Röhm plot was revealed."

"He was questioned twice by the Gestapo, but his loyalty was beyond question."

"It must have shocked him," Max repeated.

Ursule leaned over, as if confiding. "He never believed a word of it. He used to say the SA men he knew were like puppies over Adolf Hitler, but who knows? Last year, at the dinner celebrating the Midsummer Festival, Schütz was angry about Klaus's indifference to medical research. He began to throw Klaus's SA past in his face. He accused him of being a traitor and a queer. Klaus was so furious, he sobered up instantly and threw a plate of veal at Schütz. Captain von Rauschwald swatted it down—God knows why—probably sparing Klaus an assault charge. Klaus had thrown it so poorly, everyone laughed and Schütz seemed satisfied that he had successfully degraded my husband again. Poor Klaus passed out a while later." She stared at Max for a second. "You are interested in the note. Röhm's Revenge. You are really here on your investigation."

"No," said Max, touching her hand, "it was only a coincidence I saw you. I was out walking and I knew I hadn't expressed my condolences. You must believe that."

She straightened. "It's quite all right. If you come to prove our commandant killed Lila, it will simply make him pay for his two murders."

"Two?"

"Yes. Lila and my Klaus. My Klaus was dead for the past year. Schütz did that. You look at me and you see a fat woman. Klaus used to look at me and see love. Even when Schütz drained his will, air bubble by air bubble, and the alcohol slowed him down, Klaus still loved my body. He is the only man I would ever feel comfortable with. I know that to be true. I was not pure when I married, I admit it freely, but I have always been faithful, because that is true." She began to weep. Max picked at his apple cake until she quietened. She wiped her face with her sleeve. "I'm sorry." She stood. "Oh, the coffee will be too strong. I've waited too long."

"I prefer it strong," said Max, watching her pour it through a strainer. "That is the way the Brazilians brew it. Very strong." He put down his cake. It was stale. "I am sorry to have upset you. It seems your marriage with Dr. Frank was the only happy one in Ostheim." She placed the coffee in front of him. The scent was heavenly, whatever the quality, if only because it was coffee. "And, if you'll forgive me, it occurs to me that the doctor may have confided some things in you that he did not have the opportunity to tell me."

"Ostheim is not a Swabian village. You cannot expect anyone to act normal here. We live inside fences. We smell the dead burning. We are abused and insulted by a petty man. We can't get a decent piece of meat, or a kilo of vanilla sugar, or a pot of Darjeeling. I am lucky Klaus confined his interest to alcohol, Count von Prokofsk."

"Here, it seems, many people escape into the boudoir."

"Perhaps. It was Lila's way. Maybe it's the SS way. Do you think the murder had something to do with sex?"

Max shrugged. "I once had a professor who said everything had something to do with sex. I suspect so in this. Do you?"

She didn't answer. "I didn't mind her turning up her rear to any man with a stiff bird. You can't be around the profession of medicine very much and be too harsh on people. It's not for me to judge. It depends who I am thinking about. I think Schütz got what he deserved. On the other hand, I feel sorry for Bette."

"Why is that?"

"The captain. He and Lila carried on quite a dance."

"They had an affair?"

"He flaunted it. She didn't much care."

"How do you mean 'flaunted it'?"

"Exactly that. Once I saw Lila wearing a beautiful filigree ring with a girasole in the center, and a matching necklace. I asked her where she had gotten them. She winked and said Joachim had found them in the lining of a prisoner's coat. She laughed and said they were supposed to be state property, but Joachim didn't care."

"This is what she said?"

"Yes, but later, out back here, I saw him on his hands and knees kissing her ring, like she was a cardinal, and when he noticed me, he smiled at me. He didn't care if I saw him, not a whit."

"And he did this flaunting more than once?"

"He hinted at it constantly. Double entendres. Once he's supposed to have bragged to his men that he was the only man who could wear out Lila Schütz." Ursule flushed slightly.

Max perused the kitchen stove to avoid her eyes and soften her embarrassment. "That's interesting," he said. "Very interesting." He was trying to think of a reason for Bette's telling him that her husband was incapable of sex, for he could find no reason for Frau Frank to lie. It might be, given his situation, that he would want his men to think he was still a man, but why the private scene Ursule had stumbled into? And why would Lila play along with his masquerade? It made more sense that Bette had lied, but the why of that wasn't easy to parse.

He asked her many other things and she seemed relieved at having someone to talk to. Bette had kept her company for most of the day after Dr. Frank had been killed, but, later, when she thought Ursule was asleep, she had slipped away. Bette often took walks late at night, said Frau Frank, and this was no surprise, though, naturally, after Lila's death a late-night walk took on more meaning than it had before. Ursule was, however, surprised to see Bette sneaking in early that morning, as she would have been "walking" for some seven or eight hours. Max began to suspect that Ursule might have been conducting a little investigation of her own, so he tried to blunt her curiosity by a frontal assault: "So where do you think she was?"

"I don't know. Perhaps she has taken a lover." Ursule no longer seemed coy. Max no longer thought she was trying to get him to admit Bette had been with him.

"Ah," he said. "She doesn't seem the type."

"Every woman is the type, especially in times like these." She thought for a moment. "Except me. I'm not the type. Klaus was the only man for me."

Max nodded. "Surely her husband noticed her going and coming."

"Who can say?" said Ursule. "Schütz often puts him on night duty. And then, he plays his records so loud."

"He is fond of his music."

"And then, thinking as a nobleman, he may consider it bad taste to inquire as to his wife's excursions."

Max smiled. "I assure you, Frau Frank, the romantic escapades of the nobility, at least what I have seen of them, are neither more nor less frequent than those of watchmakers and everyone else."

"You've barely touched your apple cake," she grinned. "I would think those women would take away my appetite, if I were a man."

Max blinked. He hadn't known that she had seen him come from the brothel. He quickly tried to decide what he wanted

Frau Frank to believe about it. He concluded that if she thought she were his confidante, she might tell others anyway, but be more convinced of his alibi for last night. He winked. "I was investigating."

"That," she said pleasantly, "goes without saying." Almost immediately after the words came out, a cloud passed over her face. It didn't seem right to be enjoying herself with her husband dead less than a day.

He left her half an hour later and set out again for Schütz's office. Just as he climbed up the stairs to the door, however, he heard a young voice with a Slavic accent.

"Herr Colonel! Herr Colonel!" It was a Ukrainian SS private. He didn't look a day over fourteen, though his neck was inflamed from a dull razor. "Heil Hitler."

"Heil Hitler. What is it?"

"Sergeant Klimmer has been looking for you, sir. A message has come from Berlin, sir."

"From Lieutenant Colonel Oskar Hüber?"

"I don't know, sir."

"Thank you, private," he said, rushing past the boy without saluting. He was out of breath when he entered the communications room. The surly man and woman who had been there when he had finally gotten through to Oskar the first time were writing on yellow paper.

"I understand there was a message for me."

"Heil Hitler," said the woman.

Max saluted impatiently. "There was a message for me."

"Yes."

"Well?"

"Well what, sir?"

"Give it to me!"

"We passed it to your sergeant."

"Yes, fine, now give it to me."

"We cannot do that, sir."

Max stepped to the center of the room. "Excuse me?"

"Our orders are to take all communications and convey them to the addressed officer or his aide. We are not, under any circumstances, to repeat a message once it is delivered."

"What?"

"I think I have made myself clear."

"And I am making myself clear. Tell me what the message was."

The spectacled woman was amused by Max's frustration. "It was decoded, then written down. You can appreciate how the exact wording of military messages is crucial. A wrong word might lead to thousands of deaths."

Max lifted his finger and prodded the woman in the middle of her forehead. *"You* are playing games. I am not amused by your playing games. If the message came from Berlin, it was from the Reichsführung SS. Do you propose to obstruct the Reichsführer's will? I can make it extremely unpleasant for you." He poked her again for emphasis, but she was uncowed.

"Colonel," she said, "it's not the Reichsführer I must live with. It is Commandant Schütz. I will not violate my orders. Berlin is a long way."

"But Berlin has very long arms. I will make certain they reach here. You'll pay for your petulance."

Suddenly, the man spoke. "What is the harm? Colonel Hüber says you should finish your investigation and return, as quickly as possible."

"Is that all?"

"Well, it isn't word for word. Your sergeant has that."

"Did he say why?"

The man shrugged. Max turned to leave. The woman spoke behind him. "You have no right to threaten a soldier of the SS." Max stopped, but did not look back.

"Sssh," said the man.

"He'll be out of here by tomorrow, you'll see."

Max glanced back. "You had better hope so," he said.

He found Kleini waiting outside his office. The sergeant's face was pasty and sagging, but despite the visible hangover, he was cheerful. He plunged his hand into his pocket and took out the message. "We are going, colonel," he said with relief. "They want to bury Frau Schütz forever."

Max read: "THE OPPORTUNITY IS ENDED. CONCLUDE INQUIRY AS SOON AS POSSIBLE AND RETURN TO BERLIN. HÜBER."

Kleini drew his thick hand over his face as if trying to smooth out the haggardness. "Thank God," he said. "Thank God. We can't leave this place too soon."

Max said nothing for several seconds. What had initially

flashed into his mind was not his desire to punish Schütz in any way possible, nor a wish to avenge Frau Schütz, nor any feeling that the possible injustice done to the three prisoners mattered. Instead, it was simply the feel of Bette's damp thigh across his own, her breathing in his ear. All the other ideas then followed this simple image and he crumpled the message in his hand, waving it in front of him like a flag. "What sort of game is this!? God damn them! They give me no choice. They send me halfway to China to look into a murder they don't seem to care about, then tell me to forget it! God damn them! God damn you, Oskar Hüber."

"At least we're through," said Kleini. "A month of Ostheim is enough."

Max paced, thumping his stiff leg on the floor as if he wanted to break it. "No," he finally said. "No. Not now. Ostheim is an abscess. I mean to find out as much as I can. Somebody cut Frau Schütz to pieces, Kleini, and it wasn't the men they hanged for it. Hüber says to leave as soon as possible. It's simple enough: it isn't yet possible."

"You can't be serious, colonel. You never wanted this."

"I never wanted to lead men to their deaths, but I did it, maybe a hundred times."

Kleini shook his head as if he were not hearing correctly. His jowls fluttered. "That isn't the same. You know that. That was your duty as an officer. What is this? A police matter. You said that yourself. And you've given enough to duty. You've even been wounded again because of this farce. This isn't your duty. Use your common sense for once and stop acting out of some mad sense of heroic nobility."

"You know I have never—never—claimed anything more for myself because of my bloodline."

Kleini spread his hands. "And that's just part of your living up to it. Just because of your father and all the von Prokofsks back to whomever, you have to prove you're noble, that it isn't just hereditary. It's absurd."

Max's jaw tightened. "You are exceeding your rank, sergeant."

"Oh, so it's 'sergeant' now. All this talk about how I should be promoted, how I saved your life—"

"Stop it!" shouted Max. "This is nonsense. Don't you care that someone took a woman apart with a scalpel? That he carved her child from her belly and threw it on her face? Do I have to show you the photograph again?"

"You're asking me? A sergeant? I don't care. Murder is the way of life here. And what makes this murder different from what goes on with the prisoners? Or in a battle? I have seen ordinary, dull men go mad with the smell of blood and hold target practice on a British cook before I could stop them. Could I have done justice for this cook by charging the men with disobeying orders? If they're not now dead or imprisoned, they're likely ordinary, dull men again—no harm to anyone. How can you playact? I have told you what I saw with the prisoners, but that you ignore."

"I intend to take it up with Schütz, at the right time, and Lieutenant Colonel Hüber, if necessary."

"At the right time? I beg you, let us go, simply put it behind us. The longer we stay here, the dirtier I feel."

"And you, Kleini, you say you've not participated, so what dirt could be sticking to you? We *are* in a war. Things get out of hand. You're right—ordinary, dull men do get carried away. What is so damning about these acts of brutality? We haven't done them. In fact, it was the foreigners in the SS you observed. We are not responsible. It has happened in Schütz's command. He is responsible."

"We are Germans. That makes us responsible. When the Russians finally get here do you think they will say, 'Oh, you're Wehrmacht, we know you wouldn't kick babies into a fire. Let's have a beer'? Splitting hairs won't matter. We are the Germans. We did it." He began to plead. "Colonel, I love you like a brother, but you won't face up to this. What do you think they are doing in Buchenwald and Auschwitz and Maidanek? I have talked to these men. In some camps they don't even bother to work the prisoners to death, as they do here. They have gas chambers. They don't throw the bodies in a pit, either. They have vast crematories. They kill thousands a day. We are the Germans. We did this. We are doing this."

"If these things are true, Kleini, those responsible will pay."

Kleini took off his cap and crushed it in his hands. "Don't you see? *We* are responsible. We knew they were taking our enemies away, but we had no interest in what they did with them. We didn't ask. We got hints of it or were told things, but it was too easy to brush them off. Like you. I tell you what I saw, and what have you done?"

"I told you, I will confront Schütz."

"If you really thought it was serious you would have done something already."

"It was only yesterday."

"You see? Excuses."

Max stared into Kleini's face. Once again he found himself thinking about his feelings, rather than feeling them. It was true he was no longer shocked by any violence he was faced with. Well, no. There was the incident in the garden when they had "saved" a prisoner, though probably only for one of Dr. Frank's air bubbles. And the photograph of what remained of Frau Schütz still gave him a small shiver. He also considered how frightened he had been last night when Bette had sneaked home. No, he was no longer the hollow shell he had once been, but he could not honestly say that if the SS killed half of Europe he would be any more outraged by it than by any other atrocity. Nor could he feel, by being one of millions whose language happened to be German, that he was somehow culpable for another German's acts.

"Kleini," he finally said, "perhaps if I do something about this one murder a little balance can be restored. Someone systematically, calculatedly butchered Lila Schütz. It seems different to me. I feel I must do all I can."

"I beg you, colonel. Let's get out of here. Do you think what they are doing to the prisoners is not calculated and systematic? Do you think simply because you can't put a face to all these deaths that they don't matter? When this war is ended, how many millions will have died? It doesn't matter whether it's combat or old age or starvation or illness or being burned alive. Who will worry about some slut's murder? She was looking for it."

"Her fucking around," said Max, "isn't much different from your getting drunk yesterday."

"Or taking morphine?"

Max clenched his fist. "You have no right to say that."

"No? I waited in your room for a while this morning. I cleaned up a little."

"You can see the vials were unopened."

"Possibly."

"I don't even have a needle, only the hypodermic. How dare you snoop around?"

"You know I wasn't snooping. You also know how I sat on you when the need for the drug drove you mad."

"You exaggerate."

"You forget. Why would you have morphine if you're not using it?"

Max dropped his eyes. "I don't know. I—I stole it. I maybe wanted to prove I could keep it without ever using it. I felt strong, like I could control myself."

"And do you feel this way now?"

"Yes."

"Then why don't you get some sense and get out of here? A place like this would drive anyone to the needle. I was drunk for two whole days, colonel. I was happily sleeping in my own puke when the strafing woke me."

"I want to know who killed her, Kleini. I may not succeed, but no woman deserves what happened to Frau Schütz. I don't care what a couple of barracks moralists have to say."

"And the prisoners," said Kleini, "don't deserve what is happening to them. We can't do anything here. Let's go."

Max slowly shook his head. "No. Not yet. For the moment I will play this out. I can send you back if you like. I want you to go. You have no reason to stick this out."

Kleini was silent for several seconds, then he dropped into a chair. "And who will type your goddamned report? Fine typist you'd be with one hand. And who will drag your majesty out of here when the Red Army comes charging through the gates?"

"I can order you to go. I can commandeer a typist. I will certainly know when the Russians break through in this sector."

"Pah!" said Kleini, throwing up his hands. "You'd be too busy playing detective to notice. If you're stupid enough to stay, I'm stupid enough to take care of you."

"You shouldn't call your officers stupid," said Max quietly.

"I know. But not because they aren't." He crossed his arms and rocked back in the chair, disgusted by his own loyalty.

For a long time, they said nothing further, and avoided each other's eyes. Max listened to Kleini breathing. The sergeant eventually hissed through his nose and spoke.

"By the way," he said, "one of the guards brought your cane." He reached for it, leaning his chair against the wall, and snapped it up. He tossed it. Max caught it.
"Thank you," said Max. "Thank you."
Kleini grunted.

· *Fifteen* ·

After sending Kleini to eat, Max waited for an opportunity to study the prisoner records unhindered. After
lunch, there was a greater chance that Schütz would not be
in, and Max did not want a confrontation until he had gleaned
all he could from the records. He propped up his feet on the
desk and dozed for forty-five minutes or so. In some ways, the
argument with Kleini had calmed him by bringing to the
surface many of the things that were burrowing in his mind
like insects through dark soil. Exposed, they became creatures that could be dealt with immediately, or postponed until
he was strong enough to face them. Further, he was sore all
over, languid with a pleasant weariness from the previous
night.

The second time he awoke—it had seemed hours from when
Bette had pulled him atop her—he lifted his head, and looked
at her serene face. He wanted to be able to find a word for that
face, the paleness of the skin, the firm line of the lips, the
gentle upward turn of the nose. "Classical" was what came to
mind: the ideal proportions of Praxiteles, a face not blatantly
sexual or overtly distinctive, without the distasteful, flamboy-
ant beauty of actresses in motion pictures, yet definitely
beautiful—the Platonic face, the eternal essence. He impul-
sively kissed her. Her eyes blinked open and she ran her
fingertips down his back. "Again?" she whispered. He felt a
sudden humiliation, as the image of himself lying atop her
came over him. The scars she caressed, the truncated and

bandaged arm pressing her side. Hephaistos and Aphrodite, the vulgar blacksmith on the divine body: and the gods laugh and they laugh and they laugh. He had buried his face in her shoulder. But her lips sought his throat, wetly breathed in his ear, and the humiliation faded. He only thought of pleasing her, of being her man, of possessing her while enslaving himself to her, of losing identity in the point where all the universe is one.

Rocked back in the office chair, he relived the feelings and images, smiling at his own awkwardness in trying to make love in the way he had always done it before the war. It wasn't easy without an arm. He had collapsed on that side twice, once painfully mashing her breast. Also, moving his hips had been curiously arrhythmic with the stiff leg. Yet, the ridiculousness of all that disappeared in the vortex. Everything but the pleasure was forgotten, and he dozed as if he were swaying in a hammock on a warm day in Manaus.

Max had just left his office when he saw the commandant getting into a car. Max stepped back behind a corner until it paused to pass through the gates into the prison area. "Bad day for you," he mumbled, thinking of the prisoners, "good luck for me." When he opened the door, the ever-present Gissinger was working in his ledgers, this time with long columns of figures. He snapped to attention, his arms at his side.

"Herr Colonel von Prokofsk, Commandant Major Schütz is not in."

"I am not here to see the commandant. I am looking into prisoner records. With his permission, of course."

Gissinger relaxed for a second. He seemed to be thinking. "The commandant did not say you would be doing so, sir; however, I will be pleased to assist you in any way possible."

"Good. First, I would like to know about the three men executed for the murder of Frau Schütz."

"Do you know their numbers?"

"No."

"It is easier if the numbers are known, but, never fear, I shall find them." He scurried to a set of cabinets filled with ledgers. He moved about half a dozen off the top, then looked inside the one underneath. "Let's see . . . ah, here." He picked up a pen and a notepaper. "The first was a Gypsy, 175267.

The second, a political, 172532. The third, another political, 173544."

"Did they have names?" asked Max.

"Sometimes," shrugged Gissinger. "I will get them. They're in another book."

"Why?"

"Because this is just the book of criminal executions."

"And those other books?"

"Deaths of other sorts."

"What other sorts?"

"Deaths," said Gissinger.

"Executions? Accidents?"

"I believe the usual cause is typhus."

Max picked up the top book. It was dusty. "Do you mean to say that typhus has been epidemic since the camp was founded?"

Gissinger licked his cracked lips. "Yes."

"And the prisoners haven't been fumigated?"

"Every week, sir."

"Then the typhus shouldn't have spread."

Gissinger shrugged.

"These sanitary measures should have stopped the typhus."

Gissinger shrugged.

"Do you know what I think? I think if there were this much typhus in the camp that it would constitute a danger to the guards and the officers. Have any of them ever come down with it?"

"I wouldn't know, sir. I'm just a clerk." Gissinger tried to go for another set of books, but Max held his arm.

"Tell me, with no evasions, how one dies of typhus here."

Gissinger's face was emotionless. "Each morning the commandant vets the work force. Those whose work has slowed are obviously suffering from typhus. In order to protect the others, those who are infected are removed. Some days it is only two or three. On other days, none. Usually it is more."

" 'Removed' means killed?"

"Yes, sir." The clerk's face remained a blank. "You seem surprised," he finally volunteered.

"Why does he bother with calling it typhus?"

"Because it is, sir."

"But it isn't."

"If you say so, sir."

"Very well," said Max, letting him go.

Gissinger pulled down another set of books. He opened the first and put it aside. He opened the second and put it aside. In the third his skinny fingers trailed across the pages until he found 172532. "Here. A Communist. Draga Komnoliakov. Born approximately 1930. Occupation: carpenter's apprentice. Uncircumcised."

"He was fourteen?"

"It isn't certain."

"That's impossible."

"Impossible, sir?"

Max held his thought. "It just seems unlikely a fourteen-year-old could be much of a Communist."

"It does not say the circumstances of his arrest, but I can obtain those records if you like. I suppose the previous clerk could have made a mistake in recording the birthdate."

"Never mind."

"They're in the storeroom in the next building."

"Go on with this."

173544 was a Bogolyub Chirkin. Born 1884, he was an uncircumcised church janitor. The word "Communist" was also the only description of his crime. 175267 was known only as Tallinn. Birthdate unknown. Occupation: itinerant sign painter. It did not say he was uncircumcised, though a Gypsy would presumably be so. Perhaps it was only Communists who were also suspected of being Jews, thought Max.

"I am somewhat surprised," ventured Max. "They seem an unlikely group of conspirators."

"I am sure there are many unholy alliances in Ostheim. Among the prisoners, I mean."

"Ah." Max scanned the stacked ledgers. He had an idea. "Are these cross-indexed for occupations?"

"Of course, sir. I implemented that procedure myself. When a particular skill is needed—"

"Good. Find me the sign painters."

"Would you be needing a sign made, sir?"

"Find them." Max waited in a chair until the clerk had finished. He came up with three. Only one was still alive. Max then asked for a list of anyone who might have similar skills, such as artists, book illuminators, printers, calligraphers. Ten artists were found and three printers. All were dead.

"Artists have weak constitutions," shrugged Gissinger.

"The typhus," said Max.

"Of course," said Gissinger.

Already an hour had passed, but Max was afraid to think what would have been involved if the records were not so carefully kept and cross-indexed, something Gissinger took obvious pride in, though he was quick to say it was all done by Schütz's orders.

"All right, then," said Max. "I want to know about the women assigned to the brothel, particularly since last May."

"Do you know their numbers?"

"No. Nor their names. I simply want to know who was there and where they are now."

"This may take time. May I get you some tea? Would you like to return later?"

"No. I will sit here. Just pretend I'm not here."

"Yes, sir."

While Gissinger scurried from stack to stack and ledger to ledger, occasionally pausing at the file cabinet to check the cross-indexing, Max drummed his fingers on the desk top and considered the case. The most obvious thing these records had brought to light was the age of the "conspirators." The photograph of the three men dangling from the cruel loops of barbed wire ordered by Captain von Rauschwald showed two men probably in their twenties and one much older. Yet the documents said they were a teenager, a sexagenarian, and one whose age was about fifty. It would make a peculiar group to attempt an escape together. The two politicals might find common ground with the Gypsy, and it was even possible that three men of various ages would ally themselves under the circumstances, but even allowing for the tortured, starved expressions, the shaved heads, and the protruding tongues, it was obvious two of the hanged men were in their mid-twenties. Either the wrong men had been hanged, or the wrong men had been recorded as hanged. Why? Could it be that Schütz had arranged the murder of his wife and then protected the murderers by hanging three other prisoners at random? How could he do that? Max perused the clerk scribbling, scurrying, scribbling. Was Gissinger an accomplice? All

this cross-indexing could easily ferret out the hardened criminals willing to butcher Frau Schütz, but Max couldn't put it
all together. If the hanged men were the murderers, executed
to silence them, why pretend they were a carpenter's apprentice, a church warden, and a sign painter? If the hanged men
were Komnoliakov, Chirkin, and Tallinn, why did only one
appear to be the right age? The older man could be Chirkin,
but the other two? Once again Max felt he was missing
something any policeman would have noticed immediately.
He struck the table. "Damn!"

"Sir?"

"Nothing. Are you finished yet?"

"Only a minute, sir. Only a minute."

Max perused the ledger Gissinger had been working on.
"Clerk," he asked, "what is this?"

"Those? The efficiency reports."

"Explain."

"Well, sir, the relative output of labor is carefully calculated
with breakdowns as to age group, nationality, sex, and previous occupation. Ratios are done according to the expenses—
food, clothing, barracks, etc.—and the work output. This way
analyses can be done as to which national group is most
useful in getting certain assignments done."

"Oh?"

"Yes. For example, this month's figures indicate a clear
superiority of Byelorussian Communists at quarry work,
whereas Ruthenian farmers, as might be expected, are best at
hauling heavy loads."

"What is meant by 'clear superiority'?"

"It is a formula, devised in Berlin, which combines four
important categories of success: food intake, longevity, work
accomplishment, and servility. Each is given a score from one
to five, which is multiplied by—"

"And what is the goal of all this?"

"I cannot speak for the overall intention, as I am merely an
accountant, so to speak, but it is my understanding that, as
larger areas come into the dominion of the Third Reich, it will
be easier to use the subjugated peoples to the best advantage."

"Ah," said Max.

Gissinger eventually finished his notes. Nearly twenty-five
women had worked at the brothel since May 1. Most did not

last more than a couple of weeks. A twelve-year-old, one of the toughest, had lasted nearly a month before becoming one of the five who were all reassigned in the four days following the murder. Nearly half had lost their jobs after catching a disease. They were reassigned to the infirmary, where they inevitably died of the illness. "Are these illnesses recorded somewhere?" asked Max. "Are there death certificates?"

"Yes," said Gissinger. "The certificates themselves are in the storeroom."

"Please get them."

"I am not supposed to leave."

"You are under orders."

"Yes, sir. I will hurry, sir."

The women held nothing in common besides their deaths and their endless, doleful nights. They ranged in age from twelve to forty-two. Their weights, hair color, and nationality varied. One ledger even recorded the dimensions of their bodies, including the diameters (when extended) of the anal and vaginal orifices. They were indicated to have accepted duty in the brothel as volunteers. Max considered that likely, given the alternative. For all the details, however, there was nothing to indicate any relationship between the prostitutes and the hanged men. Several of them had been married, but there was no indication to whom. There were no names anything like Komnoliakov, Chirkin, or Tallinn.

Max closed the ledger with disgust. Another dead end. He sat still for a moment. It seemed silly, but he felt like crying. He was six again and his nurse had just died. He was twelve and his father had barely noticed the birthday gift Max had chosen for him. Max stood and paced furiously. These pendulum moods, swinging without warning, confusing whatever rational processes he needed, they had to end. The stiff leg was always with him, the missing arm was always missing, but these emotions randomly raising and lowering him were worse torment. He deliberately thought of Bette in an attempt to break the morose spirit that had seized him, but, like all loves, there was a germ of sadness in it too. In the end, one is always alone.

Gissinger finally returned. He held out a sheaf of papers, many of which had already yellowed on the edges. "The certificates, sir. Just as I promised. All twenty-five."

Max snatched them as if annoyed, then leafed through them. Two died of septic abscesses several weeks after the transfer. Six had died of "injuries sustained in road construction." Ten had died of the ubiquitous typhus. Seven, including the five who had been transferred out of the brothel after the murder, were said to have died of syphilis.

"This is ridiculous," said Max. "No one dies of syphilis this quickly."

"The deaths were all certified by Dr. Frank, sir."

"They could be certified by Hitler himself and still be ludicrous. Syphilis is a slow, progressive disease. That is its horror."

"I wouldn't know, sir," said Gissinger. "Perhaps they were not in condition to resist it."

Max closely studied Gissinger. "So, you trusted Dr. Frank?"

"Of course, sir," he said blankly.

"No. I don't mean 'Of course, sir,' I mean you trusted him in a way you would not trust, say, Commandant Schütz or Captain von Rauschwald or Lieutenant Pevner."

Gissinger's eyes flicked from side to side. "I trust all of you, sir, but—"

"But?"

"But Dr. Frank was a humanitarian. We are all sorry for his death."

Max thought of the air bubbles. Perhaps the fat drunk *was* a sort of humanitarian. His signatures on the death certificates grew progressively more illegible. For the five who had "died" after Frau Schütz, Max couldn't make out the letters of Frank's name. He considered the possibility that the illegible signatures might be forgeries, that Frank never saw these five women, but rejected it. A forger, after all, would make certain that Frank's signature was legible. The most telltale sign was on the certificate of the girl who had started at age twelve, one of the middle letters of the signature trailing down into a single line, dropping off the bottom of the sheet like a bird shot out of the sky. Frank had obviously passed out in the middle of his name and finished it later.

"He was somewhat annoying, however, sir. Commandant Schütz had to reprimand him for being so slow at filling out the certificates. It interfered with the records process."

"He was," said Max slowly, "very busy."

"There were sometimes several hundred to be filled out per day."

"I understand," said Max. "He had no other doctors to help him."

"Usually prisoners with medical experience would assist him, administer injections, and so forth. For several months, a veterinarian from Lemberg assisted in the operations, but he caught cold and died of pneumonia."

"There are—what?—five thousand inmates here?"

"As of this morning, precisely four thousand, nine hundred and eighty-two."

"That is like being one doctor for an entire city."

"And then there are five hundred and seventy-two staff, excluding the officers' families and the desertions last night."

"Desertions?"

"Some of the young Byelorussians were panicked by the bombing. Two were caught." Gissinger looked at the clock. "They will have been executed by now, sir."

"Clerk, tell me, if there are some five thousand prisoners, why are they assigned six-digit numbers? Is there any significance to them?"

"Many people pass through Ostheim, sir."

"Not a hundred and seventy-five thousand!"

"No," said Gissinger. "About twelve thousand have been here since the founding. I have the exact figures—" He scurried after one of his ledgers.

"Seven thousand have been killed?"

"Died, sir. Quarry work, roadwork, is dangerous. Many get ill."

"And the numbers?"

"I believe, sir, that Commandant Schütz has chosen six digits with an eye to the future. Numbers are, of course, more efficient than names, which are similar sometimes." He patted the tattoo on his forearm. "But this cannot be defaced. And how many possible combinations are there in six digits? You see what I am saying, sir."

"The commandant expects to have had a million inmates at some time?"

"His stated goal is a permanent population of twenty thousand in Ostheim, then he will open his second workplace, three hundred kilometers further east."

"Ah. In the middle of the Red Army. Herr Schütz is quite a dreamer."

Gissinger shrugged. It was not a humorous shrug, thought Max, nor one that held any hope the Russians might end the war and Gissinger's imprisonment. Curiously, Gissinger was showing pride in his juggling of figures for Schütz. He could be sent back into the other compound at any whim of the commandant's, yet he went on quietly doing his statistics and keeping his records like any bureaucrat in Vienna or Berlin or Prague.

Max shuffled the death certificates. "God! I must be losing my mind. You haven't given me any of the records of the madam, this Tanya, as she calls herself."

Gissinger bobbed his head, as if tentatively bowing. "I'm sorry, sir. My stupidity, absolutely. I assumed you meant only the workers. Tanya is on the level of a barracks orderly, and therefore falls into a different category. Barracks orderlies, as trustee prisoners, are referenced in—" He pulled down a ledger with a blue stripe. "She shouldn't be hard to find. There aren't many female barracks orderlies. . . ."

"And what is your interest in our Tanya, colonel?"

Max almost dropped the sheaf of death certificates. Schütz stood in the open door, his bald forehead beaded in sweat.

"Why, it is part of the investigation. Of your wife's murder, major." He inflected the last word in a weak attempt to regain some of the advantage seized by Schütz's sudden return.

Schütz raised an eyebrow. "Yes, well. You have taken care of that for a while, haven't you? My enemies will be pleased with their little count." He gestured at Gissinger in irritation. "Put that away. The Wehrmacht colonel and I—the SS major—will talk." He walked straight into his office. Max glanced at Gissinger, who slowly closed his ledger, then followed Schütz.

"Close the door," said Schütz. "Sit." He poured himself a glass of water. He waited for Max to settle into the chair in front of the desk, then paced to his own chair, slowly drained his water, and sat. "Well, my little count, you have scuttled me."

"I am afraid I don't understand you."

"Don't you?" Schütz reddened. "I asked you to please get this ridiculous investigation over with. I begged you to consider the impact that dragging it out might have."

"Asked?" said Max. "Begged? You were curt, abusive, and not at all helpful. Perhaps if you had—"

"Nonsense. It never mattered what I did. Never! I know why you're here. You may mince around here trying to look busy, but I know exactly what you are. You were sent here to keep the cloud of my wife's death over Ostheim and my eastern colonization plans. That's all. No one in Berlin cares about Lila's death. It's just political. You cannot deny it."

Max spoke coldly. If he had ever seemed "formal" as Bette had said, he wanted to seem absolutely glacial to the commandant. "I know only that I have been sent here to look into your report. If you would care to illuminate for me my actual motives, I shall be happy to consider the rightness of your analysis."

"Stop it," said Schütz with dismay. "Your mouth's so full of shit you're stinking up my office. You have succeeded, colonel. You may now take all the time you wish. In the end, you will go back to Berlin and tell them with all earnestness that a lengthy and extensive study has proven that, indeed, three prisoners murdered Frau Schütz."

"I do not know that for a fact, major. I may never know who killed your wife, but I find it quite unbelievable that the three hanged men did it."

"Please! You can stop now. The Führer isn't coming."

"Excuse me?"

"The Führer. His office now claims to have other business. He will not be coming as scheduled."

Max's mind flashed over Oskar's cryptic messages. "Adolf Hitler was coming here?"

"It took me months to persuade him. I had to bribe his secretary out of my own pocket to get my letters to him."

"The Führer was coming all the way to Ostheim?"

"You play the dupe quite well, colonel. Of course he was coming."

"I did not know."

"Undoubtedly."

"I swear to you I did not know."

Schütz grunted.

"Why would the Führer come to Ostheim?"

"To tour it. To see the possibilities in building a string of camps all the way to the Yellow River. To see that my leader-

ship qualities have been unjustly neglected." Schütz plucked
a framed note off the wall and shoved it at Max:

This SS Major Schütz's colonizing the East seems worth
looking into.

The Führer

"You see he has a particular interest in Ostheim."
"This hardly seems a strong endorsement."
"It got Ostheim founded."
Max thought of the way subordinates always rush around
pretending to understand not only their superiors' remarks,
but even their vaguest wishes. It led to command errors all
too frequently. Hitler had said Ostheim was worth looking
into, then someone had ordered it be built, then further down
the chain someone with actual knowledge of supplies, etc.,
had tried to patch it together out of misfit soldiers and baling
wire. He almost laughed. "Forgive me, commandant, but if I
were the Führer, I don't think I would be very interested, at
the height of the war, in taking a tour of this camp. Especially
since there are other camps, as I understand it, much closer
to Berlin."
"You imagine the Führer of the German people is afraid of
bombs? Nonsense! Four days ago, the Allies massively bombed
Munich. Yesterday, they did it again. Do you think our Führer
will stay out of Munich? Of course not. I have it on the best
authority that he, in fact, may visit the city in full splendor,
merely to raise the spirits of the population. Can you imagine
our Führer's sense of duty is such that he would scurry
underground at the sound of planes? Nonsense!"
"But he must stay near his general staff. I repeat: there are
camps closer to Berlin, aren't there?"
"And so far as I know he has never been in one, personally.
Why should he not, therefore, come to see the only one built
with an eye to the future."
"My God, man, the Russians are practically over the hill. I
would think the strafing had more to do with the cancellation
than any suspicion that you might be a murderer. You have
murdered seven thousand people here. What would my investigation matter?"
"Murder? I have murdered no one."

"And what is it you think you are doing with your prisoners?"

"This is a work camp. They are the workers. Some of them are obviously genetically inferior and need to be removed. If you have a chicken and it ceases to lay eggs, you throw it in the pot. If you have a cow and her milk production drops, you turn her into stew."

"Please. Next you'll be saying that the weakest of your slaves should be ground into sausage."

"In fact," said Schütz casually, "I know that at some of the other camps quite useful bodily products have been made from the inmates: leather, for example. Wigs."

"Very funny."

"Oh, don't get upset." Schütz was amused. "We are not discussing cannibalism. I would never corrupt a fine German sausage with the putrid flesh of these creatures."

"Why not, major? They are merely breeding stock, according to you."

"I would think, for an anthropologist, that the breeding of good stock should not seem so unusual to you, that the process of natural selection could be infinitely improved by human intervention. Consider these Americans. Do you think they could have produced physical specimens like Jesse Owens and Joe Louis without the advantages of the selective breeding of slaves? There are no remarkable athletes among the Africans. Instead you get deformities, like Pygmies."

Max thought to say the Bantus were extraordinarily tall, the Zulus physically formidable, but he merely shook his head. To say anything like that would be participating in Schütz's argument. It was not the point whether Africans were inferior to Aryans, or Pygmies degenerate. It was somehow the idea that a beady-eyed, bald sausagemaker had taken it upon himself to decide who deserved crossbreeding and who didn't. He inhaled deeply. "And you purport this to be the policy of Berlin? To exterminate the inferior?"

"Inasmuch as they are not useful. We have seized history, my little count. We have dared go beyond the conventions of morality. I know your type. You prefer to imagine cognac when you taste cheap brandy. But what did you think was going on? You knew. Somewhere deep in you, you knew.

Furthermore, somewhere inside you, you know we are right. You are German, after all. It's in the blood."

Max spoke almost in a monotone. "You can't accuse me of that. My blood may be diluted. I was born in the Sudetes, I was educated in Austria."

"Pah! Look at you," said Schütz. "Those are all the German homeland. The Führer himself was born in upper Austria."

Max nodded.

Schütz stood and went after more water. "Would you like a drink? You seem quite dried up."

Max shook his head.

"I am operating here with many handicaps. With the right equipment, I could handle thousands more. And well. I was counting on the Führer to see that and authorize the appropriate expenditures. You have given me a momentary setback, you and your Lieutenant Colonel Hüber, but I am far from finished. I will triumph over all you petty politicians. The new world needs vision, not cowardice. Are you sure you won't have water? It is from Wiesbaden. Perhaps you'd prefer to scamper back to your room and drink brandy with your sergeant."

"He had a right to get drunk. He did *his* duty against an armed enemy."

"Next you'll be saying Klaus Frank was an eminent physician. I was really quite kind when I spoke at his grave this afternoon."

"That must have been difficult for you."

"As a matter of fact, it was. He deserved the pit."

"And after all those people he murdered for you, the twelve-year-old whores—"

"Frank did me no favors. At first, always whining about lack of supplies; later, disappearing for days and falling out of chairs. I didn't tell him what to do."

"So he didn't say thousands died of typhus on your account?"

"Typhus? Of course not. He was merely there to write the death certificate. What he said they died of did not concern me."

Max thought of the prostitutes said to die of syphilis. Was this Frank's way of leaving a message to anyone who knew about the normal course of the disease? Could he have believed that by making Ostheim appear a hotbed of typhus that he could have the place shut down? Whatever he thought he was doing, his motives were lost forever. Without looking at Schütz, Max continued in a low voice. "And you take no shame in personally ordering the deaths of so many civilians?"

"Shame? How preposterous! This is a war. Or didn't you notice?"

"I fought soldiers, not impoverished villagers."

"This isn't the Thirty Years' War, colonel. What the Wehrmacht has failed to grasp is that this is modern war, total war. The enemy is not just foreign troops. It is foreigners. It is the festering corruption of years of racial degeneracy and systemic betrayal. You cannot merely meet your enemies on a field of honor any more. Never again will the great struggles between nations take place solely between armies. This is a struggle of faith. We intend to make a new world in which the superior can advance civilization. The Bolsheviks, they wish to perpetuate their religion of the uncivilized proletariat— the gospel of weakness according to the Jew Marx."

"And the British and Americans?"

"They're both alike," sneered Schütz, "they want the world like it was."

"Like it was when?"

"Whenever. They only know the modern world makes them sick."

"And you feel not the slightest guilt that your soldiers have kicked living babies into a fire." Max said it as a statement.

"I pay no attention to how they carry out my orders. These Slavs we use for soldiers are typically dullards. They aren't German after all. It is only the result that matters."

"I suppose you enjoy choosing who will die."

Schütz finished his water and sat, lacing his fingers over his stomach. "Why do you wish to make me out to be a monster? What does enjoyment have to do with it? Each morning I study the efficiency reports. If a particular squad fails to be as productive as we require, I choose a minimum of one out of ten to be removed. It is a fine proportion, one validated traditionally and employed by the Roman Empire. I write up the list and pass it to my clerk. The next morning, at roll call, the examples are made. Rarely do I do anything personally. I hardly ever watch. I think it is better for the men to let off steam. You see, you don't have to be born a count to be an effective commander."

"And the prostitutes, major, how do you measure their efficiency? How is it that you ordered the deaths of all who were there the night your wife was killed? And how is it that you have kept this Tanya alive?"

Schütz twisted his face. "The girls pick up diseases, as I am sure you know. I suggest you read the appropriate passages in *Mein Kampf.* The Jews have spread these diseases to weaken us. We cannot allow their spreading them among the troops."

"Or the officers."

"Of course. In any case, whatever you are implying makes no sense. I usually assigned them to Dr. Frank's care."

"I see. You wash your hands of whores' deaths. You take full credit for babies."

Schütz laughed. "You are trying to anger me. I will not let you succeed. I do not recall having reassigned all of the prostitutes after my wife's death. I was upset at the time, so perhaps I did not notice."

"You were not too upset to make up your lists. You were not too upset to undertake a lengthy report on Lila's murder."

"That was my duty. My little count, I hope all this trying to make something out of nothing pleases you. It is getting on toward dinnertime. But don't let me rush you. Take all the time in the world. Now that you've sabotaged the Führer's visit, I don't care if you stay in Ostheim until the winter."

"Just one other thing. Why didn't you also eliminate Tanya?"

"And I told you I don't eliminate the whores, I merely reassign them."

"To their deaths."

"People die," said Schütz. "This surprises you?" He grinned, then picked at the edge of his blotter. "Very well. I take a special interest in Tanya. Not only is she an excellent administrator, but she has always given me special care. I don't want her passed among the troops."

"She might give them something."

"What do you mean?"

"I mean you two likely share more than a bed."

· 199 ·

Schütz gaped.

"According to Dr. Frank, Lila carried syphilis. That means, I assume, that you likely carry it, and ergo, Tanya."

"Dr. Frank was lying."

"Oh? And is that why you always drink water? It is pretty unusual for a man to drink so much water. Isn't it because alcohol is not recommended for people suffering genital diseases?"

Schütz exploded. "Slander! Slander of the worst sort! How convenient for you to say what Dr. Frank said. A dead swine supports the accusations of a living one. Mineral water purifies the body. The new Germany cannot afford decisions made by people whose bodies are corrupted. A leader has obligations you, with your private cellars and imported liqueurs, will never understand. This discussion is terminated. If you must go on with your nosing, please stop meddling in the private affairs of Ostheim's staff. Hasn't your Lieutenant Colonel Hüber told you to go?"

Max stood. "You've been reading my messages."

"So? I have a right to know what goes on in my camp."

"Those were secret messages. Your men had no right to convey them to you."

"They had every right. I ordered them. Didn't you think I would?"

Max glared at him. Of course he thought Schütz would. Those two in the communications room were obviously Schütz's puppets, but Max never expected the brazenness of the admission. "And did you search my quarters also?"

"What for? You have nothing that interests me." Nausea rose from Max's stomach. He hated this man. He hated Ostheim. He hated everything. He turned, shoved the chair aside so violently that it tumbled on its side. As he passed Gissinger, huddled over the figures in one of his ledgers, Schütz began to laugh—a great, uproarious, demonic laugh of triumph.

"Take your time, colonel!" Schütz yelled. "Take forever! It no longer matters!"

· *Sixteen* ·

Max went immediately to his quarters. The older orderly saluted him as he came in, but Max barely flicked his hand and did not say "Heil Hitler." Sitting on the edge of his bed, he rested his elbow on his knee and his head in his hand. He did not move for some time. He went through the pieces he remembered of the bewildering—what was it?— argument? discussion? It hadn't flowed so much as tumbled forward. Schütz angry, wiping the sweat from his bald head. Max angry. Schütz indifferent. Max demoralized. Every so many days, one out of ten. You, you, you, and you. Bang. Into the pit. Max's head spun. He squeezed the bridge of his nose between thumb and forefinger so strongly he almost thought he would crush it, yet he held on. If he let go, his head might burst, it might spin out of control, or he might simply wake up, and then, whatever he was, whoever he was, he could fall asleep and have this nightmare again. He could not bear to have this nightmare again.

There was a knocking at the door. He did not look up. The door opened.

"Colonel, can I fetch you any supper?" It was Kleini.

"No," said Max. "I'm exhausted. I need to sleep."

"As you say, sir. Perhaps a tray, in case you wake up?"

"No, really."

"Let me help you get undressed."

"No. Please. Just leave me."

"As you say. May I ask, however, when you anticipate leaving Ostheim?"

"I don't know," said Max. "Ask me tomorrow. I'll tell you tomorrow."

"Very good," said Kleini. "Sleep well."

The door clicked shut. Max finally looked up. Perhaps he should eat. Maybe this dizziness, this ringing in his ears came from hunger. But he did not call out. Kleini's irregular footsteps faded down the corridor. The room was silent. He felt like he was in one of the empty chambers of an enormous pyramid, surrounded by tons of stones. His breathing grew faster. His heart raced until he pressed his hand against it. Cold sweat trickled in the track of the scar from his ear to his jaw. With considerable effort, he raised himself from the bed and crossed to the dressing table. He paused for a moment, looking at himself in the mirror. Grim eyes, hollow eyes. The flush across his forehead and on his cheeks seemed almost separate from the pale cast of his skin, as if it were a reddish slick floating on the layer of sweat.

He opened the drawer quickly and pulled out his shaving kit. He lifted the lid and took one vial of morphine. He froze, staring at it for some time. He licked his lips. He drifted backward to his bed and sat again, still staring into the vial as if it might, like a crystal ball, reveal the ultimate meaning of it all: what people are capable of, what makes them capable of it, what was left when you peeled a person to the bone, and what was left when a mind was peeled to the bone. He murmured to himself:

> (Come in under the shadow of this red rock),
> And I will show you something different from either
> Your shadow at morning striding behind you
> Or your shadow at evening rising to meet you;
> I will show you fear in a handful of dust.

His hand closed on the vial, squeezing it, squeezing it, as if he could crush it and the cool death of morphine could penetrate his palm and flood into his brain. He squeezed until his arm ached, until the veins on his hand and wrist looked ready to burst, then he groaned and fell back on the bed, the morphine hot under his now weakened and quivering fingers.

Sometime after that, he fell asleep. When? For how long? But fingers were gently unbuttoning his tunic. He jerked. A moist palm pressed against his lips. Ssssh! said the woman.

"Bette," he said, dropping his head back.

"Sssh, you were dreaming," she whispered. "You were talking. I think you were giving a speech. You used words like 'the Fatherland,' 'Teutonic,' and 'salvation.' You said something about an Ulf Biedermeyer."

"Ulf Biedermeyer died," said Max. "Many died."

"Rest," she said. "I will undress you."

"Ulf was a lieutenant. He had big green eyes. He was hanging a grenade on his belt when it went off. No one knew why."

"Rest," she said.

He lay peaceful for a moment, then suddenly sprang up. He grasped her shoulder, dropping the vial of morphine to the floor. "No," he said. "We must go."

"Where?"

"Anywhere. Away from here. I know a clearing in the jungle. There's an abandoned rubber plantation there."

She stretched over him, groped, and picked up the vial. She read it, then looked at him in alarm. "You've poisoned yourself!"

"No," he said. "No." He pulled her close, pressed his cheek against hers. "No. I couldn't leave you here. I'd be alone wherever I went. I love you."

Her answer was somewhat detached. "You want to make love again?"

"No. Not now. I want you to go and get your things. I want to get you out of here as quickly as I can. Everybody wants me to leave, why shouldn't I?"

She pulled away and examined his face. "But Lila's murder . . ."

"It doesn't matter—how can it matter? Let the dead bury the dead; there's certainly enough of them."

"What will I tell Joachim?"

"Tell him you love me. Do you love me?"

"I don't know. I don't think you really know. There's been so much happening. Everything that seemed so hopeful five years ago has fallen to pieces. It's natural we should try to find peace in each other. We could be mistaking these moments of peace for love."

He tried to raise himself again. "Why do you say these things? Last night was the only full time of joy I have known for years. Maybe ever. You gave me back my life. Your coming to me again can give us both another. Ostheim is hell. Let's put it behind us and find some place to wait out this war."

"And my children?"

"Bring them too. We will take them to my home. I think I will like children. I used to watch the Carachacho children playing near the camp fire. Yes, I think I will like children. There are many rooms in my house, and the Sudetes are lovely in the summer and fall."

"Joachim would never let me take his children. Commandant Schütz would never let one of his marriages break up."

"What has Schütz to do with it? We will leave, pure and simple. We will take your children and leave."

"I've thought about it all day. Part of me aches to run away with you. Life was one monotonous note until you came. Now it's like there is music in things. Everything is different, but—"

He clasped her neck and pulled her mouth to his. She immediately softened. They kissed desperately. They fumbled with buttons and belts and uncooperative sleeves, barely separating their lips to slip clothing over their heads. They made love with her astride him, her breasts teasing his face, forgetting that his trousers were only pulled below his knees and that he was still wearing his boots. As they finished, she settled atop him, her knees bent up on each side of his hips, her moist collarbone against his forehead, her hands squeezing his shoulders. He felt the warm fluid draining from her belly into his pubic hair and tasted the sweat on her throat and breasts.

"We must get away," he whispered. "We must."

She began to weep. She bit her lower lip and sniffled. He kissed her tears. "All right," she said. "All right. But you must give me a few days. Then we'll go. Just a few days."

"I will work on the report nonstop," he said. "But as soon as I reach the last sentence we will go. No matter what."

She nodded, biting her lip again. She wept, her body quaking with the effort of suppressing it.

"What's the matter?" he said, as if soothing a child. "What's the matter?"

"I've been married so long. So long."

"But that is over," he said quietly. "You have a future now. You must forget the past. We both have a future."

They slept then, with Max carefully wrapping his arm around her waist. He wouldn't let her slip away this night. He wouldn't let her sneak out of his window and walk home in the dark. Just before dawn, she stirred. She changed his bandage carefully, then they dressed, and he walked her out his door. He could hear her take a deep breath as if she were plunging into icy water, but the orderly was snoring loudly and they slipped away, apparently unseen, just before they heard the guards begin rousing the prisoners. She led him to the back of her cottage, then paused. She leaned close, pecked him on the ear, and said only, "Good night." The door closed. He stood alone in the early morning light, the scent of her hair lingering in his nostrils, frozen momentarily by the sensation of a vacuum where she had been.

The squawk of a raven startled him. He looked about, then quickly walked back to his office. He took a sheaf of paper from the desk. He carefully filled his fountain pen and thought. His strategy, he finally decided, was to state the facts as simply and as objectively as possible. He would not introduce theories. Though he might point out the more dubious of Schütz's conclusions, he would not imply the commandant had engaged in anything other than some questionable reasoning. The prisoners, after all, might have killed Lila Schütz, despite Max's strong feeling they hadn't, and, as repugnant as Schütz was, there was nothing provable to connect the commandant or anyone else to that night. The point, after all, was to forget Lila Schütz and get himself and Bette out of Ostheim. Nothing could help Lila now. If he worked hard enough on the report, he might wear down whatever scruples he had about ending his investigation this way. From the beginning, he should have faced the fact that he was no detective and should not have let his instant dislike of Schütz or his pleasure at playing Sherlock Holmes hold him in Ostheim for the past month. Kleini was right. He should get out of here, as soon as possible. Write the report and go. It was ironic, he thought, that once Schütz did not care whether he stayed or not, he had determined to leave as quickly as he could.

Max had written very little by eight-thirty, however. It was always difficult to get something as complicated as this started, and he had done little more than scribble the date: "18 July 1944," and the title (he had taken too long with the title), "An Investigation into the Circumstances of the Murder of Frau Schütz, Done at the Request of the Reichsführung SS." The introductory section was to be a mere statement of his orders and that he had been personally authorized by Reichsführer Himmler himself, but he thought better of the way he had drifted into an apologia for his own inexperience as a criminal investigator—thereby calling into question Himmler's judgment and the significance of his own words—so he was in the process of striking out most of two pages when Kleini tapped on the door.

"What is it?"

"Nothing, sir," said the sergeant. "I was waiting for you at your quarters. When you didn't call for me . . ."

"I decided to get an early start."

"You have eaten?"

Max remembered he hadn't. Perhaps that was why the writing was so torturous. "I would appreciate something, in fact, Kleini. Something for energy, but not too heavy."

"I'll see what they have. And then, I believe, you want to interview prisoners?"

"No."

"Then someone else?"

"No."

Kleini waited for an explanation. Max dropped his eyes. Yesterday, he had been so determined to carry out the investigation to wherever it would reach. Today, he was determined to end it. The change might seem unstable. Kleini had seen the morphine vials. "My research in the prisoners' files," he said, pretending to study some of his notes, "obviated the need for personal inquiries. Therefore, I am beginning the report. You may get a typewriter for us, and loosen up your fingers."

Kleini almost smiled. "We will be finished soon?"

"In a few days, at most."

"That is good," said the sergeant, but he was not as happy as Max would have expected.

"What is it, Kleini?"

"Field Marshal Rommel was wounded seriously yesterday."

Max dropped his pen. After some time he finally asked, "Will he die?"

Kleini shrugged. "His car was strafed."

Max shook his head. Out of the whole bloody war a single car gets strafed and one man is hit. It might seem like fate, but it wasn't. Max sighed and shook his head again. "Let's hope he lives." Kleini nodded.

After several seconds, the sergeant opened the door. "I will fetch a breakfast for you." He was halfway through when he turned back. "Colonel, settle my curiosity, do you have enough on Schütz?"

"Excuse me?"

"Will you finish Schütz?"

"There is nothing to prove he did it."

"Too bad."

"Why?"

"I bet Duitser, and a few others, that you were the man to bring him down."

Max closed his pen. "I'm sorry. Will you lose much?"

"More than I like, but less than I expected to win."

"So the odds were against me?"

"They underestimated you. I still think so. Pah! Ostheim is a fart: it's best to leave it behind."

Max nodded. The door closed. Rommel! He was unable to write any more until Kleini returned with a warmed-over berry fritter. He turned his chair around and ate staring out the window at Baranovitch inspecting his guards. The fritter was anything but light and the berries had become anonymously acidic from sitting. The "tea" was insipid, though fortified with goat's milk. After finishing it he remained at the window for another half hour, until the fritter settled, then he forced himself back to work.

He finished his introduction about ten-thirty, and decided to begin a chronology of the events of that night as they were known. He was well into this when he decided it was important to document the source of the events. For example, if Sovolevsky had noticed the light of Koshak's cigarette along the fence at about the time Koshak said he was at that place along the fence, then it would likely indicate that Koshak was not lying. Max considered placing footnotes to indicate sources, as if he were writing a scholarly treatise, but after situating about ten in the draft decided it would take too much time in the typing. Instead, he would be careful to insert phrases like, "according to Sgt. Külm," and so forth. The prose would be burdened and slowed down with these qualifiers, but it would make it look more thorough. He wasn't, after all, writing a novel. He went back through what he had written (the account up until nine of the night in question) and larded the paragraphs with them. His head ached. His neck and shoulders were as tight as the spring on a fieldpiece. He stretched. He paced outside. Ostheim was quiet. Very quiet. They were evidently not burning very many. A thin finger of black smoke was rising from the pit, then catching a high easterly and forming the upper arm of a huge swastika. At least it wasn't blowing directly into the cottages. He wondered if Bette had said anything to her husband yet.

He returned inside and scanned what he had written. He struggled with the window, and eventually managed to open it. He noticed Pevner and several of the unmarried lieutenants joking on their way from the officers' mess. He thought to break for lunch, but the fritter still lay heavy in his stomach. No, the more he got finished, the sooner he could forget Lila Schütz. He felt guilty for thinking that, and muttered "I'm sorry" to whatever ghost might be listening. He perused his notes and picked up his pen.

He spent all of that day and the next locked in his office scribbling. It was more painful than creeping at night across the cold desert sand in order to set up a dawn ambush. One word doggedly followed another just as he had once put one elbow in front of the other—right arm, left arm; right leg, left leg—crawling ever closer to the objective. He wouldn't allow himself to think how little he had written (other than letters) over the past few years. His mind was not in shape for it, and writing carefully was difficult enough without letting doubt slip in. He had to keep pushing at all costs. When a coherent section was finished, he had the orderly call for Kleini, who typed it on one of the special typewriters with a key for *SS*. Himmler and the rest would like that, Max thought.

Each evening, expecting Bette to return, Max sat on his bed proofreading what Kleini had typed, emending it, and sketching an outline for the next day. But she did not come, and though he longed for her, he was grateful. A night of lovemaking could slow him down even more. Eventually, he slept fitfully for a few hours, leaving his curtains open so that the earliest light would awaken him, then he returned to work despite the soreness in his leg, the stiffness in his shoulders. By the second day, only these pains kept him from dozing at his desk. Often, his mind wandered as he thought of how casual Schütz was about compassing the deaths of thousands of civilians. He also thought about Rommel. He fully expected to hear of the general's death each time Kleini brought him a meal, but there was no news, and that was good news. The longer Rommel survived, the likelier he was to recover. By the morning of the third day, Max had written fifty-seven pages and was moving into an evaluation of Schütz's conclusions. This was the most treacherous part and he had only done three pages by noon. He skipped lunch in favor of a pot of weak German tea. He was feeling stronger, however, as he could finally sense the end. He savored a vision of Bette and himself strolling among the horses on his lands. Soon Bette and he would be on their way west and he would be a father. To girls. How did one rear girls? Especially a six- and a seven-year-old?

At one-twenty, there was a commotion on the parade ground. Max had been trying to assess the necessity, in a report that would go on permanent file, of discussing Lila's sex life. It seemed cheap to make this gossip official, yet it was certainly relevant as a possible motive, either on Schütz's part or some overly serious lover's. The noise, however, frustrated him. He angrily turned to the window. Men were rushing to the communications room. The nasty woman with spectacles emerged and told them something. The Ukrainians and Byelorussians seemed confused and were translating for each other with animated gestures.

Peace? Max asked himself. My God, the war is over. But the faces weren't joyous, just confused. Rommel, he then thought. Damn.

He picked up his cane and rushed outside. He was in such a hurry, he nearly fell stepping off the porch. Schütz emerged hatless from his office with Gissinger behind him. He charged at the growing crowd: men in full uniform, men in their long underwear, Pevner trying to restore some semblance of order. Schütz pushed them aside, shouting. Some were astonished by this and immediately saluted him. Others merely stared, forgetting military protocol. Schütz entered the communications room. Several tried to crowd in after him, but with faces like two breeds of bulldog Pevner and Baranovitch pushed them back and off the porch.

Max grasped a young private as he ran by. The boy had an empty socket where his right eye should have been. "What is it?" said Max. "What has happened?"

"Hitler," gasped the boy. "The Führer is dead."

"What?"

"The Führer is dead."

Max let the boy's arm go and watched him run toward the gates, where the guards stared down from their towers to find out what was wrong. Max pushed his way through the group, accidentally kicking several men with his stiff leg. "Is it true?" he asked Pevner.

"There is a message the Führer has been assassinated. We are trying to get details. It could be some hoax. It must be a hoax. I don't believe it. Do you? What a cruel hoax!"

Max looked up at Baranovitch. The sergeant seemed unperturbed, but barely cocked an eyebrow as if to say, "What next?"

"We don't know it is true," said Pevner to the men. "It's some Russian or British hoax. The radio man said the voice sounded funny." He poked Baranovitch. "Tell them. They don't look like they understand."

"They understand," said Baranovitch.

"Tell them anyway."

Baranovitch's voice rumbled out only a few sentences, presumably in Byelorussian, and his men quieted, though they continued whispering among themselves or staring dumbfoundly at the door. Max noticed several prisoners who had been pulling thistles around the foundation of Schütz's stone office building. They, like Gissinger upon the porch, stood absolutely still, staring at the hubbub as if it were a supernatural manifestation.

Ten minutes passed before Schütz emerged. "Attention!" shouted Pevner, and all the soldiers snapped straight, even those in their underwear.

"We are having considerable difficulty in getting through to Berlin," said Schütz. "However, with great sadness I must report that the army units confirm this report. One unit has told me that a bomb was placed under the floor of the Führer's meeting room in Rastenburg. This is not proof, of course, but the likelihood of its being true is increasing. We must simply wait. I prefer to believe this is a hoax. Only a Jew would do something as cowardly as placing a bomb under the Führer's feet, and I frankly don't think it is possible."

"Herr Commandant!" shouted the radio man. Schütz went back inside. Max sighed and fell back against the wall. If Hitler were dead, the war was over. It would be Germany's way out. An end to the madness, finally.

Schütz emerged some time later with a slip of paper. He held it out at arm's length and read solemnly. "It seems that the report is true—that a bomb has killed our Führer. Evidently, the assassination has been accompanied by a putsch of some kind. The word 'Valkyrie' has been transmitted to various army groups, indicating that the Wehrmacht was involved." He crumpled the paper in his hand and threw it to the ground. "And we need ask why the Bolsheviks, the Americans, the faggot English have been pushing the German army back? Traitors! Traitors everywhere." He glared at Max so sharply that all heads turned. Max said nothing.

"Well, Colonel von Prokofsk, perhaps you already know what this 'Valkyrie' means."

Max stared back, but tried not to confront the commandant. He finally spoke, trying to sound naive. "The only Valkyries I know are on Captain von Rauschwald's records."

"No doubt," snapped Schütz. He spun on his heels and marched toward his office.

"Return to your posts," said Pevner. "We will keep everyone informed. There is much confusion." He too glared at Max, then went indoors. Baranovitch remained as expressionless as usual.

If the army had engineered the coup, Schütz might take revenge on the only army man available. Max decided to return to his room. He walked quickly. God knew what ideas the sight of Max's uniform might bring to Schütz's mind. Where was Kleini? What was the possibility of fleeing while Schütz was still lost in his amazement at Hitler's death?

A staff car rushed through the gate and came to a dusty stop just in front of Max. Von Rauschwald leaned out the window. He blinked his single eye as the dust swirled about them. "Is it true?" he asked.

"Evidently," said Max.

"Incredible!" said von Rauschwald, thinking. "Where are you going?"

"To my room. It is—it is quite a shock."

"No. Come with me. It's been weeks since we've had a drink together. You look like you need a drink. Incredible!"

Max numbly climbed into the car with von Rauschwald. He thought perhaps the captain's cottage was a better place to lie low than his own room, where Schütz could easily find him. Further, it might be useful to play up to von Rauschwald. Schütz might try anything now that the German state was headless. Max did not know exactly how much protection he might expect from the man he had cuckolded. It depended on what the captain knew. "My sergeant, Sergeant Klimmer," said Max, "do you think he may be in any danger?"

"What do you mean?" said von Rauschwald.

"If it turns out to be a Wehrmacht plot, will the men try to take it out on him?"

Von Rauschwald laughed. "Oh no. You underestimate the SS. This is a relief. We're not glad Hitler's dead, understand, but we're not sorry either."

"And what of your oath? How do you mean this?"

"The SS still holds the power, I would think. Himmler will be the new Führer. My loyalty will be to him. It is inevitable that the leader who is in power when things fall apart will bear responsibility for them, will pay for them whether he deserves it or not. Hitler has paid. The nation is renewed. Hitler alone was not Germany. He had, however, turned into a kind of invalid uncle lingering in his bed. You are sorry when he finally coughs his last, but you're relieved he is no longer suffering. Don't you agree?"

"I don't know," said Max carefully. "He has held us together for quite a while now."

"That's true," nodded von Rauschwald. "We had no future when he began."

"But what is our future now?"

"I don't think it may be as inauspicious as you do. A peace

· 212 ·

with the west, perhaps, then a common union against the Reds. After all, Britain and France are only allied with Stalin for convenience's sake."

"And the United States?"

"Will sail home and close themselves up, just like after the first war. I understand they sympathize with us anyway."

Max was about to say, "You've certainly thought all this out," but the car stopped in front of the "village" and children and wives rushed up to it. Little Klaus Frank had tears in his eyes. The boy had never known another leader. He had never known another form of government. The von Rauschwald girls, Greta and Hedwig, were holding each other around the waist. They didn't fully appreciate what was wrong, but their eyes flicked from side to side as they watched all the older people acting peculiar. Max noticed, however, that they did not rush to their father, as might be expected, but stood in the gate, often glancing back at their mother, who waited next to Ursule Frank. "Is it true?" asked Little Klaus.

"We think so," said von Rauschwald.

The boy clenched his fists and ground his teeth, his face reddening in futile adolescent rage. He choked up and ran away. Frau Kurzner called after him. "Little Klaus! Little Klaus!"

"Let him go," said Max. "It has been bad for him lately."

Frau Kurzner nodded.

Von Rauschwald walked past his girls without speaking. Bette did not seem disturbed that both her husband and her lover were approaching.

"So, someone got him," said Ursule.

"We think so," said von Rauschwald. "We don't yet know who is in charge."

"Will this end the war?" asked Bette.

"We can only hope," said Max.

"Do you really think so?" said the captain. "That would be too bad."

Max considered that, yes, some people had no real life without war. Von Rauschwald was one of them. "Yes. I think it will end."

"Too late for my Klaus," said Ursule coldly.

"What are we to do?" asked Bette.

"Wait," said von Rauschwald. "The colonel and I will have a drink. My driver is to keep me posted."

"And Schütz?"

"He is in his office."

"He is likely imagining," sneered Max, "that his enemies assassinated the Führer simply to close Ostheim."

"Come inside," said von Rauschwald.

Ursule gestured at the lawn table. "Why don't we all sit out here? I'll bring tea. I've made something like gingerbread."

"I'm not in the mood for a picnic," said von Rauschwald sharply. "After you, count?" He extended his arm in the direction of his cottage.

Max looked at Bette. If she was nervous about Max and her husband being together, she didn't show it. He said, as a reflex, "Won't you join us?" and then was horrified at the vision of the three of them together in a room.

"Thank you," she said, "but I'd prefer to be outside. I must watch the girls."

In the parlor, von Rauschwald carefully placed his hat on the arm of the chair and promptly crossed to the buffet. Although his head could easily clear the heavy cottage beams, Max lowered his head slightly and went to the settee opposite the huge fireplace. The room was as claustrophobic in the daytime as at night. The portrait of Hitler over his shoulder made him uneasy.

"Somewhere here is a recording of Siegfried's funeral march," said von Rauschwald. "It seems appropriate to the occasion. Ah, here it is." He took out his phonograph.

"It is inevitable that it will be played at the real funeral."

"It will be quite a state occasion." Von Rauschwald handed Max a very large Armagnac. "And what other music than Wagner? Surely your Mozart, your Bach never wrote such funeral music."

"They are your Mozart and Bach too. You forget Mozart's *Requiem,* and what of the *St. Matthew Passion?*" Max sipped the brandy cautiously. He was not about to get drunk with Bette's husband, even if there was no sign she had yet spoken to him. Why not? It had been over two days.

"Are you equating Hitler with Christ? That is clever. The *Hitler Passion.* He who lays down his life for the German race."

"That is hardly what I had in mind," said Max. "I was merely comparing Bach to Wagner. Each great composer has his own merits."

"Still," said von Rauschwald. "It is clever. Ah, imagine that as the centerpiece of a great eulogy. If only I were in a position to write such a speech! I could be sublime."

Max watched the motes swirling in the sunlight angling in from the back rooms. "I'm certain you'd do better than the type who usually makes speeches at state funerals."

"Do you think so?"

"Eulogies are usually so mechanical."

"This is true. I am a person of great passions. That is what Germany needs. The world thinks the Germans are intellectual, scientific, logical. That is only our disguise. We adopt it to conceal that we are really dominated entirely by passion, much more than the so-called Mediterranean hothead. National Socialism allows us to get in touch with ourselves. That is what Hitler unleashed. But," he added ruefully, "here I am in Ostheim." He quickly placed the needle upon the record and sat down, closing his eye. The strokes of the initial low kettle drums made von Rauschwald flinch, then the solemn music began to rise in its swirling intensity. When the woodwinds played their somber melody, Max's fingertips felt the vibrations in his glass. Von Rauschwald was totally involved, like a man breathlessly careening toward a sexual climax. When the recording ended, the needle scratched back and forth, tick-tick, tick-tick, maybe a dozen times before von Rauschwald finally opened his eye.

"There," he said. "That is the spirit of Germany. Its soul."

And Mozart? And Bach? thought Max, but he did not say it. The whole argument was academic. What was spirit after all? What was a nation's soul? He merely nodded, smiled, and sipped. Von Rauschwald lifted the needle.

"Doesn't it bother you, Captain von Rauschwald, that Wagner chose one of the few mythologies I know of in which the gods destroy themselves?"

"What do you mean?"

"The Götterdämmerung. When I was in Brazil, the Carachachos explained certain natural phenomena, such as the disappearance of certain animals, as the gods devouring their children: the gods would periodically run mad and consume their own children. It took some time for me to understand why the Carachacho did not see this as horrific. It was a kind of cycle. Madness takes over, but when it ends, things are clean, ready to be restored, if you see what I mean."

"I see. And you perhaps see the Führer's death as a similar moment on a cycle?"

"Well, perhaps it could be seen this way, but I really was comparing again. In Wagner, the gods bring about the end of Valhalla. It is a definite end, not a moment before a rebirth. If Wagner explains us, is it possible he also explains an impulse to self-destruction?"

"But those are the old gods," said von Rauschwald. "We can learn from their fall. In any case, I'm not certain how you mean what you are saying."

Max pondered for a moment. "Nor am I." He smiled. "I suppose I am rambling a bit. Tiredness. This day has had its shocks."

Von Rauschwald raised his glass to the portrait. "Heil Hitler," he said.

Max raised his glass over his shoulder. "Heil Hitler."

"Let's listen again." Once more von Rauschwald was as if in a trance. The music played through, and, as before, it took the captain several seconds to lift the needle.

"I suppose," said Max, "that this could change all our circumstances. What will you do after the war?"

"If it ends, I will continue to serve the Fatherland. I will remain in the SS, of course, and wait for the next war. And you?"

"I? I suppose I will return to my lands. I'm of no use to anyone as a soldier now. One eye may be enough, but one good leg and one arm . . ."

"No matter your wounds," said von Rauschwald, "there is always a way to serve."

"I am more of a burden than a soldier."

"But what about an investigatory role? Yes. Perhaps you should enter the SS. One doesn't need to be unscarred to serve in such a way."

"I doubt my accomplishment on this investigation will give much to recommend me."

"You cannot alter the facts. The prisoners did it then?"

"I don't really believe so, but I have nothing concrete to

contradict it. If there were witnesses, for example, among the prisoners, and Schütz was involved, he had merely to order their deaths."

"I know," said von Rauschwald. "You think it was our beloved commandant?"

"I don't know what to think. At different times I think almost anyone could have done it. Murderers don't wear cuff-titles to announce themselves. Do you remember the Düsseldorf Ripper? No one suspected him. Not even his wife."

The captain laughed. "Only an unmarried man could expect husbands and wives to know each other very well."

Max hesitated for a moment, then sipped his brandy. He took in more, perhaps, than he ought to have, but the resinous warmth spreading through him gave him nerve. He tried to be casual, as if the question he had in mind did not matter. "I hope you don't think I'm prying, understand, but there seems to be a common impression that you were Lila's lover. Is that true?"

Von Rauschwald smiled enigmatically. He stood, moved to the front door, then back to the kitchen. "Children have big ears," he explained, almost tasting the pleasure of what he was to say next. "She was utterly mad for me."

Max watched him sit. The captain leaned forward, almost begging Max to ask more. "I don't know what to say," said Max. "She was rumored to be quite promiscuous."

His smile collapsed. "It was a game she used to play. She liked to make me jealous. It was merely a game, however."

"And when she went home to her husband?"

"They had abstained for years. Lila found me. Schütz kept a whore."

"Tanya? In the brothel?"

"I believe so," he said distastefully.

"So then Schütz was not jealous of you?"

"He hated me. He did not have to be jealous."

"Ah," said Max.

Von Rauschwald's gloom vanished quickly. He lowered his voice like they were conspirators. "I could make her sing like a canary, four, five times in an hour."

"Ah," said Max. "You were lucky. After my wounds, I found sex extremely difficult."

Von Rauschwald blinked. "A pity," he said. "But some of us

are bulls. It takes more than a shelling to put us out of commission."

"And Bette, your wife, did she know about you and Lila?"

"Perhaps. It doesn't matter. You see, I have it on good authority that after the war, loyal SS men of the correct racial type, war heroes, will be allowed to have two wives."

"Two?"

Von Rauschwald went on to explain that an old friend of his who worked in filing for the SS had read memoranda proposing such an allowance in order that the deaths of German warriors did not diminish the next generation. Women would outnumber men by war's end, and if they could not marry they could not fulfill their role as mothers. The best men under such a plan would be allowed to increase their offspring twofold. Lila and Bette had been great friends, said von Rauschwald, and would have been marvelous partner wives.

All that Max could think of during this lengthy explanation was what Bette had said, "He pisses like a woman." Yet he planned to sire more children with two wives? Hitler dead, war heroes with more than one wife—Max shook his head. The Armagnac was causing hallucinations.

Von Rauschwald noticed. "What are you thinking?"

"I am thinking we shall all be Mormons," said Max, then found himself having to explain his joke, since the captain had never heard of them.

"Ah," said von Rauschwald. Had he now taken to imitating Max? Or was he mocking him?

Enough. You won't trap me, thought Max. I'm not interested in uncovering any more of Ostheim's secrets. I am going to write my report as quickly as possible and leave with your wife. It is simple enough.

But he was nagged by the idea that Bette had lied. Why? Did she merely want Max to feel more free in the adultery? It was an extraordinary lie, if that were all she wanted: "He pisses like a woman."

Von Rauschwald had just placed another recording on—the overture to *Lohengrin*—when his trance was shattered by pounding on the door. He angrily threw it open.

"The Führer!" gasped his driver. "The word has just come. He's alive! The Führer is alive!"

· Seventeen ·

The bomb had failed. The putsch had failed. The very evening of the day Hitler had stood in a room with an explosion meant solely for him, he made a speech on the radio. Schütz had the spectacled radio woman copy out all of it she could hear through her earphones, then he stood on the porch in front of his office and read it out. Revenge would be taken, he promised. And then some, thought Max. The assassins and their accomplices, like Satan and his angels, would be swept away by the broom of a wrathful god. By ten o'clock, even the prisoners must have begun to wonder if the Führer were immortal. That he was wounded at all had begun to seem incredible, and was likely to inspire new enthusiasm for a crumbling war effort. Max, who had thought he no longer believed in a grand plan to the universe, was stirred by a sense of destiny in it all. He could not accept it as a destiny of heroism or glory or triumph—those things were empty mouthings—but a kind of tragic destiny, which ennobled the Germans only because they were forced to endure. Like blind Oedipus, like tormented Orestes, like Tiresias with his wrinkled dugs, they wandered on. Max lay on his bed and imagined what it might be like in 1950, when the war still continued. Or in 1955. Or 1960. Would Hitler create a line of warrior kings that would make the Hundred Years' War seem like a skirmish? Is this what the Thousand-Year Reich meant? In ancient times, would his worshippers have proclaimed him a god?

Kleini checked in at about eleven. Despite all that had happened, he had slipped away to type what Max had written that morning. It didn't come to much and he wanted to know if Max had done more. "You will give me no peace," said Max, "until we are on the train to Berlin." Kleini smiled, then smiled more broadly when Max promised to finish within two days. "Now," he added, "to accomplish this, I need my rest."

"Oh yes, sir," said Kleini happily.

As he closed the door, Max called out. "By the way—"

"Yes."

"Be careful. Some of these SS might hold any army man responsible."

"Don't worry," winked Kleini. "I am totally shocked and outraged by this treason."

"Good. Keep saying that."

A strange silence had settled onto the camp. Even Sgt. Külm's dogs seemed aware something momentous had transpired and the absence of their usual barking was more disturbing than the noise. Despite Max's uneasiness, however, the writing, the Armagnac, the intensity of it all had drained him. He dreamed of Vienna. He was old and fat and eating pastry with both hands. Both hands? He said to the waiter that he wasn't supposed to have two hands and the waiter said he would not charge him for the extra one. Meantime, outside the pastry shop, Sgt. Külm was leading a parade. Külm was the new Führer and his legions were composed of a superior breed of Alsatian shepherd that marched on its hind legs and shot with unerring accuracy. They had just conquered India and were leading elephants in chains. The waiter brought Max an enormous Napoleon with chocolate swastikas painted into the icing. He cut it into sections, one swastika to each, and went from café table to café table, feeding hundreds of patrons with one Napoleon.

His door clicked.

He was instantly awake, but did not move. The food thief? He wasn't equipped to wrestle the person down, but he would wait until he was fully in the room, startle him, then perhaps get a good look. The door closed. Whoever it was moved straight toward him, then paused. He held his breath for several seconds, then saw a flicker of light. A reflection off metal. He instinctively rolled off his bed and crashed into the figure, fumbling with his hand for the arm that held the knife. He heard a short cry of pain, felt cloth in his face, and the tangle of limbs and skirt.

"Bette?"

"Of course! What are you doing?"

There were footsteps in the corridor. Max shushed her. The orderly had come to investigate. He tapped timidly. "Colonel?"

"Yes."

"Are you all right?"

"Yes. I—I bumped a chair in the dark."

The orderly hesitated, then his footsteps receded.

Max fumbled for the light switch. When it came on, Bette was sitting on the floor, a light pullover twisted around her neck and shoulders.

He settled to the floor with his back to the dresser. "What were you doing?" he whispered.

She angrily pulled her arm from the sleeve. "I was getting undressed. You could have hurt me!"

"I was startled," said Max. "I thought I saw a knife."

"Couldn't you call out? Didn't you think it might be me?"

"I didn't know. I'm sorry. I thought perhaps you would stay away until we were ready to leave."

"My life has been empty too long," she said, slipping the sweater off her head. She wore only a chemise under it. The hard tips of her nipples poked the sheer cloth.

There was nothing else to say. He could feel warmth spreading from his loins. He rolled sideways and lowered his lips onto her shin. He kissed it through the stocking, then kissed the small stitched hole on the side of her knee. He slid forward and lifted her skirt. He held his breath and looked at her face. She reddened and closed her eyes. He dropped down and kissed the naked flesh next to her garter strap, inhaling the scent of her thigh and groin. She lifted his head, held him before her and said, "The bed."

"I want you on the floor," he said. Without answering, she wrapped her arms around his neck and pulled him on top of her. Their mouths held together for a long time, dizzily breathing each other's breath, while he, then she, fumbled her panties and stockings down around her knees. The awkwardness, however, made her break the kiss and roll him onto his back. Stepping out of her stockings, she straddled him.

They were finished only moments later. Almost gasping, she dropped forward, brushed his face with her breasts still covered by the chemise, then cradled his head in her arms and kissed him hungrily.

"Can we get into bed now?" she whispered.

"I don't know if I can move."

"You must."

"Why?"

"I think I have a splinter in my ass," she said.

"Is that why you climbed on top?"

She reached behind her. "I only just noticed it. I had an impulse. I have never done it on a floor."

"Nor I," he said. "It was *incredible.*" Uneasiness flickered across his face: the phrase Oskar and he had affected when gadding about Vienna. He did not want her to infer he thought of her as a whore, but she took the words only as a compliment.

"I feel free with you." She smiled. "You do not have to have a certain way of doing things."

"I thought you said I was formal."

"When your clothes are on. Come on. Into the bed."

"If we must. I could sleep here for a week."

They peeled off what was left of their clothes and climbed up. He offered to find the splinter. She lay on her side and pointed in the center of her buttock. He squinted at the tiny black line, picked at it with his fingernail, then resorted to the pin on the back of the medal for valor he had received from the Italians. She jumped slightly when the splinter finally came out. A small drop of blood appeared on the skin. He kissed it as if it were her mouth.

"Umm," she said. "Get in here. I want to lie beside you."

"I could kiss every inch of you."

She pulled him up and tangled herself all around him. "You know, it's these afterwards I enjoy most. Just lying warm beside you, feeling your heart beat. That is what a woman likes. The afterwards."

He hugged her. The light annoyed him, but getting up seemed too arduous. He pressed his face against her shoulder. They remained silently locked like this until he abruptly rolled onto his back.

She nudged his ear with her nose. "What is the matter?"

"My hand is tingling. My missing hand. Sometimes you can still feel the body parts you've lost."

She lifted her head and peered at him.

"I'm serious. It's not unusual at all." The conversation he had earlier had with her husband entered his mind.

"Does it bother you?"

"It goes away eventually. It's only momentarily annoying."

"You are thinking of something. You are suddenly sounding formal."

"I—I don't know—I was wondering. You have said Captain von Rauschwald has no, ah, organs."

"Yes, but he has never mentioned feeling it as if it were there." She closed her eyes. "God! What a torment that would be. Do you think he ever sees anything with the missing eye?"

"I don't know," said Max. "I only know about phantom limbs. Bette," he added carefully, "if Joachim is without the necessary parts, why does no one else know this? Why are so many people under the impression that he and Lila were lovers?"

She sat up and glared at him. "Can't you leave it alone? He doesn't want anyone to know. SS heroes are supposed to have dozens of children. Can you imagine how Schütz would have tormented him? Why do you bring this into our bed?"

"I'm sorry. There are things that have to be asked."

"So you can humiliate him in your report? I shouldn't have told you."

"I will not write unnecessary gossip into the report, but surely his medical records—"

"Yes, yes. And are you fucking Frau Frank for information too?"

He clasped her by the shoulder and flung her back. "I could hit you for that! I love you. These questions have nothing to do with that. If you suspect me you should leave."

"You've bruised my shoulder," she said fiercely.

"I'm sorry. You had no right to say that."

"But you have a right to interrogate me in bed? God, Count von Prokofsk, if you want to know what is there why don't you order Joachim to drop his trousers? Or is it too horrible for a man to see?"

"I would not humiliate him without reason."

"As if the military does not exist to humiliate! He has one

testicle, Max-Baldur. It hangs like a cat being carried to the river in a sack. It's important, Max, for without it he'd be an SS capon, fat and sweet-voiced and soft-fleshed. Eh?"

"Please, Bette."

"No. Hear me out. Above this is a nub. Oh, German surgeons are clever. Without them, he would have died, mercifully. But they gave him all the reconstruction they could. A nub. No bigger than the end of your thumb. Not big enough to hold when he pisses. From the front it looks like a tiny set of puckered lips." She abruptly covered her face with both hands. "Oh God!" she whimpered, "and all those white and fishy scars. Those white and fishy scars."

Max turned his back to her. He peered at his own scars. At the scab where the Russian bullet had scraped him. He hunched over, as if self-consciously trying to hide himself. He listened to her weeping and considered whether she had been making love to him as a substitute for her husband. They were similar in build, both decorated with scars. The difference? Von Rauschwald had two hands. Max had a penis. He cringed, but he inhaled deeply and pursued it. "Is this why?" he asked quietly. "Is this why you haven't told him?"

"I tried," she sniffed, "but I couldn't. I couldn't. He might keep the girls. You don't know what it's like to carry a child in you. When my brother died, my father was brokenhearted. *I* was brokenhearted. But my mother! You'll never know what it is for a woman to lose a child. I can't let him take them from me."

"You don't know that he will."

"He can never have another."

"It isn't like they are sons. These SS types all want warriors. They don't care about girls."

"But he might keep them. Just to punish me. Just to hurt me." She touched Max's shoulder. "Can't you see how his pride will be hurt? It isn't like he is normal."

Max jerked his shoulder away. "You said you loved me."

"I do."

"Then you must leave with me. You must tell him you're leaving with me. If you don't, I will tell him."

"No! That will be worse."

"I will. Then you will have to choose, won't you?"

Her dark silence endured for at least a minute. She picked

up her chemise. "All right. You tell him. You crush his spirit. Do you think I could stand by for that? Do you think I could love you as much after that?"

"I'll have to take the chance. What's another risk in my life?"

She cocked the hand holding the chemise on her naked hip. "My, isn't that heroic!"

He looked away. The combination of the attraction of that body and his anger was like two enormous steam engines bearing down on each other. He did not know what would happen if they collided. He tried to think of anything at all, anything that could insulate him behind the formality she always accused him of. "One other thing, Frau von Rauschwald. I've been meaning to ask you. On the night of Frau Schütz's death, a woman about your size and weight was seen walking between the quarters about nine-thirty. Was this you?"

She slipped on the chemise, then slapped him hard across the face. "You've fucked me," she said. "Isn't that enough?"

He touched his stinging face, then reached for her waist. She backed away and he caught only the hem of her chemise.

"Sssh!" she said, pulling toward the door. There were boots in the corridor, and not just the orderly's. Many boots.

They held their breaths, then jumped at the sharp rap. The chemise pulled between Max's fingers as Bette quickly snapped out the light.

"Yes?" shouted Max.

"Commandant Schütz! Open the door."

"Just a moment."

"Open it or I shall."

"I am undressed."

The door flew back. Schütz entered behind two Ukrainian privates holding their rifles in front of them and nervously licking their lips.

Max covered himself with his blanket. "What is the meaning of this?!"

Schütz triumphantly switched on the light. Max blinked. The commandant, who was just about to speak, raised his eyebrows, then tipped his hat. "Good morning! The Frau von Bitch! What a surprise!"

Bette stood by the open window, naked from the waist down,

her clothes clutched in front of her hips. The helmet of a soldier was just visible outside, the tip of his rifle pointing up at her. She lowered her eyes.

"Well, my hero Wehrmacht colonel," said Schütz, "you are under arrest. How the tables have turned!" He laughed.

Behind him, Joachim von Rauschwald stared at his wife, his face pale and hard, his eye fixed and cold. Slowly, slowly, with one gloved finger, he smeared a bead of sweat across his glossy brow.

· *Eighteen* ·

In his underwear, Max was tossed like a sack of potatoes into a root cellar. He squinted into the dark of his "cell" and thought how inconvenient it was for an institution like the SS to have its preconceptions disturbed. Despite its brothel, despite its kitchens, despite its tailor shop, infirmary, showers, cottages, garages, communal outhouses, and prisoner barracks, Ostheim had no jail. In a sense, it was entirely a jail, but its intention was the imprisonment of a class of inferiors: Jews, Communists, Gypsies, homosexuals, insolvent Slavs, Seventh-Day Adventists, thieves, black marketeers, murderers (of the everyday type), and anyone else who irritated the Third Reich like sharp pebbles in the boots of its march to destiny. But in imprisoning a class of enemies, in seeing all opponents as the same, Schütz had made no provision for the incarceration of individuals.

If Schütz had acted out of any authority (which was almost certainly the case), they were likely arresting hundreds of people: purging the body politic of its ill humors, as the Nazis had done every few years. The fact that an individual might have placed the bomb would be swallowed up by the notion of collective guilt, and those at the top would go on believing that the mystic unity of Germany had been threatened by an evil race, class, gang, group, conspiracy, that could easily be defined to include Max-Baldur, Count von Prokofsk, shivering atop a barrel of pickles, listening to the movements of rats among the stores. He tried to tell himself that Schütz was not stupid enough to summarily execute someone who had been so widely publicized as a defender of the Fatherland, but it was hard to be optimistic when you were already underground. People had been known to disappear, after all. Into the cellar, into the void. One colonel, far out to the east, could be easily lost. He wondered if any fool would be sent to verify Schütz's report. All Schütz had told him was that he had been arrested on suspicion of complicity in the assassination attempt on the beloved Führer.

As the day lightened, he was gradually able to pick out the details of his prison. Sacks of potatoes on his left. Barrels and crates of meat tins on his right. Occasionally rats stood on their hind legs and sniffed the peculiar scent from the center of the room. Max talked to them. He asked each one if he were the rat who planted the bomb, though he began to think maybe he was interrogating the same rat over and over. When they didn't answer, he tried asking them in English, then Portuguese, then Carachacho. One seemed interested in the latter. "You're a long way from home," said Max. "But, of course, I am a German. I am in my traditional homeland. Literally *in* it." He scratched the end of his stump, and tried to shake the increasing soreness out of his stiff leg. If he were lucky, he thought, they'd shoot him before it got too uncomfortable.

He heard footsteps and fumbling with the latches on the heavy door. Light filled the room like an explosion. "Company!" laughed a man with an accent. A shadow blocked the light momentarily. A man tumbled down the uneven stairs and lay flat on the floor. Darkness again. The fastening of the lock.

Max raised himself to his feet. "Good day," he said drily. "Welcome to Rio."

The figure tried to move, made a noise like "oof," then flopped back on the floor. The narrow slit under the door let in enough light so that Max recognized the uniform. "Kleini? Kleini!" He dropped to his good knee and pulled at his tunic. It was wet in some parts, stiff in others. When Kleini finally spoke, his voice was slow and unclear, as if he were speaking through a pillow. "So, colonel," he said, "you're still alive."

"What have they done, Kleini?"

"Ooof! My head feels like a pumpkin." Kleini groped for the stairs. He settled back against them with a sigh.

"What?"

"A pumpkin. Pump-kin."

Max had just begun to make out the puffiness around his eyes, the swelling around his split lip.

"These boys aren't much fun," said Kleini. "Let's go home." He suddenly gritted his teeth and pressed his side with his hand.

"Schütz will pay for this!"

Kleini weakly laughed. "Give the devil his due, colonel."

"They had no right to beat you."

He laughed again, then coughed. "I don't think they knew that. They told me you were dead." He stretched out his hand and fumbled until he found Max's stump. "That *is* you. You aren't a ghost, are you?"

"Why did they tell you I was dead?"

"Papa Schütz wants to know what you and Colonel Hüber were up to."

"Up to?"

"He wants to know what the messages meant."

"And they beat you for that? My God, I don't even know what they mean. 'The Führer'! Was that supposed to tell me that Hitler was coming to visit? If that's what it meant, what difference could that make? The Führer wasn't blown up here. And what did the second message say, other than 'give up'?"

" 'Come home.' " Kleini coughed. "I think they broke a rib. Bastards. A rib will heal. Usually. But my foot, they broke my foot."

"The real one?"

"No, my wooden one. I'll have to get another one or I'll face the firing squad on one foot. I'll be unsteady. They'll think they've frightened me. The pigs!"

"What else did they want to know?"

"That's all. Schütz, ah well, he doesn't like to think I know nothing."

"He just enjoys the beating."

Kleini sniffed. "He's just a Bodo."

"What do you mean?"

"I mean people live up to their names." He pressed his side. "There was a Bodo in our village. Silly. No nerve. When

Chamberlain made us part of Germany again, Bodo got a suit. He strutted around like he owned the Sudetenland. A couple of peasants got pissed at him and pitched him in a shit pile. He came back with six of the Hitler Youth and beat them up."

"I don't understand."

"No balls. He didn't get even himself. He liked to watch the others. That's our Schütz. Bodo Schütz. A real Bodo."

Max took down an empty crate. "You should get off the floor."

"I'm fine. It feels cool."

Max sat on the crate himself. "Too cool."

"Nice," said Kleini.

"Do you think," asked Max, "that a Bodo could butcher his wife?"

"Oh good," said the sergeant, clearing his throat, "let's play detective. It's one way to wait to die. They'll be here for you soon. Then you can accuse Schütz to his face. That is, ah, before Baranovitch breaks your nose."

"Still, it might prove interesting."

Kleini reached out and clapped Max's shin. "Congratulations."

"Excuse me?"

"For tapping the captain's keg. He is not a happy man."

"He'll probably hurt her. God!"

Kleini said nothing, but the way he sighed indicated assent.

"I'll probably never see her again."

"At least, ah, at least you had a good one before the end. A week ago I finally tried the whorehouse." He coughed. "Like screwing a fish."

"Bette and I fought."

"No need for regrets, then."

Gradually, as the time passed, they began to recognize that any interrogation of Max was going to be delayed. Kleini revealed that von Rauschwald had spent as much time trying to find out the details of his wife's affair as Schütz had spent on Oskar's messages. Kleini had told him nothing. Because, Max thought, he knew nothing, but Kleini said he had seen her sneaking in one night. If the captain didn't kill her, said Kleini, her face would never be the same.

Max, shivering with the combination of his frustration and

chilliness, tried to pace but kept faltering on the uneven earth floor. They reminisced about North Africa: the time Ulf Biedermeyer bought an Arab girl while drunk and couldn't find the seller, the time they chased a British patrol through ancient ruins, and the beaches—those hot, clean beaches. Kleini remembered Rommel slapping him on the back, and Max recalled the general's praise after they had captured an Australian patrol. Eventually, Kleini dozed off. Max couldn't tell how hurt the sergeant was. If the blows to the head were severe enough, he could be going to sleep for good. Otherwise, he would need the rest. Perhaps dying, in this situation, was better. They had likely beaten Kleini and tossed him in here in order to make Max think about the consequences of not immediately confessing to everything and anything, including the creation of all Jews. Aristocrats were supposed to be more afraid of violence than ordinary men. He began to think, however, that his only defense might be an offense. Prove Schütz murdered Lila and shout the idea until someone listened. Then it might seem Schütz was manufacturing charges simply to stop the accuser.

Several more hours went by. He thought he heard thunder in the distance. He reviewed all the evidence. Röhm's Revenge. The scalpel. The syphilis. The fetus. The "reassignment" of the prostitutes. The executed prisoners' ages. The SS dagger. The dogs. He went from one elaborate construction based upon speculation to another. Each construction would eventually collapse, simply because of what he did not know, after all these inquiries. Who was the father of Lila's baby? What explained the prisoners' ages? What had the prostitutes known? He thought of the American mysteries he had read in Brazil, how one salient fact whose importance was adduced by the detective revealed the entire complex structure of evil. But Charlie Chan and Philo Vance worked in hermetic environments: locked rooms, limited suspects, clear motives. There were hundreds, maybe thousands of people in Ostheim with motives, and the only locked rooms were not where the murder had taken place. It was a miracle that real crimes were ever solved. Max had a vision of the universe filled with criminals, all with secrets, and only the unlucky ever being caught. Maybe the only differences between the soldier and the dockside cutthroat was that the latter could be hanged for fewer acts of the same crime.

Later, the alarm went off. An escape? There was much running again. Max crept up to the bottom of the stairs and tried to peek under the door. He could only see the shadows of boots. It seemed to be late afternoon. Perhaps they had just found Bette, sliced into small pieces. The dizziness of the thought made him roll onto his back. His foot clipped Kleini, who said "What the—?"

"I'm sorry," said Max.

"I thought it was a rat. Have I slept long?"

"Yes." He heard Kleini move, then grunt with pain.

"Have I missed the schnitzel?" he finally asked. "The potatoes with butter? The cabbage in wine?"

"Please," said Max.

"I've got to piss."

Max heard Kleini struggling to stand. "Let me help you."

"I've got it. Ooof!"

Max's fingers brushed the sergeant's tunic as he hopped out of reach.

"Damn. Why is the ceiling so low?"

Max heard the spattering of urine.

"There," said Kleini, "may Schütz eat one of my christened potatoes."

"You didn't!"

"Of course I did. May my piss be carrying—"

The door rattled. Max eased himself back down the stairs. This was it. The beating.

Light filled the room again, but it was golden. The sun was going down. Baranovitch stood alone in the opening and blocked most of it. He held out Max's uniform. "Here," he said. "Put it on."

Max again heard the low rumble he had mistaken for thunder when the door was closed. "Shelling," he said.

"The Bolsheviks," said Baranovitch.

"How close are they?"

"Close enough to be here in an hour," said Kleini, listening.

"Too close," said Baranovitch. He slammed the door.

"Pigfucker!" said Kleini. "I'll help you."

"I can manage."

"If they leave us for the Reds, we'll wish Schütz was back."

"We'd be another sort of prisoner," said Max.

"Not quite. Duitser told me they used to shoot commissars on sight. It was policy. I doubt the Reds have forgotten that."

"I see."

It took a long time, but Max managed to feel his way into his clothes. There was a new sound, along with the chaos of running and the thunder. Trucks and cars were being moved. Max and Kleini sat silently, lost in their own thoughts. After a while, intermittent flashes came under the door. They heard the muffled crackling of distant machine guns.

"Maybe they have left us," said Kleini.

"I don't think so."

"Let's try to break the door, or dig out."

"They haven't moved the trucks yet."

"Maybe they aren't going to."

"I don't think so."

"Well," said Kleini, "if I can find a stick to dig with, I'm digging." He broke a piece off one of the crates, and, somewhere near the potatoes, began huffing and coughing as he jabbed at the dirt under the foundation. Max tried to ignore it for a while, then decided he might as well help. He was just rising when the door opened again. Schütz stood several meters behind Baranovitch. *Hieronymo's mad againe,* thought Max.

"Come out, Colonel von Prokofsk." The commandant waved Max's cane. "Sergeant Klimmer too."

Max peered back at Kleini. "I want you to know," he said, "that one of the greatest treasures of my life has been knowing you."

He could barely see the outline of the sergeant's head, but it slowly dropped.

"Stop this high-class posturing, will you, and give me a hand."

Schütz was pacing impatiently. "Out!" he shouted. "Now!"

Max slipped his arm under Kleini's and awkwardly hopped him up the stairs. The scene that faced them was chaos. Soldiers were running in all directions, mounting machine guns on the backs of trucks, lifting in crates of ammunition, and pushing against each other's field packs to get in. There was shouting in three or four languages. Only minimal lights were on, and to the north the sky flashed under an intense bombardment. As soon as Max and Kleini were clear of the cellar door, two uniformed men carrying explosives clattered in.

"I guess the rats have had it," said Max.

Schütz poked at the two of them with Max's own cane. "I'm certain you know that the putsch has failed. Whatever your role in it, you will pay. The executions are going on all over the Reich, and not a single conspirator will escape—even if he works in the Reichsführung itself. Adolf Hitler is our Supreme Commander now."

Max tossed his head toward the east. "And look how things have improved."

Schütz, to Max's surprise, was not overtly angered. "I am certain that this is a momentary withdrawal. I can sense a new commitment among the troops, now that the Führer has taken charge."

"The Russians," said Max, "will find Ostheim useful."

"You," barked Schütz, "will remain silent. You are under arrest."

"When a man's about to be killed," said Max, "he feels chatty."

"You counts always feel chatty. In any case, you still have a trial coming. After that, you will die. Painfully, I understand. The Count von Stauffenberg was lucky in being shot last night. Others may not be so. He at least had the courage to do the dirty work."

"The Count Claus Schenk von Stauffenberg?"

"As if you didn't know. Your bomb-thrower."

"I am very interested to know this, but I fail to see what it has to do with me."

"Have you no courage left? It is only a matter of time until those messages from your Lieutenant Colonel Hüber are deciphered."

"And has Lieutenant Colonel Hüber been arrested?"

"That is not my concern. You were obviously sent here to wait for the Führer. When that failed, another count was called into action. In the meantime, Lieutenant Colonel Hüber tried to use you to discredit me. He who is my enemy is the Reich's enemy. It is only logical you are guilty of complicity."

"Colonel," said Kleini, "what a bad little boy you've been!"

Max laughed. "I? Assassinate Hitler? Here? Don't be absurd! Oskar probably wanted me to ingratiate myself with him by being the only civilized human in Ostheim."

"It won't be so funny in the courtroom. The convoy will be leaving soon. You will be under the guard of Sergeant Baranovitch. He will shoot you if you attempt to escape. There is no place to escape to, anyway. The Reds have no mercy for us. Under these circumstances, Captain von Rauschwald has said you would normally, as a gentleman, be offered a pistol with a single bullet. But I think such a privilege should be reserved only for SS men. In your case, I thought this might be more appropriate." He held out Max's shaving kit. Max slid his arm from around Kleini and took it. He couldn't open it, so he merely stared at Schütz with a quizzical expression.

"Morphine," said the commandant. "There is enough in it to kill you several times. I have provided a needle. Why not save the sergeant here the trouble of guarding you? Further, there might be mercy on this fat aide of yours, and whatever family you have."

"You pig!" said Kleini.

Schütz turned and calmly shoved Kleini with the point of Max's cane. Kleini thrashed his arms, then toppled to the ground.

"I believe you are mistaken," said Schütz. He threw the cane at Kleini, then saluted Max. "Heil Hitler!"

"Heil Hitler," said Max coolly. Schütz marched away in a hurry.

"All in all," said Kleini struggling upright, "he's a bit cranky today."

"I don't know," said Max. "Hieronymo seems rather subdued."

"Who?" asked Kleini. He did not wait for an answer. "He's lost his kingdom."

"He's stunned. You can see that, but he obeys."

Baranovitch stepped forward. "Come on," he said. "The car's at the rear."

"We have a car?"

"Yes. Come on."

"Excellent," said Max. "We can die in a crash."

"You can die here," said Baranovitch without twitching an eyelid.

"Sergeant Klimmer can't walk unless I support him. Will

you take out the morphine so I can put it in my pocket?" Max lifted the shaving kit out in front of him.

"What do you need that for?" said Kleini. "For God's sake!"

"You never know," said Max. "It's not easy to get."

"Throw that shit away! You're innocent. No court will convict you."

"No one is innocent," said Max. "No court can make you innocent." He gestured back at Baranovitch. The big man looked suspicious, but he unloaded the case and dropped the vials and hypodermic in Max's pockets. They bent over together to help Kleini up. For a moment, Baranovitch, with his hands full of the sergeant, had his face right where Max could have smashed it with his fist. Max hesitated, however, and with Kleini leaning against him lurched off in the direction Baranovitch indicated, wondering why. Maybe it was just the madness of thinking anyone Baranovitch's size could be leveled with one punch.

They moved along the line of trucks. Sitting ducks for a good pilot, thought Max, but all of the tower spotlights were pointed into the prisoners' compound, either to offer them up to any fighter that came along or to make a pilot pause before strafing the camp. Along the fences, thousands of men had gathered. They watched without expression, their eyes large and white, their cheekbones almost tearing through their tissue-paper skins. This, thought Max, is what the underworld would look like: thousands of anonymous faces, hands hardened into claws hanging limply at their sides. Would a people who had endured so much ever recover? Or would they come back into life as erased sheets of paper, smudgy, with only the vaguest outlines of whatever they had been? With the train out, there was no way to evacuate these ghostly men, and perhaps Schütz's last act at Ostheim would be to order the machine guns turned on them. It would be merciful, Max said to himself. The Russians, he had read, often shot anyone they suspected of being tainted with Fascism, including their own men who had been imprisoned by the Reich, and the Soviets had no love for Jews, Gypsies, Poles, or any of the others. But that was not why it was merciful. Killing them would simply end the nightmare. Doctor Frank's air bubbles no longer seemed as cruel as they once had.

With a grunt, Baranovitch indicated that they could rest

against one of the trucks. Max was dripping with sweat, and Kleini was puffing like a locomotive. It was while settling Kleini on the running board that Max heard a child crying. A staff car was positioned in the space between the two barracks where the unidentified woman (Bette? Lila?) had been seen. The rear door to the car opened, bumping the wall, and Bette stepped out, holding Hedwig in her arms.

"Let me speak to her," said Max.

Baranovitch shook his head.

"What can be the harm?"

Baranovitch looked at Max, then at Kleini. His slow brain ground for a second. He flicked his head to the side.

Max was nearly to the building when Bette finally noticed him. Her face froze in a mixture of shock and bewilderment. She peered into Hedwig's face and bounced the child, who had reduced her loud wailing to an occasional whimper and gasp for air. Max stopped by the masked headlight. Ursule Frank, in the front seat next to Little Klaus and a German driver, pushed her son forcibly when the boy pointed to Max and attempted to speak.

"The girl," said Max, "she isn't hurt?"

Bette smiled wanly. "We had to leave her clock. Her grandfather gave her a clock. There isn't much room . . ."

"You should have been evacuated months ago."

"We never should have come." She glanced awkwardly at anything but him.

"You are all right?" he asked.

She nodded. "A little embarrassed." The girl wanted to get down. She put her in the car, then placed both hands on top of the door, peering at him directly. "Good luck, Max-Baldur," she said.

"Wait," he said. "There are things I want to say."

"I know." She bit her lip and turned to enter the car.

He said loudly, "When the war is over—"

"You will be dead, my little count." Captain von Rauschwald had entered the alley. Bette twisted to see him, then quickly climbed in with her children. "Oh, don't get in," he said, "I have come to get you. A wife's place is at her husband's side."

"If you were any kind of husband, you would never have brought her here."

"Those were my commandant's orders, my little count. Now

I am convinced of the wisdom of it. So convinced, in fact, she shall not leave without me." He banged the car top with his fist. "Out! The others can go ahead."

"For God's sake," pleaded Max. "Get her out of here. You know what the Russians do to women."

"She will be honored to die at my side, if necessary."

He jerked her out by the arm.

Max instantly understood why Bette had not yet suffered from her husband's rage. He was saving her for worse than a beating. He was going to abandon her to the Red Army. He moved forward, but suddenly felt himself constrained by Baranovitch's big hand. "You won't hurt her, von Rauschwald. If I have to come back from the dead, you won't hurt her."

"Well, I suppose you'll have to then." He tipped his hat.

"What the hell are you doing?!" It was Schütz's voice. "You need to have a tender parting with that whore?" He came along the side of the barracks. "I ordered you to collect all the records!"

"My wife is going to help, isn't that right, darling?"

"He wants to leave her here!" shouted Max.

"There is no time for this foolishness," said Schütz. "And why is this traitor running loose?"

Baranovitch grabbed Max more forcefully and began to drag him back. Max lost his balance and fell. Schütz ignored him, however, and charged at von Rauschwald. "Let that bitch go and come with me immediately."

"I want her to stay," said von Rauschwald.

"I don't care what you want. All our records must be taken to Berlin. Only with them will we be able to prove how well Ostheim was run. Over there! Immediately! Or I will have you shot on the spot!"

Von Rauschwald's face was cold and white. "Very *well!*" he shouted, shoving Bette against the car. She gave a small cry of pain as her mouth struck the edge of the door. Von Rauschwald saluted and spun on his heels. Schütz glanced back at Max. "Get up!" he said. "Or I'll see you never need a trial!" He then followed von Rauschwald.

Baranovitch lifted Max by the arm. Max barely had time to mumble good-bye before Baranovitch whirled him around and shoved him in the direction of Kleini, who had raised himself by means of the door handle.

They lurched off again in the direction the Byelorussian indicated. They finally reached the staff car. Max recognized it as Schütz's own. "We are riding with Schütz?"

"No," said Baranovitch. "Not enough room for his papers."

Max helped Kleini into the back seat. "The traitors get the limousine," said Kleini, "the emperor gets a truck."

Baranovitch leaned against the rear wheel well and pulled out a cigarette. "We wait," he said. Kleini leaned over Max and asked, "Have you got another one of those?"

"Not until your firing squad," said Baranovitch.

"It's a nasty habit," said Kleini. "Bad for the lungs."

Max fidgeted. "Aren't we leaving?"

"All at once. We may be surrounded."

"Wonderful," said Max drily.

"The Russians came quick," said Baranovitch. "There were only Hungarians protecting our front. They aren't worth spit." As if to emphasize the point, he spat. That was Baranovitch, Max thought. Though one might suspect his glowering reticence concealed a certain wisdom or knowledge, he always proved he was exactly as he appeared.

"When are we going?" asked Max.

Baranovitch shrugged.

Max idly moved to the front of the car and sat against the big radiator. He looked in the direction of the garden. Soldiers were coming from the family quarters. They had likely wired several Hitler portraits, like those in the von Rauschwald parlor. When an angry Russian ripped it down: boom! The Supreme Commander's revenge. He peered at the prisoners. Though they did not seem to have moved, several of them were now wearing signs around their necks. Max remembered something he had almost forgotten. In the train station in Vienna, just as he was departing for North Africa, a thin, attractive woman in pigtails, with bruises on her arm and face, was shoved along the platform by SS men. She wore a cardboard sign on her neck that said, "I am a pig who sleeps with Jews." Behind her was a man, also with a sign, "We Jew boys always prefer a German girl." No one seemed to pay much attention to this procession, except for a tourist who snapped several photographs and an old woman who yelled something at the Jew.

The prisoners, however, were wearing neatly lettered signs

that said, "Comrade!" and "Communist." Some simply had a hammer and sickle on theirs. Max wandered back to Baranovitch. "Waiting for the Reds," he said.

Baranovitch put out the end of his cigarette with his fingers and stuck it in his pocket. "We should have finished them when we had the chance."

"The Russians may do it for you, I understand," said Max. "Doesn't it strike you as sad that a simple cloth or cardboard sign can be the difference between living and dying?"

Baranovitch said nothing, then muttered, "Bolsheviks killed my brother because the milk he sold them was sour. He was in the wrong street that day."

"I didn't mean it wasn't true," said Max. "It's just sad. We'd like to think dying occurs for important reasons, not just because some soldiers think it's funny to shoot at the sign that's supposed to save you."

Baranovitch grunted and peered down the line to see if there were any chance of the convoy's moving.

Max suddenly stepped away from the car. "Come with me," he said to Baranovitch. "Come on!" The sergeant looked momentarily confused. He took his rifle off his shoulder, however, and followed.

"Stop!"

Max glanced back. "Come! It's important."

"We wait, by the car!"

"Come!"

When the prisoners saw that Max was headed straight for them, some of them awkwardly pulled off their signs. Most simply stared. Max walked directly up to the fence. "You," he said. "Where did you get the sign?"

The prisoners backed away a step, but said nothing.

"Please," he said. "I do not care what you have on it. I merely want to know where you got it."

Baranovitch came up behind him. "Back to the car!" he barked.

Max ignored him and continued to speak with the prisoners. "I beg you. No one will be harmed. I simply want to know where you are getting the signs."

The prisoners rustled. "What do you care, German?" shouted one. "You want one for yourself?" Someone laughed giddily, as if he were the only one who understood that the order of the camp was about to be reversed.

Max singled out a cadaverous man whose right eye was swollen shut. He had the red triangle of a Communist over his heart, but wore no sign. "You! Here!" Max gestured, indicating the man should approach the wire. The man hesitated, but the other prisoners drifted back, avoiding his eyes as if he were already dead. He did not hesitate long. The weeks, months, perhaps years of obedience drew him. "Come closer." The man was already a meter from the fence. "Closer. Closer."

Max's arm snapped out between the wires. He caught the prisoner's filthy collar in his fist and held him. Baranovitch audibly gasped and raised his rifle. The prisoner's puffy eyelid twitched open, revealing a red slit. His left eye rolled from side to side at the electrified wires centimeters from his face. Max, the prisoners, Baranovitch—all stood absolutely still as a single spotlight glided across them.

"Sir," whispered Baranovitch. "The electricity." He pointed with his rifle. Max's outstretched arm hovered inside a square barely large enough to fit a book. Movement in any direction would touch it. The prisoner's chin quivered. Max tightened his grip.

"Who is the sign painter?" said Max.

The prisoner's feet edged back but Max held him fast.

"The sign painter!"

"No German." His whisper quavered. "No German."

"I'm under arrest," said Max. "You understand?" He spoke so that everyone could hear. "I could be dead before most of you. Who is the sign painter?"

"Why should we tell you?" The voice came from among the prisoners. It was deep, with a Russian accent. The prisoners separated and a bullish man stood alone, smoking a cigarette. He reached behind and handed it to another prisoner, then he strolled forward until he stood in the light. He was obviously better fed than most of the others and had vaguely Oriental features.

"A woman was murdered," said Max, without moving.

"We should care about this? And what has a sign painter to do with it?"

"I think you know."

"Me? I am just a prisoner."

"I doubt that. You are either an officer or a commissar."

"Perhaps."

"And you must have some desire to get even with Commandant Schütz."

The man grinned. "Oh, we will get even. With all of you."

"He is a murderer, isn't he? Schütz had the sign painter Tallinn letter him a paper that said 'Röhm's Revenge.' He then stuck it to his wife's body."

"He saved us the trouble of executing her, then. You are all murderers. Why should we care about her?"

"She's a victim. Like you." Max quickly flicked his wrist. The prisoner he had been holding toppled backward. The man scurried on all fours into the anonymity of the dark. Max coolly pulled his arm out of the wires. Baranovitch's huge body sagged with relief. "Tallinn isn't dead, is he?" asked Max. "He will not be harmed if he just comes forward, if he just tells me what I need to know."

The man laughed, revealing crooked and yellowing teeth. "German promises!"

"I was sent here by the Reichsführer himself. I—"

"Save your breath. We know, Count Max-Baldur von Prokofsk, hero of this, that, and the other. You have some very pretty medals. Soon you will be begging to trade them for morphine, and you know what? No one will accept. Where will you be then?"

Max blinked. "It was you, then. *You* searched my room."

"Me?" The man grinned. "How would I do that?"

Max swept his hand across the prisoners. "You do more than you let on. You play docile, but you manipulate your guards. You *wanted* me to know you were in my room."

"Perhaps someone wanted to open your eyes. Perhaps someone was merely curious."

"No." said Max. "It's more. You wanted to know if I was one of them."

"Aren't you? You wear their uniform."

"I am a German, but I have never been a Nazi."

The man's eyes flashed. "And when did you stand up and say, 'Stop'? It is too late for these distinctions."

Max spun away. He squeezed the bridge of his nose until it hurt. He was silent long enough that Baranovitch stepped forward. The sergeant squinted at the prisoner and threw the bolt of his rifle. "You," he said to the Russian, "have no right to judge *us*."

Max shoved aside Baranovitch's rifle. "No," he said. "Let's go. We must evacuate."

"He is one of their commissars," hissed Baranovitch.

The prisoner stepped forward. "Let us suppose, Colonel Count, that we find out who is scheduled to die."

"He is stalling," said Baranovitch.

Max ignored the sergeant. The puzzle was beginning to make sense. "The clerk, Gissinger?"

"As a hypothesis, let us suppose we always find out about death warrants. Let us suppose they are for healthy men, good party members, and that it is clearly not in the interest of the party that they die."

"Gissinger alters the records," said Max.

"Men who are already dying are regularly substituted. Their deaths keep others alive."

"And they volunteer, I suppose," Baranovitch said sarcastically. "They are all good Communists."

"Their sacrifice makes them martyrs to the revolution. They, ah, become good Communists. The committee democratically selects who shall be so honored."

"Doesn't it bother you to sacrifice the weak and innocent?" said Max.

"Chivalry is dead, Herr Archduke. We take care of our own. Such choices don't bother you, do they?"

Max ignored the remark and stepped closer to the wire. "So Chirkin, Tallinn, and Komnoliakov are still alive?"

"No," grinned the Russian.

"Theoretically, then," said Max in exasperation, "it is possible that the men who *were* Chirkin, Tallinn, and Komnoliakov are alive?"

"Theoretically. Except for Chirkin, the traitor."

Baranovitch craned his neck to see if the convoy was moving. There were soldiers running and orders being shouted. The towers were being abandoned. "Hurry up!" he barked.

"Well?" said Max.

"Chirkin thought he was clever. He thought only of himself. He thought he could bargain with the devil. He arranged for the commandant's knife to be stolen and for Tallinn to make the sign. He was promised freedom. What he got was a wire noose. We would have killed him if von Rauschwald hadn't. He would have betrayed us eventually."

"So Chirkin killed Frau Schütz?" Max looked at Baranovitch, who glared at the prisoners with hatred. "Schütz was right?"

"No, no, no." The Communist shook his head. "Chirkin thought he had a deal with von Rauschwald."

Baranovitch pointed at the trucks. They were starting the engines. "He is stalling us!"

"Wait," said Max. "I'm confused. Explain. The roll call. The escape attempt."

The Communist sighed. "Are you stupid as well as blind? There was no escape. Chirkin supplied von Rauschwald with the knife, the scalpels, the sign. Von Rauschwald tells Chirkin that he will sneak him and Tallinn out of the camp in his own automobile. He tells Chirkin to hide under the infirmary with Tallinn."

"And Komnoliakov?"

"Chirkin had a big mouth. Komnoliakov nosed in."

"And then?"

"Von Rauschwald calls a surprise roll call. He had already arranged for the death warrants, even before the killers were identified. He killed them"—the prisoner made a motion as if garroting someone—"without interrogation. Not a single question."

"But the captain had never seen Tallinn or Komnoliakov. So you fed him two innocent typhus patients? Your committee voted two sick men should be executed wrongly and you feel morally superior to us?"

"And who created this fine situation?"

"Von Rauschwald took great pleasure in killing them. I suppose that amused you."

The prisoner grinned. "No. Killing you, that would be amusement."

"Why should I believe you? You are simply trying to turn us against ourselves."

"There's no need to do that to cannibals."

"You knew why I was here. You had only to reveal this. You cannot believe we approve of butchering women," said Max.

The prisoner laughed mockingly, his yellow teeth glaring.

He turned his back and disappeared into the shadows of the faceless crowd.

"We must go," barked Baranovitch. "There's no time."

Max stared at the prisoners. He felt small, ridiculous, humiliated.

"We must go!" Baranovitch jerked Max's arm. The first trucks were grinding their gears. Gunfire crackled not far away, behind the northern rise. Baranovitch shoved him.

"No," said Max. His teeth were clenched, his eyes wild. "I want von Rauschwald."

"Get him later."

Max pulled his arm loose. "We may be dead later. I want him now!"

"No!"

"Leave me then. Take Kleini and go. I want von Rauschwald!"

The sergeant glanced at the headquarters, then at the receding convoy. He muttered gutterally and ran for the car.

Max limped toward the headquarters as quickly as possible. The ridiculousness of sending Baranovitch away did not occur to him until he saw Kleini leaning out the window of the car, speeding through the gate. The camp was deserted now, except for the truck. No one seemed to be loading it. No one seemed to be guarding it. Surely neither Schütz nor his second in command would be the last out of Ostheim. That was stupid militarily. It showed what an idiot of an officer Schütz really was: a read Bodo, as Kleini had said. And what would the prisoners do when they finally knew they were unguarded? One arm, a stiff leg, and no weapon. Max, you've really done it this time, he thought.

He circled the truck and noticed a detonator hooked to a pair of wires. Two more pairs lay neatly beside it. The small truck was about half full. Crates in which ledgers had been tossed, file cabinets, and trunks were strapped in with fat ropes. The eastern sky lit up with a red flare. If it were the enemy's, they couldn't be more than minutes away. Under that curious light, it was as if the war had paused to catch its breath, and Max had the sensation he was utterly alone, that no one was in Schütz's office, that he was abandoned in an empty corner of hell. But the flare dropped somewhat, a machine gun rattled, rifles cracked, and the sharp smell of gelignite rolled through on the wind.

He clambered up the steps and across the porch. The area in which Gissinger had kept his careful ledgers seemed twice as large with all the empty shelves on each side. Bright light, however, streamed through the partially open door to Schütz's office. When he shoved it back, he was blinded. Then, as the scene gradually became clear, he was frozen by the strange tableau.

Every light in the room was lit. To Max's right, in the midst of three shadeless floor lamps, von Rauschwald hunched his shoulders over, his eye pressed close against a small camera. Two muffled clicks followed in rapid succession. He was photographing Schütz, motionless upon the desk, a single bullet hole over his right eye, the framed Hitler note lying on his chest, his trousers pulled down around his boots. An overturned inkwell dripped one last, slow drop to the floor. It barely missed a wide stream of blood that flowed from the heels of Schütz's boots onto an amorphous blob of flesh on the floor. A dark hole stared where the commandant's genitals should have been.

"My God!" exclaimed Max.

Von Rauschwald dropped his camera. "The Russians!" he said. "I had just gone to tell the convoy we would catch up with them—"

"Russians?" Max stared at him.

"Yes. An advance patrol."

"And you are taking photographs?"

Von Rauschwald bent and picked up his camera, but he did not take his eye off Max. He cast a few furtive glances at it, then caressed it to see if it was broken. There was fresh blood on his hands and sleeve. "Why are you here? They could be back any moment."

"But you have time for photographs."

Von Rauschwald pulled his pistol. "So. You've escaped. That was foolish of you."

"Yes. I suppose it was," said Max weakly. "I came back to arrest you."

"Arrest me?" He laughed.

"You murdered Frau Schütz, and now, I presume, Commandant Schütz."

"And soon, you may presume, yourself." Von Rauschwald shrugged as if to say he was sorry.

Max had made the most fundamental military error: don't get so interested in your objective that you charge into a trap. Once there, however, what? Evasion? The unexpected assault? His stiff leg couldn't move him fast enough for either. Delay was the only alternative. Delay in the hope that the situation would change.

"And do you intend to mutilate me, as you have mutilated the Schützes?"

"Now, now," said von Rauschwald. "The prisoners mutilated Lila. The Bolsheviks mutilated the commandant, who was courageously, like a ship's captain, determined to be the last to leave. You, perhaps, simply escaped, or deserted to the Red Army."

"I thought you'd want souvenirs of my death."

"Souvenirs?"

"The camera."

"It occurred to me how grateful they would be to have actual photographs of Soviet brutality. It would be quite a spur to the troops, don't you think? They may give Schütz a medal, when I get through with my tale. Me too. I, of course, having fought to rescue him, may be assured of a place back in the front line."

" 'Front-line swine.' "

"Yes. I like being a 'front-line swine.' Schütz and others may joke about the men who do the real fighting, but we all know who wins wars. It isn't the Schützes with their damned papers!" He kicked at Schütz's boots. The heel swung slowly, tapping the side of the desk three times before it stopped. "You and I understand war. One-armed, you would happily return to combat, would you not?"

"My fighting days are over."

"Your days are over." Von Rauschwald lifted his pistol to aim it.

"As one officer to another," asked Max quickly, "would you do me the courtesy of explaining a few things."

"Explaining?"

"Yes. I know you murdered Lila, but I don't understand much of it." Act inferior, thought Max, entice his vanity.

Make him want to toy with you. "You see, I'm not much of a detective. I could not put it all together."

Von Rauschwald laughed. He mockingly looked around him. "And where is the microphone hidden? Isn't this where I confess and the police rush in?"

"I am obviously alone and ill-prepared."

"I'm disappointed in you, then. I won't explain how difficult it all was, how I deliberately complicated the evidence, how I set up the appearance of an escape, or how I got all that blood off me without being seen."

"That's a pity," said Max. "I would like to know."

"You were never any match for me."

"That seems obvious, given our situation."

"It is to your credit, Count von Prokofsk, that you settled upon me at all. If you hadn't seen Schütz here . . ."

"You misunderstand. I came to arrest you. I already knew."

"Nonsense."

"I expected Schütz to assist me."

"Did you? You see, you have overestimated him again. He was incapable of killing Lila. Oh, he was fine at getting others—the very people he disdained—to do his killing for him. This prisoner to the left, this prisoner to the right, kill all those on the left. Then he'd stand there watching until he was bored and go back to his office. He hadn't enough heart to kill as I kill. He felt nothing, ever!"

"You prefer the personal touch."

"And who has the right to kill without hating? Eh? You cannot say that in Africa you became a hero by being indifferent."

"I cannot say I hated anyone I killed, either. I am a soldier."

"And I am not? Look at you. You had only to enlist and you were an officer. Your family assured that. Even the SS has been filled with noble families, especially at the top. It is easy to recognize the natural nobility, if one makes an effort, but they've gotten lazy. They merely check pedigrees, like at a dog show. Every step of the way I had to prove myself to idiots and inferiors, like Schütz. I, who had the greatest feeling for the soil and blood of Germany, had to kowtow to insensitive slobs who were only interested in dressing up and strutting around."

"And this is why you killed Lila?"

"I owed her everything. I had no feeling for myself as a man. Life mocked me. Bette could only offer pity. I wasn't worthy of love or contempt. Lila, however, gave me back my feeling as a man. She didn't treat me like I was sick and had to be babied."

"I understand how the right woman can restore a man's identity. Bette did that for me. That is why I love her." He didn't know exactly why he chose to say this to von Rauschwald, unless it was some sort of attempt to take her away from her husband at the last moment, in some metaphysical sense.

Von Rauschwald sneered. "How romantic we Germans are!"

"But if Lila gave you so much, why kill her?"

"She betrayed me. Betrayal is a capital offense." He said it as if any fool could see it.

"And how could she betray you?"

"As every woman can betray. As Bette betrayed me."

"And that is why you wanted Bette to wait with you? Another 'execution'?"

"I had a special death planned for her." Von Rauschwald's face was almost dreamy. Max shivered, though sweat was trickling into his eyes.

"The child, then," said Max carefully, "was not yours."

Von Rauschwald slumped into a chair. He seemed exhausted. "She did not know. She said she had fucked a Jew, a syphilitic Jew."

"Ah. She admitted, then, to having syphilis."

"Yes."

"And did you not seek treatment?"

"From whom? That slob Frank? No doctor will ever touch my body again."

"Years from now the disease will catch up with you."

"I will find out what to take and buy it on the black market. No doctor will ever touch me."

"I sympathize," said Max. "I have felt much the same. And you, you have lost too much." He stared coolly until the full impact sank in.

Von Rauschwald bolted to his feet when it did. "You know!" he said. His single eye narrowed. He was shaking uncontrollably. "How do you know?" The gun barrel traced circles and figure eights. "How?"

"Someone saw you bathing."

"That's a lie. I have never bathed anywhere I could be seen."

"There is always somewhere to be seen. Further, it is likely in the records in Berlin."

"Yes, but not in Ostheim. I made certain of that. Only Bette could have told you."

Max was silent.

"Oh, yes, in a moment of passion. She leans over. She whispers. You laugh."

"I never laughed. Never. I have lost too much to laugh. A slight twist of fate and you would have your eye and I my arm. . . ."

Von Rauschwald sagged and seemed almost to be speaking to himself. "Sometimes"—he licked his upper lip—"I ejaculate. Isn't that ridiculous? It happened as I was cutting her. It builds up and builds up and then it happens. It happened twice with Lila before it was necessary to kill her. I wanted to cup it in my hand or a glass, then put it into her. I wanted her to have my son. But she liked to humiliate me, she liked to keep me on my knees. She told me the child was one of the prisoners'. She said she wasn't sure which, because there had been too many."

"Perhaps she was lying. Perhaps it was Bodo Schütz's." Max gestured at the blue-white commandant.

"What difference would this make? Either way was betrayal. I told her to meet me in the garden. I wanted to spread her on the ground, drive the scalpels into her cunt, and the note into her mouth. I planned it for two weeks. I dreamed of it. But she wouldn't listen to me. She wanted to go somewhere where there was a chair."

"A chair?"

"Where she could humiliate me again. Hold the knife against the side of my throat and make me lap at her until she was exhausted. It was our game. But she was unfaithful. I couldn't take her humiliating me any more. She held the knife out and poked at me. She called me Herr Rausch, playfully, and rubbed her knee against my crotch. I took the knife and drove it into her chest. She fell too quick. She gave me no pleasure by suffering."

The photograph of the dead woman flashed into Max's mind. "So you mutilated her?"

"Not immediately. My eyes had grown accustomed to the

dark. She looked peaceful. She was almost smiling. I had prepared it all carefully: 'Röhm's Revenge' and the scalpel would point to Dr. Frank, but she looked too peaceful, too serene. You wouldn't know she'd betrayed me. She was like a statue of the Virgin." Von Rauschwald stared into the corner, as if he were seeing her there.

"And you wanted Frank to take the blame?"

"He's a doctor," said von Rauschwald matter-of-factly.

"Ah," said Max. "But it was Schütz whom everyone suspected."

Von Rauschwald laughed. "Yes! People are so stupid. I prepared it all so carefully, and they came to the wrong conclusion!"

"Obviously, not everyone thinks as you do."

"That is their loss. We shall have to do something about it in the next phase of the Reich." He lifted the gun, as if he suddenly remembered he had something to finish before the Russians arrived. "And you, I'm afraid, will never know how great Germany shall be."

Max could think of nothing more to delay the inevitable. Von Rauschwald would soon accomplish what the entire British army had failed to do. They had snatched away pieces of him, but von Rauschwald would take away his life, and then, if the mood struck him, chop off parts of what was left. Max pointed at the window, mirrorlike because of the bright lights. "Look, Rausch," he said calmly, "the bombardment has ended."

Von Rauschwald turned, turned back, and turned again. The momentary confusion about his name and the opaqueness of the glass gave Max a second. He dived across the open door at an angle, losing his balance. Von Rauschwald fired once, then twice, splintering the door frame. Max was already down, however, trying to crawl into the darkness of the clerk's room. Von Rauschwald stepped forward and reached for the doorknob. Max, now on his back, kicked the oak door as hard as he could. It cracked into von Rauschwald's face. Max heard him fall back against a chair as the gun went off. He grasped a shelf, desperately trying to stand. He was halfway up when he heard von Rauschwald coming again. He was crawling across the floor in a nightmare in which everything moved at one-tenth normal speed, when von Rauschwald kicked his arm out from under him.

"You pig!" shouted the captain. "I even liked you." He kicked Max in the side, rolling him over. Max peered up at the shadow looming over him. Von Rauschwald leaned over and grasped Max's tunic. He stood him up and backed him against an empty file cabinet.

"And now!" he said. "You will tell me how you knew it was me. If you do, you will die easy. Do you understand?"

"If I don't answer," said Max, "you will always know that there is a loose end. You will not know what it is."

Von Rauschwald struck him hard across the face with his pistol. Max tasted blood. The captain would not make Max's dying easy, no matter what he said. The escape had failed. The game was lost. But Max wanted von Rauschwald to know that at least in one way he had failed to cover all his tracks. At the very least, knowing this would have to make him wonder what else might have slipped his attention. It was the only revenge Max might have.

"Röhm's Revenge," gasped Max. "A nice touch, but too nice. All neatly lettered. It had to be something to distract."

"Is that all? How does that mean me?" His breath was hot in Max's face. The gun barrel stabbed at Max's nose.

"It doesn't."

"Well?"

"The letterer is alive."

Von Rauschwald hit him again. "I hanged him myself!"

Max shook his head. "Chirkin was only a go-between."

"I know. I hanged the Gypsy also."

"He's alive. You should have checked the number on his arm. Schütz would have. You hanged the wrong man. At this very moment, my sergeant is taking him to Berlin."

The lie worked. Von Rauschwald backed away and loosened his grip on Max's tunic. He was thinking. Hard.

"You shouldn't have wanted such a dramatic note. Why didn't you do it yourself? I'll tell you. You like to make everyone share in your crime. You like to run a thread so that your suffering is everyone's."

"Shut up!" His hand drifted to his pained head, as if he once again felt the shrapnel that the doctors had told him could not be there.

"Now," said Max, wiping at the blood on his lip, "kill me. But you'll never get the man who made your little note, Herr Rausch."

"You pig!" Von Rauschwald was already on him, crashing his knee into Max's groin, when the door cracked open. Von Rauschwald spun away from Max. A shot. A second shot. Von Rauschwald grunted as if he had been punched in the belly. He fell. The gun skittered into the blinding light of Schütz's office. A Soviet soldier with a pasty face tried to make out what else was in the room.

Max sprang for the pistol. He tumbled over von Rauschwald. The soldier recovered his senses enough to fire. Max had his hand on the pistol. He raised it. He fired—once, twice—as he toppled backward. He raised himself on his elbow and watched the motionless soldier crumple, bullet holes under his eye and in his cheek. When he fell on his face, the entire back of his head was mush.

If there was one, there were others. Max looked around, then lurched through Schütz's blood to jerk out the light cords. One behind the desk did not go out. Its diffuse golden light spread under the desk and barely reached the corners. It cast the silhouette of Schütz's body on the ceiling. Max thought of the Russians and how stupid it was to announce his presence by turning out the lights. They were likely cautiously approaching the building with grenades. Eyeing the window, he dragged himself to the door and closed it. He was raising himself with the help of the knob when von Rauschwald cried out, "Nooooo!" The word was helpless, pathetic, the scream of the trapped fox who must gnaw off his own foot.

Max pointed the pistol at the shadowy captain, then knew that the man was going nowhere. He lowered himself next to him. Von Rauschwald coughed and weakly laughed. "You are Death?" he asked.

"Colonel von Prokofsk."

"I want to hear—"

"Yes."

"Siegfried's funeral."

"We cannot have it here."

"Ba-bumm! Ba-bumm!" Von Rauschwald coughed, then shrieked again. His hands were crossed over his belly. He seemed to be holding it together.

Max thought of Lila Schütz. "The pain is less than you deserve, but don't worry, it won't last much longer."

"I don't want to die."

No matter how tormented their lives have been, thought Max, they never want to die. Death was a woman easy to love from afar, easy to flirt with, but always terrifying to embrace. He felt dirty for what he had said. "I'm sorry." That sounded stupid, so he took a telephone from the clerk's desk and placed von Rauschwald's hat on it. He lifted the captain's head and rested it on the hat. "The Russians will be here any minute. I have to go."

Von Rauschwald cried out again. It was so loud, Max looked around, fully expecting the Reds to come crashing in. He thought about the ridiculousness of his situation. He couldn't drive a truck, could he? One leg couldn't work both the clutch and accelerator. How far could he get on foot? Further than if he sat. Perhaps if he headed into the thickest part of the woods . . . "I have to go," he said.

"Don't leave me," begged the captain.

"I must."

"Please. Don't let them operate on me."

Max patted von Rauschwald's shoulder as if he were dismissing a boy who had brought him a newspaper. "It won't be long. You'll soon be in Valhalla, eh?" He began to raise himself. He thought of the Carachacho Indians. "Or somewhere in the river mist," he muttered to himself.

An engine roared across the parade ground. It wasn't as loud as a tank or truck, or so he thought, but he swung the office door open for a rear escape. He took shelter behind the clerk's desk and aimed for the center of the door. Footsteps approached rapidly, then more slowly. Von Rauschwald screamed again, but it was as if Max did not hear him. Max seemed to be watching himself from a great distance. He was surprised how calm he appeared.

The doorknob turned. Then someone kicked the door back, carefully staying out of the frame. It bounced off the dead Russian's heel. "Colonel?" said a low voice. "Commandant?"

"Baranovitch?" said Max without moving. "Is that you?"

The sergeant stayed out of sight for several seconds, then quickly popped his head in and out. "I can't see you."

Max stood. "Von Rauschwald killed Schütz. A Russian got him. We may be surrounded. Why in hell are you here?"

Baranovitch's huge body loomed in the doorway. "I didn't want them to get you. They shot two boys for nothing. They were just afraid."

Max remembered the two deserters Schütz had executed after the strafing. Like so many, they must have been boys playing soldier who suddenly awoke to real war. "Where is Kleini?"

"With the convoy. I heard shooting. I think the Bolsheviks may have taken it. There is an old road I know. It may be good enough to take us to Uzhgorod. Come!"

Von Rauschwald screamed again. The Byelorussian peered at the dead Soviet, then at the captain. He lifted his rifle and aimed at von Rauschwald's head. Max struck it down.

"What are you doing?"

"It's only a matter of time."

"Let him suffer," said Max.

"Let the Bolsheviks have him, then."

Max looked into Baranovitch's rough face. "No," he finally said. He reached into his pocket and took out a morphine vial. He tried to hold it under the stump of his arm, but it moved. "Here." Baranovitch took it while Max clutched the hypodermic between his teeth and attached a needle. With the sergeant holding the bottle, he drew the entire contents into the hypodermic. He then dropped to his knee. Baranovitch guarded the door. "Give me your arm," he said to von Rauschwald. "There will be no pain." Von Rauschwald, however, was muttering.

"This proves absolutely I am the descendant of Erdewulf, Count von Rauschwald. Absolutely. Read it yourself."

"Hurry up!" said Baranovitch.

Max pushed the needle through the captain's upper sleeve. Von Rauschwald jerked when it went in, though how he could feel the needle in addition to all his other pain was bewildering. Max emptied the syringe and hoped he had struck a vein.

Von Rauschwald screamed again, almost sat up, then fell where his face could be seen.

"Hurry up!" said Baranovitch.

"Erdewulf's grandson, he was a—he was Wulf the Lion. He

had many children. He had many bastards. They called them Rausch, you see, and—"

"I think I see them," said Baranovitch.

Max watched von Rauschwald die. It only took a few seconds, and he could have told himself that it was impossible for even that much morphine to have worked so quickly, but he did not. If you set out to kill a man, even a murderer who is dying, the responsibility lay on you. You had to live with that. Dr. Frank had understood that, but wasn't very good at living with it. Schütz and the others would have passed their responsibility on to abstractions like "orders," or "the future," or "the resurrection of Germany." Max, who was feeling the pain of knowing that he could never take back the morphine now in the captain's blood, kept telling himself this was no different than pitching a grenade into a British foxhole, but it felt different nonetheless. When von Rauschwald's eyes rolled oddly up at the last moment, only the whites of his eyes were visible.

O you who turn the wheel and look to windward/ mumbled Max, *Consider Phlebas, who was once handsome and tall as you.*

"Now!" said Baranovitch. "Now!"

"It is finished. Let's go."

Baranovitch charged out the door and hid against the truck. Max too now saw movement in the brush beyond the outer fence. To his left, the prisoners stood numbly watching. Baranovitch waved him on. Max limped up behind him. They eased around to the back of the truck. "The car is fast. We will run for it."

"Wait," said Max, touching one of the ledgers.

"We can't take the truck!" Baranovitch was exasperated for the first time Max had ever noticed.

"We must destroy these records."

"What?"

"The Russians must not get them."

"You think this is the only death camp?"

"It is the only one I've been in."

"What do I care about Germany?"

"You are fighting for us."

"I am fighting against *them;* I am fighting for Byelorussia. I'm fighting for my life."

A rifle cracked. About half a dozen Soviet soldiers were charging the fence. Baranovitch fired twice. The Russians dropped to the ground. Max snatched a grenade from Baranovitch's belt, stuck it in his tunic, and limped to where the detonator and wires had been spread on the ground. Bullets crashed into the front of Schütz's headquarters. "The car," shouted Max. "The car."

Baranovitch, cursing in his native language at incredible speed, fired several times, then ran toward the car. About halfway there, he dropped to the ground when the Russians opened up again. By now, Max was flat on his belly, holding the detonator against the ground with his chin, and wiring all six leads. He watched the windows of the staff car shatter, just as Baranovitch climbed into it, but somehow the car began to move. The Russians charged the fence again. One of them vaulted over the concertina wire and hit the fence. Sparks flew as he quivered and fell, electrocuted. In the momentary confusion, the car turned across the front of the headquarters, driving across the wires. Baranovitch, twisting his enormous size below the seat, shouted, "Get in, you idiot!" and reached out, flinging glass all around him.

"Down!" shouted Max.

When he pushed the detonator, there was an odd fraction of a second, just time enough for Max to think, *Shit! It's wired wrong.* But then it was as if the universe had exploded. In a great wash of light, Max had the sensation of being flipped in the air like a doll bumped off a comforter. His back was pelted by sticks and smoking fragments of stone and metal. He lifted his head and saw dust: sooty, brown, sulfurous, opaque. His eyes stung. His ears were singing in a high squeal. Gradually he recognized the silhouette of the car against the fire in what was left of one of the barracks. Baranovitch slowly groped toward him, picked him up by the neck, and threw him in the back seat. Max raised himself up and shouted that he had to get near the truck as Baranovitch jammed down the accelerator.

He couldn't hear his own voice over the ringing, and Baranovitch seemed to pay no attention, even when Max prodded him with the grenade. The sergeant, however, pulled up beside the truck and Max leaned over and rolled the grenade underneath. He was immediately flung back by the sergeant's popping the car into gear. They crashed forward into the smoke and Max somehow scrambled up to look out the rear. There was a flash where the truck would have been. The car was careening forward into the rolling dark as if Baranovitch did not care what he might hit. The ruins of a stone hut appeared. They swung left. The gate tower appeared. They clipped one of its legs and spun the tail so that Max thought they were going to roll. The rear wheel well struck a pole, however, and Baranovitch accelerated again. The clouds broke away as if they had crashed through a wall. They were on the road in crisp darkness, Max bouncing in the glass on the seat until his palm was bloody, Ostheim swallowed in a fading haze of fire behind them. The prisoners! he thought. Surely they hadn't wired the prisoners' compound; he couldn't have unthinkingly blown them up. No, he decided, they couldn't have. The explosion was too small. It must have been too small. It had to have been too small.

It wasn't until the sergeant found the overgrown cutoff to Uzhgorod that Max noticed the burning in his upper thigh. He had been wounded again, on his left side. It wasn't until he had climbed, tumbling over, into the front seat to help Baranovitch feel his way along the rutty road that he thought of Bette, then Kleini, then all the others in the convoy. He had an odd series of sensations and gradually realized he was crying, out loud, but couldn't hear it. When Baranovitch stopped the car and took him into his massive arms, he could feel the sergeant's breath on his ear and knew he was soothing him, though he couldn't hear a word of it.

· *Epilogue* ·

The rabbi and the old man were dozing on the balcony of the hotel. They had said nothing to each other of the past that had brought them to Vienna. It was not necessary. The bond between them existed because of what they understood about that past, something impossible for anyone who had not lived through it to fully grasp. Instead, the old man had chatted about school days, about cafés that had once been filled with artists, about professors who built up their own self-importance by humiliating students. The rabbi had talked about Toronto: growing up in the Jewish community there; how his great-uncle had seen Babe Ruth hit his first-ever home run in that city; how, on his last trip there, he had been amazed by the traffic on the Queen Elizabeth Way. Whenever the conversation drifted toward the only thing the two men had in common, it was as if they felt the heat from it, and backed away. When the rabbi had begun to tell of how his brother had been threatened during the worst part of the Free Quebec movement—because he was stubborn about not Frenchifying the name of his small laundromat chain, "Cleanarama"—the old man had suddenly gotten out of his chair and limped to the window. The rabbi cut short his story and suggested they go look for some of the places the old man had known when he was in school. The old man had nodded. They wore themselves out trying one street after another, overindulging in pastries, and studying maps with their cab drivers while trying to locate the old man's former lodgings, a notorious cabaret, the small park where a band had once played Strauss ad nauseam. Could it be possible that this concrete and steel office building stood on the site of Frau Janos's boardinghouse? Nothing looked the same anymore, the old man said.

The rabbi was watching a pigeon mercilessly peck at an aspidistra on the next balcony when there was a knock at the door. "I will get it," he said.

"She is right on time," said the old man.

A darkly tanned woman in her thirties, slim and moderately attractive, tilted her head to one side and looked in. "Papa?" she asked, as if her father had now metamorphosed into the rabbi in front of her.

"He is sunning on the balcony. It is very pleasant. Come in. You are Frau Vilalta?"

"Yes." She extended her hand, shook his politely but quickly, then headed straight for her father.

He looked up from his chair. "You didn't have to come," he said.

She touched the adhesive bandage on his left cheek. "Oh Papa!" she said. "You should be ashamed!"

He twisted his mouth sheepishly and turned his head away as she hugged his neck.

"We were so worried. When Jorge was transferred here, we wanted you to come along. You and Mama always talked about coming home, but you are driving us crazy!"

"I can take care of myself."

She rolled her eyes and faced the street.

The rabbi stepped onto the balcony and timidly said, "Frau, your father is a brave man. He is speaking for what is right."

"I think he is just trying to find something to do now that Mama is dead. Isn't that right, Papa?"

The old man lifted himself to his feet. "Your mama would have understood. She was there with me. It must never happen again. Now, if you will excuse me, my ancient bladder—"

The bathroom door closed. Frau Vilalta stood silently peering at the building opposite, her arms crossed.

"You must understand," said the rabbi. "As he said, it must not happen again."

"He will be all right when he gets back to São Paulo."

The rabbi gently touched her head with his finger. "It is all in there for him. He cannot run away. The righteous man will fight the demons, no matter what it costs."

"It is Mama's death. She just wasted away. It was a strain on all of us. Papa has become a stranger."

"It is a hard thing to lose a wife."

She nodded. "They were a happy couple. They weren't happy by nature, like Brazilians are supposed to be—they retained the Old World brooding, especially Papa—but they were very much in love, I think. He used to say she was the only jewel he had carried from the muck of Europe."

"But you must understand," said the rabbi, "your father isn't doing this only out of grief. It is true I have only known him for, well, not even two days, but I feel sure the wife of such a man would approve of what he has done."

She looked straight into the rabbi's eyes. She smiled sadly. "He wrote constantly, to everyone, about what was happening to the Amazon Indians. And she typed every letter."

"You see, he is seeing the possibility of it all happening again. Those of us who were close to it can never consider it impossible again."

"But it was so long ago. Isn't a man entitled to peace? If he would just talk about it, not keep it all inside."

"Who knows how we get peace?" shrugged the rabbi. "But, consider, maybe this is his way of talking about it."

She leaned against the balcony railing hesitantly. "Do you know it was we sisters who insisted upon learning German? Greta and Hedwig were like different people, who had almost forgotten what little they knew. I had only heard it between Mama and Papa. He thought we should know English, and, of course, Portuguese, but he did not care about German. It has turned out well we insisted. My husband got the transfer because I could teach him. We are returning next month. Our children, well, it's amazing how they learn: Portuguese, German, French, and terrible English."

The old man had been listening from just inside the doors. "The boy," he said pleasantly, "can quote Baudelaire, Camões, Goethe, Eliot, even Shakespeare. He has a memory like an Indian."

The rabbi looked at Frau Vilalta. "A memory can be a blessing."

"Ah," she said. She smiled and kissed her father on the

forehead. "Well, let's get you packed, before you get in another fistfight."

"I have to learn I'm outnumbered." The old man raised his artificial arm.

"But that's tougher than knuckles," said the rabbi.

"And a great deal slower."

The daughter offered to pack while her father showered. The rabbi remained on the balcony, trying to get a clearer idea of what the old man saw in Vienna, and knowing full well that whatever was in a man's head would always be a mystery to others. Did he see a city, a nation, a group of people permanently tainted by what had happened forty years before? Or did he see the possibility of redemption? When the rabbi had announced his intention of returning to Germany during his family's Seder, his aunt had fainted. His uncle, who had been one of the lucky few Jews admitted into Canada in 1939, turned white and said he would never allow the name of Germany, or those who lived there, to be mentioned in his house. But to be a German and bear the curse of your fathers was different from being a Jew who must never forget what being a victim had meant. This old man, with his artificial arm, with his stiff leg, what did he feel? What did he know? What did he see?

The old man was in the balcony door. "Rabbi, our train is the late one. Won't you join us for supper? I have promised Gabriella one of the finest meals in Vienna."

The rabbi raised his hands. "After all those pastries? You must be hollow. Go. Spend time with your daughter. You have exhausted me."

"Perhaps we should take my bags."

"Nonsense. You will eat, come back, then say good-bye."

"You are very kind," said Gabriella.

"I am supposed to be," he laughed.

He sat on the balcony until twilight, then moved inside. The old man's luggage sat by the end of the bed. Gabriella had closed it too quickly and the corner of the dark brown folder stuck out. He sat on the divan opposite and tried to read the newspaper. He shouldn't touch the valise, though he should point out the problem when they returned. Nothing in the paper interested him. He was tired of the election. Well, perhaps if he opened the valise and shoved the folder back inside, there was no harm in that, was there? He lay the bag on the divan and popped its latches. When he did, the folder fell out and once again its contents scattered on the floor.

He picked them up slowly. There were many photographs. The photograph of a young Afrika Korps officer that had stunned the rabbi before. Yes, he was heavier, and much more harried-looking, but it was unmistakably the same man. There was a picture of him with his arm around a short, curly-haired sergeant. They were in the desert. There was a clipping, very brief, about the Goebbels' gemütlich dining with Max-Baldur, Count von Prokofsk, recent hero of the North African Campaign. Mrs. Goebbels was "charmed." From a magazine, there was a photograph of the count shaking hands with several Nazi officials, including Reinhard Heydrich. There were a number of photographs of various people, including the count, now wounded, sitting at a table in front of a pretty cottage having tea. His mother? What did all of this prove? The old man had waved these in his attackers' faces and said they were the proof. Of what? Newspaper clippings of eyewitness accounts by several survivors of Ostheim filled much of the folder, but they could be found in any library.

There was also a letter. It was brown with age and very brittle. The rabbi hesitated for a moment. It might well crumble if unfolded. He yielded, however, and delicately opened it after clicking on the lamp. The handwriting was difficult, but he finally made it out.

17/11/45

Am shocked to find out you are still alive. More shocked than to think I am still alive. It is easy for you now. Rest out your internship in Switzerland, then, under no circumstances allow yourself to return to the Sudetenland until the Reds are out. Your old friend, you see, would like to keep you alive, even though you seem to be impossible to kill. I really thought they got you in '44. When what was left of the Ostheim personnel reached Budapest, your Sergeant Klimmer and the others claimed you were certainly dead. I hope you heard of the little tribute on Berlin radio. They made you out as having died in single-handed combat against a platoon of Bolsheviks. I have little time or I would write more, but we shall never see each other again, and the essentials must be taken care of as Professor Popkin used to say. In fifteen minutes I will be meeting a priest who has arranged for my new life in some country that I've never seen and cannot speak the language. I suspect I may end up eating crocodiles with your redskins, but it is my only chance. There is too much certainty that the Allies will finish up us officers—especially those in the Reichsführung SS.

The irony! The stupidity! You will find me ludicrous. I had intelligence, believe it or not, Maxy, that a colonel, injured in Africa, of noble rank, had told a hitherto unknown (to us) group that he was going to kill the Führer if he could just get close to him. I thought it was you. I swear! I never considered anyone else. War changes men after all. Before, you were not capable of such plots, but you had, after all, been through so much—the morphine and all that. When you came to me that night, you did seem peculiar, and Breda hinted you had lost more than an arm. Forgive me. We were looking for an unimpeachable figure to clear up the Ostheim business. Knowing the planned visit, I placed you there. Imagine how I felt when we found out Stauffenberg placed the bomb! Imagine how I felt that you might have been killed by the Russians because of my mistake! With Hitler gone, our chicken farmer would have seized power. I might have ended up a cabinet minister. But the bastard, like you, wouldn't die. How do we know he's dead even now? And I, it seems, may end up a chicken farmer: Führer of the Coop! What your father always said has come to pass: Oskar has come to a bad end.

I must close, old friend, I think I see the priest. It was such a relief to get your note from Zurich but I would have been much more interested to read how you got there from Ostheim than I was in your dutiful confirmation of Commandant Schütz's report. Who else but Communist prisoners would have done such a thing? You will understand why I cannot give a return address. O.H. is a memory, Maxy, and I hope not too poor a one for you. I should have known you better.

The letter was unsigned. The rabbi delicately folded it. He closed the valise tightly and placed it back where it was. He had never heard of Ostheim, or Oskar Hüber. Perhaps this old man had somehow been involved with the underground. He thought to ask him outright, but decided not to. Perhaps, despite the good intentions, the old man's underground affiliations felt treasonous. The old man had told him as much as he had wanted. When Gabriella's husband returned to Brazil, perhaps this Max-Baldur von Prokofsk would sit on the beach and let the sun bleach away some of his worst memories before he died. This, thought the rabbi, was simultaneously humans' greatest blessing and most horrible curse: the ability to forget. If we could not remember, we were cursed to suffer the same agonies again. If we could not forget, we were cursed to suffer the same agonies again.

The rabbi decided to walk to the theater district. He wanted to see people happy, driving shiny cars, laughing and winking and sipping beer, as if there were no yesterday.